PT 405 PRE

Studies in European Culture and History

edited by

Eric D. Weitz and Jack Zipes
University of Minnesota

Since the fall of the Berlin Wall and the collapse of communism, the very meaning of Europe has been opened up and is in the process of being redefined. European states and societies are wrestling with the expansion of NATO and the European Union and with new streams of immigration, while a renewed and reinvigorated cultural engagement has emerged between East and West. But the fast-paced transformations of the last fifteen years also have deeper historical roots. The reconfiguring of contemporary Europe is entwined with the cataclysmic events of the twentieth century, two world wars and the Holocaust, and with the processes of modernity that, since the eighteenth century, have shaped Europe and its engagement with the rest of the world.

Studies in European Culture and History is dedicated to publishing books that explore major issues in Europe's past and present from a wide variety of disciplinary perspectives. The works in the series are interdisciplinary; they focus on culture and society and deal with significant developments in Western and Eastern Europe from the eighteenth century to the present within a social historical context. With its broad span of topics, geography, and chronology, the series aims to publish the most interesting and innovative work on modern Europe.

Published by Palgrave Macmillan:

Fascism and Neofascism: Critical Writings on the Radical Right in Europe
by Eric Weitz

Fictive Theories: Towards a Deconstructive and Utopian Political Imagination
by Susan McManus

German-Jewish Literature in the Wake of the Holocaust: Grete Weil, Ruth Klüger, and the Politics of Address
by Pascale Bos

Turkish Turn in Contemporary German Literature: Toward a New Critical Grammar of Migration
by Leslie Adelson

Terror and the Sublime in Art and Critical Theory: From Auschwitz to Hiroshima to September 11
by Gene Ray

Transformations of the New Germany
edited by Ruth Starkman

Caught by Politics: Hitler Exiles and American Visual Culture
edited by Sabine Eckmann and Lutz Koepnick

Legacies of Modernism: Art and Politics in Northern Europe, 1890–1950
edited by Patrizia C. McBride, Richard W. McCormick, and Monika Zagar

Baader-Meinhof and the Novel

Narratives of the Nation / Fantasies of the Revolution, 1970–2010

Julian Preece

palgrave
macmillan

BAADER-MEINHOF AND THE NOVEL
Copyright © Julian Preece, 2012.

First published in 2012 by
PALGRAVE MACMILLAN®
in the United States—a division of St. Martin's Press LLC,
175 Fifth Avenue, New York, NY 10010.

Where this book is distributed in the UK, Europe and the rest of the world,
this is by Palgrave Macmillan, a division of Macmillan Publishers Limited,
registered in England, company number 785998, of Houndmills,
Basingstoke, Hampshire RG21 6XS.

Palgrave Macmillan is the global academic imprint of the above companies
and has companies and representatives throughout the world.

Palgrave® and Macmillan® are registered trademarks in the United States,
the United Kingdom, Europe and other countries.

ISBN: 978-0-230-34107-4

Library of Congress Cataloging-in-Publication Data

Preece, Julian.
    Baader-Meinhof and the novel : narratives of the nation, fantasies of
the Revolution, 1970–2010 / Julian Preece.
        p. cm.—(Studies in European culture and history)
    Includes bibliographical references and index.
    ISBN 978-0-230-34107-4
        1. German fiction—20th century—History and criticism. 2. Rote
Armee Fraktion—In literature. 3. German fiction—21st century—History
and criticism. 4. Literature and society—Germany. 5. Left-wing
extremists—Germany. I. Title.

PT405.P73 2012
830.9'3581—dc23   2011036880

A catalogue record of the book is available from the British Library.

Design by Newgen Imaging Systems (P) Ltd., Chennai, India.

First edition: May 2012

10 9 8 7 6 5 4 3 2 1

Printed in the United States of America.

For Pippa as always

CONTENTS

ACKNOWLEDGMENTS

I began reading for this book during a period of research leave in 2001 while I was working at the University of Kent. It benefited from a small research grant from the British Academy. My Swansea colleague, Tom Cheesman, read drafts of this manuscript and made some judicious interventions, for which I thank him. I would also like to thank the following for encouragement, useful reading suggestions, or other help and advice: Georgina Blakeley, Martin Brady, Neil Burgess, Seiriol Dafydd, Osman Duranni, Kat Hall, Stephen Hayward, Sara Imperatori, Stefan Neuhaus, Alan O'Leary, Astrid Proll, John Wieczorek, Jochen Wittmann, and Ute Wölfel. Once again, George Stern proved an invaluable proofreader.

Some of my initial findings were published in advance. As a consequence, traces of the following can be found in this book:

- "Between Identification and Documentation, 'Autofiction' and 'Biopic': the Lives of the RAF," *German Life and Letters* 56 (2003), 363–76;
- "Death and the Terrorist in Recent German Fiction," in *Politics in Literature: Studies on a Preoccupation from Kleist to Améry* (Munich: iudicium, 2004), ed. Rüdiger Görner, 171–86;
- "Die Terroristin als alter ego in den ‚bleiernen Zeiten' und andere umgewandelten Motive in Dea Lohers Zeitstück *Leviathan*" (The Terrorist as Alter Ego in the "Years of Lead" and Other Reworked Motifs in Dea Loher's Political Play *Leviathan*), *Monatshefte* 99:3 (2007), Special Issue on Dea Loher, ed. Birgit Haas, 375–90;
- "Reinscribing the German Autumn: Heinrich Breloer's *Todesspiel* and the Two Clusters of German 'Terrorist' Films," in *History and Cultural Memory of German Left-Wing Terrorism, 1968–1998*, The *German Monitor* 2008, eds. Gerrit-Jan Berendse and Ingo Cornils, 213–30;
- "Lives of the RAF Revisited: the Biographical Turn," *Memory Studies* (2010), 151–63;
- "RAF-Revivalism in German Fiction of the 2000s," *Journal of European Studies* 40:3 (2010), 272–83.

ABBREVIATIONS AND
SPECIAL TERMS

APO, Außerparliamentarische Opposition (Extraparliamentary Opposition), term coined during the Great Coalition of SPD and CDU 1966–1969, usually applied to the Student Movement and associated with figures such as Rudi Dutschke

Bewegung Zweiter Juni (June 2nd Movement), a violent West-Berlin-based group, named after the date of the killing of Benno Ohnesorg in 1967; founded in 1972 out of the remnants of such groups as the *Blues* and the *Tuparmaros*. Merged with the RAF in 1980

BKA, *Bundeskriminalamt* (Federal Bureau of Criminal Investigation)

Bundesamt für Verfassungsschutz (Federal Office for the Protection of the Constitution); usually abbreviated to *Verfassungsschutz*, from which *V-Mann* and plural *V-Männer* (undercover secret police agents or informers, always male in fiction)

CDU, *Christlich Demokratische Union* (Christian Democratic Party, conservative)

Fatah, a prominent faction within the PLO (see below)

FDP, *Freie Demokratische Partei* (Free Democratic Party, or the Liberals)

FRG, Federal Republic of Germany or, up to 1990, West Germany

GDR, German Democratic Republic or East Germany (1949–90)

German Autumn, *Deutscher Herbst*, the events that took place over 44 days in 1977, starting from the kidnapping of Hanns-Martin Schleyer on September 5, and including the hijacking of the *Landshut* passenger jet on October 13 and its successful liberation four days later; the suicides in Stammheim Prison of Andreas Baader, Gudrun Ensslin, and Jan-Carl Raspe the same night; and Schleyer's murder by the RAF on October 18

GSG-9, *Grenzschutzgruppe 9* (Border Police Group 9), special counterterrorist unit

Kommune 1, a West Berlin commune in the late 1960s which specialized in outraging respectable opinion with street actions and media hoaxes

Die Linke, the Left, political party formed in 2007, consisting mainly of reform communists from the East German Party of Democratic Socialism (PDS), formerly the SED or *Sozialistische Einheitspartei Deutschlands* (Socialist Unity Party of Germany)

LKA, *Landeskriminalamt* (the state equivalent of the BKA)

PFLP, Popular Front for the Liberation of Palestine

PLO, Palestine Liberation Organization

RAF, *Rote Armee Fraktion* (Red Army Faction), known too as the Baader-Meinhof Group after two of its leaders, Andreas Baader and Ulrike Meinhof

RZ, *Revolutionäre Zellen* (Revolutionary Cells), a loosely connected network of militants, associated with Frankfurt and West Berlin

SDS, *Sozialistischer Deutscher Studentenbund* (Union of Socialist German Students)

Situationists, Paris-based activist-artists who sought to turn everyday situations into revolutionary events

SPD, *Sozialdemokratische Partei Deutschlands* (Social Democratic Party of Germany, the moderate Left)

Spontis, a vaguely anarchist grouping who believed in "spontaneous" revolutionary acts

Stasi, *Ministerium für Staatsicherheit*, MfS, the East German (GDR) secret police

Tupamaros, inspired by a group of Uruguayan revolutionaries, Movimento Liberacíon Nacional-Tupamaros, who named themselves after a rebel Inca leader, Túpac Amaru II. Offshoots in Munich and West Berlin

A Note on Translation and Citation

For the sake of simplicity, though admittedly not always that of elegance, I refer to the novels and films that are the main focus of my study by their English title, followed by the author or director's surname and date of publication or release, thus *A Hero of Internal Security* (Delius, 1981) or *Knife in the Head* (dir. Hauff, 1978). All the translations are my own. I have used the published translations of novel and film titles, where these are known to me, and give the details of these translations in my bibliography, alongside the original German titles. The novel editions that I cite in the text, however, are sometimes different than those in the bibliography and the details of these cited editions are given in the end notes. For ease of orientation, it may be useful for the reader to refer to the bibliographies and filmographies at the end of the book, which I have arranged in chronological order.

PREFACE

My reason for writing this book is not an interest in terrorism per se, but rather in German politics and literature in the 20 years either side of German reunification in 1989–1990. The book began as a project on writers and the German Student Movement and the impact of the protests associated with the year 1968 on literature. This period seemed to have shaped contemporary Germany and influenced its writers more than any other since World War II. Yet, as others before and after me have discovered, the argument, as it is conducted by novelists, is not about 1968 or the Student Movement, but about "Baader-Meinhof." Politically motivated violence is what novelists have written about, indeed it has become a defining theme in contemporary German literature. One of the purposes of this book is to find out why this is so. At the outset it was clear that the significance of left-wing terrorism could not be practical politics (the terrorists had little direct influence) or collateral damage (they did not kill many people). But, as a character based on Andreas Baader reflects in one of the key novels, *Ascent to Heaven of an Enemy of the State* (Delius, 1992), "statistics are irrelevant in this football league."[1] It is my contention that the meaning of this terrorism was symbolic and thus was located in their contemporaries' imagination. As novels explore symbolic meanings, Baader-Meinhof invites investigation by novelists; this book attempts to evaluate these meanings over the last four decades.

For works of imaginative literature, most of the novels stick remarkably close to the known facts, but they re-present these facts in the context of fiction. I have identified plot lines and narrative patterns, tropes, motifs, and stock characters, as well as omissions and strategies of denial or disavowal, and tried to make sense of them. In my penultimate chapter, I turn my attention to international fiction on the same subject. A portrait of contemporary Germany—its neuroses, blind spots, and aspirations—is what I hope will emerge.

My first step was to locate novels in which a character associated with Baader-Meinhof terrorism is depicted. My corpus is as comprehensive as I have been able to make it, but doubtless I have missed one or two. The space devoted to individual novels is one indicator of my estimation of their significance, aesthetic or thematic, but I have also treated popular formats such as thrillers seriously and subjected them to the same style of analysis. Germanists, especially German Germanists, do not do this very often. Where it helps to categorize the novels, I compare them with films that depict terrorists, of which there are many, and with plays, of which there are only a few, as well as with popular works of historiography, sometimes because novelists have drawn on these or been inspired by them. Novels, however, are at the center of my inquiry for a number of reasons. I am better qualified to assess them. There are more of them (just about) than films, and their authors are often freer to develop their own expressive ideas than filmmakers are. Baader-Meinhof has been turned into myth and is the subject of those contemporary legends also known as conspiracy theories. The terrorist has been appropriated into the literary canon and popular culture, inserted into national history, and made into a figure from either farce or tragedy. All this is more comprehensively apparent in novels than in films.

In my use of some key terms, I take advantage of the softening of attitudes that has taken place since the German Autumn in 1977. We are no longer under the terminological constraints that Erin Cosgrove satirized not so long ago in her spoof campus romance *The Baader-Meinhof Affair*, where her heroine receives this stern piece of advice:

> You *never* call the Baader-Meinhof Gang terrorists. They were heroes, activists, vanguard, or revolutionaries. But they were never terrorists. In fact, don't ever call them the Baader-Meinhof *Gang*. That was the moniker given to them by the fascist *Springer Press*. They are a *group*, *not* a gang.[2]

For me, "terrorist" denotes an activist or militant who uses isolated acts of violence to draw attention to a cause, to sow disorder, to make a point, to challenge the status quo, or for some other possibly quite private reason. I try to use the word dispassionately and do not imply a value judgment. In the 1970s, even the designations "Baader-Meinhof Group" and "Red Army Faction" (RAF) were contentious. The German authorities insisted that they were pursuing a *Bande* (as in "bandit"); calling them a "group" bestowed a degree of legitimacy. To say "RAF" (either phonetically as *raff* or enunciating the letters as *err aa ff*) could be thought tantamount to expressing allegiance. "Baader-Meinhof" was always a misnomer anyway. Gudrun Ensslin was arguably more influential than either Ulrike Meinof or Andreas Baader. Early press reports called them "Baader-Mahler," after the lawyer Horst Mahler, who made common cause with his clients in the summer of 1970 (and who is now an *eminence grise* of the extreme right).

After 1977 Baader, Ensslin, and Meinhof were all dead (and Mahler had defected), but the group originally named after two of them continued to operate for 21 more years. I use "Baader-Meinhof" to refer to all the left-wing terrorist groupings over the whole period in question. The two most important of these, at least as far as the novels are concerned, were the *Revolutionäre Zellen* (RZ, or Revolutionary Cells, sometimes called the Red Cells), which existed for more than 20 years, sometimes in collaboration with the RAF, and the *Bewegung Zweiter Juni* (June 2nd Movement), which merged with the RAF in 1980. There were also the shorter-lived *Tupamaros*, and the West Berlin based *Blues* and the *Umherschweifende Haschrebellen* (the Wandering Hash Rebels), whose heyday was 1968–1969. These are the groupings that impinge on the fiction. Where it is necessary to distinguish between them, I do so. Otherwise I intend "Baader-Meinhof and the novel" or "Baader-Meinhof fiction" to be inclusive. My dates neatly encompass four whole decades, beginning with the birth of the Baader-Meinhof Group itself, whose roots reached back of course much earlier, and ending with the publication of what (for now) is the last Baader-Meinhof novel. If one part of my theory is correct, novelists' fascination with Baader-Meinhof is now over. There were no new German novels in 2011 and only one in 2010.

One problem with my plot-focused methodology is that it risks making all the novels sound of equal quality, or, in other words, that I make no aesthetic judgments. For the record, I can state that I admire everything written by F. C. Delius and the old masters Günter Grass and Heinrich Böll. Of the novels I discuss in depth, I recommend *My Sister, My Antigone* (Weil, 1980), *The Mountain Pass* (Klöppel, 2002) and, most highly, *Part of the Solution* (Peltzer (2007). *Schäfer's Torments* (Haderer 2009) is the best *krimi*. I have found most of the others rewarding to read and have only given up before the end on two occasions (I had better not say which, but some readers will be able to tell).

JULIAN PREECE
December 2011,
Swansea

A BRIEF HISTORY

Much Baader-Meinhof history is known more or less by heart by West Germans who were in their twenties in the 1960s or 1970s. As some of it is key to the novels that I discuss, a summary will be useful to readers born elsewhere or at a later date. What follows is highly selective and only includes episodes or individuals depicted in the novels themselves.

June 2, 1967: A plainclothes police officer called Karl-Heinz Kurras shoots the 27-year-old Benno Ohnesorg at a demonstration against the state visit of the Shah of Iran to West Berlin. At the time of the shooting, the Shah, his wife Farah Diba, and their host Willy Brandt, until recently mayor of West Berlin, now foreign minister in a "grand coalition" of Christian and Social Democrats, are watching a production of *The Magic Flute* at the Deutsche Oper on West Berlin's Bismarckstraße. Ohnesorg was shot in the back of the head at point-blank range. He was unarmed and was taking part in his first demonstration. Dozens of other students were beaten, both by Iranian security personnel, members of the notorious SAVAK, and by the West Berlin police. The journalist Ulrike Meinhof condemned the Shah's visit in an article that was distributed to demonstrators. After the demonstration and the shooting of Ohnesorg, Gudrun Ensslin is recorded as saying about the German authorities: "This is the generation of Auschwitz. You cannot conduct arguments with them."

April 2, 1968: Gudrun Ensslin and Andreas Baader, assisted by Thorward Proll and Horst Söhnlein, plant homemade incendiary devices in two Frankfurt department stores, timed to explode in the middle of the night. The resulting fires trigger sprinklers, which causes damage worth millions of marks, but no one is hurt. The action is inspired by a spoof pamphlet, *Burn, warehouse, burn!* written by pranksters inspired by French Situationists led by Dieter Kunzelmann, the leading figure in West Berlin's Kommune 1, and is meant to draw attention to the American bombing of Vietnam. The arsonists are arrested two days later. At a trial in September, where they are defended by Horst Mahler, they are sentenced to three years in prison.

April 11, 1968: The attempted assassination of the student leader Rudi Dutschke outside the offices of the SDS on West Berlin's Kurfürstendamm. The would-be assassin, Josef Bachmann, had acted on increasingly febrile calls in the popular press to "Stop Dutchske Now!" Dutschke's supporters responded by laying siege to the West Berlin printing presses of the Axel Springer media corporation. Some of the Molotov cocktails were passed to the protestors, who included Meinhof, by the agent provocateur and police informer, Peter Urbach, who was employed by the *Verfassungsschutz*.

May 1968: Revolution on the streets of Paris.

March 1969: The election of Gustav Heinemann to the federal presidency begins the *Machtwechsel* (change of power), which takes place in September when Willy Brandt, Social Democrat leader and former resister against the Nazis, wins his first term in office at the head of a coalition of Social Democrats (SPD) and Free Democrats (FDP).

June 1969: Baader and Ensslin are released, pending a review of their sentences. They work on a social project in Frankfurt aimed at integrating adolescents brought up in state "care homes." These *Fürsorgeheime*, which are designed to discipline wayward working-class youngsters, are a site of state oppression in the eyes of the Left and were a key cause for the nascent RAF. One of these adolescents is Peter-Jürgen Boock, who will play a key role in the kidnapping of Hanns-Martin Schleyer in September 1977. In November, the review turns down Baader and Ensslin's appeal, and they are required to serve out the remaining 20 months of their sentences. They abscond to Paris and Rome, resurfacing in West Berlin in February the following year, where they stay with Meinhof and her twin daughters. Meinhof is writing a play on life in a girls' *Fürsorgeheim* called *Bambule* (meaning "riot")

April 4, 1970: Baader is rearrested as he returns from a nocturnal mission to a graveyard where, according to Urbach, weapons have been buried. He is stopped for speeding and is unable to recite the details on the borrowed driving license he has with him.

May 14, 1970: Baader is freed from jail by his friends. Meinhof had written to the prison governor requesting an interview with him, showing a copy of a contract for a book on *Fürsorgeheime* that she claimed to be writing for Klaus Wagenbach's Rotbuch publishing house. Baader is allowed to go to the library of the Institute for Social Affairs in Dahlem, West Berlin, to meet her. After less than an hour, Ensslin and four accomplices arrive to help Baader escape. The 60-year-old librarian, Georg Linke, is badly wounded when the only man in the group fires at him. Meinhof joins Ensslin and Baader in leaping from the first-storey window and running towards the waiting getaway car. In this moment the Baader-Meinhof Group is born.

June 8–21, 1970: Two groups, including Baader, Ensslin, Mahler, and Meinhof, fly from East Berlin to Beirut, where they proceed to a Fatah guerilla training camp in the Jordanian desert. They are not the first (or by any means the last) German revolutionaries to make this journey. Their first association with the Palestinians is not recorded as harmonious or productive, but they continue intermittently to work with anti-Zionist (and often anti-Semitic) forces in the Middle East for the next two decades.

September 1970: Journalist Stefan Aust, who had worked with Meinhof at the left-wing magazine *konkret*, retrieves Meinhof's twin eight-year old daughters from a beach commune on Sicily on behalf of their father, Klaus Rainer Röhl, Meinhof's estranged husband. According to one report their mother intended them to be transferred to a camp for Palestinian orphans in Jordan.

October 8, 1970: Arrest of Horst Mahler.

July 15, 1971: 20-year-old hairdresser Petra Schelm, who was a member of the group that traveled to Jordan, is shot in Hamburg.

September 1971: Horst Herold becomes President of the *Bundeskriminalamt*. He instigates the technique of *rasterfahndung* (pattern searching), which boils down to treating all West Germans of a certain age with some features in common with RAF members as suspicious. He uses new technology to store and match data and becomes associated in the public mind as the RAF's number-one adversary; for his critics, he is the head of a "surveillance state." His techniques are successful, but inflammatory and ultimately counterproductive.

October 22, 1971: Police officer Norbert Schmid is shot in Hamburg.

December 4, 1971: Georg von Rauch, a leading member of the *Blues* with links to the RAF, is shot in West Berlin.

January 28, 1972: The so-called "Anti-Radicals Decree" *(Radikalenerlass)* becomes law; it requires anyone wishing to join state service to declare loyalty to the *Grundgesetz* or Basic Law (the supposedly interim constitution the Federal Republic adopted in 1949).

March 2, 1972: Thomas Weisbecker, who is associated with the *Tupamaros*, is shot in Augsburg.

May 11–24, 1972: In the RAF's so-called "May Offensive," four American soldiers are killed in attacks on military bases in Frankfurt and Heidelberg. Other bombs explode in Karlsruhe, directed against a federal judge; at the Springer media concern's offices in Hamburg; and at police headquarters in Augsburg and Munich.

June 1–15, 1972: On the eve of the fifth anniversary of the Ohnesorg shooting, Baader and his two key comrades, Jan-Carl Raspe and Holger Meins, are arrested after a siege in a Frankfurt suburb. Responding to a tipoff, the police ambush them when they come to retrieve explosives deposited in a garage. The siege is broadcast live on television. Ensslin and Meinhof are arrested over the next two weeks. Herold is triumphant. Now begins, however, the more effective phase of the RAF's campaign, which will last more than five years. RAF prisoners are distributed across the republic, to stop them from fomenting trouble among other inmates. While awaiting trial, they are kept largely in solitary confinement. They carry out numerous hunger strikes. The authorities make mistakes. The photographs of Meinhof and Margit Schiller at the moment of their arrests reinforced the perception that the prisoners were subjected to mistreatment.

June 25, 1972: Police in Stuttgart shoot dead the young British businessman Ian McLeod, wrongly believing him to be a member of RAF.

September 5, 1972: The massacre of eleven Israeli athletes at the Munich Olympics. Eight militants from the Palestinian Black September group break into the Olympic Village, shoot two and kidnap nine Israeli athletes with the aim of securing the release of Palestinian and other comrades held in Israeli and German jails, including Meinhof and Baader. The day ends at Furstenfeldbrück airfield when the athletes are killed by their kidnappers during a bungled police rescue attempt. The crack commando unit GSG-9 is formed as a result of this public debacle. Writing from prison, Meinhof supports the kidnapping unequivocally.

June 5, 1974: Murder of Ulrich Schmücker in West Berlin, a member of June 2nd Movement, who agreed to cooperate with the *Verfassungsschutz* after his arrest and imprisonment two years earlier. The precise circumstances of his murder and the degree of secret service complicity remain unclear, despite four trials in the longest-running criminal case in the history of the Federal Republic (1976–1991).

November 9, 1974: Death of Holger Meins from self-induced starvation in Wittlich prison. Allowing him to die of starvation made him into the RAF's most effective martyr.

December 4, 1974: Hans-Joachim Klein, a member of the Revolutionary Cells, chauffeurs Jean-Paul Sartre to visit Baader in prison in Stuttgart-Stammheim.

February 27, 1975: Kidnapping by the June 2nd Movement of the Christian Democrat candidate for the mayoralty of West Berlin, Peter Lorenz. In exchange for his return, five terrorist prisoners are released and are flown to Yemen. RAF prisoners are from now on placed in a prison in Stammheim on the edge of Stuttgart, where they inhabit single cells on the top floor of the same building. For the first time in modern German history, male and female prisoners live next to one another. If their conditions up to now were often difficult, from this point they are the best-kept prisoners in the land.

April 24, 1975: The "Holger Meins Commando" storms the West German Embassy in Stockholm. They demand the release of 26 RAF prisoners. Two diplomats are killed before the terrorists accidentally detonate one of their own bombs and the siege is ended. One terrorist is killed instantly. Another dies of his wounds days later. RAF supporters denounce the Swedish and German authorities for transporting him to Germany in a critical state.

May 21, 1975: The trial of Meinhof, Baader, Ensslin, and Jean-Carl Raspe begins in a specially built court room in Stammheim.

July 31, 1975: The June 2nd Movement raids a West Berlin bank, getting away with 100,000 marks and distributing marshmallows to passersby.

December 21, 1975: Hans-Joachim Klein and Gabriele Kröcher-Tiedemann, both members of the Revolutionary Cells, join Illich Ramirez Sanchez ("Carlos the Jackal") in a raid on the headquarters of the Organization of Petroleum Exporting Countries (OPEC) in Vienna's Obere Donaustraße, killing three. Backed by the new Iraqi leader Saddam Hussein, the aim of this PFLP action is to press wealthy Middle Eastern states, in particular Iran and Saudi Arabia, to show more hostility to Israel. The Austrian government flies out terrorists and hostages to Algiers that evening, including a badly wounded Klein.

May 9, 1976: Ulrike Meinhof is found hanging dead in her prison cell. The circumstances surrounding her death, which were not professionally investigated, are among the most mysterious in Baader-Meinhof history. Street protest is widespread. *Sponti* leader Joschka Fischer narrowly avoids responsibility for the death of a police officer in clashes on the streets of Frankfurt.

June 27–July 4, 1976: An Air France passenger jet carrying 248 passengers, including 92 Israelis and 12 crew on a flight from Tel Aviv to Paris is hijacked on June 27 by two members of the Revolutionary Cells, Winfried Böse and Brigitte Kuhlmann, and two Palestinians from the PFLP. After refueling in Libya, the plane lands in Entebbe, Uganda. Idi Amin's forces cooperate fully with the terrorists, who demand the release of political prisoners held in five different countries. Most prisoners are Palestinians jailed in Israel, but they include six Germans, including Jan-Carl Raspe, though not Baader or Ensslin. On July 1, the non-Jewish hostages are released and flown to Paris. Most of the remaining Jewish hostages are freed in a raid by the Israel Defense Force in the night of July 3–4. All the terrorists, three hostages, one Israeli (the elder brother of future Israeli Prime Minister Benjamin Netanyahu), and at least 20 Ugandan soldiers are killed.

April 7, 1977: Federal State Prosecutor Siegfried Buback and his driver and bodyguard are shot by a killer on a motorcycle as their car waits at a traffic light in Karlsruhe. Christian Klar and Brigitte Mohnhaupt are later convicted of the killings.

April 28, 1977: Baader, Ensslin, and Raspe are sentenced to life imprisonment for four murders, thirty-nine attempted murders, and causing six explosions.

July 30, 1977: A bungled attempt to kidnap Jürgen Ponto, the spokesman for the board of the Dresdner Bank, results in his killing. The killers were accompanied by Ponto's goddaughter, Susanne Albrecht, who arrived at his door bearing a bunch of flowers. Klar, Mohnhaupt, and Peter-Jürgen Boock are later convicted. Albrecht eventually seeks refuge in the GDR, where she is rediscovered after the state's collapse in 1990.

September 5, 1977: The beginning of the "German Autumn," exactly five years after the massacre at the Munich Olympics. Industrialist Hanns-Martin Schleyer, a former SS officer and now president of the Employers Association, noted for his hard-line stance in labor disputes, is kidnapped in a Cologne suburb. His driver and three armed bodyguards are shot by his kidnappers, who include Boock. They demand the release of the RAF prisoners in Stammheim. The authorities open negotiations, but also impose a news blackout and refuse the prisoners contact with each other or their lawyers, which is illegal. The BKA fail to find Schleyer.

October 13, 1977: A Lufthansa passenger jet (the *Landshut*) carrying 86 Germans from Majorca to Frankfurt is hijacked by a Palestinian commando named "Halimeh" (after the *nom de guerre* of the RZ activist Brigitte Kuhlmann killed at Entebbe). The plane lands at Rome, Lanarka, Dubai, Aden, and finally at Mogadishu in Somalia. The hijackers' demands include the release of the RAF prisoners. The pilot Jürgen Schumann is shot dead in Aden on October 16th. After the hostages have been doused in duty-free alcohol and explosives have been installed around the plane, it is stormed by the German police commando unit GSG-9 at five minutes past midnight German time on 18 October. The operation is simpler than that mounted by the Israelis at Entebbe, as the Germans are assisted by the Somalis. All passengers, the remaining crew, and one wounded hijacker survive. That morning, Baader, Ensslin, and Raspe are found dead or dying in their cells. They did their best to make their suicides look like murder. The following day, the police receive the news that Schleyer's body can be found in the boot of a car in the French border town of Mulhouse. This terminates the events which will come to be known as the German Autumn.

November 9, 1977: Kidnapping of millionaire Austrian businessman Walter Michael Palmers, owner of a retail chain specializing in women's underwear, by the June 2nd Movement in league with three Viennese students. Palmers is ransomed for 30 million schillings (approximately 2.5 million dollars); the students are immediately arrested.

November 19, 1979: RAF member Rolf Klemens Wagner and three accomplices raid a branch of the Swiss Volksbank in Zurich, taking 473,000 Swiss francs and shooting dead a passerby, injuring another as well as two policemen as they flee. Wagner is arrested.

June 2, 1980: Merger of RAF and the June 2nd Movement.

May 11, 1981: The economics minister for the state of Hesse, FDP politician Heinz-Herbert Karry, is shot dead in bed at his home in Frankfurt. The Revolutionary Cells claim responsibility some two weeks later but no one is ever arrested for the crime.

By November 1982 all those responsible for the killings during the "German Autumn," including Christian Klar, Brigitte Mohnhaupt, and Peter-Jürgen Boock, are brought to justice. Over the next decade, the next generation of the RAF carries out a number of attacks against NATO; American soldiers; and German politicians, diplomats, and businessmen. These attacks are anonymous and often are ruthlessly efficient. No new leadership emerges to rival that of Baader, Meinhof, and Ensslin.

June 17, 1988: Andrea Klump and Horst Ludwig Meyer plant bomb in a discotheque frequented by American soldiers in Rota, Spain. It fails to go off and both escape.

November 30, 1989: Three weeks after the fall of the Berlin Wall, Deutsche Bank boss Alfred Herrhausen is murdered in Bad Homburg as he is being driven along a suburban street in his armor-plated Mercedes. The attack is highly sophisticated and is detonated by the car passing through a beam of light emitted from a bicycle parked on the pavement. Herrhausen's chauffeur is unhurt. The RAF claim responsibility for the attack.

June 1990: Four months before the unification of the two German states is officially sealed, ten former RAF members are arrested in the German Democratic Republic, including Susanne Albrecht, Silke Maier-Witt, and Inge Viett. They have lived in the GDR under new identities for ten years.

April 1, 1991: Murder by unknown gunman of Detlev Karsten Rohwedder, head of the Treuhand agency, charged with transferring former GDR state enterprises into private ownership. The shooting, from a distance of more than 60 meters, is as professional as the dispatch of Herrhausen, which feeds speculation that the RAF, which again claims responsibility, did not act alone. In 2000 the BKA announces that new forensic techniques have enabled them to identify a hair found at the murder site as belonging to the RAF member Wolfgang Grams.

January 1992: The Revolutionary Cells announce their dissolution.

April 10, 1992: The RAF announces a halt on attacks on leading government and business figures.

June 27, 1993: Despite—or perhaps because of—the presence of 97 officers from the BKA, GSG-9, and the Federal Border Police, Wolfgang Grams and GSG-9 officer Michael Newrzella are killed in a bungled attempt to arrest Grams and Birgit Hogefeld at Bad Kleinen railway station in Mecklenburg. The circumstances of Grams's death have never been clarified to the satisfaction of all parties. Nine leading officials, including Interior Minister Rudolf Seiters and Federal State Prosecutor Alexander von Stahl, resign in the aftermath.

April 20, 1998: The RAF releases a communiqué announcing its own dissolution.

August 1998: Hans-Joachim Klein is arrested in France.

September 1998: Helmut Kohl of the CDU is replaced as federal chancellor by Gerhard Schröder of the SPD, at the head of a Red–Green Coalition that includes Ensslin's former lawyer Otto Schily as SPD minister of the interior and former Frankfurt street-fighter Joschka Fischer as Green foreign minister.

September 1999: Horst Ludwig Meyer is killed in a shootout in Vienna, and Andrea Klump is arrested.

October 2000: The trial of Klein begins; Foreign Minister Fischer is called as a witness.

March 25, 2007: Brigitte Mohnhaupt is released from prison after serving 25 years.

May 8, 2007: President Horst Köhler refuses to pardon Christian Klar.

December 18, 2008: Klar is released.

May 2009: A chance discovery in the archives of the East German secret police (Stasi) shows that Karl-Heinz Kurras had been an East German agent when he shot Ohnesorg on June 2, 1967.

Note: This brief history was compiled from Butz Peters, *RAF. Terrorismus in Deutschland* (Munich: Knaur, 1993); Stefan Aust, *Der Baader-Meinhof Komplex*, 2nd edition (Hamburg: Hoffmann & Campe, 1998); Hans Kundnani, *Utopia or Auschwitz: Germany's 1968 Generation and the Holocaust* (London: Hurst, 2009); and Ron Augustin, *Labourhistory.net/raf/chronology.*

Introduction: The Baader-Meinhof Myth Machine

The idea of armed urban guerillas waging an underground war against the state has fascinated many of Germany's leading contemporary writers. The original leadership trio of the Rote Armee Fraktion (Red Army Faction, or RAF, also known as the Baader-Meinhof Group) have consequently been depicted in more novels than any other Germans from the second half of the twentieth century. Why this should be so is at second glance puzzling. The outline history of German left-wing terrorism is undoubtedly exciting, but Andreas Baader, Ulrike Meinhof, and Gudrun Ensslin exerted no real influence on German politics. They left behind no great works. The RAF, which was their creation, enjoyed no mass support and never posed a great danger either to the state or to the public. The total number of fatalities in the 28 years of the RAF's existence is little more than the number that can die on the roads in Germany in a bad week.[1] Over roughly the same period more than 3500 people lost their lives in the Troubles in Northern Ireland. In Italy between 1969 and 1983, five times as many are estimated to have died in unrest involving extreme right-wing and left-wing "terrorists."[2] The leading historian of the German Student Movement, Wolfgang Kraushaaar, has called the RAF "in their basic characteristics autistic and thus at their core unpolitical."[3] In the showdown with the West German state, which lasted for 44 anxious days in September and October 1977, the release of their own prisoners was the sole issue at stake.

Another leading critic, Klaus Theweleit, has argued that the RAF's lack of a political standpoint was precisely how and why they enjoyed support:

> The abstract identification of so many who had "radical feelings" with the RAF could only function as well as it did because there was, especially on the RAF's side, zero politics. I consider this point to be crucial. The "anti-imperial struggle" against the capitalist Federal Republic [...] did not articulate a single demand, only abstract phrases such as "fight with weapons," "unconditional struggle," "never give up, persevere at all costs."[4]

Here perhaps we have one of the reasons that German left-wing terrorism has proved such a rich source of myths. To a considerable degree, novelists have been able to add their own political content. "Baader-Meinhof" is a semi-blank screen on which they project ideas, scenarios, and fantasies. The terrorists' actions themselves were already rich in possible meanings because they operated in the shadow of Nazism. The RAF, for example, used the martyr politics of historically resonant dates, as terrorist and liberation movements tend to do. Holger Meins starved himself to death on November 9, 1974, which was the anniversary of the abdication of Kaiser Wilhelm II (1918), Hitler's Beer Hall Putsch (1923), and *Kristallnacht* (1938). Meinhof hanged herself in the night of May 8–9, 1976, 31 years to the day after the end of the war in Europe (for Germany either a day of liberation or of capitulation, depending on your politics); and what was left of the RAF finally announced its disbandment on April 20, 1998, which was Hitler's 109th birthday. Baader-Meinhof reinscribed German history, partly counteracting Nazism, but sometimes even reenacting it. Imprinted on this historical backcloth, their actions were interpreted through or against it, often to the point that they became burdened with too much meaning.

Baader-Meinhof also enthralled segments of two generations of West Germans because they acted out a drama of revolt. They posed fundamental questions to the rest of the German left. Whom do you support? Them or us? The crypto-fascist state or the revolutionary vanguard risking all to defeat it? The questions were false on all counts. There were indeed still old Nazis in powerful positions, and the anticommunist Anti-Radicals Decree (*Radikalenerlass*) of 1972 criminalized some left-wingers. Sections of the press dominated by the Springer media concern used incendiary rhetoric against students that had no place in a democracy. But the Federal Republic of Germany was not fascist and none of the violent left-wing groups was in the vanguard of anything. What the RAF performed after the arrest of its leaders was the categorical rejection of the state, which ended in the leaders' own self-destruction. After seeing where this route led, their contemporaries gradually engaged with the state that they instinctively distrusted. By the end, once the generation of 1968 (or 68ers) finally formed a government in 1998, they had embraced it.

The decade and a half after the "German Autumn," as the sequence of bloody events in September to October 1977 came to be known, during which occasional assassinations and other violent attacks continued, plays a different role in the political imagination. From the perspective of the 2000s, when most Baader-Meinhof fiction was written, the assassins of the 1980s offered a rebellious alternative to compromise with a capitalist and imperialist system that was still perceived as corrupt. As this phase of RAF history is less well known (and, as few charges have been brought with respect to the murders that occurred then, it is up to a point less knowable), the 1980s are the favored decade for more recent Baader-Meinhof novels. There are a number of reasons for the glut of Baader-Meinhof fiction in the 2000s. One critic identifies a gap in literary production between 1978 and 1988 and offers a number of explanations, such as exhaustion, resignation, and the "shock" of 1977.[5] The resurgence of interest after 2000 indicates a belated readiness to incorporate the terrorist "years of lead" fully into the national imaginary. It part of the continued preoccupation with all aspects of the recent national past, which is far greater in Germany than in more self-confident nations. The made-for-television docudrama *Death Game* (dir. Breloer, 1997), was the first German Baader-Meinhof film intended to appeal to a wide audience. It countered lingering suspicions that the supposed continuity between the Third Reich and the Federal Republic, reflected in the personnel in elite positions, made the RAF's actions comprehensible, even justified. Breloer shows the ex-*Wehrmacht* lieutenant Chancellor Helmut Schmidt saving the republic in the name of democracy and the rule of law. The experience of military combat as a young man under the Nazis steeled him for his defense of republican democracy. Breloer's narrative shows growing general confidence in the state.

Interest in Baader-Meinhof history intensified after the formation in 1998 of a government of 68ers, in the shape of a coalition between the Social Democrats and the Green Party, which had grown belatedly out of the protest movements of the late 1960s. A favorite plot idea in a number of recent thrillers involves middle-aged figures from the professions or business who fear that their past Baader-Meinhof connections will be exposed. The idea was taken from life. In 1977, the new chancellor, Gerhard Schröder, had defended the student publishers of the so-called "Mescalero Letter" in court. The notorious letter began by conceding "very secret joy" (*klammheimliche Freude*) on hearing the news of the murder by the RAF of the state prosecutor Siegfried Buback, before its author rejected such murders as both ineffective and illegitimate. Despite its message of antiviolence, the confession contained in its opening phrase became notorious. Jürgen Trittin, the second most senior Green Party politician in the cabinet, had been a student activist at Göttingen University at the time that the letter was published in the student union magazine. The presence in the new cabinet of Joschka Fischer as deputy chancellor and foreign minister and of Otto Schily as minister of the interior signaled that the 68ers had arrived. The life paths of public figures such as Fischer appear to invite literary reinvention, and Fischer undoubtedly inspired some writers. Wolfgang Kraushaar presents Fischer's life through that of the nineteenth-century radical turned Bismarckian *realpolitiker*, Ludwig von Rochau.[6] It is a narrative technique worthy of the great novel of German reunification, *Too Far Afield* (Grass, 1995), which is included in this study because of its fictionalized account of the shooting of Karsten Detlev Rohwedder in April 1991, the last RAF assassination of a leading business figure, which the novel lays at the door of an anonymous worker inspired by a fictional nineteenth-century forebear. Fischer had been a *sponti* militant whose street-fighting protest on the day of Meinhof's death resulted in a young policeman narrowly escaping death. He also knew various members of the Revolutionary Cells (*Revolutionäre Zellen* or RZ for short). Schily was Ensslin's defense lawyer from 1972 to 1977; he became a member of the *Bundestag* for the Greens before switching to the Social Democrats and serving as an authoritarian law-and-order interior minister in the Red–Green Coalition.

In contrast, their former ally Horst Mahler was a teenage nationalist from a Nazi family; he became a radical left-wing lawyer who first defended members of the future RAF before joining them. It was claimed in 2011 that Mahler possibly had links with the Stasi in the late 1960s. Mahler distanced himself from the RAF once in prison and reentered public life as an extreme nationalist in the late 1990s, thus ending up ideologically back where he started.[7]

The right-wing press set out to discredit Fischer. But he emerged strengthened from the exposure. He could explain how and why his views had changed; his political maturation followed a pattern that mirrored the evolution of the state itself. With this normalization of the terrorist past came a greater willingness to say and imagine things about it. Baader-Meinhof is a peculiarly German story, because it is predicated on German history and on German responses to it. Writing about it in a work of fiction entails posing the national question, whether novelists are aware of it or not.

Another reason for renewed literary interest in the RAF after 2000 was the political disagreement over the economic model that the new Berlin Republic should adopt, which reached crisis point in the election year of 2005. Democratic institutions are securely anchored at every level of German society, but in imaginative works by a number of leading German writers, there is an alternative to them that can be brought about through means that include guns and bombs. More important perhaps is the fact that by the turn of the twenty-first century, the RAF was well and truly consigned to history. Once it no longer posed any sort of threat, the time was ripe for its symbolic value to be charted in literature. As poetry is "emotion recollected in tranquillity," novels on historical subjects tend not to get written until the historical chapter is closed. The process shows some of the hallmarks of trauma: Before you remember, you have to forget. The past is repeated in the medium of literature in part because the events were not properly concluded, worked through, or discussed at the time. The cause of the trauma was enacted in 1977, in particular the murder of Hanns-Martin Schleyer. For a number of years after 1977, representing terrorism became taboo. Even today, Schleyer himself never features directly as a fictional character, despite writers' fascination with him.

All writers who engage with Baader-Meinhof, not just novelists, employ an unusual range of literary tropes in response to the terrorists' provocative deeds. The first history was written in English by Gillian Becker, a Jewish South African novelist. She showed in her title that she was narrating a tale about a generational drama inextricably linked with the Nazi past; *Hitler's Children*.[8] Others have interpreted the events as a violent Freudian family romance, in which the sons and daughters rose up against their sinful parents.[9] Stefan Aust's standard history, *The Baader Meinhof Complex*, first published in German in 1985, consists of a series of semiliterary vignettes. The idea of a "complex" originated with the *Bundeskriminalamt* (the BKA or Federal Bureau of Criminal Investigation), which borrowed it from US President Eisenhower's warning against a military–industrial complex threatening to take over America.[10] *The Baader Meinhof Complex* has been the best-selling book of nonfiction in postwar Germany, and it is a key source for a number of novels. Its author became the editor of the weekly news magazine *Der Spiegel,* which regularly led with RAF-related news stories.

Aust's book is also littered with references to books by the RAF leaders' favorite authors, such as Herman Melville (*Moby Dick*), Thomas Wolfe (*You Can't Go Home Again*), Bertolt Brecht (*The Measures Taken*), and Jean Genet (*The Maids*). Baader, Meinhof, and Ensslin all left substantial book collections in their cells in Stammheim Prison. According to Elfriede Jelinek's *Ulrike Maria Stuart* (2006), Aust's account of the conflict between Meinhof and Ensslin that preceded Meinhof's suicide borrows from Schiller's drama about Elizabeth I and Mary Queen of Scots, *Maria Stuart*. A double biography of Baader and the BKA chief Horst Herold, *Baader and Herold: Description of a Struggle* by Dorothea Hauser,[11] refers to the events of 1977 as a "state foundation myth," because the result was an emphatic victory for the government, which gained legitimacy as a consequence of its crushing of the terrorists. This interpretation of the events is now a widely held view. The biography concludes with a dramatic sentence: "Andreas Baader and Horst Herold never met each other in person." The author may have little new information on either man, but the lack of new information reminds us that what is sometimes needed more than new facts are narratives that account for what is already known. The subtitle, "Description of a Struggle," is borrowed from Kafka.

Likewise the subtitle of Gerd Koenen's triple biography of Gudrun Ensslin and her two lovers, Andreas Baader, and Bernward Vesper, *"Urszenen des deutschen Terrorismus"* ("Ur-scenes of German terrorism"), is adapted from Freud.[12] This famous triangular love story has recently been made into another major film: *Who If Not Us?* (dir. Veiel, 2011). It is one of the Baader-Meinhof narratives that appears never to grow stale, no matter how many times it is retold on the printed page or re-presented on screen. There is something archetypal in the perceptions of both Baader and Ensslin. Each was good-looking and was associated in the public mind with both sexual prowess and androgyny. Baader was a force of natural energy with a devil-may-care attitude. He exuded the charisma of an American film star (Marlon Brando, Humphrey Bogart, and James Dean were repeatedly cited as comparators or role models). Ensslin was cool and calculating, at once, in male eyes, dominatrix and femme fatale, perhaps more Shakespeare's Lady Macbeth than Schiller's Elizabeth.

The film version of Aust's book (dir. Edel, 2008) is a fast-paced series of tableaux depicting incidents that have been pored over by journalists and sympathizers as if they were scholars examining the manuscript of an ancient text. No single moment caught onlookers' imagination more than Meinhof's leap from the window of the library in the Institute for Social Research in Miquelstrasse in the Dahlem district of West Berlin on May 14, 1970. The incident is rendered memorably in Uli Edel's film. Dea Loher made it into the basis of a neo-Schillerian play in 1993 entitled (after Hobbes and Melville), *Leviathan*.[13] An American historian sees the leap as rich in meaning for both the principal individuals:

> The leap was patently metaphorical: Baader plunged into precarious freedom. Meinhof [...] leapt into an entirely new life of danger and notoriety, in which bombs replaced words as her main weapons. More than anything else, they both took a leap of faith; trusting in their cause, each other, and their comrades forming the RAF, they somehow imagined victory in a literal war against the government of the Federal Republic.[14]

But the idea that Meinhof decided in that split second to exchange her conventional existence as journalist and mother for the life of a revolutionary on the run from the law is contested.[15] It is a fiction that makes sense only in the imaginations of those looking on at what she did and projecting their own feelings on to her deed.

The RAF wanted to author history through their deeds. Their notorious communiqué announcing where Schleyer's body could be found has attracted attention for its callous account of Schleyer's murder ("we have ended his corrupt existence").[16] But in the first part of their statement, the RAF refers to the government's own *dramaturgie*, which included the storming of the hijacked Lufthansa jet *Landshut* in Mogadishu, which was followed by the deaths in Stammheim of Baader, Ensslin, and Raspe, which the RAF was determined the world should believe were murders.[17] From the Frankfurt Arson Trial in 1968 to the Stammheim suicides in 1977, the RAF dealt in images and impressions and their own effect on public opinion. Their actions and the reactions to them took the form of bloody performances to be photographed, discussed, and interpreted—which is of course the purpose of most acts of terrorism. Their story is sometimes relayed in images made famous through repeated showing in the media, which is the effect that Leander Scholz aims to emulate in his much-discussed novel *Rose Party* (2001). Images were all-important to the founders of the 2nd June Movement, who chose that name because whenever it was mentioned it would be necessary to explain that it commemorated the day in 1967 that Benno Ohnesorg was shot. In this climate, Holger Meins's death by self-starvation can be transmuted into murder (instead of sacrificial suicide). Perhaps the RAF's greatest coup of all, which took the form of an especially macabre work of art, was to convince much of the world that their three leaders had been murdered on the night of October 17–18, 1977. The alternative to victory was self-destruction, which is part of another richly resonant narrative. According to Gerd Koenen, the seventh floor of Stammheim's high-security wing, where the RAF were incarcerated, became a second *Führerbunker* in the subconscious minds of the RAF leadership[18]

Inserting these events into a satisfactory historical narrative preoccupied writers in the years that followed 1977. The film critic Thomas Elsaesser sees multiple mythological and literary narratives at work, linking national history to psychoanalysis, inherited guilt, the "return of the repressed," and Shakespearean and Sophoclean archetypes (such as *Hamlet* and *Oedipus/Antigone*):

> It was as if the events—at once demanding an explanation and in their emblematically dense textuality, inviting hermeneutic excess—had proven so eminently interpretable because they also inscribed themselves in several other histories, where revolutionary violence, the 1960s student protest movement, and even the phenomenon of international terrorism and government reprisals figure only obliquely.[19]

For the historical sociologist Norbert Elias, the generational conflict recalls a classical tragedy.[20] Both sides resembled more and more closely their adversaries' negative image of them. Elias was right about tragedy, insofar as its purpose is to cleanse its audience of unwanted emotions, which are acted out for them by others. Many German Baader-Meinhof narratives have sources in classical literature, religion, or mythology. The greatest mythologizer among the historians is Koenen, who presents the German Autumn as the Wagnerian climax to "the years of lead" ushered in by the Student Movement in 1967–68. His chapter title "Black Milk of Terror" is a reference to a line in Paul Celan's most famous poem about the Holocaust.[21] F. C. Delius gives the events mock-Christian symbolism of sacrifice and redemption in *Ascent to Heaven of an Enemy of the State* (1992). Both the terms "German Autumn" (for September–October 1977) and "years of lead" (for the longer period characterized by Baader-Meinhof violence and the state response to it) were popularized by film directors, who adapted the phrases from Romantic poetry.[22]

Some of the events and individuals seem to have been taken from a work of fiction. On the evening of June 2, 1967, a character in *Eros* (Krausser, 2006) muses about whether Benno Ohnesorg (whose surname means "without worry" or "carefree") would have become a martyr had his parents given him a more ordinary name: "Holger came into the room and bellowed, they have killed *Benno*, he—and many others after him— talked about *Benno* as if he were a close friend."[23] The last name of Petra Schelm, the pretty young hairdresser who was the first RAF member to be shot dead by the police, means "rogue" or "vagabond" (a *Schelmenroman* is a picaresque novel). The surname of the first casualty on the other side, the librarian in the Dahlem Institute, Georg Linke, means "left" or "leftist" and has connotations of clumsy (*linkisch*). He confronted the young women who arrived at his door to free Baader, thus showing what twentieth-century Germans have often been accused of not possessing, *zivilcourage*, or the courage to perform one's civic duty. But if Linke was the left, like the SPD-led coalition that composed the West German government in 1970, then where did that place the RAF? One answer is clear: often in some unsavory company. An RZ member who collaborated with a Palestinian commando to hijack an Air France airliner in June 1976 was named Winfried Böse (*böse* literally means "evil"). At Entebbe, where the airliner was awaited by the Ugandan dictator Idi Amin, it was none other than "Mr. Evil" who divided the Jewish from the non-Jewish passengers.[24] Here there is a problem in the literary and cinematic material. The events at Entebbe barely feature in German fiction or historiography. In English-language accounts they often have pride of place. German authors also largely ignore the massacre of Israeli athletes at the Munich Olympics in September 1972. As well as imposing narrative patterns or interrogating existing patterns of historiographic meaning, novelists select which events and characters to include in the first place. One finding of my book is that as soon as terrorist actions have a bearing on memories of the Holocaust, anti-Semitism, the contemporary Arab-Israeli conflict, or the Jewish presence in postwar Germany, German novelists do their best to pretend that they have not noticed.

However novelistic much of the history may be, not all episodes have found authors as readily as others. Hans-Joachim Klein, for instance, was a working-class member of the Revolutionary Cells whose mother survived Ravensbrück concentration camp, where she was sent for having a sexual relationship with a Jew. She killed herself shortly after her son was born, leaving him to be brought up by his policeman father, who regularly beat him. A year after driving Jean-Paul Sartre to visit Baader, "Klein Klein," as he was condescendingly nicknamed, found himself assisting Carlos the Jackal to hold up the Vienna conference of the Organization of Petroleum Exporting Countries (OPEC) on December 21, 1975. Klein's memoirs, which he wrote in hiding from both the police and his former comrades, are the rawest of the terrorist autobiographies and the most insightful.[25] Yet it took a Dutch documentarist until 2005 to depict Klein's experiences on-screen.[26] Only parts of the history of West German terrorism appear suitable for literary or cinematic treatment. The role played by comrades from the Middle East, such as Saddam Hussein, or groups operating in the Yemen, and the undesired connections with the Holocaust have often been omitted, repressed, or distorted. In *Dreamers of the Absolute* (2008), Michael Wildenhain belatedly fills a number of these gaps, even sketching a line of continuity between the Revolutionary Cells and al-Qaeda.

The unfurling of Baader-Meinhof history has had many twists and subplots. The subject has refused to go away in the two decades since German reunification. The Rohwedder assassination has generated almost as much written and filmic material as the German Autumn. The RAF remained a current topic after the death of Rohwedder's presumed assassin Wolfgang Grams in 1993 and even after the RAF's formal disbandment in 1998. Throughout the 1990s and 2000s, controversies centered on the events surrounding the bungled operation to arrest Grams and the role of the GDR in harboring RAF fugitives. A publicly funded Berlin exhibition entitled *Mythos RAF* caused a furore in 2003 because the organizers appeared too close to their subject, writing of the terrorists' "ideals" in their advance publicity.[27]

The Berlin Republic has measured itself against its terrorist past, confronted chunks of it, but also comforted itself, at least in fiction, with the thought that both parts of the new state shared a revolutionary past. East German communism collapsed before the RAF did, but it was essential for the RAF's existence from the beginning. The two histories are intertwined, albeit not to the extent that some recent novelists have made out. It is still not known whether there was a connection between Karl-Heinz Kurras's killing of Ohnesorg and Kurras's work for the Stasi.

Nonfiction authors who approach the subject autobiographically reconstruct fragmented memories of mediated events that they only partially comprehended at the time. What is remembered is not the author's personal experiences, but the coverage of events on television and in the newspapers. Dorothea Hauser explains that she was a twelve-year-old schoolgirl in 1977, unaffected by the ideological and emotional battles then being waged, but marked nonetheless by images and reports. Anne Siemens (b. 1974) begins a book of interviews with the relatives of RAF victims by recalling how as a child she saw the ubiquitous WANTED posters of RAF terrorists and on November 30, 1989 even heard the explosion that killed leading banker Alfred Herrhausen.[28] When the 41-year old detective Anton Glauberg in *The Last Performance* (Woelk, 2002) explains to his colleague, an East German ten years his junior, that he has "got little more to do with terrorism than you have. I was seven when Benno Ohnesorg was shot," she points out that this made him "seventeen when Schleyer was murdered. Old enough to take sides."[29]

In the 1990s the RAF began to be approached through "memory." As well as memoirs by former participants, there were book-length interviews with prisoners and ex-members. In the 2000s there was a trend for biographies. Since 1997 there have been at least seven biographies of Meinhof and numerous biographical accounts of Baader, Ensslin, and Vesper, as well as biographies of their most prominent opponents and victims, such as Schleyer and Herrhausen. Victims and bystanders came to be the subject of books or even wrote their own. Some of the paradigms in operation, such as "victim fiction," are borrowed from those devised to work through the memory of Nazism. The three volumes of essays entitled *After-Images*, edited by Inge Stephan and Alexandra Tacke, indicate the trajectory of their conceptual thinking: the first volume is on National Socialism; the second on the Turn or *Wende*, as the changes of 1989–90 are usually termed, and the last is on the RAF.[30]

The 1990s and 2000s witnessed a wave of novels about the Nazi past, which explore the individual involvement of family members in the Third Reich (dubbed the "new German family novel"). The central characters in several recent Baader-Meinhof novels also have personal connections with the terrorist past, which they learn about in the course of the action. Similar scenarios can be found in a number of popular films from the late 2000s. The favorite plot type involves a parent, usually a mother, who may not have played a role in the child's upbringing or who is mistakenly believed to be dead, and who turns out to have been a terrorist. There is an urge at work in this fiction to bring what is left of the estranged family back together again. Above all, mothers have to go back to being mothers. To make the emotional connections tangible in fiction, atypical family links are needed. The difference between the RAF and both Nazism and the *Wende* is that the latter were both experienced by everyone alive at the time. All Germans had memories of World War II, and the life of every

East German was turned upside down in 1989–1990. In contrast, only a tiny proportion of the population was even indirectly connected to any of the terrorist groupings, to their victims, or to the police who pursued them. The idea that contemporary Germans need to "work through" the terrorist past by finding out about their parents' involvement is absurd. Memories of the RAF are secondhand, because experience of terrorism was mediated through the press and television. Everyone followed the key events as they were reported in the media; they discussed them and formed opinions, backing one side or the other or identifying with some of the participants. The memories may be vicarious, but they are none the less powerful for all that. The guilt for a past deed that animates a number of these novels is historical guilt, the roots of which may ultimately lie in the Nazi period. If these family-based plot types are fanciful, it is because their function is symbolic: It is an idea of the national family that is being reassembled.

The very first book on the RAF, published in 1972, was not an overtly symbolic narrative at all, but a supposedly factual report commissioned by the BKA that was called simply *The Baader Meinhof Report*.[31] It is marked nonetheless by the polarities that shaped West German society in the early 1970s. As it embarked on its third decade, making it a few years younger than its self-styled militant adversaries, the Federal Republic was hardly a state that was comfortable in its own skin. *The Baader-Meinhof Report* was completed in July 1972, one month after the final arrest of the group's leading members. Its anonymous authors drew on reports from undercover agents, so-called *V-Männer*, working for the Federal Office for the Protection of the Constitution (the *Verfassungsschutz*). Perhaps surprisingly for such a publication, the report showed a broad interest in psychological motivation and historical precedents. The authors referred to women's lib as well as to the Oedipus complex. They even ventured into literary criticism, declaring themselves unimpressed, for instance, by how the Student Movement's guru Herbert Marcuse wrote German, and dismissing Meinhof's screenplay for the television film *Bambule* [Riot] as "childish."[32] Through their concern with the terrorists' private lives, the authors also show that they have the makings of a certain sort of novelist. Their approach was typical of instant Baader-Meinhof historiography as reproduced in the popular print media.

The Baader-Meinhof Report is prefaced by a statement from Horst Herold, then the BKA's new president, who proudly declares his faith in the police's ability to understand the behavior of militant groups on the political fringes who threaten state security. This is because, in Herold's opinion, "there is no other organ of the state that has so much insight and knowledge of aberrant behaviour patterns at its disposal, or that has its hand so close to the pulse of what is going on in society." The key word here is "aberrant" (*abseitig*), because what really characterizes their findings is not understanding at all, but the opposite. *The Baader-Meinhof Report* got it wrong on just about every count. Had its authors shown a novelist's empathy for their subject, the history of the FRG could have been quite different. A cleverer police force would have helped to defuse the critical situation instead of allowing it to escalate.

An officer who appears in a Baader-Meinhof thriller from 2003 illustrates the BKA's way of thinking. He explains that the police purposefully intimidated everyone under the age of 35: "Each one of them was made to look into the barrel of an automatic pistol. Each one of this corrupted generation." He then claims that the BKA was successful:

> And they all got the message. We showed them the instruments and they all did as they were told. It should be called the "German Spring," not the "German Autumn." In an enormous operation we, the police, saved society. Afterwards they respected law and order. And we separated the next age groups from the corrupted generation.[33]

The problem was that such talk made matters worse. The understanding of the BKA man (and it is always a man) for his terrorist adversary will become a topos in films and novels. Herold himself is the model for a series of such characters. But in July 1972 he had not yet got the measure of his enemy. In prison over the next five years, the RAF played on their compatriots' insecurities, portraying themselves as victims of a vicious "pig system" that was reverting to fascist type. Allegations of "isolation torture" and "extermination confinement" became unifying causes for a new generation of recruits. The RAF prisoners called on their comrades outside to respond by showing resistance, as their parents had failed to do under Hitler. In other words, they staged a performance and invited the audience outside the prison to project meanings onto their actions and to invest emotionally in them.

In West Germany in 1972, the Nazi legacy was felt in most walks of life, often most poignantly, according to middle-class twenty-somethings at the time, in the family. Yet *The Baader-Meinhof Report* begins by referring to that other organization that used the famous RAF initials first and which visited its own destruction on the same city of Frankfurt 23 years before Baader and Ensslin planted two incendiary devices in the Schneider and Kaufhof department stores at Easter 1968. The same rhetorical ruse of pretending to confuse the two RAFs is played in a novel by the rebel poet Peter-Paul Zahl, *The Happy Ones* (1979), which he wrote while in prison on charges related to terrorism, which underscores how the lines of ideological demarcation between the two sides can become blurred.[34] After all, *all*

Germans had recently been victims of a much worse RAF than that led by Baader, Ensslin, and Meinhof. In the course of World War II, His Majesty's Royal Air Force destroyed or damaged far greater chunks of real estate than the Red Army Faction ever did afterwards. Many of the Frankfurt firemen who put out the twin blazes caused by Baader and Ensslin on April 4, 1968 had cleared up after those more serious World War II fires. After 1945, a shining new city was built on the ruins and the corpses. The survivors were proud of their achievement, but wanted the past to remain buried with the rubble. The student radicals, on the other hand, wanted to dig it all up. They saw that both East and West Germany were still occupied by the Allies, the most powerful of which was now engaged in similar bombing missions in Vietnam. One reason for the new RAF's choice of name was to remind Germans of their own recent wartime suffering: what the Americans were now doing to the Vietnamese, the Americans and the British did to the Germans not so long ago. Another reason for the choice of name was to frighten the German public. It brought to mind the Soviet Red Army, which had conquered the eastern part of Germany to set up what they called the first "workers' and peasants' state on German soil." The German RAF has been accused of possessing a nationalist, anti-Western streak, for which, at least subconsciously, the Vietnam War was a convenient excuse. Once the RAF adopted Palestine as their second great cause, their anti-Israeli rhetoric could echo the anti-Semitism of their parents' generation, whether they intended it to do so or not.

Most striking in *The Baader-Meinhof Report* is the attitude of the report writers to gender and sexuality. Its authors speculate, for instance, that the Palestinians at the Fatah training camp in Jordan did not like the "dominant" German women who visited them in the summer of 1970 in order to learn the techniques of guerilla warfare. But they reacted differently to the group's male leader, the report speculated: "The Arabs, for whom homosexuality has been second nature for thousands of years, could only have found Baader attractive, with his very feminine manner and smooth complexion."[35] To its critics, the RAF was as sexually perverse as it was criminal, and Baader's own criminal perversity is reinforced by his alleged resemblance to "the Arabs." All subsequent reports on the nascent RAF's ill-starred mission to the Jordanian desert (and there are many) say nothing of their hosts' liking for their supposedly androgynous male leader. As Baader is said to have clashed with the Palestinians from the start, this attraction can only be the BKA's fantasy. *The Baader-Meinhof Report* gives details of the sexual behavior of the Baader-Meinhof women that could never be corroborated. Most are said to be inclined to lesbianism or bisexuality. Ensslin, for instance, seduces men but keeps favorite younger women as lovers. West-Berlin's notorious Kommune 1 corrupted her and, like other women in the radical subculture, she overcompensated for her sex by becoming more masculine than the men themselves. The contraceptive pill is seriously put forward as a reason that German women turned to terrorist violence (since they needed new thrills now that they no longer needed to be concerned about unwanted pregnancy). The absurd proposition is then rejected on the illogical grounds that Meinhof was a criminal before the pill was widely used and, like Ensslin, is a mother.[36] Here the report's authors, whether wittingly or not, are on to something. German fiction of the 2000s is still fascinated by terrorists being mothers, a theme that international novelists have all but ignored.

Both the BKA in *The Baader-Meinhof Report* and the advocates of armed struggle were out of step with mainstream developments in German politics. In September 1969 a former anti-Nazi resister named Willy Brandt succeeded an ex-Nazi party member, Kurt Georg Kiesinger, as federal chancellor. Brandt's spontaneous kneeling before the monument to the victims of the Warsaw ghetto while on a state visit to Poland in December 1970 was a more politically meaningful gesture than Meinhof's earlier leap from the Dahlem window. Brandt's visual indication of penitence signaled a new phase in relations between West Germany and the Communist bloc, his vaunted *Ostpolitik*, and a new attitude towards the Nazi past. Brandt's credentials as a left-wing leader were impeccable. But his crime in the eyes of the Extra-Parliamentary Opposition (the APO) was to have joined a coalition in December 1966 with Kiesinger's Christian Democrats. For his party's mainstream, this was a stepping stone to forming a government with his own Social Democrats as the senior partner, which happened in 1969. For his left-wing critics, like Ensslin, who had worked with the SPD at the elections in 1965, it was proof that the party was no better than the old Nazis who comprised the elites. As foreign minister, Brandt also hosted the Shah of Iran on his visit on June 2, 1967, which ended in Ohnesorg's shooting.

Brandt's party, the *Sozialdemokratische Partei Deutschlands* or SPD, has never controlled the German left unchallenged. The terrorist period is another episode in the schism of the German left that began during World War I. For many, the party betrayed the progressive cause in 1914 by voting in favor of war. Its leaders then sided with the reactionaries in the Revolution of 1918–19, when the crypto-fascist militias in the so-called *Freikorps* crushed worker insurgents in Berlin, Munich, and elsewhere. The second schism occurred after December 1966 when Brandt embarked on his coalition with the Christian Democrats in the CDU and endures to this day. But the Greens were founded only once the forces to the SPD's left recognized that violence and extremism resulted in marginalization. It is no accident that writers' interest in Baader-Meinhof intensified after the

SPD split for a third time in the mid-2000s, when its former leader Oskar Lafontaine defected to form *Die Linke* with the East German reform communists. There are various clues in the *The Baader-Meinhof Report* to suggest how the BKA got it so wrong. Its authors criticize the republic's two leading politicians, Chancellor Brandt and President Gustav Heinemann. In March 1969, Heinemann became the first postwar Social Democrat to become head of state. Heinemann, however, had defended Meinhof in court when she was sued for libel by Defense Minister Franz Josef Strauss in 1963. Brandt's own son was defended in court by Horst Mahler, who later defended Baader and Ensslin in the Frankfurt arson trial. As *The Baader-Meinhof Report* was being written, Mahler was safely behind bars, serving a fourteen-year prison sentence. (In 1980 he himself would be represented by future SPD Chancellor Schröder).[37] The personal links between the RAF and the country's highest office-holders show how left-wing terrorism came from the center of society, from the elites themselves, rather than from the "aberrant" fringes. As was pointed out repeatedly by conservative opponents, the terrorists were on the whole middle class, well educated, and economically privileged. Many of the first-generation novelists knew one or more of them personally. The problem with the first narrative account of Baader-Meinhof terrorism is that it does not do justice to the evolving republic's conflicted self-understanding. Its grotesque bias against its subject is part of the problem that it purports to address.

The early novels are similarly interventionist and partisan, though from the opposite perspective. *The Lost Honor of Katharina Blum*, (Böll, 1974) states its purpose in its subtitle, which is to show "how violence comes into being and where it can lead." The story of an innocent woman's revenge on the reporter who ruined her reputation because she spent the night with a young man who is believed, wrongly as it turns out, to have terrorist connections is a denunciation of the misogynist journalistic practices of Axel Springer's *Bild-Zeitung*. Heinrich Böll reacted with horror a couple of months after *Katharina Blum* was published to the suggestion that his short novel might condone politically inspired murder. In November 1974, the same year that Böll was awarded the Nobel Prize for Literature, Berlin's most senior judge, Günter von Drenkmann, was killed in cold blood as revenge for the death of Holger Meins. In the RAF's eyes, *Katharina Blum* articulated a moral justification for "shooting a representative of the ruling apparatus of coercion."[38] Conservative critics all too eagerly agreed.

Distinguishing the legitimate left from the bomb-throwers is a preoccupation of other early novels with a broadly terrorist theme.[39] Their focus is often on the state response to the terrorist threat, the support the terrorists enjoyed among sections of the public, or the effect on society of the government's countermeasures. Some are highly introspective, showing the *betroffenheit* (emotional concern) of a first-person narrator, which can deteriorate into paranoia and nervous breakdown. Other novels explore a historical parallel. Most of these are included in Thomas Hoeps's ground-breaking survey.[40] I do not consider them directly in this book because the subject that interests me is taking place at best in the background.

The contemporary novel that is most often invoked in discussions of terrorism also does not come within my orbit for similar reasons. The contents of Bernward Vesper's autobiographical *Die Reise* (1977, meaning *The Journey*, or *The Trip*) and the circumstances of its production belong to Baader-Meinhof history, but it was written too soon to depict the RAF as the RAF. Vesper committed suicide in May 1971. He is portrayed in a number of the filmic and literary treatments.[41] His self-destruction aided his book's status when it was finally published in August 1977. Its fragmentary rawness betokened authenticity to radicals suspicious of bourgeois aesthetics. *The Trip* is a cult book rather than a classic, mixing accounts of drug-taking with soul-searching recollections of Vesper's childhood and relationship with his Nazi father, who was a celebrated poet during the Third Reich. He also shows glimpses of his romance with Ensslin, who left Vesper for Baader shortly after the birth of their son. The most compelling sections, which resonated with Vesper's peers, are those about his aging father's child-rearing methods. On the whole, however, the fascination of Vesper's subject matter is not matched by his novel's readability. *The Trip* has been a best-seller twice. In 2003 Gerd Koenen, working from Vesper's original manuscripts, retold much of its contents as if the material were unknown, which may show that it is more interesting than Vesper was able to make it.[42] He shows too that Vesper was disingenuous in recalling his hostility to his father. Koenen gives rather more details of Vesper's work with his father's old Nazi networks, showing that his emotional entanglement with his father had ramifications that he failed to explore himself. Vesper's own contempt for ordinary Germans is expressed through his calling them (in English) "vegetables," in his view, the brain-dead automata of Americanized Coca-Cola culture. Traces of Nazi rhetoric are sometimes not too far beneath the surface. Another recent book on his shared student years with Ensslin reveals how the couple championed Will Vesper's poetry. The postwar neglect of an old Nazi poet was Ensslin's first cause.[43]

If there is a canonical German novel that could shed light on the allure of terrorism for the German literary imagination, it is one written in Switzerland in the aftermath of World War I, at a time when street violence and assassinations were more prevalent in Germany than in the 1970s or 1980s. Hermann Hesse's *Steppenwolf* (1927) explores the dichotomy between the integrated bourgeois, who owns property, has a profession and career, and is married with a family, and the intellectual outsider who opposed the war and despises conventional society for its smug hypocrisies. The hero Harry Haller thinks of himself as half man, half wolf from the wild Siberian steppes and lives on the fringes of society in a garret apartment. For more than a generation, *Steppenwolf* was required reading for students across the West, not only in Germany. Meinhof's liking for Hesse during her student years is well documented. Gillian Becker, in *Hitler's Children*, turns it against her and her fellow undergraduates, quoting a passage that shows Haller revealing the causes of his latent anarchism, which is one aspect of his contradictory character. She explains that Hesse was

> a pacifist, whose romanticism particularly appealed to [Meinhof and her friends], warming their feelings, who were already emotionally in heat. He wrote about individuals who were different from (better than) most people [...] Steppenwolf, who is a "genius of suffering," and who despises those who do not suffer, who are bourgeois—which is to say smug, vulgar, little, brash, insensitive, American, ordinary, dull, lukewarm, or engaged in the bakery business. He exhibits the snobbery of the romantic egotist.[44]

At the end of *Steppenwolf,* Harry is introduced to the "Magic Theatre," which is a performance of his own soul, a voyage into the recesses of his mind and personality. According to one interpretation, he is being tested by his new friends, who show him the hundreds of different signs on the doors to the theatre's auditorium, such as "All girls are yours." Harry chooses one marked "Hunt the Cars" and finds himself in the midst of a futuristic civil war, firing on a vehicle carrying a state prosecutor.

Hesse writes in the tradition of German "artist novels," which present the artist as deracinated and opposed to the unreflective bourgeois mainstream. In the opposition between the alienated creative spirit and the contented but shallow-minded and compromised majority, there is a connection with Meins's notorious last words:

> either person or pig
> either survival at any price or
> struggle to the death
> either problem or solution
> there is nothing in between.[45]

In *In His Early Childhood, a Garden* (Hein, 2005), the father of a presumed terrorist sees the distance between his deceased son's values and those of society as unbridgeable. The chasm is not political or moral, but existential. Only after years in prison would his son have been prepared to make his peace with the rest of society, but then on terms that would likely cost him his self-respect:

> If he comes home from prison, he will certainly be a broken man and perhaps embittered and in despair, but I hope ready to come to terms with a life which today he finds unacceptable and contemptible. So contemptible that he has become involved with people who, no matter what they may think themselves to be doing, are in fact nothing but criminals.[46]

At the end of this novel, the father too has gone over to what Hesse calls "the other side." Yet German novelists do not in the main pursue the connection between art and political violence, which has been explored in terrorist novels written in other languages by authors such as Dostoyevsky, Henry James, and Joseph Conrad, or latterly J. M. Coetzee.[47] German novelists rarely even acknowledge the international tradition. The German novels are particular to their own national context and are responsive to their own set of political circumstances.

Filmmakers reacted more quickly than novelists to the RAF: film thus often got there first, and images from the key films are imprinted on the consciousness of the novelists and their readers alike. Many of the films were viewed by art-house audiences around the world, their supposedly radical politics matched by an avant-garde aesthetic. They are likely to be cited as the first points of reference in a historiography written in English.[48] *Mother Köster's Trip to Heaven*, (dir. Fassbinder, 1975) shows how the widow of a factory worker who suddenly kills his manager before committing suicide is exploited by the press, by a middle-class Communist couple, and finally, by a group of anarchists. Fassbinder continued in *The Third Generation*, 1978) and in a famous sequence in the collaboratively directed *Germany in Autumn* (1978). Fassbinder knew Baader in Munich and once remarked that he himself didn't throw bombs, he "made films," by which he meant that his art was a reaction to post-Nazi West German society in the same way as the RAF's violence was.[49] The same was true of Fassbinder's fellow directors: the list of makers of films about the RAF reads like a roll call of the New German Cinema Movement. Volker Schlöndorff worked with Louis Malle on *Viva Maria!* (1965). Schlöndorff then codirected the film version of Heinrich Böll's *The Lost Honor of Katharina Blum*, 1975) with Margarethe von Trotta; collaborated on *Germany in Autumn;* and returned to the topic 20 years later with *The Legends of Rita* (2000 known in German as *Die Stille nach dem Schuss* or *The Silence after the Shot*). Trotta directed *The Second Awakening of Christa Klages* (1976), which she followed in 1981 with the seminal *Die bleierne Zeit* (known in English as either *The German Sisters* or *Marianne and Juliane*), both of which explore doubled terrorist identities. Reinhard Hauff made *Knife in the Head* (1978), on the subject of an intellectual (played by Bruno Ganz) who is caught between ruthless radicals and a violent state, from a screenplay by the novelist Peter Schneider. Hauff also made *Stammheim* (1985), from a screenplay by Stefan Aust. Several of these films influenced the novels that are the subject of this book. After the release of *The Journey* (dir. Imhof) and *Stammheim* (dir. Hauff), both in 1985, there were only two more Baader-Meinhof feature films before *Death Game* (dir. Breloer, 1997), initiated a second wave (one was a Swedish–German coproduction and the other was a minor experimental film).[50] Each post-Breloer Baader-Meinhof film responded visually or thematically to one of the classics made between 1975 and 1981.[51] The new films thus reenvisioned the terrorist past for a new generation of audiences by reinscribing the well-known images. From this point, novels are richer and more varied and no longer reliant on film for their imagery.

According to Meinhof's ex-husband Klaus Rainer Röhl, her love affair with political violence began with *Viva Maria!* In Louis Malle's film, the Revolution is female (in the shape of the two Marias played by Brigitte Bardot and Jeanne Moreau) and the use of weapons in its service is highly eroticized. No one appears to get injured; the good gals (and guys) belong to an international circus troupe that takes up the cause of the Latin peasants in their struggle against a corrupt priest. Rudi Dutschke's widow recalls that he saw this "wonderful romanticisation of the Third World" four times. It briefly gave its name to an offshoot of "subversive Aktion," the "Third World working group" where comrades from faraway lands gave "talks on their countries."[52] Röhl speculated in 1974: "In the beginning there was a film. Would it be surprising if at that the end there was another film, another legend about two women who know how to use explosives, assisted by a couple of swarthy journeymen?"[53] If one reads the next dozen years from 1965 to 1977 through the iconography of *Viva Maria!*, which anticipates the literary and cinematic portrayal of the actions it perhaps helped inspire, one can see that Röhl had a point.

RAF members too were more likely to be interested in film and acting than in writing. One of Ensslin and Baader's two accomplices in the Frankfurt arson attacks in 1968 was Horst Söhnlein, who ran Munich's Action Theatre, which competed with Fassbinder's troupe in the underground of the Bavarian avant-garde. The double documentary biopic *Black Box BRD* (dir. Veiel, 2001) of Alfred Herrhausen and Wolfgang Grams captures several of Grams's old friends recalling his interest in acting. Contemporaries recall that Baader wrote a screenplay for a "socialist film," handing over a manuscript to the director Peter Fleischmann.[54] Holger Meins went to film school in Berlin with Wolfgang Petersen, who went on to direct *Das Boot* and to work in Hollywood. *Starbuck*, the documentary of his life, entitled after Meins's code name, was directed by another former student, Gerd Conradt, but the code name was given him by Ensslin from Melville's *Moby Dick*. Ensslin herself appeared (naked) in an absurdist film-school short a year and a half before she helped plant the incendiary devices in two Frankfurt department stores. Meinhof's *Bambule* would have been broadcast on May 24, 1970, had she not taken part in the freeing of Baader from jail ten days earlier. It took 27 years before it was eventually shown on German television. The lag indicates how long the RAF cut themselves off from the mainstream, but the fact that the film was made and was scheduled to be broadcast shows that alternative channels of expression were open to them at the time.

Early fiction on the RAF is full of references to film: the undercover existences, aliases and false identities, the fear of tapped phone calls are all highly cinematic.[55] Their interaction with film and film history was both serious and deadly. Meins and Raspe once pretended to need props for a film about the revolution when in fact they were ordering equipment which was useful for hot-wiring cars.[56] That Baader's presumed cinema role models are from Hollywood tells its own story of the German reaction to the Americanization of culture after 1945. Writing in the *Süddeutsche Zeitung* in February 1972, Günter Grass took the film comparison a step further. He argued that the RAF's degeneration since May 1970 followed the script of the 1967 gangster road movie, *Bonnie and Clyde*, in which robbing banks began as eroticized social protest before becoming an end in itself. The RAF also was set to cause more and more damage before their spree ended in a fatal shootout.[57]

Ensslin and Baader were consummate celebrities. Films as far apart in time and as different in conception as *Stammheim* (dir. Hauff, 1985) and *The Baader-Meinhof Complex* (dir. Edel, 2008) were accused of glamorizing them. When the first full biography of Baader was published in 2007, two of its most revealing findings involved cinema. The most significant male involved in his upbringing was an uncle, the actor Michael Kroecher, who among other roles played Lord Stanhope in Werner Herzog's *The Enigma of Kaspar Hauser* (1976).[58] His nephew's favorite film, however, was Gilles Pontecorvo's *The Battle of Algiers* (1965), which explores the dynamic of terrorism in the Algerian war of independence. Baader's biographers speculate that he was aware of parallels between a number of his key exploits and episodes in this film.[59] As there are so many films about them, it is as if, having stepped off the big screen into real life, the RAF stepped right back on to it.

Some people associated with terrorism did write books, however, even novels. Marianne Herzog, who spent more than a year in prison for her membership in a criminal association, published three books after her release, two of which are indirectly autobiographical.[60] Before and after her prison term, she was engaged in legitimate campaigning. Herzog's boyfriend from the late 1960s was Peter Schneider, who went on to write a classic literary account of the student movement (*Lenz*, 1973) as well as two novels, published 30 years apart, with a more direct bearing on terrorism, ... *already you are an enemy of the state* (1975); and *Scylla* (2005). Other writers got caught up in violence. When she was put on trial in France in the mid-1980s and risked deportation to Germany, Katharina de Fries was offered asylum by the Greek minister of culture, Melina Mercouri. The Writers' Association had drawn Mercouri's attention to the plight of one of its members.[61] The actor Christof Wackernagel joined the RAF in the summer of 1977 and was arrested on November 10th of the same year in a shootout in Amsterdam. Sentenced to ten years in prison, he began to write, publishing two volumes of fiction before his release. After resuming his acting career, he now lives in the capital of the Saharan state of Mali, where he has continued to write. One of the films released on the thirtieth anniversary of the German Autumn was a documentary on his life: *White Man with Black Bread; Chistof Wackernagel in Mali* (dir. Grosch, 2007).

One major Baader-Meinhof novel, *The Happy Ones* (Zahl, 1979), was written in a prison cell. The half-Jewish activist Peter-Paul Zahl was not part of a terrorist group, but as a poet and publisher, he operated at the heart of the radical scene, printing the RAF's first communication after the Baader liberation, for instance. Zahl was also carrying a gun in December 1972, which he pulled out and fired when challenged by police. *The Happy Ones*, which has become something of an alternative classic, draws clear lines of demarcation between the left-wing criminal rogues, who are the heroes of his Kreuzberg picaresque panorama, and "the Unnameables" who literally emerge from underground through the drains and are engaged in their parallel struggle against the state. Peter-Jürgen Boock is a quite different case. He was close to Baader and Ensslin from the summer of 1969 onwards, when they befriended him during their work with Frankfurt adolescents. The self-conscious delinquent teenager became part of the RAF second-generation inner circle, which carried out the Schleyer kidnapping eight years later. His autobiographical novel *Descent* (1988) has some powerful passages, but its purpose is self-justification and its first-person narrator has no self-insight or capacity for reflection: he is the victim of history and gets shot on the novel's final page in the attempted kidnapping of an American NATO general. Although Boock does what no professional German novelist had hitherto attempted, which was to depict a RAF cell from the inside, the result is strangely unrevealing. Good writers do not have to be honest about themselves and their involvement in their topic, but perhaps it helps bad writers if they are. Boock continued to publish after his release. A "documentary fiction" on the Schleyer kidnapping followed on the 25th anniversary in 2002. Most of the book is taken up by discussions with Schleyer, which took the form of "interrogations" and mock trials, during which Schleyer impressed his captors with his intelligence, empathy, and humanity.

Perhaps the most interesting writer to become entangled with terrorism was Corinna Kawaters, who in the mid-1980s was the author of two feminist detective novels set among radicals and squatters. Her amateur detective Zora Zobel is named after the heroine of a children's political adventure novel by German-Jewish author Kurt Kläber, first published in 1941.[62] *Red Zora* was the name taken by an all-woman offshoot of the Revolutionary Cells that carried out bomb attacks against commercial targets. In Kawaters's novels, Zora's heart certainly beats on the left, but she has no patience with contemporary left-wing mores and she challenges prejudice wherever she encounters it. In December 1987, Kawaters fled Germany when she was tipped off that the BKA was searching the Bochum offices of the alternative newspaper *die tageszeitung,* where she worked. When they found an alarm clock of the type the *Red Zora* was known to use in their bombs, she was not surprised that she became a wanted person: "I knew what they could be used for."[63] She spent the next eight years avoiding arrest in France and Spain before giving herself up in 1995. *Der Spiegel* calls her a "amateur author," but she was published by the cult publisher zweitausendeins, and *Zora Zobel Finds the Corpse* (1984) sold 24,000 copies.[64]

The existence of these "novelist-terrorists" does not demonstrate an essential connection between the decision to commit acts of violence and the urge to write a novel. It does represent, however, the extreme end of the spectrum of the fascination that terrorism has exerted on German novelists.

One of the arguments of this book is that German novelists turn to Baader-Meinhof terrorism in order to represent contemporary national politics rather than to make specific interventions. The subject gives them an opportunity to explore far-reaching social and economic questions or matters as diverse as sexual morality, the Nazi legacy, relations with the communist East, and the viability and desirability of the status quo. The questions that the terrorists through their very existence posed to the West German state and then to the reunified German state and its system of social and economic organization were, after all, apparently fundamental. As they never represented a special interest, their aims were never limited to a set of demands that could be negotiated. But their challenge to the state presupposed that there was an alternative way of ordering politics and that they knew what that was and how it could be brought about. At a point in history when the working classes were happily integrated, terrorists insisted that radical change could be effected by individuals acting together on basically moral impulses. Indeed, individuals could decide for themselves whether they should offer resistance to an exploitative system by relinquishing their compromised existences and taking up arms against oppression. Meinhof's jump from the window of the Dahlem library is emblematic for that reason. The wider scenario is rich in novelistic potential.

One of Germany's leading contemporary novelists, Bernhard Schlink, employs a series of highly traditional tropes in a Baader-Meinhof novel that was a follow-up to the best-selling work of German fiction of the 1990s, *The Reader*. The tight narrative structure of *The Weekend* (Schlink, 2008), its symbolic use of location, and the transformative effect of the two days the characters spend together recall two classic novellas from the last two centuries, Eduard Mörike's *Mozart on his Journey to Prague* (1856) and Günter Grass's *The Meeting at Telgte* (1979). Both conclude with art asserting a Pyrrhic moral victory over philistinism or war. Schlink was inspired by the debate in the summer of 2007 over whether President Horst Köhler should pardon Christian Klar and Brigitte Mohnhaupt, who masterminded the assassinations and kidnappings in 1977 and had been in custody for 25 years. Köhler paid a visit to the imprisoned Klar but refused him a pardon. In *The Weekend*, Jörg is released because he has inoperable prostate cancer and thus no longer poses a possible threat. He is, however, the center of narrative attention and the novel's pivotal point. All the other characters who gather to welcome him back from prison want something from him, owe him something, or are owed something by him. Karin, now a bishop, reminds them all that the armed struggle played a role in their imaginations and the way that they perceived the world and its possibilities: "We all believed that we had to leave bourgeois society behind us if we wanted to lead an uncorrupted life."[65] Jörg represents something that Karin and the other university friends could have become. Through him they are connected to high politics. He is also connected through them with the church, business, the professions, and the media. By dipping back into their pasts, however, the friends emerge stronger, finally ready to take their lives in new directions.

The Weekend underwhelmed German reviewers in 2008. They saw it as opportunistic and adding little to the media debate about releasing unrepentant middle-aged terrorists. In 1995, the German press had been no more impressed by Schlink's *The Reader*, which only became a runaway bestseller in English translation. For contemporary German tastes, Schlink's first serious novel (he was already established as an author of crime fiction) let Nazi perpetrators off too lightly. The connection between the two novels is through Germany's defining 68er generation, whose Baader-Meinhof fiction is the subject of my first chapter. *The Reader's* central character is Michael Berg, the eponymous *vorleser* of the German title, who became emotionally entangled at too tender an age with the manipulative Hanna Schmitz, a former SS underling and Auschwitz guard. Michael never recovered from the encounter. If *The Reader* is an allegory of intergenerational German relationships, then Michael's feelings of love and disgust for Hanna are what most Germans of his age felt for the country of their birth as it was defined by their parents. The friends in *The Weekend* are Michael's contemporaries. Each is thwarted because of something that happened in their shared youth. Karin is dissatisfied with her life, even though she has been made a bishop, because she could not have children after a botched abortion, which is her secret from her husband. Henner may be a successful journalist, but he is single and also childless, and discontented in his personal life. He began an affair with Christiane, which she broke off mid-embrace, only now explaining to him that it was because she glimpsed Jörg gazing at them as they made love. Ilse has not found anyone else since she stopped loving Jörg. Christiane's life has been dominated by her preoccupation with her younger brother, whom she secretly betrayed to the police to save him from getting killed, which is her secret from him. She is a variant of the Antigone figure in German Baader-Meinhof literature (which is why she shares a name with Gudrun Ensslin's older sister), except that she colluded with the state rather than rebelling against it. Only the businessman Ulrich, who is accompanied to the gathering by wife and teenage daughter, appears to have thrived, but his verbal combativeness suggests that he is overcompensating for his switch in allegiance.

The Reader ends with Michael's cringing failure to find common ground with Hanna's surviving Jewish victim after Hanna has killed herself on the eve of her release from jail. Jörg, who is sentenced to a longer term behind bars than Hanna, makes it out of jail only because he is going to die in a few months. At the end of *The Weekend,* all the characters cooperate with one another to clear up after a violent rainstorm has caused a flood in the basement of Christiane's new countryseat. Three are from the younger generation, one is an East German, and another, who has only months to live, is fresh from a 25-year jail sentence. Schlink's Germany is finally pulling together and moving on. *The Weekend* is a state-of-the-nation political novel. In terms that I will develop in the course of this study, it is a "national-unity closure narrative" because it brings both sides of the formerly divided country together and consigns Baader-Meinhof to the past. Not all novels follow that trajectory, however, as I will now attempt to show.

CHAPTER ONE

AVOIDING THE SUBJECT:
SIX TROPES IN 68ER FICTION

The tropes that I characterize in this chapter come from novels either written by members of the generation of 1968 themselves or by slightly older contemporaries. Born in the 1940s, the 68ers had childhood memories of the war, in particular, of the Allied bombing, followed by postwar deprivation. They often grew up without fathers, or with parents who had been damaged by the war and the aftereffects of Nazism. The family, as Wilhelm Reich did not always need to teach them, was a site of oppression. They entered adulthood at a moment when West Germany was changing, authority being challenged, and the whole postwar settlement was being questioned. Some of their anger could have been sparked by resentment for the hardships they suffered as a result of Germany's losing the war. They both despised and pitied their parents. The student movement experience in the second half of the 1960s was *their* experience. The 68er novelists are writing about a part of themselves and their own past when they write about Baader-Meinhof. Many knew individual RAF members: Ulrike Edschmid attended Berlin's *Film- und Fernsehakademie* with Holger Meins, for instance. Uwe Timm, in contrast, studied with Benno Ohnesorg.[1] Günter Grass knew Ulrike Meinhof and campaigned with Gudrun Ensslin on behalf of the SPD in 1965, as did Peter Schneider and F. C. Delius. Peter O. Chotjewitz was one of the German writers who helped Baader and Ensslin when they arrived in Rome with Astrid Proll in November 1969. When Baader was arrested in West Berlin, it was a driving license stolen from Chotjewitz that he showed to the police.[2] All empathized critically—and sometimes uncritically—with the terrorists. Chotjewitz (1934–2010, an exact contemporary of Meinhof's) and Christian Geissler (1928–2008) belong to the latter category; Heinrich Böll (1917–85) and Günter Grass (b. 1927), to the former.

The novels' publication dates span most of the 40-year period I am investigating. Some 68er novelists, such as Schneider and Timm (both

b. 1940), returned to the topic in the 2000s, after broaching it 20 to 30 years earlier. Grass waited until *My Century* in 1999 to allude directly to it. Although Peter-Paul Zahl (b. 1944) depicts the Kreuzberg milieu that regards the (terrorist) "Unnameables" to need resocialization, it was left to the cartoonist who illustrated Zahl's *The Happy Ones*, to publish the autobiographical follow-up, *The Black Star of the Tupamaros* (Seyfried, 2004). Delius (b. 1943) made the German Autumn his own topic in three novels written between 1981 and 1992, which are the subject of the next chapter. By the 2000s, this generation presents political violence as a youthful aberration that belongs well and truly to the past. Except when they are nostalgic, like Seyfried (b. 1948), these autobiographical novels aim for historical closure.

The fiction published in the 1970s and 1980s, in contrast, adopted a variety of strategies in order to avoid the subject: the terrorist as terrorist is largely a chimera, as the focus is on characters who interact with terrorist figures that emerge from the shadows or disappear down the sewers; who are already dead; or who are not really terrorists at all (any more). British and American writers take a different approach, as I show in Chapter Five; but in Germany, it was the fascination with the phenomenon that seems to have been significant from the literary point of view.

Terrorist as Woman

At the birth of what became the RAF on the morning of May 14, 1970, four women, Ulrike Meinhof, Gudrun Ensslin, former inmate of a *Fürsorgeheim* Irene Georgens, and medical student Ingrid Schubert, accompanied by an unidentified man, took part in the freeing of Andreas Baader. Their getaway driver was Astrid Proll, who waited outside at the wheel of an Alfa Romeo. That 5:1 female/male ratio was not typical of the future RAF's makeup or of that of any of the related terrorist groups, but it underlines women's prominence. Every poster of WANTED mug shots, which soon came to be displayed in public buildings the length and breadth of the republic, featured rows of young female faces. The media and police offered often bizarre explanations for why this was so. Novelists are not better able to explain why the most gender-blind organizations of the period dedicated themselves to political violence designed to overthrow the state. While the RAF officially believed feminism to be a bourgeois distraction, their turning to a life of illegal revolutionary activity came at the same point that the modern German women's movement was born. The situation appalled mainstream conservatives, but the ways German girls were brought up in the shadow of Nazism must have had something to do with their readiness to join up.[3]

The representation of Baader-Meinhof terrorism is bound up with attitudes to gender. There may be more sophisticated ways of dividing up novels than by the sex of the authors and that of the central characters, but the picture that emerges by doing so with this fiction gives some useful pointers for the discussion in the rest of this book. For instance, since the year 2000, women writers have contributed a number of biographies and historical works, but little fiction to the Baader-Meinhof literature. After a burst of attention from feminist writers in the 1980s and 1990s (such as Grete Weil, Eva Demski, Judith Kuckart, and Ulrike Edschmid), the interest of women novelists has not matched the prominence of women among the terrorist groups. The situation is a little different for playwrights (see Dea Loher and Elfriede Jelenik), and recently even for filmmakers.[4] In the 2000s, *The Mountain Pass* (Klöppel, 2002); *The Photographer* (Chaplet, 2002), and *The Pale Heart of the Revolution* (Dannenberg, 2004) were the only novels by women to address any aspect of the theme until *Murderer's Child* (Mayer, 2009), which was written for use in schools.

When women novelists do depict terrorists, they are hardly ever interested in men and they rarely fictionalize, instead sticking closely either to known facts or to their own experiences. Their emphasis is on female self-empowerment. Christine Brückner makes Ensslin into a courageous martyr in a collection of monologues by women who made an impact on history but who have somehow either been written out of it or not given their own voice.[5] The intergenerational *Choice of Weapons* (Kuckart, 1990), which draws heavily on Ensslin's biography, and the documentary fiction *Woman with Weapon* (Edschmid, 1996), based on interviews with Astrid Proll and Katharina de Fries, show the life paths that can lead women to commit acts of violence from political conviction.

Male authors of the first wave of Baader-Meinhof fiction (in particular Böll, Degenhardt, Röhl, and Zahl) also all favor women terrorists, but for different reasons. Only Chotjewitz bucks the trend, but his Andi is clearly based on Baader, whereas the women terrorists in the other novels are all fictitious. Male novelists are likely to base male terrorist characters on a real individual: on Baader (in five novels), Grams or Klar (in two each).[6] Their female terrorist characters, however, are nearly always fictitious. The result is that in the German literary imagination, Baader-Meinhof is not merely gendered, it is "othered" or allegorized. This produces a variety of projections and disavowals. Contrary to what one may have expected, the female terrorist is rarely idealized, demonized, or eroticized in male fiction; far more often, she is domesticated, thus disarmed and rendered harmless. Readers are led to conclude that she didn't really mean it, her lover led her astray, she's sorry now, and, anyway, she always acted from the most upright motives. She was misguided and is now penitent. As a tragic victim of circumstances, she can be redeemed and become a reliable member of society once more. What is at issue is the reestablishment of gender norms and conventional gendered behavior. The terrain was staked out in the first Baader-Meinhof novel. *The Lost Honor of Katharina Blum* (Böll, 1974) shows how the modern-day witchhunt relies on a battery of rhetorical defamation, which allies female sexual freedom ("whoring") with political depravity (communism).[7] This becomes a self-fulfilling prophecy: when the heroine is accused of loose sexual morality, she resorts to an extremist political deed. The plot of *Scenes of Fire* (Degenhardt, 1975) concerns the attempts made by two men to persuade a former girlfriend to give up violence and to warn her that her cell has been infiltrated by the *Verfassungsschutz*. Both men want to save her from herself (and in this instance they fail). Zahl's Gabi is rehumanized by her former friends as if she were an underworld Pygmalion. This role could easily have been made male within the context of *The Happy Ones* (Zahl, 1979). Various characters in *Safety Net* (Böll, 1979) discuss the local boy turned terrorist Heinrich Bewerloh, with whom Veronica Zelger has disappeared to Istanbul, taking her son from her first marriage with her. Bewerloh and Zelger belong to a cell that plans to make an attack in Germany. But Bewerloh does not appear in the novel himself. While Bewerloh blows himself up in Istanbul, Zelger returns with her son to Germany to turn herself in. Böll adapts a standard narrative, which saw the leading RAF women (Meinhof and/or Ensslin), both of whom abandoned young children for the revolutionary life, as dupes of Baader. Zelger's surrender may be depicted in the same spirit of reconciliation between the two sides that pervades the whole novel, but the gender politics are conservative. Böll is able to have it both ways: the "bad" terrorist is a man, the "good" one is a woman, whose maternal instincts finally triumph. The female warrior turns out to be a bearer of humane values after all. Delius uses the same turning away from violence by the female terrorist in *Ascent to Heaven of an Enemy of the State* (1992). In popular fiction, the corresponding impulse is to redomesticate the aberrant woman by reintegrating her into her family and/or reminding her of her maternal obligations.

Not Really a Terrorist

Until recently, German novels stepped back from depicting life on the run, imagining ideological discussions, presenting characters faced with moral dilemmas or choices, or with the original decision to join the underground struggle itself. This results in a peculiar absence from the early literature, that of the terrorist figure himself or—more likely—herself. One explanation is pragmatic, since to depict a terrorist in fiction *as a terrorist* would have been construed as provocative and would have resulted in rhetorical defamation, even judicial reprisals on the author and publisher.[8] There is a scene in *The German Sisters* (dir. von Trotta, 1981) when the imprisoned Marianne finds out that her journalist sister Juliane has written about her in a feminist women's magazine. Marianne denounces Juliane as the worst kind of traitor. There were a number of real cases that could also have acted as a deterrent. The journalist Horst Rieck was beaten up by a gang that included the *Blues* activists Georg von Rauch and Bommi Baumann because they believed him to be the author of a report on an attempted bombing campaign in West Berlin in the autumn of 1969. Films that broke the taboo of representation, like the American *Raid on Entebbe* (dir. Kershner, 1977) or the German *Stammheim* (dir. Hauff, 1985), sparked violent protests when they were screened in Germany.[9]

In prison after his arrest in 1979, Peter-Jürgen Boock left the RAF. While he did not become a *kronzeuge* (prosecution witness) by giving the police information in return for a reduced sentence, his reputation among leftists never recovered from his decision to talk and publish about his experiences. His was a betrayal of a different sort to Julianne's in *The German Sisters*. Boock reaped the rewards in publicity by turning his RAF life into a commodity for consumption in the media. Christian Geissler recognizes that he could fall into the same trap and gets round it by devising a debased, alienated language to narrate the main body of *Kamallata* (1988). This is underlined when he turns to the language of the media for the terrorists' actual attack. The problem was that the mimetic space was occupied by the ideological enemy and novelists were too ambivalent in their attitudes to terrorism to attempt to reclaim it.

Sometimes novelists concentrate on the periods immediately preceding or following that spent as an illegal militant. In *The Comrade* (1975), Klaus Rainer Röhl presents Katharina Holt (based on Meinhof, his ex-wife) once she has regretted her involvement. In contrast, Peter Schneider in...*Already You Are an Enemy of the State* (1975) only hints in his final paragraph that his young left-wing teacher, who falls foul of the overzealous implementation of the Anti-Radicals Decree, has "gone underground." In *Safety Net*, Böll introduces Veronica Zelger only at the moment she has decided to give herself up. Similarly, while Zahl in *The Happy Ones* articulates a series of arguments against the RAF's tactics, Gabi, "No. 3 in Dr. Herold's hit parade of the most wanted people," only appears once she has delivered herself back into the hands of Zahl's vagabond heroes, who rehabilitate their former friend.[10]

In *The Gentlemen of the Dawn* (1978), Chotjewitz depicts Andi as an imprisoned victim of state oppression, but does not reflect on why he finds himself there. The character hiding from the police in *My Sister, My Antigone* (Weil, 1980) is a terrorist at one remove. She is wanted only because she herself has provided shelter to another person on the run (as Katharina Blum did).

Delius ignores the RAF altogether in *A Hero of Internal Security* (1981), concentrating on a witness to the main events rather than a participant. The terrorists are all Palestinians in *Window Seat at Mogadishu* (Delius, 1987). In *Ascent to Heaven of an Enemy of the State* (Delius, 1992), Sigurd Nagel, who is modeled closely on Baader, reflects posthumously on society's obsession with him as he floats heavenwards above the celebrations of national unity prompted by his death. The terrorist Conni in the same novel, who is hiding in a cupboard at a sympathizer's flat during Nagel's funeral, expresses her regret for her part in the kidnapping of the industrialist Alfred Büttinger, whose humanity in captivity forced her to reconsider her commitment to violence. Delius thus presents her not as an active threat to society or potential killer, but as remorseful former accessory to killing.

Novels from the 2000s break with the practice of nonrepresentation completely. As some foreign novelists had taken a different approach already in the 1970s and 1980s, it appears to have been a German inhibition. Nonrepresentation can be part of a strategy of denial, a deflection of attention from the violence itself. More pertinently, it is a sign that what the terrorist groups actually did was less important than the role they played through their very existence in their contemporaries' imagination.

The Only Terrorist Worth Writing about Is a Dead One

This third trope is related to the second. A remarkable number of the novels by writers who experienced the period are elegiac or therapeutic acts of mourning. Their usually first-person narratives are prompted by the death of a character associated with terrorism who was once linked to a narrator who in turn bears some resemblance to the novelist. Some of these novels were written in the aftermath of the German Autumn (those by Chotjewitz and Demski), others at the beginning of the 2000s (those by Timm, Seyfried, Klöppel, and Woelk). The fictional survivor has a general representative function, not merely as a cipher for the novelist. The history of German left-wing terrorism cannot be disentangled from the deaths of its militants. The most famous are Petra Schelm, Thomas Weissbecker, Georg von Rauch, Holger Meins, the Stammheim suicides (Meinhof, Baader, Raspe, and Ensslin), and, sixteen years later, Wolfgang Grams. The dead terrorist can take on the role of moral savior for the survivors, who in turn feel guilt for not preventing his or her death. As the terrorists are not deemed to be responsible for their own deaths, even when they take their own lives, they can be presented as victims. The death can force the survivor to reflect on his or her own life and relationship with the deceased and on the ideas or emotions that drove him or her to take the path that he took. Fictional dead terrorists are more likely to be male than female, whereas the reverse is true of fictional live terrorists. The reason may be the need to allegorize the living terrorist figure, while the dead one is mourned as if he were a substitute redeemer.[11]

References to redemption come in various forms. Delius develops Easter and Whitsun imagery: Nagel/Baader takes the sins of the nation on himself, dying so that his compatriots can redirect their lives. In *Choice of Weapons* (Kuckart, 1990), Katia investigates the life of her former au pair after hearing of her death in Lebanon. "You will not deny me three times," Katia imagines her saying, which casts the older woman unambiguously in the savior role and the survivor Katia in the role of the unworthy disciple.[12] The murder of the American venture capitalist in *Death of a Truffle Pig* (Weiss, 2007) happens on Good Friday. *Dead Alive* (Demski, 1984) begins on Easter Saturday with the unexpected death of the central character's estranged husband, who had become entangled with "the Group." The novel moves through twelve days to his funeral. We are told several times that both spouses were aged about 30, the age that Christ began his teaching mission in the world. *Dead Alive* is unusual for a novel published while the third generation RAF was still active in that the survivor rejects her husband's legacy. The grain of the novel runs against the Easter imagery: the husband's death brings no new life or hope for the future. The wife does not understand how her husband, whose views she once shared and who left her on account of his erotic attraction to young men, can have been drawn to "the Group." She is inclined to feel inferior because she approached life differently:

> [He] took the Group more seriously than the woman did. The woman always had a guilty conscience when she came into contact with the Group's stringency, its unlikeable vocabulary, its lack of neediness. She thought that she herself resembled too much a sort of happy jellyfish, that she did not have enough courage, even if she had found out what she needed the courage for.[13]

This peculiar form of survivor guilt informs *The German Sisters*. Juliane is closer to Marianne when she in jail than she was when she was still on the run. She is closer to her still after Marianne is dead, when she decides to devote herself to bringing up her son, whom she rejected while her sister was alive, and to finding out how she died in prison, strongly suspecting that it was not suicide. Peter O.

Chotjewitz and Eva Demski conclude with recreations of the funeral of Baader, Ensslin, and Raspe, as shown in the final documentary sequence of *Germany in Autumn*. *Ascent to Heaven of an Enemy of the State* (Delius, 1992) is set at an imaginary version of the funeral. It was while filming the funeral that von Trotta met Christiane Ensslin, to whom she dedicated *The German Sisters*. The only shot of the real Ensslin in *Germany in Autumn* is of her contorted head after she is dead; and it is from the point of view of this baroque death mask that *The German Sisters* is narrated. Juliane is still mourning her dead sister at the end.

Gerhard Richter's 1988 sequence of paintings, *18. Oktober 1977*, ends with an image of the funeral; of the fourteen other paintings six are based on photographs of the dead Meinhof, Ensslin, or Baader. One of Richter's aims was to defamiliarize well-known media photographs, but the paintings, like the elegiac novels, are about mourning the dead, which has been a preoccupation in German fiction since the 1950s. Instead of being killed in the course of World War II, however, in Baader-Meinhof novels individuals die for a cause that was intended to compensate for that war. Seen in that light, the victims have a moral integrity, at least posthumously, and can be mourned with a clearer conscience. Postwar grief has been reattached to them.

All this begins to change in the fiction published after 2000. Now the central characters are likely to be cleared of responsibility for the terrorist's death and begin to live fulfilled lives as a result. Solving the murder of his former terrorist brother has a morally cleansing function for Glauberg in *The Last Performance* (Woelk, 2002). The novel that shows how a process of prolonged but secret guilt-ridden mourning can come to a fruitful end is *The Mountain Pass* (Klöppel, 2002), published by the legendary Rotbuch imprint, founded by Klaus Wagenbach. According to the dust jacket, Renate Klöppel (b. 1948) is a psychotherapist and has written no other fiction, which may be why her elegantly written novel has gone unnoticed in the critical writing.

In the 1970s and 1980s, Wagenbach, who faked the book contract for Meinhof so she could gain access to Baader in May 1970, also published Schneider, Herzog, Chotjewitz, Zahl, and Geissler. Delius worked in his editorial department. By issuing Klöppel's closure narrative in 2002, the veteran leftist gives it a symbolic seal of approval. The mountain pass in question is in the Himalayas, where former activist from the Revolutionary Cells Anna takes part in an organized trek, after her latest attempt to pursue a career has ended in failure. The novel consists of two parallel narratives, one set in Nepal, in which Anna succeeds in reaching the tour party's high-altitude destination, and another which takes place in her memory as she relives her involvement with violent direct action more than 20 years previously. Anna feels responsibility for her friend Madeleine's accidental death in an explosion in a Hamburg metro station at five minutes past midnight on New Year's Day 1978. The exact time is significant, because the hijacked airliner *Landshut* was stormed in Mogadishu on the previous October 18, 1977 at five past midnight German time. Part of the novel is a requiem for Madeleine, whose rebellious charisma pulled Anna in to terrorism. The narrative of the novel is her delayed confession, which she posts to Madeleine's former partner Rainer, who is also on the Nepalese trek with his and Madeleine's grown-up daughter, and with whom Anna now conducts a brief and unsatisfactory affair.

The Mountain Pass narrates a typical terrorist biography: Anna reacted against her upbringing by opting for violent protest, but her present feelings about her past are at the forefront. Her guilt for Madeleine's death is entwined with a series of distancing strategies that made Madeleine, rather than Anna, responsible for her actions as a young woman. Anna thus discreetly disavows the violence that she once advocated. It is important to her that she never held a gun herself, although she was the getaway driver when Madeleine and their friend Jan held up a provincial savings bank and opened fire on a passerby who got in their way. Anna also learnt how to make bombs. She feels that she was pulled into taking part because she was used to doing what others wanted: "I had forgotten how to have a will of my own. I wanted to be involved, to be taking part. But all the rest? It was others' expectations which determined my deeds."[14] Within their cell it is Jan who takes the lead, issuing orders and practising psychological terror on both women. Anna does what she is told but claims that she never integrated into the group. When she performs an action against the use of atomic energy on her own initiative, without telling the others, by attempting to bring down some power cables, she makes mistakes and the rest are angry with her. She resents what she sees as their ungrateful non-acceptance of her. Terrorism is one phase in a life that is characterized by low self-esteem. After Madeleine's death, Anna enters an unhappy marriage with a dominant man, whose politics are apparently very different from hers. He wants her to wait on his guests, echo his every word, and have no life or opinion of her own unless first sanctioned by him. She is attracted to him, however, because he can offer her the materialistic trappings of a prosperous bourgeois lifestyle.

The Mountain Pass is set 20 years after Madeleine's accidental death. The time lapse must be important, as it is repeated several times. It makes the present 1998, which is the year that the RAF formally declared its own dissolution. Anna rejects her past and the use of violence, including violence against things, which in theory distinguished the Revolutionary Cells from the RAF, who were prepared from the start to take human lives in the pursuit of their cause. Anna is damaged and compromised, but beginning to face up to the secret blot on her conscience, having now talked through her past and finally mourned her friend. She can finally take her life forward in a new direction. In the 2000s, the purpose of this first-generation trope is to draw a line under the past.

Mirror Images

One common view, which in itself has much literary potential, is that both sides, the state and the political outlaws, needed and fed off each other, each seeing somehow reflected images of themselves in their adversary. There was, in other words, a mutual fascination between police and terrorist. The cliché beloved of conspiracy theorists that the state needed a terrorist threat in order to justify escalating security measures is served up by the "Prof" in *Descent* (Boock, 1988). There are more credible sources for it. It is the ostensible conclusion to the film *The Third Generation* (dir. Fassbinder, 1978) and to the novel *The Happy Ones* (Zahl, 1979). This critique comes from an anarchist Left that held that the RAF discredited left-wing protest and played into the hands of their opponents, who welcomed the excuse for repressive countermeasures. The RAF, for its part, contended that these measures would radicalize the masses and produce a revolutionary situation. There is no doubt that it was a self-perpetuating conflict. Police repression during the German Autumn radicalized Wolfgang Grams, for instance, rather than political events in the world outside. In *Window Seat at Mogadishu* (Delius, 1987), Andrea Boländer muses that the confrontation between the terrorists and the state has nothing to do with her as a German citizen. Both sides are equally unattractive in their tendency to extremism, and are wrapped up in their own concerns without regard to the wider public they are purportedly either addressing or protecting. The *Verfassungsschutz* was originally at least in part responsible for protests turning to violence through the work of an *agent provocateur*, Peter Urbach, who inspired the depiction of Baader as an infiltrator working for a worldwide right-wing conspiracy in *The Comrade* (Röhl, 1975). A novelist has little need to elaborate on the image of Urbach handing Molotov cocktails to Meinhof outside the HQ of the Springer media concern in West Berlin after Dutschke's shooting in April 1968. In popular conspiracy fiction written in the 2000s, the villains are all working for the state.

The motif of "a plague on both your houses" was popular with filmmakers, who once more showed the way forward to novelists. In both Reinhard Hauff's films, there are parallels in the two sides' behavior, which in itself is a basic device of critical perspective. Neither Judge Prinzing, who steps down as trial judge after seeking to manipulate the outcome, nor the four accused emerge with enhanced reputations by the end of *Stammheim* (dir. Hauff, 1985). *Knife in the Head* (dir. Hauff, 1978) ends with the recovering Hoffmann and the policeman who shot him locked in combat. *Mother Köster's Trip to Heaven* (dir. Fassbinder, 1975) shows the working-class Frau Köster being taken advantage of by both sides. In the end she is shot after a group of anarchists have enlisted her help to hold the journalists hostage that are responsible for vilifying her deceased husband. Glimpsing her son in the crowd of spectators, she runs towards him, only to be shot; whether it was by the police or by the anarchists is immaterial. These films are exploring an independent political or ideological position that follows neither side.

In the 2000s, the identification between investigator and terrorist becomes overt in films such as *Baader* (dir. Roth, 2002) and *What to Do in Case of Fire* (dir. Schnitzler, 2002). In the literary thriller *The Execution* (Brenner, 2000), a character based closely on Herold explains: "In my head I became a terrorist myself. I read what they read. I ate what they ate. I would have lived like them too if my job had allowed it."[15] It is the fate of the BKA man not to be listened to by his superiors or society at large. In the detective's mind, the terrorist is a fellow outsider who is single-handedly trying to put the world to rights. This trope remains quite constant from the 1970s to the 2000s. When they look back at the defining events in the recent terrorist past, novelists and filmmakers identify BKA and RAF with each other, which underlines the symbolic significance of the German Autumn in the national memory. By the 2000s, Horst Herold has become a semitragic character.

Nobody Was Supposed to Get Hurt, or the Legend of the Perfect Terrorist Action

Gregor Schnitzler's 2002 Berlin film *What to Do in Case of Fire* concerns a group of Kreuzberg squatters from the late 1980s who plant a home-made bomb in an abandoned villa in the upmarket district of Wannsee, primed to go off when the front door is opened. The villa stands empty and the door is unopened between 1988 and 2001, the time span that saw German reunification and then witnessed Berlin resume its role as national capital. The film picks up its story at a historical moment, when capitalism is triumphant and most of the former radical squatters have made their professional way under the prevailing system. When a well-dressed estate agent steps inside the villa with an elegant-looking would-be buyer, most of the building is demolished in the explosion. Yet the two potential victims emerge from the rubble as if they are characters in a cartoon and are barely injured. Had they been killed (as they surely would have been in real life) the cops-and-robbers comedy caper that ensues simply could not have taken place. *The Edukators* (dir. Weingartner, 2004), released in Germany as *Die fetten Jahre sind vorbei* or *The Years of Plenty Are Over*, works from a basically similar premise. The actions of the trio of antiglobalization protesters are mini-performances, designed to relay a message to their wealthy victims, who return home to find their expensive possessions extravagantly rearranged but undamaged. When one day everything goes wrong and they end up having to take a millionaire villa owner their prisoner, the days of fun protest should be over, but at the end of the film they are setting off another mission.[16] These two popular films from the 2000s reenact the original founding myth of Baader-Meinhof violence. All the terrorist groupings had basically similar views on what forms of violence were permissible and what were not. In 1970 in West Berlin, *Der Blues* and their comrades in the *Tupamaros* foreswore the use of firearms. Yet, like the Revolutionary Cells, June 2nd Movement, and the Heidelberg Socialist Patients' Collective, they grew violent, or leading individuals found themselves endangering and taking lives. The difference between legality and illegality, between a communard ready to throw a stone at a demonstration or smash a department store window in the dead of night and an armed bank robber or political kidnapper was not always obvious.

The operation in May 1970 to get Baader out of jail was intended to be victimless. Meinhof fooled the prison authorities into bringing Baader to the Institute for Social Affairs in Dahlem, where he could be freed more easily than from Berlin's Tegel Prison. Take away the badly wounded librarian, Georg Linke, and you have the perfect terrorist act, the immaculate performance. It has been thought ironic that the shot came from the unidentified male accomplice who was brought along because he knew how to behave with guns in extreme situations. Perhaps the reverse is true, and he was alone in not having grasped that it was not supposed to be for real. The myth of the victimless Situationist prank should have died at this point. Somehow it proved remarkably resilient.[17] The pre-RAF student radicals took the view that violence was justified because the state employed it on them. Violent direct action was understood as "counterviolence" (*Gegengewalt*) as opposed to that practiced by the state or incited by the tabloid press. Those branded *terrorist* had not started or sought the confrontation. The revolution, which they saw as imminent, could not be brought about by entirely peaceful means. The reality of killing still came as a shock and lost them support. After the RAF's "May Offensive" in 1972, members of the public cooperated with the police. Günter Grass's chapter for 1972 in *My Century* (1999) is narrated by the Hanover school-teacher who has decided that his loyalty now lies with the state.

In *Scylla* (Schneider, 2005) the narrator is horrified to be confronted with Paul Stirlitz, a contemporary from his radical past who tells him that he took his slogan *Sprengt Springer* ("blow up" Springer) seriously and has made a bomb to leave outside the newspaper's West Berlin headquarters.[18] Now a successful lawyer with a younger wife and preoccupied with reno-vating a second home in Italy, the narrator tries to recall what he meant to say as a leading student radical all those years ago. Surely it was clear to anyone listening to him that he was speaking metaphorically. Stirlitz placed his bomb in a baby's pram, like the one used in the ambush of Schleyer's limousine. It was intended to damage the building, but when it accidentally toppled over, a passing car stopped to check on the baby and two people were killed. Stirlitz was lucky, as the explosion was blamed on criminals fighting a turf war. Like Anna in *The Mountain Pass*, Stirlitz has a guilty secret and is haunted by the prospect of being found out.

Perhaps one reason for the obsession with death in fiction is that it came—however perverse this may seem—unexpectedly, initially at least. Although it condemns the RAF, *The Happy Ones* (Zahl, 1979) condones acts of "victimless terrorism:" "the only thing is that when you carry out actions like that... you just must not harm *any* human beings" (231). In *Red* (Timm, 2001), Aschenberger was planning to blow up a symbol of Germany's military and imperial past, Berlin's Victory Column, but it had to be at a time when its destruction would not endanger life. This idea is familiar from the American Paul Auster's novel *Leviathan*, where the cen-tral character's erstwhile friend destroyed replicas of the Statue of Liberty. The terrorist as nonviolent saboteur also is central in the first piece of German prose fiction on terrorism, Günter Herburger's "Lenau," in which the sabotaging hero is said to have leapt from the window of the courtroom with his accomplices: "They screamed for joy, it said in the newspapers, like Red Indians [...] Guards looked on dumbstruck or they applauded their audacity and cleverness."[19] The episode is based on the exploits of Tommy Weissbecker and Georg von Rauch, who were both dead by the time the book was published.

Cold-blooded killing fitted neither the RAF's own image of itself nor the image that others wanted to project onto it. Meinhof won no new sup-porters when she explained a month after the Baader liberation that it was legitimate to shoot policemen. The first "actions" committed by Ensslin and Baader were directed against property, the material goods on sale in the two Frankfurt department stores where they planted incendiary devices in April 1968. It was not hard to connect these explosions with the anarchist pamphlets "burn, warehouse, burn!" written by Dieter Kunzelmann and

Kommune 1 in May 1967, ten days before Ohnesorg was shot. After nearly 300 people had been burned to death in a fire in a department store in Brussels, Kunzelmann linked the horrific scenes with the Vietnam War and made out that the fire had been started deliberately in order to give Europeans a feeling of what it was like to be in Vietnam: "Our Belgian friends have finally worked out how to let the population really participate in the fun goings on in Vietnam: they set a store on fire, two hundred [...] citizens end their exciting lives and Brussels becomes Hanoi."[20] The leaflet was a classic Situationist hoax, and its authors were cleared in court of incitement to violence. Kommune 1 members soon did turn to violence, however. Baader and Ensslin were inspired by the leaflet.

One terrorist career that has inspired at least two films, one play, and several novels, illustrates this paradox better than any other.[21] Inge Viett took part in the successful kidnapping of Peter Lorenz in February 1975, which all involved took to be an exemplary action because it achieved its objectives without injuring anyone, let alone killing anybody.[22] Lorenz was the Christian Democrat candidate for the mayoralty of West Berlin. He was held by the June 2nd Movement in a Kreuzberg cellar for seven days, until five terrorist prisoners were released and put on a plane to the Middle East.[23] Nobody was hurt during this action, which depended on the kidnappers' ability to blend in with the cityscape. They played the part of Robin Hood, sending 700 marks they found in their victim's briefcase to a woman whose appeal to him for help they also found among his papers. Their five jailed comrades were flown to Yemen under the tutelage of Pastor Heinrich Albertz, former mayor of West Berlin, who had resigned in the wake of the Ohnesorg shooting, who was instructed to utter the code words for the all-clear when the prisoners had safely arrived: "It was a day as wonderfully beautiful as today." The Lorenz kidnapping has pride of place in ex-terrorists' memoirs, because it is paradigmatic of what they thought could be done, though what the second-generation RAF failed to recognize was that the state would not let them repeat the performance by releasing the RAF's biggest fish in return for Schleyer, two and a half years later.[24] The episode has appealed to novelists: Jette in *Choice of Weapons* (Kuckart, 1990) is one of the released terrorists. Jenny in *The Black Star of the Tupamaros* (Seyfried, 2004) is one of the kidnappers. The Schleyer kidnapping, in contrast, began with the killing of a chauffeur and three bodyguards, which accounts for its entirely different place in the literary historiography.

In July 1975, Viett took part in two successful bank raids, during which chocolate marshmallows were distributed to passersby and bank customers to demonstrate their solidarity with everyday citizens. She gained further notoriety by twice escaping from West Berlin's Lehrter Women's Prison.

She was part of another team that helped a number of comrades escape from neighboring Moabit Prison; she raised money for her group by leading a kidnapping of an Austrian businessman. These actions were all committed in a spirit of international solidarity with oppressed peoples in the Third World. Viett's life would be the stuff of Zahl's Kreuzberg vagabonds or Louis Malle's two heroines in *Viva Maria!* were it not for the fatalities: at the British Yacht Club in February 1972, when a boat builder was blown up by a device intended to damage only property, what Viett calls "a fatal accident" for which she felt no responsibility;[25] and in the Grunewald in June 1974 when an erstwhile comrade, Ulrich Schmücker, was "executed" for betraying the group to the *Verfassungsschutz*. Schmücker and Viett had been arrested together in May 1972, a fact she mentions in the Chronology appended to her memoirs, but not in the narrative itself. The *Verfassungsschutz* regularly approached arrested terrorists; they presumably recruited him after his arrest with the offer of favorable treatment and reduced punishment. Viett justifies Schmücker's shooting with a dark metaphor: "He evidently died from a bullet with which the so-called guardians of the Constitution had been playing billiards and which had rolled off their table" (97). Viett blames her state of mind in August 1981 for her own shooting of a Paris traffic cop, at a point when she recognized that the "armed struggle" no longer had any connection with legal left-wing campaigns. He and a colleague had seen her riding a moped without a helmet and had signaled for her to pull up. She fled, losing one pursuer by kicking him from his bike, but the second cornered her in an underground car park. She shot him down in order to get away. She concedes that she had made a mistake, buying a Suzuki that she was not permitted to ride, and not realizing that a helmet was a legal requirement, but she is not prepared to accept responsibility for condemning her victim to spend the rest of his days in a wheelchair. He was, she noted:

> Not a concrete person, not even the concrete enemy. He just turned up fatefully for a moment in my life and this fate became determined as his own [fate] as a result of decisions which essentially were his own. A tiny shift in how things turned out and his fate could easily have been my own. (258)

The June 2nd Movement did not set out to kill anyone, but real people had a habit of getting in the way of the bombs and the bullets.

The Black Star of the Tupamaros gives the fullest portrayal of non-RAF terrorists in the 1970s. Gerhard Seyfried explains that his second historical novel is written "from the viewpoint of the time which is depicted," which means the narrator is not blessed with the wisdom of hindsight.[26] It seems fair to assume some autobiographical overlap, as the main character is born the same year as Seyfried himself. His novel combines a number of other common tropes. His central character Fred falls in love with the slightly younger and very beautiful Jenny as they are spraying political slogans around Munich by night. The terrorist is, as so often, a beautiful woman, which places the autobiographical narrator at one remove from terrorism. The year is 1974. Jenny and Fred are outraged by the CIA-backed military coup in Chile, which began the previous September. They are inspired by films such as Costa-Gavras's *State of Siege* (1972) about the original Uruguayan Tupamaros and by Hans Magnus Enzensberger's documentary novel on the Spanish Civil War, *Durruti or the Short Summer of Anarchy* (1972). Their protests take numerous forms, such as breaking shop windows, setting fire to newspaper kiosks, and torching a politician's expensive car. Newspapers print lies about them; the politician has made comments that they see as demagogic. They admire the June 2nd Movement marshmallow stunt, which the RAF condemned as "pure populism" (161). The reaction of like-minded comrades to ticket price increases for Berlin public transport is quoted with approval in a "News" section midway through the novel: "At the beginning of July [1975] the Revolutionary Cells hand out leaflets and 120,000 forged multiple tickets for Berlin Public Transport to a value of 360,000 DM; ticket machines are disabled and advice about travelling for free is distributed" (155). Taking part in one of these actions is how Madeleine was killed in *The Mountain Pass* (Klöppel, 2002).

Torching the politician's car is reported in the press as endangering the car owner's life, even though the car was empty and neither its owner nor anyone else was in its vicinity. Setting fire to newspaper kiosks is an "attack" and allows police and media to tar them with the terrorist brush. The demarcations between actions against things (*Sachen*) as opposed to actions against people (*Menschen*) become fluid. Jenny is prepared to cross the next boundary when she produces a gun and asks Fred, who knows about guns from his brief period of military service, to teach her how to use it. He also helps her to steal cars and to rob a bank. When she is arrested a mere week after she became an illegal, he goes on the run himself with a suitcase that she entrusted to him containing two pistols and a stack of fake driving licenses.

In the novel's frequent "News" sections, which are printed in bold type and capital letters, comrades' arrests, prison escapes, and deaths are reported, along with "actions" such as the storming of the West German Embassy in Stockholm in 1975, and the sequence of shootings that culminate in the German Autumn. Seyfried does not ignore the killings, but when Jenny disappears from Fred's field of vision, she disappears from the reader's too, which means we are unaware of what she is doing. Fred is not sure, since he does not ask and she does not tell him, about the level of her involvement in the Lorenz kidnapping or, two and a half years later, of her involvement in the kidnapping of Schleyer. Even though he visits her in prison and after her escape in East Berlin and Yugoslavia, she never confides in him. There are hints that the project has failed and that the characters regret what has happened. Fred and Jenny's friend Sandra comes closest to admitting this, but immediately corrects herself.

"The best thing would have been if the whole bloody thing had never started." She laughs but has tears in her eyes. "No, I don't mean that. It wasn't us who started it anyway, but the others hounding us, bashing us with truncheons, shooting people up, Ohnesorg and Dutschke. But how it has turned out now, oh God." (285)

Even if the other side did start it, it could still have been better for it never to have started at all. That there is no link in logic between the two halves of her statement does not seem to matter. When Fred learns on the last page that Jenny has been shot, the reader shares some of his sadness, but the novel has no more capacity for critical reflection than Fred appears to have himself. What it shows is the perennial wish that it be possible to be a revolutionary who takes the fight to the state without causing injury or loss of life. Seyfried is alone among this generation of writers to continue to hold this view now.

Rejected Selves, or the RAF as "Poison Containers"

In a lecture at the Berliner Ensemble commemorating the 20th anniversary of the German Autumn, the psychoanalyst critic Klaus Theweleit argued that the affective bonds between terrorists and their nonimprisoned supporters were pathological. The RAF prisoners functioned as "poison containers" for those on the outside. That is they became, like other charismatic figures from politics and public life (he cites the recently deceased Princess Diana), repositories for others' unwanted feelings. Drawing on a psychological theory of voters' changing emotional responses towards elected leaders, he explains the shifting attitudes of would-be or onetime supporters. "Both the supporters and all the others who behold them in public, pour ('project') certain things into them, offload fantasies, delegate wishes, tasks, prohibitions."[27] The terrorists acted out roles, first that of political outlaw and then that of victim of state repression, on behalf of others who identified with them, rejected them, and then felt overwhelmed with guilt as these human "poison containers" languished and died in prison. Identification with the terrorist victim in prison and his attendant martyrdom was part of a much wider "complex."

For Theweleit, there were three ingredients in October 1977 in what he describes as a ritual of purification. The state too played a role:

> This sort of collaboration between political outlaws, who deliver the transgressions, a state, which carries out the sacrifice ceremonies, and a group which is emotionally attached to the outlaws and which (after a great hue and cry) is left over and, purified, carries on in another direction is textbook poison-container politics: textbook acting out of social group fantasies. (50)

Wolfgang Kraushaar explains the appeal that Baader and Ensslin exerted over their contemporaries at the time of their first trial in 1968 in similar terms:

> They acted out something in their attacks and actions that many in the SDS were thinking but were not brave enough themselves to carry through: that it could at some point be necessary, in the struggle against a political system that in the face of the atrocities in Vietnam stood accused of not disconnecting itself from Auschwitz, to put one's own life at risk.[28]

Thomas Elsaesser echoes the same thesis: "A significant element in the RAF's popular appeal lay in the many kinds of vicariousness their emergence onto the scene permitted their own generation to engage in."[29] None of these theorists deals at any length with literary fiction, but their ideas approximate the narrative trajectory of a number of novels.

Baader-Meinhof novels frequently focus on the fascination that the life of a terrorist figure exerts over a narrator or central character, who further can serve as mediator between the author and the fictional terrorist. The generational proximity of the author and the central characters is the decisive factor for this biographical portrayal. Writers born after the 1940s are unlikely to employ such mediators. The pattern was first established in by Günter Herburger in "Lenau" (1972), in which a writer is obliged to put up a young man who is on the run and turns up from nowhere on his doorstep. Herburger (b. 1932) dramatizes the position of the intellectual supporter, torn between his own work and the effort involved in sheltering a political fugitive. As the narrator complains of Lenau's demanding, even parasitic behaviour, he acknowledges that "the more I defame my friend and comrade Lenau, the more vulnerable I become to criticism."[30] Chotjewitz's semiautobiographical narrator invents a succession of alter egos to engage with "Andi," the terrorist friend whose legal executor he becomes. Through his narrator, Chotjewitz thus approaches his onetime friend Andreas Baader, at two or even three removes:

At the beginning of December 1977, Fritz Buchonia had completed the draft of the first five chapters of the book. He was reluctant to write the account in the first person, as he believed the topic to be sensitive. For that reason he invented a character to think, say and experience everything that he was afraid of and with which he did not want to be identified.[31]

Dead Alive (Demski, 1984) is also autobiographical fiction inasmuch as the central figure, the unnamed "wife," shares a number of biographical markers with Eva Demski herself.[32] In the course of twelve days between her husband's death and funeral, she not only encounters figures from each area of his life, she reflects on their common political background and traces his political development from the mid-1960s to the autumn of 1974 when he died. Unlike the characters in Chotjewitz's novel, the wife succeeds in liberating herself from her husband's entanglements. A similar narrative configuration is present in *Red* (Timm, 2001). Linde, his central character, is confronted with his own past when he learns of the death of his long-lost friend, Aschenberger. Linde, who has made his living as a professional funeral orator, had either forgotten or transcended that past when he stumbled across a package containing explosives when clearing out his deceased friend's flat. Demski's "wife" also finds herself the unwitting custodian of a package, but is only half-surprised to find out about her husband's connections. In both these novels, there is a sense in which the surviving friend or widow is mourning a potential side to himself or herself, and realizing that he or she could have taken the same path on account of a shared political background. "'You know,' muses Linde to himself, 'this Aschenberger is a kind of Doppelgänger for you, he is pressing down on your conscience.'"[33]

The narrative pattern is not unique to German fiction.[34] Margaret Scanlan identifies the "motif of the writer as the terrorist's victim, rival, or double" to be intrinsic to terrorist novels, first appearing in "Dostoevsky's *Demons*, James's *The Princess Casamassima*, and Conrad's *Under Western Eyes*." She diagnoses "both writers and terrorists in these novels as remnants of a romantic belief in the power of marginalized persons to transform history."[35] There are several German novels that conform up to a point with her pattern, except that the accent is more likely to be on the writers' failure. *The Gentlemen of the Dawn* (Chotjewitz, 1978); *A Hero of Internal Security* (Delius, 1981); *Choice of Weapons* (Kuckart, 1990); *Too Far Afield* (Grass, 1995); *Red* (Timm, 2001); *The Assassin's Library* (Sonner, 2001); *Eros* (Krausser, 2006); and *Part of the Solution* (Peltzer, 2007) all feature writers who are the terrorists' counterparts, opposite numbers, or other selves. *My Sister, My Antigone* (Weil, 1980) is narrated by a writer who rejects her fanatically moral "sister," one of whose contemporary embodiments is named Gudrun Ensslin. This trope is deployed most influentially in the film *The German Sisters* which depicts two forms of commitment: one with the pen, one with the gun. The film is told from the point of view of a journalist, who also plays the role of mediator between the filmmaker and the terrorist figure. The distance between Juliane and the film's director Margarethe von Trotta is similar to that between Chotjewitz and Buchonia, Demski and "the wife," or Timm and Linde. Von Trotta's own heroic view of the other sister, Marianne, is indicated by her casting Barbara Sukowa, who played Marianne, as the title figure in her next historical biopic, *Rosa Luxemburg* (1986). While Marianne's actions are said to be wrong, her motives, which are the same as those of her journalist sister, are not questioned. Juliane at one point even claims that violence is the easy way. Werner, the father of Marianne's son, who kills himself at the beginning of the film, claims that Marianne's ideas are shared by both him and Juliane. Unlike Marianne, however, they are both too cowardly to act on them.

Three prominent first-generation novelists waited two to three decades before writing their most personal novels on the subject of terrorism. *Scylla* (Schneider, 2005) follows *My Year as a Murderer* (Delius, 2004) and *Red* (Timm, 2001). All three novelists were activists in the mid- to late-1960s who have made significant contributions to the theme of this book already, Delius in the *German Autumn Trilogy* (1981–1992), and Timm in two seminal novels on the student movement, *Hot Summer* (1974) and *Kerbel's Flight* (1980). *My Year as a Murderer* is called "a novel" but is presented more as a confession, and the narrator shares some well-known features with Delius himself. The narrator presents himself as a stereotypical intellectual unsuited to any sort of action:

> I did not even have the courage to pick up a cobblestone in my hand, let alone throw it. Me as perpetrator, murderer, this idea was more than foolhardy, it was impossible, mad, crazy. But, looking back today, perhaps because of its absurdity it produced a few sparks in my mind and ignited my imagination.[36]

Read autobiographically, Delius's career-long engagement with the RAF in his fiction shows an ever-increasing critical distancing. For Sven Kramer, Delius's "sympathy for armed opposition is tangible" in the title poem of *A Banker on the Run* (1975).[37] *My Year as a Murderer* certainly enacts a typical emotional development, compressed into a single year. The reader traces the evolution in the thinking of a left-wing author, whose original instincts were both antistate and antibusiness, but who makes his peace with a republic that itself evolved dramatically over the period concerned.

Peter Schneider's engagement with terrorism is arguably greater still. In *Lenz* (1973), he articulated the intellectual dislocation of student activists trying to forge alliances with the working classes. His confused hero wonders about throwing a stone at a demonstration. After Schneider's epistolary novel... *Already You Are an Enemy of the Cconstitution* (1975), there followed an appearance in *The Second Awakening of Christa Klages* (dir. von Trotta, 1976), where he plays a pastor who gets a knock on the door late at night from a fugitive. Schneider then wrote the screenplay for *Knife in the Head* (dir. Hauff, 1978).[38] This shows how an intellectual gets caught in the crossfire between violent radicals and the police. The plot reads like an autobiographical allegory that accounts for the predicament of many other left-wing writers in the late 1970s. In an exchange of letters with jailed RAF member Peter-Jürgen Boock in 1985, Schneider is at his most candid. When approached by a former friend who joined the underground struggle, he refused to follow him for what he calls a "hedonistic" reason:

> I imagined that, if I followed this acquaintance, I would never again be able to sit on the muddy beach at Ostia with a glass of white wine on the table in front of me and look out to sea without having to be afraid that the shadow that some stranger or other behind me was casting onto the terrace belonged to someone pursuing me.[39]

Twenty years later, this becomes the main plot idea for the novel *Scylla*. The collaboration with Boock that resulted in the exchange of letters was to have been a televised interview, but permission was refused on the grounds that Boock was facing trial. Schneider explains his motivation: "In the television interview I wanted among other things to signal that millions of Germans for almost two years defined a good part of their political identity by distinguishing themselves from 100 desperados but did not have the opportunity of looking one of them in the face."[40] This is a prearticulation of Theweleit's thesis: had they not first felt an affinity, there would have been no need to distinguish themselves from the *desperados*.

Schneider's memoir, subtitled *My '68*, published in 2008, the fortieth anniversary of the year of failed revolutions, attracted widespread attention, as his books usually do.[41] His main title, *Revolt and Delusion*, shows his distance from his former self. Violent direct action is a recurrent theme. He retells the well-known anecdote of how the Italian publisher Giangiacomo Feltrinelli came to the Vietnam Congress in February 1968 with a present of several sticks of dynamite for Rudi Dutschke and how the explosives were hidden in his baby son Hosea Che's buggy. Dutschke, who is sometimes portrayed as an almost saintly pacifist, was not above smashing shop windows.[42] As a spokesman for the student movement, Schneider shared responsibility for preparing the intellectual ground for the use of illegal political violence in some circumstances when he coauthored an article published in *konkret* entitled "Gewalt" ("Violence"). The other authors included Ulrike Meinhof, who had recently stopped writing columns for the magazine. Sarah Colvin concludes that the "article was remarkable for its decisive move away from the students' taboo that forbade violence against other human beings."[43] The "delusion" with which the memoirs begin is that the revolutionary left will assume power very shortly. But it is the love story at its heart that gives the book its shape and connects Schneider's biography with terrorism. The woman he refers to as "L.," as if she were a character in his own *Lenz* or a nineteenth-century fiction, was stunningly beautiful and briefly worked in an antique shop. She was invited for dinner at the house of none other than Axel Springer after he came to the shop. Schneider recalls his jealousy, how he waited up for her return, and her reluctance to tell him much about Springer's less-than-subtle attempts at seduction. With hindsight, Schneider sees that their love had no future once he had obliged her to have an abortion, which was at that time illegal in the Federal Republic. After they moved apart personally, they took different political paths. L. joined the RAF and is none other than the writer-terrorist Marianne Herzog.[44] Schneider stepped back and became a socially committed writer instead of a man of violence.

This trio of 68er writers made their peace with the republic. Their successor generation was caught up in 1977, rather than 1968. The novel that could have been the last word on the terrorist as alter ego is *Checked* (Goetz, 1988), which works through the complex from the point of view of a younger character, who experiences the events through the media and believes he is being manipulated (controlled or "checked") by them.[45] The idea is that the whole thing was a con as both sides were staging a performance that manipulated the rest of the population, which needed to free itself from the fascination they exerted. It took more than two decades after 1977 for writers to show in their novels that they had done this.

CHAPTER TWO

FROM STECHLIN TO STAMMHEIM:
F. C. DELIUS AS PIONEER

A trio of novels by F. C. Delius, published between 1981 and 1992, which were presented as the German Autumn Trilogy in 1997, are the main subject of this chapter.[1] Theodor Fontane's state-of-the-nation novel *Der Stechlin* (1898) is my initial point of comparison, because of its symbolic use of a large family house and the connections that Fontane (1819–1898), the great chronicler of Bismarckian Prussia, makes between local and global events. Like Heinrich Böll in *Safety Net* (1979), to which Delius alludes, Helmut Krausser in *Eros* (2006), and Bernhard Schlink in *The Weekend* (2008), Delius uses symbolic structures to demonstrate power, durability, tradition, moral value, or—equally likely—the lack of these. Delius stuck with the theme of the German Autumn at a time when few other German writers were interested in it and commercial rewards were not as significant as they would have been with other subjects. All novelists and filmmakers who come after him stand in his debt. Building on the film *Germany in Autumn* (dir. Kluge et al., 1978), Delius made Horst Herold and Hanns-Martin Schleyer (though not Helmut Schmidt) into literary characters, elaborated what has since become the national commemorative narrative of "Mogadishu," which shows German democrats triumphing over evil outsiders behaving like Nazis, and explored in depth a number of other myths and tropes. The penitent female terrorist and the disengaged writer as onlooker are two of the most prominent of these. Above all, the three novels stand out because of the stubborn focus on the 44 days in 1977 from the kidnapping of Hanns-Martin Schleyer on September 5th to the freeing of the hijacked Lufthansa passenger jet *Landshut* on October 18th and their memoralization, which makes historical figures and events into components in contemporary national mythology. Delius comments critically on that mythologization at the same time that he helps to create it.

The key symbolic structures or locales in the trilogy are: the headquarters of an imaginary confederation of leaders, which is situated in Cologne on the banks of the Rhine (*A Hero of Internal Security*); the fuselage of the hijacked Lufthansa passenger jet *Landshut* (*Window Seat at Mogadishu*); and the city of Wiesbaden, capital of the state of Hesse, and site of the central offices of the BKA (*Ascent to Heaven of an Enemy of the State*). Delius's three novels are set at different points in September and October 1977. *A Hero of Internal Security* happens over a few days in mid-September, immediately following the kidnap of Alfred Büttinger (a cipher for Schleyer); *Window Seat at Mogadishu* occurs over the four days of the *Landshut* hijacking in mid-October; and *Ascent to Heaven of an Enemy of the State* takes place at an imaginary version of the funeral of Baader, Ensslin, and Raspe towards the end of the same month. Delius follows the drama as it unfolds, each time from a different and original perspective, but the shape and slant of each novel are also determined by the evolving politics over the eleven years that he took to write the three novels. These are: the end of the Social Democratic era in 1981 or the so-called *Tendenzwende* (change of direction) and return to conservative, Christian Democratic values (*A Hero of Internal Security*); the high point of West German economic success under CDU Chancellor Helmut Kohl in 1987 (*Window Seat at Mogadishu*); and the timorous sense of a new beginning for a unified German state in 1992 (*Ascent to Heaven of an Enemy of the State*).[2] In the first two novels, Delius explores his main characters' emotional contradictions as partial expressions of the national psyche. In the third, he is both more formally experimental and directly political, presenting four interlocking and mutually complementary perspectives.

Fontane's last novel, *Der Stechlin,* is set in the post-Bismarck era, partly in Berlin and mainly at the remote location on the edge of Brandenburg, from which it takes its name. The title could refer either to a lake or a wood, as both words are masculine in German, or to one of the two male members of the Stechlin family, but not to the family residence since both "Haus" and "Schloß" (castle) are neuter. *Der Stechlin* is a novel about political transition; on the eve of the calamitous twentieth century, it looks forward cautiously to modernity and at the same time back to the rhythms of life at the rural heart of historic Prussia, whose conflicted rise to European preeminence was Fontane's lifelong theme. Fontane's concerns are the interplay between tradition and change, the local and the global. He is also the first German novelist to depict a democratic election, which the patrician Dubslav von Stechlin loses to a Social Democrat candidate. Delius drew on a ballad by Fontane for his first post-*Wende* fiction, *The Pears of Ribbeck* (1991), which is an allegory of reunification, as Günter Grass drew on Fontane's whole life and works for his reunification novel, *Too Far Afield* (1995).

Fontane describes the Stechlin building before he has introduced a single character.[3] Every small detail is meaningful and connected with the identity of the border region between the provinces of Brandenburg and Mecklenburg. Local and national history are etched on to it. Like much of Germany, the original castle had been destroyed during the Thirty Years' War (1618–1648), to be rebuilt along more modest lines after the founding of modern Prussia in the early 1700s. Now in the 1890s, as the newly unified German Reich has swallowed up Prussia and is characterized by accelerating industrialization and crass militarism, the premises face decline rather than destruction. Dubslav von Stechlin is short of funds and is uncertain whether the next generation in the shape of his only son will show interest in the family home. The modern world is alien, which is underscored to the family when Dubslav's son Woldemar becomes engaged to a Swiss woman brought up in England. Yet England and Switzerland are the two countries most associated in this era with democracy, freedom, and progress, and the fruits of this union are likely to be more robust than the original Stechlin stock. By the end of the novel, after Woldemar has married his Swiss wife, and when Dubslav shortly afterwards dies, the mood is optimistic. The newlyweds move into the ancestral seat, which they set about renovating. Prussia too will not disappear but rather will be renewed; the Social Democrats are not after all about to tear it all down. *Der Stechlin* is Fontane's last work and his only remotely utopian novel.

In *Safety Net, Eros,* and *The Weekend,* there is a representative family residence called a "Schloβ" (castle or country seat). In *Safety Net,* Böll's Tolmshoven stands in the western Rhineland, on the edge of the political power base of the old Bonn Republic. Böll emulates Fontane in his concentration on family, generation, the primacy of a particular place, and the links outwards to the worlds of politics, religion, and business. Fritz Tolm's roots in his locality go back as far as Dubslav von Stechlin's did in Brandenburg. The oldest section of Tolmshoven dates from the twelfth century. Like Dubslav von Stechlin, Fritz Tolm shares his family name with the place he lives in, and his friends joke that he should be called "Tolm zu Tolm." But the shortening of his name from Tolmshoven indicates a reduction, and may be a sign that things do not quite fit anymore. The continuity that Fontane affirmed is broken; life will have to continue without Tolmshoven, which, had it not been set alight on the terrorist Heinrich Bewerloh's orders, would have been demolished by the state after the discovery of brown coal in the area surrounding it.

A grand representative family residence and the family who live in it are also Krausser's starting point in *Eros.* Fontane's unity has still not been restored. The "Ice Palace" separates the von Brückens from the workers in their factory, who include the parents of future RAF member Sophie Kurtz. The "ice" indicates the lack of love in the wealthy industrialist family, and the palace burns down in the dying days of World War II, in apparent defiance of its nickname. The fire is a symbol of the fall of Germany, and the confusion over its cause recalls the debate over responsibility for the war. At the end of the novel, we learn that it was Alexander von Brücken's father, in disappointment at the fall of Nazism, who lit the fateful match. Through his hobby of architecture, von Brücken senior is linked with Hitler; his other views and interests are of his time. His son's postwar castle is a fairytale construction he calls the *Eulennest* (owl's nest), which brings to mind Hitler's summer residence in Berchtesgaden, nicknamed the Eagle's Nest. As von Brücken dictates his reminiscences to a novelist whom he entrusts with turning his life into literature, he is also building a mausoleum. Both the *Eispalast* in Nazi times and the *Eulennest* in the old FRG cut their powerful inhabitants off from the rest of society, which was not the purpose of the castle in Fontane's *Der Stechlin*.

In *The Weekend*, Schlink shifts the focus from the Rhineland, favored by Böll and Delius, to Brandenburg, the historic center of Prussian power, and resettles it with West Germans. Terrorism is now seen an illness from which the body politic has all but recovered. The released terrorist Jörg himself is dying and Jan, who disappeared more than 30 years earlier, is imagined to have died in the Twin Towers on September 11, 2001. There is no political legacy to pass on to the next generation, but by the second day of the weekend, the assembled group of former student friends is happy to take part in prayers led by Karin, who is now a bishop, suggesting that the group members have become reconciled with traditional religion. One big problem with the past, as it is embodied by the setting, is that it is not connected meaningfully with the present. In 2007, the year when this short novel is set, the Schloß has new owners, the former West German Christiane, who is the sister of released terrorist Jörg (based on Christian Klar), and her friend Margarethe, from the former GDR. They and their guests are cut off from their history and use the premises merely as a decorative backdrop. Finding themselves somewhere in historic Brandenburg, the heart of Fontane's Prussia, which for 40 years was part of the other German state, the West Germans are disoriented, but in exploring their surroundings, they find out about themselves. The house and its grounds are a space that is divorced from their normal lives, which obliges them to behave differently and to react to each other and their unaccustomed situation. There is renovation to be done, as it has neither running water nor electricity, but at the end they all pull together to clear up the cellar after a flash flood. In Schlink's conservative symbolism, the estranged terrorist family is reconciled (the dying Jörg makes peace with his long-lost son) at the same time that the historic residence is reclaimed. Once more, like Fontane, Schlink concludes a political novel (or *Zeitroman*) optimistically. Like Böll, Delius increasingly sees 1977 as a prelude rather than an ending. Even in *A Hero of Internal Security*, which is the most socially and economically critical of the three novels, the basic narrative gesture is conciliatory. By imagining what may go on inside the head of an apparatchik of the capitalist system, Delius empathizes with "the enemy" more overtly than Böll does; Böll's Fritz Tolm (a cipher both for media magnate Axel Springer and, as a potential kidnapping victim, for Schleyer) has views very like his own. Roland Diehl is not a readily likeable character. He is emotionally repressed, sexually domineering, spiritually empty, and interested only in advancing his own career. The novel's readers are not encouraged to find him ridiculous or objectionable, however. Andrea Boländer, the 30-year-old biology researcher who plays the central role in *Window Seat at Mogadishu*, is more critical of her government than she is of the terrorists who hijack her plane, but she also appears to emerge an emotionally enriched person from her ordeal. In *Ascent to Heaven of an Enemy of the State*, Sigurd Nagel is celebrated as a unifying figure because he asked questions and posed problems that the state needed to address.

In *A Hero of Internal Security*, the symbolic "house" is the purpose-built headquarters of the Confederation of Leaders. Büttinger, as chairman of the confederation, commissioned its construction; it thus represents both his (absent) personality and his management precept of performance, which the confederation exists to propagate. The high-tech, sixteen-story glass and steel structure on the banks of the Rhine in Cologne, with its shiny surfaces and mechanical perfection, is inhuman in scale and is designed with the express purpose of eliminating the natural world. It exists in opposition to the outside world; its air-conditioned, heat-controlled environment is completely sanitized.[4] Diehl is Büttinger's speechwriter and "thinker," making him responsible for formulating the ideology of personal performance which maximizes individual and collective output. He is a pseudo-writer who serves capital on its own terms, not reflecting for a moment what motivated the kidnappers. As the novel begins, shortly after the kidnapping has taken place, Diehl is even beginning to blame Büttinger for obliging him to experience unwelcome emotions. He cannot begin to accommodate imaginatively what is happening to his kidnapped boss. Thus, as a writer and thinker he is defeated by the situation before it has barely begun.

The novel's last chapter focuses on the building, rather than on any of the characters, and on the smooth running of the confederation that is contained securely within it. Both will survive the killing of Büttinger.

The building demonstrates the confident economic power of the 1980s, which, according to Delius's thesis, the kidnapping and killing of Büttinger (Schleyer), the Stammheim suicides of the RAF members, and the storming of the *Landshut* made possible. This may be a less positive outcome than in *Safety Net*, because what was gained at the end of Böll's novel is in danger of being lost now. Tolm's enemies, represented by his business rival Amplanger, are well and truly in control. We are even further away from the integration of *Der Stechlin* or the harmony at the end of *The Weekend*.

While even tiny insects such as ants and spiders cannot find a way through nonexistent cracks in the confederation's HQ, nobody can do anything to combat the foul smell from the nearby brewery. This is described as "a proletarian stink" (*A Hero of Internal Security*, 219) which all the building's occupants are obliged to inhale. What disturbs them more than the smell is that "they could not get a better hold on the world outside the house" (220), which continues to operate according to other laws. As what has happened to their kidnapped chairman is "unimaginable" (219) to them, they prefer not to think about it at all. Unwanted emotions which he has repressed return in Diehl's nightmares, in which he confronts death, capture, and danger. His battles with his private demons are compounded by his inability to form relationships with women that are not based on sex and power. What is missing in his emotional makeup is the ability to empathize with another person. He can only dimly understand what troubles his girlfriend Tina, and he rarely tries to imagine the ordeal Büttinger may be enduring.

The increasing importance of the business ethos on the eve of the Kohl era gives the first novel of Delius's trilogy a more modern feel than *Safety Net*. Delius acknowledges Böll's influence with a reference to "Fritz Tolm," who is under consideration as a possible successor to Büttinger (80). Like Katharina Blum, Roland Diehl, who used to be a rally driver, often drives fast on the autobahn just to relax: "until the day's stress was burnt up, until the dull feeling in his fingertips disappeared, which all day long had pressed buttons on his Dictaphone, the air conditioning, the telephone" (63). Like Böll, Delius does not employ shifts in mood or tone. For the most part too he eschews irony. By the end, Diehl has grown used to the idea that his boss will not be returning to work, even though he is still alive and negotiations between government and terrorists are ongoing. Diehl is offered a promotion, which entails a move to another department and has come about as a result of the crisis. He accepts, thus profiting personally from Büttinger's plight.[5] Tina meanwhile has ended their relationship.

Delius has said that Diehl is an inverse image of himself as a writer.[6] They are the same age; their names share a majority of their letters. Like the experience of Martin, the stuttering autobiographical central character in *America House and the Dance around the Women* (1997), which is set on the day of an anti-Vietnam War demonstration in February 1966, Diehl's first experience of sex ends all too quickly as a result of his overexcitement. Diehl also once tried to address a student general meeting in Frankfurt and found the words would not come out of his mouth, which aroused the scorn of his listeners. This makes him a failed student activist. Diehl is an ideologue in discussions with colleagues, arguing that their confederation should be bold in pointing the way forward for society and not let itself be inhibited by the demands made by "the partner association," the trade unions, whom he calls "Menschen*ver*führer" (50) (*seducers* rather than *leaders* of people). Büttinger, on the other hand, once astounded his listeners by showing understanding for student radicals and recognizing his own younger self in them. Delius suggests their common ground by giving him the same initials as Andreas Baader. Andrea Boländer in the next novel, *Window Seat at Mogadishu*, even shares the spelling of his first name. Both she and Diehl, aged 30 and 37 respectively, belong to the same generation as the terrorists and have much in common with their supposedly more radical contemporaries. Diehl never knew his father, who was missing in action in the war. He never accepted his mother's second husband and resolved on no account to turn out like him. But Diehl did not rebel like his contemporaries. Instead he was determined to be successful. He joined the newly formed *Bundeswehr* as a lieutenant in the paratroopers, thus volunteering for a longer period of military service than was obligatory. His socialization took place in the army, where he internalized military values of discipline, which, like some of the songs that he learns, were directly inherited from the Third Reich. Diehl looks back proudly on his first publication, which was a letter to the newspaper *Die Zeit* on the building of the Berlin Wall, when he was 20. Delius aligns him even more closely with recent history by making his birthday June 18th: the reason Diehl remembers the newspaper reports of the workers' uprising in East Berlin on June 17, 1953 is that they appeared on his eleventh birthday, making "two historical events on one day" (53). Büttinger was born the day World War I began, making him 65 when he was kidnapped.[7]

As a bearer of the values of the economic system that underpins the republic, Diehl is moderately frightening. Büttinger, however, is different. Even though he was once a member of the SS, like Schleyer, it is hard not to admire his drive. The know-how, leadership, and determination of men like him continue to power the West German economy in the 1970s. He argues that the Nazis' failure should teach Germans to be pragmatic about what they can achieve. *Leistung* (achievement or performance) has always been his watchword; the problem for him with the Third Reich was that it did not ultimately provide a context in which *Leistung* paid off. Although he talks about his career path through the Hitler period, which makes him atypical of his generation, he expresses no remorse for the plight of the Germans' millions of victims. Action rather than reflection is Büttinger's domain, which is why his approach to the past is ethically unsophisticated. The flip side to his shallowness is that he does not complain about the defeat, as so many did. He immediately accepts the new political reality and sets about making it a success. As he is so much more attractive a character than his protégé, Büttinger's loss will be a blow to the confederation, but the system as he has defined it is bigger than any individual and will continue without him.

Delius remains the only novelist to portray a character based on Schleyer, albeit one who does not appear directly. It is a challenging and nuanced portrait, which anticipates the reassessments of Schleyer's character in the decades to follow. Yet Büttinger is present in the first and third installments of Delius' trilogy only through others' consciousness of his absence. Memories of him inhabit their private imagination as if he were a guilty secret. For Diehl, the Boss is as good as already dead; by the time *Ascent to Heaven of an Enemy of the State* begins, he has been shot. His presence in the trilogy's final novel recalls that of Schleyer in the film *Germany in Autumn,* when he speaks as if from the grave as a disembodied voice through director Alexander Kluge's reading out of passages from Schleyer's letters in captivity to his son, Eberhard. Along with Horst Herold, Schleyer is the key figure from the other side in literary and filmic accounts of the German Autumn (bizarrely, Helmut Schmidt tends to get portrayed only in film). But whereas other central episodes from Baader-Meinhof history have been represented in various genres or formats and in a number of novels, the Schleyer kidnapping has only been attempted in Part One of *Death Game* (dir. Breloer, 1997). His imprisonment and interrogation are remembered by one of his penitent kidnappers in an at times powerful fictionalized reconstruction: *The Kidnapping and Murder of Hanns-Martin Schleyer* (Boock, 2002). The kidnapping and murder have been reperformed or reenacted, however, far more times in film and fiction, with different figures assigned the various roles. In *The Third Generation* (dir. Fassbinder, 1978), the whole episode is replayed as farce, as it is in Peter-Paul Zahl's reunification play *The Blackmailers: A Nasty Comedy* (1990). The role of Schleyer is played by an authoritarian GDR headmaster in *Out of Your Skin* (dir. Dresen, 1997) and by an ex-friend of Dutschke's, now a millionaire businessman in *The Edukators* (dir. Weingartner, 2004). Schleyer's murder is emulated in the short novel *Death of a Truffle Pig* (Weiss, 2007) and his kidnapping is reenacted in *Where Will You Be* (Hammerstein, 2010).

If Schleyer's cold-blooded murder is the cause of collective trauma, then these reenactments may be symptoms of compulsive behavior typical of trauma victims, who want to repeat in their minds the original traumatic event.[8] With the possible exception of Thomas Weiss, the authors and filmmakers who have depicted reenactments of the kidnappings and murders are identified with the political left: the trauma that they express is that suffered by the perpetrators. The taboo surrounding Schleyer obliges them to avoid representing the events themselves, with the result that these are replaced by other events in the present. Over the years, the Schleyer figure has evolved from Nazi capitalist, who embodied the continuity between the Third Reich and the Federal Republic, to brave, insightful capitalist democrat who debated with his captors. This evolution occurs across the board. A biography from 2004 presents his postwar persona as complex and reveals a number of exaggerations in his opponents' account of his wartime activities.[9] Peter-Jürgen Boock recalls how Schleyer showed intellectual and even moral superiority over his captors. Alfred Herrhausen and Karl Detlev Rohwedder, the other two best-known RAF victims, who in the literature may sometimes be taken as Schleyer substitutes, are commemorated too for their reformist and liberal views. The trope of capitalist villain as quasiliberal was initiated by Böll in his portrayal of Fritz Tolm; it is carried on in *Too Far Afield* (Grass, 1995) and *Dengler's First Case* (Schorlau, 2003) in their depiction of characters based on Rohwedder, and in the documentary reconstruction of the life of Herrhausen, *Black Box BRD* (dir. Veiel, 2001). For the RAF, Schleyer was a symbol of "the system," but their misappreciation of that symbol was indicative of their misreading of evolving political consensus in the FRG.

A Hero of Internal Security breaks off before the German Autumn reaches its climax, with the hijacking of the *Landshut*, which is the point at which *Window Seat at Mogadishu* begins. In the second novel, which was published on the tenth anniversary of the German Autumn (and was just about the only publication to commemorate the date, in marked contrast to the anniversaries ten and twenty years later), the locus of the action is the fuselage of the hijacked airliner, which acquires multiple symbolic meanings. The passengers are a representative sample of Germanic humanity. One is a veteran of Rommel's North African campaign and is returning to the desert for the first time since the war. Whereas Rommel was defeated, this time the Germans win; the GSG-9 commando raid to free the passengers at Mogadishu is the first German military victory since World War II. Two passengers are elderly and do not understand what is happening, providing an occasionally poignant commentary. Mainstream ideology is represented by a group of young women returning from a beauty contest. Another woman runs a beauty parlor. The only other profession that is mentioned is Andrea Boländer's own, university biology researcher. This puts the body, in particular the female body, at the center of the novel. All the passengers are obliged to concentrate on their bodily needs and functions as their ordeal intensifies. The toilets on the plane quickly become blocked, giving off an awful stink as excrement spills out on to the floor. The temperature cannot be regulated as they sweat out an entire day on a runway in Dubai. Nobody can wash or change their clothes, eat and drink when they need to, or attend to their other hygiene requirements. The human body, along with the emotions generated by physical desires, was expelled from the headquarters of Confederation of Leaders in the previous novel, along, ultimately, with Büttinger himself and his captured body. Boländer has the opposite experience, which ultimately has some positive repercussions. She is more aware than Diehl of what the RAF is, but she affects neutrality in a dispute that she does not believe has much to do with her. At first she assumes that the hijacking of her plane cannot be linked to the kidnapping of the country's top industrialist, because the hijackers are not German. None of the other victims expresses a political opinion until right at the end, when they come to believe that their government has abandoned them.

When the plane is taken over by four Palestinians, the conditions for the 86 tourists and 5 crew resemble those that the RAF prisoners claimed that they suffered in prison, also bringing to mind a concentration camp. The leading hijacker, the self-styled Captain Jassid, is an unpredictable and all-powerful commander, described as "the machine's dictator" (248), who can be at turns both friendly and ruthless, wanting to educate as well as to terrorize the passengers and crew in his power. He "executes" the pilot for disobeying him and accuses various passengers of being Jewish. He "selects" his next victims by issuing them with numbers telling them in which order they will be shot, and he has the whole plane wired with explosives. Jassid is both anti-Zionist and anti-Semitic. He blames the Germans for the creation of the state of Israel because he believes that Israel would not have come into existence without the Holocaust, which, perversely, aligns Germans with Israelis and Jews. He borrows RAF rhetoric by presenting himself as a resister to the current neo-fascist West German regime, inviting his captives to ally themselves with him against their government. Germans are thus both oppressors (as friends of the state of Israel) and oppressed, as they are now treated on the plane as the Jews were treated by the Nazis. They are victimized, feminized, and infantilized in numerous ways. The novel's narrative takes the form of Boländer's application to the state for victim compensation. None of the Germans, the majority of whom are female, attempts to overpower the hijackers. The copilot even abandons a landing at Aden when he notices that Jassid, who is seated next to him, is not wearing his safety belt and would fly through the cockpit window.

Window Seat at Mogadishu is the first Baader-Meinhof novel to be narrated from the point of view of a victim.[10] Delius is also the first writer to imagine what went on inside the hijacked *Landshut*. Since then, there have been three other German treatments of the hijacking, two made-for-television "docudramas," and a feature film. The second part of *Death Game* (dir. Breloer, 1997) is set mainly on the plane and was broadcast on the twentieth anniversary of the hijacking, in 1997. *The Miracle of Mogadishu* (dirs. Brauburger, Halmburger, and Vogel, 2007) was commissioned by the ZDF state broadcasting company for the hijacking's thirtieth anniversary. Like its predecessor, it concentrates on the passengers, the pilot's heroism, and the Palestinians' irrational anti-Semitism. It also elaborates on the real-life love story between stewardess Gabi Dillmann and Lufthansa pilot Rüdiger von Lützau, who, unbeknownst to her, was following the *Landshut* in another plane on the orders of the government. The title echoes that of a recent popular fiction film directed by Sönke Wortmann about the first (West) German victory in the World Cup in 1954, *The Miracle of Berne* (2003). The feature film *Mogadishu* (dir. Richter, 2008) shifts the accent further onto the human ordeal, highlighting even more the bravery of the pilot Jürgen Schumann, to whom the film is dedicated, and Dillmann, played by the award-winning actress Nadja Uhl. The stewardess is even shown sheltering the plane's sole Jewish passenger, whose Auschwitz tattoo she notices on boarding. *Mogadishu* has a second hero in Helmut Schmidt. At first boxed in by foreign powers which are fearful of offending the Palestinians and Arab states under the influence of Moscow, Schmidt emerges diplomatically and militarily triumphant. Working from the same sources, Delius downplays the pilot's role and ignores the stewardess's touching love story. Jassid's suspicion that some of the passengers might be Jewish or might have Jewish connections is only one of a series of outbursts, rather than his defining characteristic.

For mass audiences, the drama on the *Landshut* has become the favored commemorative narrative. The two films from 2007/08 were bound up with the vogue for exploring German war-time suffering, which resulted in a slew of books and films on the bombing of German cities and the expulsion of civilians from the eastern territories. The four fictional treatments of the hijacking (one novel and three films), produced over a period of 21 years, show differences of nuance and emphasis, but by necessity all show the German tourists and cabin crew as victims of foreign terrorist oppressors, who are moreover not just anti-Israeli or anti-Zionist, but anti-Semitic. This national narrative thus concentrates on pulling together in the face of an outside threat, which resembles in some key respects the threat that the previous generation of Germans posed elsewhere in the world. As Christian Hißnauer has demonstrated, this narrative was not immediately apparent to opinion-makers or to the German public in 1977.[11] It has been manufactured in the intervening years.

Delius was the first writer to recognize the potential of "Mogadishu" for generating greater meanings. For him, the German Autumn was a national event; his whole trilogy is a national epic, albeit one that incorporates the dislocations of recent German history rather than attempting to smooth them out. It is unfair to claim that he is "normalizing" German history in the manner of conservatives like Ernst Nolte, whose attempt to explain the Holocaust as a preventive response to Soviet terror sparked the Historians' Quarrel in 1985, but the charge indicates that Delius is posing essentially the same national question.[12] Delius is careful with contexts and perspectives; Boländer herself is anything but triumphant by the end of *Window Seat at Mogadishu*. As she runs along the tarmac, away from the setting of her ordeal, she reflects on how she has become part of a spectacle that the rest of the world has already been watching. In other words, her experience is instantly being turned into myth by the media. That is the moment that interests Delius as a novelist, and which is brought into even sharper relief in his next novel.

The third volume in the *German Autumn* trilogy is rich in literary, cinematic, religious, and mythological allusions, most of them with a specifically German dimension. Delius is now concerned above all with how national narratives are pieced together from historical events and characters. *Ascent to Heaven of an Enemy of the State* is conceptually the most imaginative and formally experimental of the three novels. Most of the narrative consists of a monologue delivered by the deceased Sigurd Nagel, whose biography is closely based on that of Andreas Baader, on the day of his funeral. Rather than the ragged, heavily policed affair familiar to viewers of *Germany in Autumn* (dir. Kluge et al., 1978), one of Delius's key filmic intertexts, the novel presents the funeral as a cause for rejoicing that brings all parts of the nation together, even including—most improbably for 1977—delegations from the GDR. While *Germany in Autumn* intercuts footage of Schleyer's state funeral with the funeral of Baader, Ensslin, and Raspe, Delius essentially merges them, moves them from Stuttgart to Wiesbaden, and turns the two somber occasions into an ironic celebration. The encounter of the Italian Professor Serrata with the police is another allusion to Alexander Kluge's film, towards the beginning of which the Stuttgart police apprehend a Turkish immigrant. The shared intertext of film and novel is Heinrich Heine's satirical poem from 1843, "Germany. A Winter's Tale," as I will show.

Delius acknowledges being inspired by Robert Coover's *The Public Burning*, a surreal post-Vietnam political novel mixing fantasy with documentary reportage of the execution of the communists Julius and Ethel Rosenberg on June 19, 1953.[13] One of Coover's main figures is Richard Nixon, vice-president of the United States at the time the novel is set and president until 1974, three years before the novel was published in 1977. Coover is more interested in the resonances of 1950s McCarthyism two decades on than he is in Nixon's presidency. Delius's novel, although set in 1977, is an ironic commentary on the unification of the two German states in 1990, which was his theme in *The Pears of Ribbeck*, published the previous year. Delius also overwrites the theme of the Antigone/Oedipus/Hamlet drama, opposing fathers and rebellious offspring with that of sacrifice and redemption.[14] Another meaning of *Himmelfahrt* ("ascent to heaven") is suicide: a *Himmelfahrtskommando* is a suicide squad. There are some references to sacrifice in *A Hero of Internal Security*. Diehl played the role of the Apostle Peter, abandoning his leader in his time of need: Büttinger / Schleyer took the Nazi sins of the entire nation on his own head.

The Ascent to Heaven of an Enemy of the State has no single physical focus comparable to the *Landshut* or the House of People Leaders. The novel consists of four independent strands, which are narrated by the deceased Nagel / Baader; the terrorist Cornelia Handschuch (based more loosely on Silke Maier-Witt and Susanne Albrecht, both of whom regretted their involvement in the Schleyer kidnapping); the BKA chief Bernhard Schäfer (the first fictional portrait of Herold); and Maurizio Serrata, a professor of German Studies from the University of Ferrara. Serrata is in Germany to investigate the circumstances of the death of Margret Falcke (Ulrike Meinhof). His role was played in history by the unofficial international commission that published a report on the Meinhof case, but, like the other three characters, he also reflects on what the recent events say about the state of contemporary Germany.[15] The four characters do not meet, and their strands hardly even overlap; when they do, the consequences are incidental. Towards the end of the day, Schäfer receives the news that Handschuch has been apprehended. Serrata is also arrested, though not by the BKA; the police attempt to frame him for possessing heroin before releasing him a few hours later, on condition that he not set foot on German soil for six months.

On the evidence of the narrative structure, Germany has fallen apart rather than grown together. The novel is in one sense a literary counterpoint to the national political event of reunification, except that it appears once again to be predicated on reconciliation. Handschuch is penitent; Serrata cannot find any evidence that Falcke was murdered and remains a germanophile, despite his mistreatment at the hands of the police; Schäfer (whose name means "shepherd") is a benign national guardian whose priority is to avert further bloodshed by removing the motivation to commit acts of violence. At one point he imagines throwing an inkpot at Nagel, as if he were Luther and Nagel were the Devil. Schäfer is a lonely, isolated man, surrounded by computers and closed circuit television screens, who recognizes that his adversaries were strident moralists and thus more-than-worthy opponents. His ambition to keep his fellow citizens under near complete surveillance nonetheless has Orwellian overtones. This leaves only Nagel to spoil the party with some bitter humor. He, however, is dead and his spirit will soon be in heaven.

Delius challenges readers to reassess their understanding of recent history. The main characters stand for a point of view or set of forces in culture and society. They are not intended to be psychologically plausible, let alone likeable figures with whom readers can sympathize. Serrata, who once allowed RAF fugitives to shelter at his house, represents those intellectuals, at home and abroad, who sided instinctively with adversaries of the German state. His task now consists of measuring lengths of toweling that Falcke (like Meinhof) is claimed to have torn into thin strips to fashion herself a noose. It seems hardly credible that the strips would have been strong enough to take her weight; some of her injuries point to her already being dead when her head was inserted into the noose. Serrata comes to the conclusion, however, that we should believe what we want to believe about the nature of her death. The evidence is inconclusive. This debate has not progressed since 1976, when Meinhof was found hanged in her cell, or 1992 when Delius's novel was published. A recent biography of Meinhof comes down in favor of murder over suicide; a history by a respected state prosecutor entertains no doubt that she took her own life.[16] Why agents employed by the state should have picked Meinhof out at that point and risked the consequences of discovery before her trial was over is never addressed by conspiracy theorists.

Set in a wider context, Serrata's investigation concerns more than Meinhof, since several other terrorist deaths have been passionately contested. In addition to Benno Ohnesorg, the police or judicial authorities were accused of murdering Petra Schelm, Thomas Weissbecker, Georg von Rauch, Holger Meins, and of course the Stammheim trio of Baader, Ensslin, and Raspe. The government's opponents were determined to believe the worst; as a result, conspiracy theories abounded. According to one, Baader was flown out to Mogadishu on the evening of October 17th, shown to the hijackers, who trustingly released their hostages before they themselves were shot, after which Baader was murdered and returned to his Stammheim cell, where his body was discovered the following morning. The clue was the sand from the Somalian desert that was said to have still coated his shoes. Peter Schneider responded with an appeal for common sense, pointing out the many points where disbelief needed to be suspended before such a tale could be believed.[17] In a piece of ironic Brechtian prose, the poet Erich Fried picked holes in the official account of the Rauch shooting, calling it "preventative murder," which resulted in his being sued (unsuccessfully) by the chief of the Hamburg police.[18] Since *Ascent to Heaven of an Enemy of the State* was published, even more ink has been spilled on the case of Wolfgang Grams, who according to official reports shot himself in the head at Bad Kleinen on June 26, 1993. Schneider was right about Baader; Fried turned out to be wrong about Rauch.[19] Consensus has not been reached on either Meinhof or Grams. In Delius's novel, the Serrata strand still serves as a reminder that closure has by no means been reached with Baader-Meinhof history.

Cornelia (Conni) Handschuch belongs to the trope "terrorist as woman," which I identified in the last chapter. It was she who pushed the baby's pram into the road to stop Büttinger's car and to effect his kidnapping. The pram did not contain a baby, of course, but machine guns, with which Schleyer's chauffeur, the driver of the second car, and two bodyguards were killed. The real pram used in the kidnapping is today the prime exhibit in the display cabinet dedicated to the RAF in Berlin's Museum of German History on Unter den Linden. As a deadly terrorist prop, it has accrued a number of meanings, featuring in the film *Third Generation* (dir. Fassbinder, 1978) and in the novel *Scylla* (Schneider, 2005). Pushed by a woman as one-half of an apparently loving couple, the pram denotes the female terrorist as false mother and shows the RAF's cynicism in exploiting the natural human reluctance to endanger a baby. Thomas Elsaesser takes it as either an invention or a "quotation" from Sergei Eisenstein's seminal film of the failed Russian Revolution in 1905:

> Was it something the police invented, in order to show just how inhuman the terrorists were (the RAF "women" perverting the most basic maternal instincts?) or was it the terrorists, "citing" the Odessa steps scene from *Battleship Potemkin* or the 1918 Spartakist uprisings in Berlin and Munich, in order to inscribe themselves into the historical iconography of Revolution?[20]

In *Ascent to Heaven of an Enemy of the State*, Conni is hiding at a sympathizer's flat across the border in Luxemburg during Nagel's funeral. Speaking to a tape recorder, she expresses her regret for her part in the Büttinger kidnapping, explaining how she has reconsidered her commitment to violence. Delius thus presents terrorist as woman not as an active threat to society or potential killer, but as remorseful former accessory to killing. Conni recalls Böll's Veronica, who failed to get a voice to in *Safety Net*. The actions of both characters anticipate the trend in the more recent fiction to reassemble the estranged family, in particular by redomesticating the errant terrorist mother.

Nagel is the central presence in *Ascent to Heaven of an Enemy of the State*, narrating nearly half the 62 sections. He reflects on society's obsession with his life as he peers down at the celebrations prompted by his death. "I loved him," Herold is supposed to have said of Baader, which serves Delius as an epigraph. Delius recognizes that all involved with Baader saw in him what they wanted to see: the state saw a demonic adversary; contemporaries saw a possible biography for themselves, or, in Theweleit's phrase, a "poison container." Nagel, trying to make sense of the interest in his life and death, throws back this fascination in the face of those he enthralled.

> We inserted a few question marks: and if I may overstate my significance, which I have every intention of doing, then I can say: I was the question directed at you yourselves: that is why you have this love for me which is dipped in fury, hardened by contempt, and tempered with hatred. (471)

Delius reproduces slightly altered facts and statements from Stefan Aust's seminal history, but it is Nagel himself who mockingly spits out Aust's third-person narrative, as if it were his own, and as if to say: If this is how you want to see me, then it is because it helps you to see me in this way. It does not mean that you understand me. He calls himself first "an invention" (445), then "a puzzle" (507).[21] Through Nagel, Delius portrays Baader as a national spirit which has been exorcised from the body politic. He presents his life both as performance and a story that the German public told itself. The relationship between Nagel / Baader and Germany is symbiotic, which allows him to play all sorts of different roles in his contemporaries' imagination. He name-checks classic films associated with terrorism, such as *Viva Maria!* and William A. Graham's melodramatic *21 Hours at Munich* (1976). He mentions Chinese robber tales and tries out the role of Captain Ahab from *Moby Dick* (the Stammheim nickname that Ennslin gave to Baader). His first name, Sigurd (or Siegfried), is taken from Germanic legend. The Siegfried of the *Nibelungenlied* was killed because he was a threat to the king; his widow's vengeance on his murderers brought about the destruction of the entire Burgundian kingdom. Nagel, meaning "nail," brings to mind the crucifixion. As Nagel's coffin is carried to its final resting place, draped in the colors of the federal flag (black, red, and gold), Nagel takes wing as the federal eagle, quoting a line from the Romantic poem "Moonlit Night" ("Mondnacht") by Joseph von Eichendorff about the soul lifting off from the earth, best known in a setting by Robert Schumann. He also evokes the boy in the Grimm brothers' fairytale "The Juniper Tree," who is killed by his stepmother and fed in a stew to his father, after which he returns to life as a bird to wreak his revenge. These reenactments of fragments of national mythology reach a culmination once the funeral is over. Floating high above the proceedings, Nagel invites the male visitors to pay a call with him on the figure of Germania, whose tallest and most splendid monument towers above the Rhine at nearby Rüdesheim. The colossal statue was erected to celebrate the Prussian victory over France in 1870–1871 and the unification of the German Empire which followed. Nagel imagines Germania to be the national whore that German men sleep with one after the other in standing position. The scene is grotesque and obscene. It is a reworking of the last sequence in Heine's *Germany. A Winter's Tale,* in which the poet meets Hammonia, the personification of the city of Hamburg, walking the streets, before she takes him back to her rooms and shows him the future of Germany in a used chamber pot.[22] Delius is not as pessimistic, but by the end of the final novel in the trilogy, the national celebrations have descended into pornographic farce.

Ascent to Heaven of an Enemy of the State belongs with such postunification novels as *The Last Performance* (Woelk, 2002), *Eros* (Krausser, 2006), and *The Weekend* (Schlink, 2008) as a national-unity narrative. Unlike the others, it does not aim for closure.[23] Delius is above all he is still interested in ruptures and contradictions, despite a narrative urge towards reconciling the two sides. He also depicts history as process. In *Death Game,* Breloer took a number of elements that Delius employed first (whether or not he borrowed them directly does not matter: Breloer is an unoriginal scriptwriter) and sealed them shut. Nonetheless, it was the German Left in the shape of Delius's trilogy of novels that supplied the basic plot ingredients for this narrative of the new German nation. Terrorism serves essentially a double surrogate function in the later novels. While former West German novelists investigate the now unified state's shared anticapitalist past in order to bring the two sides together, former East Germans are more likely to present an alternative to the post-unification social and economic order. In the only Baader-Meinhof novel by a former East German, *In His Early Childhood, a Garden* (Hein, 2005), Christoph Hein normalizes the East German past by showing that in extreme situations all states behave in the same way. Two television productions from the mid-1990s invited East German viewers to reflect on their own past and on the past of the unified nation.[24] In film there is one collaborative venture: Volker Schlöndorff worked with the veteran GDR scriptwriter Wolfgang Kohlhaase on *The Legends of Rita* (1999). That film's final sequence shows Rita getting shot as she rides her motorbike through a checkpoint after the collapse of communism and the opening of the German–German border. The revolutionary alternative to capitalism, whether embodied in the GDR's "real existing socialism" or the exploits of the June 2nd Movement, dies with her.

In *The Weekend*, Schlink's sole former East German character is not interested in the Westerners' supposedly radical past:

> During the conversations about the RAF and the German Autumn and the pardoning of terrorists between Christiane and her friends, she again and again had the feeling that this was a sick topic and that they were talking about a sickness that had struck down the terrorists themselves at the time and that now struck down the people talking about it. (88).

By the end, this marginalized viewpoint has become that of Schlink's novel: the West Germans are cured, among other things, by East German common sense. *The Weekend* was published in 2008, when the Christian Democrats were once more the leading partner in government. The Berlin Republic was ten years old; the world financial crisis, seen in Germany as a systemic failure of Anglo-Saxon capitalism, restored faith in German economic virtues, in particular partnership between workers and employers and social solidarity. *The Weekend* is a more confident novel than any part of Delius's trilogy and than its predecessor *The Reader* (1995). Schlink, like Breloer, is a conservative. Schlink's political vision is challenged by some other writers in the 2000s, as I will set out in my last chapter, but it is in accord with mainstream thinking, as reflected in novels as the fourth decade of Baader-Meinhof fiction drew to a close. A similar development can be traced in fiction that reinterprets classical models, as I will now show.

CHAPTER THREE

RETELLING THE CLASSICS: BAADER-MEINHOF AND THE GERMAN LITERARY CANON

Political violence was one of a number of challenges that grew out of the protest movements associated with the year 1968 in the Federal Republic. More far-reaching battles were fought over the meaning of the national culture after the cataclysm brought about by Nazism. In literature, a crisis of tradition was compounded by the rediscovery of past radical periods, such as the pre-1848 *Vormärz* or even the *Sturm und Drang* from the decade of young Goethe. A contest for the national literary heritage thus opened up in the wake of the anti-Vietnam demonstrations as part of Rudi Dutschke's "march through the institutions." If the national classics were not to be tarred with the nationalist brush, they had to be rediscovered, reappropriated, and reinterpreted. It is no accident that in reimagining left-wing terrorism over the 40-year period that is our subject, German novelists often reinvented traditional forms or archetypal narratives, rewrote classics or adapted national myths. In, the 1970s the Left was showing that the classics belonged to them as much as to the Establishment they were fighting. More recently, the purpose of adaptation has been national reconciliation.

From *The Lost Honor of Katharina Blum* (Böll, 1974) to the detective thriller *Autumn Messenger* (Hoeth, 2009), German novelists have invoked past writers, such as Grimmelshausen (Zahl); Mozart's librettist Schikeneder (Woelk); Goethe (Schneider); Schiller (Böll); Hölderlin (Geissler); Kleist (Delius, Hein); Büchner (Schneider, Zahl); Fontane (Grass); and Kafka (Chotjewitz); as well the ancients Homer (Schneider, Hoeth); Sophocles (Weil); and Apuleius (Krausser). Playwrights and filmmakers look back to Heine (Kluge et al.), Hebbel (Hochhuth); and (again) to Schiller (Jelinek, Loher); and Hölderlin (von Trotta). Adapting a classical source can disguise a critique by defamiliarizing the well-known contemporary circumstances; or it can lend gravity to incidents or individual cases. It also gives them meanings that they did not originally possess. Böll's polemic in *Katharina Blum* is reinforced through association with Schiller's short story "The Criminal of Lost Honor" (1786).[1] In *The Gentlemen of the Dawn,* Chotjewitz writes over Kafka's *The Trial* (1914–1915) for similar effect. *The Happy Ones* (Zahl, 1979) quotes from Grimmelshausen's picaresque account of survival in the Thirty Years' War, *Simplicissimus Teutsch* (1668). Zahl juxtaposes fragments from the narrative of the brutal attack on Simplicissimus's family farmstead, which opens that novel, with an account of a police raid on an anarchist flat in Kreuzberg. Zahl's point is that outsiders who are counted as rogues and criminals were written about seriously in the first prose masterpiece in the German language. The first edition of *The Happy Ones* was even adorned with an epigraph from *Simplicissimus,* which bizarrely disappeared from the reprints.

One effect of adapting the classics in this context is to transmute the threat ostensibly posed by the RAF into literature or, in other words, to remove it from history into the symbolic realm. Literary works then become the cause of offense and outrage, as happened with *Katharina Blum, The Gentlemen of the Dawn* and, twenty years later, *Too Far Afield* (Grass, 1995). In German contemporary literature, Baader-Meinhof terrorists tend to be on the side of right, which lends them a legitimacy that they found harder to attain outside the pages of novels.

German novelists are not interested in the literary lineage of terrorism as a theme or existential problem. The first critic to approach Baader-Meinhof terrorism through literature says little about contemporary events in the FRG or about the people behind them, because he focuses on the wrong books.[2] Even Dostoyevsky's *Demons* (1872),[3] which is thought to be the first "terrorist novel," is not cited until *The Assassin's Library* (Sonner, 2001) and then only indirectly. German novelists ignore Joseph Conrad, who twice depicted terrorists in *The Secret Agent* (1907) and in *Under Western Eyes* (1911), as they ignore Jean-Paul Sartre and Albert Camus, who explored the ethics of assassination in plays like *Les Mains Sales* (*Dirty Hands,* Sartre, 1948) and *Les Justes* (*The Just Assassins,* Camus, 1949). None of the German novelists appears to have heard of the British classic, *The Man Who Was Thursday* (Chesterton, 1908). The German novels are too closely bound up with the German political situation to take a longer or dispassionate view of the terrorist as literary figure in the modern European tradition. Instead they take the shape of a series of national narratives, through which we can trace an evolving sense of collective political identity.

The efforts to establish interpretative legitimacy were at their keenest in the 1970s. In *Lenz* (1973), whose hero is interested in the ethics of minor forms of violence, Peter Schneider evokes the *Sturm und Drang* playwright

Jakob Michael Reinhold Lenz and Georg Büchner's novella named after him (1835), as well as the German literary tradition of Italian journeys. Schneider's hero is ultimately uninterested in either violence or in running away, but in making a difference through more mundane means. Schneider's follow-up work,...*Already You Are an Enemy of the State* (1975), is an epistolary novel, consisting of letters written by the central character to his lawyer over the course of five months. It is not thematically an adaptation of *The Sorrows of Young Werther* (Goethe, 1774), the founding work of modern German literature, but is formally imitative of it. The political import of the last sentence in the second novel is the opposite of that in *Lenz*, as the reader has to infer that the young teacher who has been banned from his profession has joined the underground struggle as a result of the state's behavior. In *Lenz*, the hero concluded by announcing his intention to stick around and make difference.

In cinema, the concern was with the historical and cultural resonance of narratives. Margarethe von Trotta adapted the phrase "die bleierne Zeit" ("the leaden time") from the Greeks via a poem by Friedrich Hölderlin ("Der Gang aufs Land," The Step into the Countryside, 1801). After her 1981 film of the same name, the phrase "die bleierne Zeit," came to be applied to the 1970s as a whole. Translated into Italian, *gli anni di piombo* gains an additional sense as the "years of the bullet," and it is applied to an even more extended period.[4] The term "German Autumn" came indirectly from Heine's *Germany. A Winter's Tale* (1844) via a political film, *Germany in Autumn* (dir. Kluge et al., 1978), which also cites Schubert's song cycle *Die Winterreise* (*The Winter's Journey*, 1827). It was the BKA who first invoked Schubert when they called the national crackdown in the wake of Holger Meins's death and the protests that followed *Die Winterreise*.[5]

In each case, the Left invokes literary or artistic tradition in order to appropriate it. Hölderlin's theme was a better world of fulfilment and wholeness, which he located in classical Greece and juxtaposed with a degenerate present that needed to be redeemed. Heine's satire of the German territories he passes through on his journey from the French border to Hamburg depicts a people in hock to petty rulers and outmoded ideologies, let down by their institutions and their intellectuals. Whether in the 1800s (for Hölderlin), the 1820s (for Schubert), the 1840s (for Heine), or the 1970s, something was wrong with the state of Germany. As the revolution of 1848 occurred in March, the preceding period came to be known as the *Vormärz* (literally "the pre-March"), which reinforces the association between political oppression with the dead seasons of autumn and winter. The connection sat deep in the national consciousness. Sönke Wortmann's film of the German soccer team's performance in the first World Cup tournament to be held in a unified Germany was called *Deutschland: Ein*

Sommermärchen (Germany: A Summer's Tale, 2006). Sixty years after the defeat of Nazism, sixteen years after reunification, Germany hosted the world's best national soccer teams and their supporters. There were no terrorist outrages, as there had been at the Munich Olympics in 1972, and for the first time since 1945, ordinary Germans proudly waved their national flag.

Injecting a radical critique into Kafka's fictions of modernist alienation was a popular pursuit for 68er writers and critics.[6] Chotjewitz cannot quite make the connection work. His Fritz Buchonia finds himself confronted by a state apparatus that conducts opaque proceedings organized by corrupt officials. Their pseudo-legal harassment is backed up by house searches, phone-tapping, the interception of letters, and round-the-clock observation, none of which, of course, feature directly in Kafka's writings. *The Gentlemen of the Dawn* is a polemic, the simplicity of its politics matched by the uncomplicated nature of its re-presentation of Kafka. When Buchonia receives his summons, he is "not unhappy about this as many other accused did not find out for years if at all what the allegations against them were when proceedings were started against them."[7] This recalls the court's failure in *The Trial* to communicate its reasons for making arrests. That fundamental breach of the law is of a different magnitude to the secret services opening a file on an individual without telling him and then collecting information to fill it, which was one of the fears that haunted contemporary German intellectuals.

The tendency in Chotjewitz's novel is to believe the worst of the state and of all who work for it. Buchonia entertains the idea that the kidnappings and bomb attacks are carried out by "officials from the questioning authority" (177) in order to sow confusion among the populace. This was a strategy employed in Italy, where Chotjewitz lived from 1967–1973. Chotjewitz's version of Kafka's first sentence ("Somebody must have been saying nasty things about Josef K because one morning even though he had not done anything wrong he was arrested") fails to replicate either the original's ambiguity or the threat in Kafka final word ("Someone must have caused Fritz Buchonia to have a bad conscience, since without his being aware of having done anything wrong, he had a dream one morning").[8] Buchonia just has a guilty conscience, which may be through no fault of his own, and then he has a dream. The novel is one person's paranoid fantasy.[9]

Appropriating Friedrich Hölderlin (1770–1843) for the Left was a more serious project than evoking Heine, Schiller, or even Kafka. Nationalists, even Nazis, had claimed Hölderlin as one of their own. Among writers and critics, Peter Weiss and Pierre Bertaux challenged their presentation.[10] Hölderlin is the originator of the title *Kamalatta. Romantic Fragment*

(Geissler, 1988). In the years of his madness in the tower in Tübingen, Hölderlin is said to have cried "I do not understand that. It is *kamalatta* language" when a friend read to him in Greek. The city of Kalamatta is where the Greek war of liberation against the Turkish Ottomans began. According to the dust jacket of Geissler's novel: "in broken language and twisted syllables Hölderlin refuses to make use of the open speech of freedom." Geissler himself refuses to write freely because he and we are not yet free: his novel is about the struggle to achieve freedom. He internationalizes the conflict by beginning in Mexico City where up to 40 protestors were shot by the army in October 1968 (the Tlatelolco Massacre). This is the event that radicalized the central character, the documentary filmmaker called Proff. The perception of the novel is that repression in both the world and in Germany has not greatly lessened since the Third Reich. The novel *Kamalatta* is modeled on *The Aesthetics of Resistance* (Peter Weiss, 1975–1981) as it not only makes great demands on its readers, it resists easy assimilation or incorporation into the literature business or any hegemonic ideology. Plot is its least important element. Geissler also enacts Adorno's understanding of Hölderlin's poetry as "paratactic," that is, that he articulated a sense which reaches beyond conventional semantics and for that reason disobeys the rules of conventional grammar.[11] Geissler took some ten years to complete his mammoth account of an imaginary attack on an international special forces meeting at the southern German spa town of Bad Tölz. Buried under his paratactic prose is the stuff of a Cold War political thriller, which in the hands of a Freddie Forsyth or John le Carré could have conveyed a ready sense of what the attack was all about through a gripping narrative. Geissler had other aims and wanted his readers to work, but prompted one major critic to call it "simply unreadable."[12]

Schiller is a point of reference for three dramatists who have portrayed the RAF on stage (Hochhuth, Jelinek, and Loher). Rolf Hochhuth has often been labeled Schillerian in his reduction of history to individual decisions taken by individuals.[13] Dea Loher makes Meinhof's decision to join the underground struggle into what Moray McGowan discusses as if it were a Schillerian moment in *Leviathan* (1993).[14] In his own plays, Friedrich Schiller (1759–1805) was interested in power, ideology, and the clash between social forces and the individual will. He depicts rebellion, intrigue, or political assassination and places the individual's moral conscience center stage. Conspiracies can bring down leaders, thereby changing the course of history. This may have been a political simplification in Schiller's own time and was clearly inaccurate in the last third of the twentieth century. The problem with reinventing Schiller is that an individual decision, even of the momentous, life-changing sort that Loher's Marie, takes is personal. It cannot have the same consequences that it did for Schiller's Wilhelm Tell, who assassinated the Habsburg governor in order to win freedom for his people. This underlines one of the theses of this book: that terrorism has loomed so large in the literary imagination as a symbolic action only.

Dea Loher is the first writer to imagine what could have passed through the minds of the main actors in the first episode of the Baader-Meinhof drama after Baader has been freed. *Leviathan* works as a drama of an individual faced with a moral dilemma. But apart from Marie (Meinhof) none of the characters develops, and Marie takes her decision between the scenes rather than as a result of what happens or is said on stage. It is not psychologically plausible that she believes the revolutionary rhetoric she suddenly begins to produce. In a drama that echoes Schiller in its title, Jelinek is interested purely in this symbolic aspect. *Ulrike Maria Stuart* (2006) is concerned with representations in contemporary media and culture of the leading RAF characters, in particular, the two principal women, who take the roles of Elizabeth I (Ensslin) and Mary Queen of Scots (Meinhof). For Jelinek, whether or not the drama in Stammheim really did reenact the power struggle between Schiller's two queens is irrelevant. What is at stake is that, following Stefan Aust, their relationship has been seen that way. In Schiller's *Maria Stuart* Elizabeth has Maria executed (as happened in British history); in *The Baader-Meinhof Complex,* Ensslin goads Meinhof into taking her own life. Elisabeth (Ensslin) may be triumphant politically, but Maria (Meinhof) is the morally superior woman. This is a powerful political myth, which is a template for the trope of "bad" terrorist / "good" terrorist, which writers like Böll gendered, presenting the female as redeemable, unlike her male counterpart. It can also be seen as a component in the masculine bias of Meinhof biography.[15] Jelinek questions the layering of meaning and the intermeshing of narratives—as Helmut Krausser does in *Eros*, which appeared the same year. By the mid-2000s, the contest for interpretative legitimacy was no longer paramount; writers could reflect on the processes through which meanings are generated.

The key Baader-Meinhof play is not, however, by Schiller, but by Sophocles. As it was translated into German by Hölderlin, discussed by Hegel, and adapted by Brecht, it has a thoroughly German pedigree. In Sophocles's *Antigone,* said to be the first political play in the western tradition, the heroine puts the bond of kinship to her dead brother, the rebel Polynices, above her duty of loyalty to the state, embodied by her uncle King Creon, by insisting that Polynices' body be buried rather than left in the sun to be consumed by the crows, as Creon decrees. The tragic conflict of loyalty can be interpreted in a number of ways: as one between reason and emotion, law and instinct, male and female values, or the ties of the family against state authority. It is also about mourning the dead. For

German appropriations of *Antigone* in the late 1970s, it is significant that the rebellion against Creon and the city of Thebes has already happened. The rights and wrongs of Polynices's rebellion are not up for discussion: Antigone is mourning the loss of a family member, irrespective of what he has done. As the situation is static and the military threat to the order of the state has subsided, what is at stake is reconciliation, catharsis, and closure. The twentieth-century German Antigone, however, was a resister. Brecht prefaced his postwar adaptation of Hölderlin's translation with a scene set in the dying days of Nazism. A soldier has been hanged for desertion and his sister wants to cut down his body, either to bury it or to resuscitate him as he may still be breathing.[16] Brecht is interested in political defiance rather than mourning, in doing the right thing rather than following the dictates of a criminal regime. *The German Sisters* (dir. von Trotta, 1981) echoes *Antigone* after the terrorist Marianne's death, when the journalist Juliane wants to find out the truth about how her sister died. Since the constellation of the two sisters in von Trotta's film is the prototype for the trope "terrorist as alter ego," Antigone is indirectly an all-but-universal figure in German Baader-Meinhof literature.

Germany in Autumn (dir. Kluge et al., 1978) includes extracts from a fictitious production of Sophocles's tragedy with the actress Angelika Winkler in the title role. She was known in the Baader-Meinhof context through her casting as Katharina Blum in the film of Böll's short novel, as well as playing Hoffmann's politically naïve ex-wife in *Knife in the Head* (dir. Hauff, 1978).[17] In the scene "Antigone Postponed," which was directed by Volker Schlöndorff from a screenplay by Heinrich Böll, a group of television executives discuss whether they should broadcast the new production of the play, in the aftermath of the Stammheim suicides. They decide against doing so because their decision would be seen as provocative. The point of the episode is to show how paranoia breeds repression through self-censorship and to ask: What point have we come to if we can no longer stage the classics?[18] The project can become overblown and the myth can be overdetermined. Klaus Theweleit mocks the film's ending, when Christiane Ensslin is given permission by the mayor of Stuttgart, Manfred Rommel, to bury her sister along with her two comrades in the municipal cemetery.[19]

Among recent critics of Sophocles's *Antigone*, only George Steiner refers to the Baader-Meinhof connection, but he mangles some of the details, calling the film *Der Herbst in Deutschland* and referring to "the "Red Fraction" and "the Baader-Meinhof band." He accepts the validity of the analogy, however, coming down on the side of Creon (the West German state) being justified in his refusal to allow Antigone (Christiane Ensslin) to bury her sibling (her sister Gudrun).[20] This does not take into account that Manfred Rommel made the opposite decision with the bodies of Baader, Ensslin, and Raspe, as portrayed in *Germany in Autumn*. As the conflict between the generations over justice runs right through the film, Thomas Elsaesser has identified Antigone as its leitmotif; he lists a number of parallels between the myth and events in Germany.[21] He argues that only the sequence in the film that is directed by Fassbinder, dramatizing his own reaction to the news of the Stammheim suicides, challenges the film's overriding interpretation of German terrorism as a revolt of the young against the state. Playing himself, Fassbinder shows that he is complicit, as a German born in 1945, in the cycles of violence and counterviolence.

The sole version of the Antigone myth to be explored in a German novel is more challenging than "Antigone Postponed," but has gone unnoticed in the general critical literature on the myth and has not received its critical due in the context of Baader-Meinhof literature.[22] *My Sister, My Antigone* (Weil, 1980) is an autobiographical novel about the novelist's memories of survival as a Jew in Nazi-occupied Holland. It is, astoundingly, the first German novel to make a link between the "years of lead" and the Holocaust and, until *Dreamers of the Absolute* (Wildenhain, 2008), the only one. Apart from *The Happy Ones*, it is the only German Baader-Meinhof novel by a German-Jewish author. It also undermines the RAF–Antigone connection by suggesting how terrible an uncompromising commitment to virtue can be. Its narrative impulse is towards reconciliation. Its elderly female narrator, who is a writer, identifies with Antigone's less heroic sister, Ismene. At the same time, she wishes that she had been more like Antigone, whom she identifies with resisters such as Sophie Scholl and Gudrun Ensslin. In Sophocles's tragedy, Ismene first refuses to help her sister out of fear of Creon, before regretting her cowardice and trying to make amends after it is too late. Weil's nameless narrator is burdened with guilt, because she did not do enough at the appropriate time to save others—in particular, her husband—from the Nazis. She is convinced that a woman like Antigone or a contemporary version of her like Ensslin would have shown more courage and decisiveness at crucial moments. Her understanding of Antigone is at the same time ambivalent, because she recognizes that that such devotion to virtue can in its own way be tyrannical.

My Sister, My Antigone is more about mourning than about resistance. Weil's narrator has been recently widowed for a second time. She is preparing her thoughts about her life for another book about her past because time is running out for her too. She reflects repeatedly on her age and its physical effects, such as her poor hearing, which prevents her from taking part in public discussions. She finds it unfair that she is treated differently by others because she is old, as she still has her mental faculties and is fit enough to ski. At times her comments on her age read like displaced references to her Jewish identity: her age makes her different from others in their eyes, but not in her own. But she downplays any suggestion that postwar Germans are anti-Semitic, implying that other Jews come back to Germany, looking to take offense where none is intended. She may protest too much on this point.

My Sister, My Antigone is set over a single day in November (the year is not specified, but Ensslin is referred to in the present tense, as if she is still alive). The narrator has returned to Frankfurt from Switzerland, as she does at the end of every summer, which means that we find ourselves once more in an autumnal Germany. The narrative is framed by references to the younger generation. The narrator's old school friend Trudy refers (in English) to "that terrible generation," adding that they are "dirty, work-shy rabble."[23] The narrator, in contrast, shows a liking for the young, confessing that she yearns to run her fingers through their beautiful long hair. At the end of the day, she relays another conversation with Trudy, who has said that "if they catch a terrorist, they should put him up against the wall immediately. If an innocent person gets caught in the crossfire, that is just something that happens" (216). The narrator does not like Trudy and does not share her opinions. Trudy is a non-Jewish German whom she knows from her schooldays in pre-Nazi Germany. We may assume that Trudy represents a mainstream strand in German opinion and that her attitudes have not changed in the last half-century. The narrator has no wish to end their friendship, but cannot align herself with her. While the root of the narrator's problem lies in the German past, she is not integrated into its present, as the disagreement with Trudy highlights.

The narrator projects her own ostensibly better self onto an imaginary heroic other, whom she identifies with Antigone. Antigone stood up for herself and her beliefs, she spoke out, showed defiance, and in the end took her own life rather than be bowed; in Nazi-occupied Amsterdam, the narrator did none of these things. Her husband was deported to Mauthausen concentration camp and murdered, which she believes she could have prevented had she persuaded his boss to intervene on his behalf with the Gestapo. She meanwhile survived because she made compromises. She was a member of the Amsterdam "Jews Council" (a notorious *Judenrat*), which organized deportations on the Nazis' behalf in order to have a degree of control over what happened. The narrator failed to go underground (*untertauchen*, which literally means "to dive under"), join a resistance group, and live clandestinely. But this was not out of fear; as a non-Jewish friend told her, her duty was to help her mother get through the war. For every Jew who disappeared, the Nazis executed a relative who was left behind. Had she murdered a Gestapo officer when she had the chance, the consequences for her mother would have been much worse. Knowing this, the narrator still suffers from chronic "survivor's guilt," blaming herself as much as the Nazis for what happened.

Towards the end of the novel, Weil includes an authentic eyewitness report by a German soldier of the massacre of the inhabitants of a Polish ghetto. The narrator knew the soldier's Jewish girlfriend in Holland. Neither survived the war. Even though its author admits that he took part in the mass shooting, the Jewish narrator identifies with him, because he participated against his will. She explains: "We let ourselves be abolished. You as a German soldier, I as a persecuted person" (134). This idea of self-obliteration is central to her understanding of her identity. She "abolished" her integrity through her wartime actions, which resulted in her own physical self-preservation: "Thus I save my life, thus I do away with myself" (128), she recalls. After 1945, when she returned to Germany, she did not make amends or change her ways through civic action of any sort. Compared with both the mythical Antigone and with the contemporary Ensslin, she says she has "licked my wound, all my life long. Played with an unavailable revolver. Only dreamt of fire. No attempt to exterminate myself, no attempt to demonstrate in public" (156–57).

The narrator imagines Antigone as a real person, a contemporary with her own values and wants. She is a foil as well as an ideal other self. It is Brecht and Böll's Antigone, the resister against tyranny, battling for the people like a modern-day freedom fighter. But the narrator recognizes that her ideal other self would be insufferable if she met her in real life. Her absoluteness would be dangerous. The difference with her is that the narrator "always made compromises, as we all make them, those of us who do not take morality that seriously. We healthy, realistic ones, who have not been robbed of our reason by the gods" (140). At the end she recognizes that her projected image of moral perfection is unattainable. In the words of an American critic: "She is not Antigone, she is herself, like Ismene, full of compromises, and she finally accepts this."[24] In Holocaust literature, whether memoir or fiction, satisfactory resolutions can never be achieved. At the end of *My Sister, My Antigone*, the narrator dreams that she confronted the SS officer with a revolver and shot him, after reversing Antigone's famous sentence to Creon by saying: "I am here to hate, not to love."

The narrator compensates for her past failing by agreeing to shelter a young woman who is wanted by the police. Her goddaughter explains that "Marlene" is in trouble for sheltering a man they are looking for. The narrator knows that this means the RAF. Thus if Marlene is involved in terrorism at one remove, the narrator is removed twice over. She disagrees with everything that she assumes Marlene believes and is supporting, but

"A fugitive does not show the door to another fugitive" (118). Although she wants an end to violence, she helps someone involved in this violence. She is withering on the connection between contemporary terrorism and resistance: "History writers do us the favor of calling our terrorism resistance" (163). She explains herself:

> I would like to shake Marlene awake and say: Get up and get lost. I am a tired old woman. I don't care what happens to you. Even though you have told me nothing, I know you are a terrorist's girlfriend. I am against violence and people who sympathize with violence. I am against your belief that we can have a paradise on earth and even more against your hellish route to this paradise. You are playing at war. And I want peace.
> But I cannot say it. My wound makes it impossible. Marlene needs help and so I help. Without asking about ideology. (164)

The purpose of resistance in the present is to compensate for failure in the past, which is a common proposition in Baader-Meinhof literature. *My Sister, My Antigone* is different because, uniquely, it is written and narrated by a Jewish German. Weil's intention of harmonization and reconciliation is all-encompassing. She rejects the German fixation on Antigone and embraces a mode of ethical behavior that can recognize compromise as a valid alternative to absolute virtue. The legacy of Antigone in German thought and literature is thus the problem that has to be overcome, according to this insightful novel.

Reconciliation is the opposite of what concerns Rolf Hochhuth. Given that his career as a dramatist spans the decades of the RAF's existence and that he returns repeatedly to questions associated with it, it is strange that his name is rarely mentioned in accounts of literature and terrorism. Hochhuth has been the best-known living German dramatist since his first play, *The Representative* (1963), which centers on the Pope's complicity in the Holocaust. It was first produced by Brecht's avant-garde stage designer, Erwin Piscator. Since this debut, Hochhuth has regularly provoked controversy and arguably has been more successful as a campaigner than a dramatist. The only time that a German politician ever resigned from office because of his links with Nazism was thanks to Hochhuth's intervention, when he revealed in 1978 that the minister president of Baden-Würtemberg, Hans Filbinger, had imposed death sentences on deserters in the dying days of World War II. The allegations were true, but Filbinger was foolish enough to sue.

Since the collaboration with Piscator, Hochhuth's plays have not enjoyed critical appreciation, but he nonetheless has a knack for expressing what his audiences may be thinking and may want to see presented on stage. His obsession with political assassination was also fed in part by the RAF. What makes the RAF admirable in Hochhuth's eyes is that they succeeded in killing a number of prominent leaders while their compatriots under the two dictatorships either did not succeed (during the Third Reich) or did not even try (in the GDR). *Wessis in Weimar* (1993), the most talked-about play on the subject of German reunification, includes a scene depicting the mysterious shooting of Karsten Detlev Rohwedder on April 1, 1991. In *McKinsey Is Coming* (2003), William Tell, Stauffenberg, and the killers of Ponto, Schleyer, and Herrhausen are all possible role models for the unemployed at the beginning of the twenty-first century. Hochhuth's point is that individuals still can make a difference and that individual moral decisions for that reason still count. This is what draws him to the classical dramatic tradition, whether embodied by Schiller or, as in the case of *Judith*, by Friedrich Hebbel.

The proposition that the assassination of an unjust ruler (*tyrannenmord*) can be justified powered Hochhuth's contribution to the debates surrounding the 1980s Peace Movement in the commissioned play *Judith* (1984). Here Hochhuth focuses on plans to assassinate an American president modeled on Ronald Reagan because of NATO's decision to deploy weapons of mass destruction in West Germany. As German left-wing terrorism moved into a new decade, this was the new cause for Baader-Meinhof's third generation.[25]

Judith is an adaptation of the Old Testament story, which entered the German canon in a version for the stage by Friedrich Hebbel in 1840. The Biblical Judith saved her people the Israelites by seducing the Assyrian general Holofernes, getting him drunk, and chopping off his head as he slept. She is an undercover heroine and the original honey-trap.[26] Hochhuth makes a number of melodramatic connections. The Judith role is played by an American journalist who is a widow, one-quarter German (and a fluent German speaker), and the daughter of an ambassador. Her fiancé Gerald is secretly working for the CIA, but her brother has been crippled by his own side's chemical weapons in the Vietnam War. Judith has an opportunity to assassinate the president in order to prevent the resumption of production of weapons of mass destruction similar to those which crippled her brother. What interests Hochhuth, however, is that these weapons will be stationed in American bases in the Federal Republic. They will be aimed eastwards, in the first instance against targets in the GDR, which increases the likelihood that West Germany will in turn be targeted by Soviet forces, using weapons based in East Germany. This makes the German-American Judith into an all-German anti-American resister.

In Hochhuth's *Judith*, the Biblical story is reenacted twice. Like Weil, he presents contemporary terrorism in the historical context of Nazism. The ideological implications of his contextualization, however, could not be more different. The first reenactment, based on historical fact, is set on the Eastern Front in 1943. Jelena Masanik, a Russian partisan, takes the role of Judith, while that of Holofernes is played by the Nazi commander in Kiev. The Germans are the oppressors; the partisans fighting on behalf of the subjugated population of East European *untermenschen*, including the exterminated Jews, are the oppressed. Jelena succeeds in planting a bomb in the bed of the Nazi chief. Unlike the work of the Biblical Judith, Jelena's deed achieves nothing except the commander's death, which results in reprisals that claim the lives of up to 12,000 local Belarussians. The only political moral for Hochhuth to explore (and he brushes it aside) is whether such assassinations can be condoned, let alone encouraged, given the Nazis' reprisal policy.

As this action is presented as a prologue, Hochhuth invites us to see the present time (1984) through the lens of 1943. He makes historical comparisons between the Americans in the 1980s and the Nazis, as well as between the assassination of an American president and anti-Nazi resistance. His play suggests that by reenacting Jelena's political murder, the contemporary Judith (a German American) is resisting the present Nazis (the Americans) on behalf of her oppressed people (the Germans). Indeed, by killing the American president, Judith is compensating for the German failure to kill Hitler. This redressing of past failure is at the heart of much Baader-Meinhof literature. The problem is that history may not have repeated itself. The Americans were, moreover, Germany's liberators from Nazism in 1945.

Hochhuth taps into a discourse that sees the Germans in the 1980s as victims of the unscrupulous Americans:

> *Professor*: [...] we have not merely two oceans
> But above all these
> Unbelievably stupid Germans, who store our poison
> As if it were beer.
> A herd of lemmings
> —since they stopped being a bandit gang
> Incomprehensible people:
> Their stupidity today is almost like
> Their cruelty under Hitler.[27]

Hochhuth takes his argument a stage further. Gerald, Judith's fiancé, offers the view that the people who used gas in Auschwitz should not cry "crocodile tears" if they themselves are now subjected to a gas attack:

> *Judith*: You would not be permitted to talk like that
> Even if you were Jewish...

Gerald: Jews are among those
Who are making the plans
—just as the Jews helped make the atom bomb. (2227)

The Germans are now potentially the victims of the Jews. In Act 2, Judith confirms to Teiresias who it was that invented the new neutron bomb, which could kill people while not harming property:

Teiresias: The man who invented it, do you know him too?
Judith: No, I never saw him, Dr. Cohen. (2254)

The Jews are now responsible both for the possible destruction of Germany in 1984 and for the invention of the new bomb. The heroine of German resistance is fighting against them. Hochhuth's anti-American rebellion is a nationalist enterprise, which brings out what some critics have felt was latent in the RAF itself. *Judith* has received scant critical attention, although the original German productions were widely reviewed.[28] It articulates, however, a strain of thinking which will come to the surface once more in *Death of a Truffle Pig* (Weiss, 2007), in which the American villain, this time a capitalist predator, is possibly of Jewish descent.

Like Hochhuth in *Wessis in Weimar*, Günter Grass presents the Rohwedder assassination as revenge for the destruction of the East German economy at the hands of the Treuhand which Rohwedder headed. *Too Far Afield* (Grass, 1995) was greeted with hostility in the press because it was a substantial work of fiction about reunification by the country's leading writer who refused to welcome the events of 1989–1990 with enthusiasm.[29] The novel centers on an elderly man, Theo Wuttke, alias Fonty, who relives the life of Prussia's most accomplished nineteenth-century chronicler, Theodor Fontane (1819–1898) one hundred years after him. Everything Fonty (b. 1919) experiences through seven decades of twentieth-century German history has a parallel in either Fontane's life or in his novels. *Too Far Afield* reimagines German history and national identity as expressed through Fontane. With regard to the assassination of the Treuhand boss Rohwedder, Grass refers to two lesser known Fontane novels, *Quitt* and the posthumously published fragment, *Mathilde Möhring*.[30] He invites his readers to reconsider what the novels are really about, as well as explaining the assassination and revealing the identity of a fictitious assassin.

In real life, Rohwedder's killing was the work of a trained marksman who fired in darkness from a distance of some 60 meters, killing his victim instantly with his first bullet. No one has been prosecuted for this murder. Although the RAF claimed responsibility, there were suspicions that it could have been carried out by former Stasi operatives, perhaps working in tandem with the RAF (it would not have been for the first time). In a populist book published in 1992, a trio of conspiracy theorists argued that the German state wanted to eliminate Rohwedder.[31] Although for leftist critics, Rohwedder carried out his job with little regard for the human consequences in the increasingly desolate former GDR, for economic conservatives he did not get on with his task fast enough. In *Too Far Afield*, the assassin, a reincarnation of Fontane's Mathilde Möhring, gets her revenge on behalf of her countrymen who have been thrown out of work as a result of the Treuhand reorganization, including her husband,.

In his early fiction, Grass showed how respectable citizens came to participate in state-sponsored political violence under the Nazis when he was a child and adolescent. A number of characters in these novels can be identified as terrorists. One of the first to make an appearance in *The Tin Drum* (1959) is Joseph Koljaizcek, the narrator's maternal grandfather, who is an arsonist and Polish nationalist wanted by the German gendarmes. The student novel *Local Anaesthetic* (1969) depicts two forty-something school-teachers debating the pros and cons of their seventeen-year-old pupil's plans for violent public protest against the Vietnam War. Irmgard Seifert supports Scherbaum's idea to set fire to his beloved pet dachshund before the eyes of the fur-coated ladies who eat cake in West Berlin's expensive Café Kempinski, because Seifert is ashamed of what she did at his age in the dying days of World War II. The young radical will compensate for her own moral failing under Hitler. Eberhard Starusch, formerly known as Störtebeker in *The Tin Drum* and *Dog Years* (1963), committed random acts of arson, which he would like in retrospect to call anti-Nazi resistance, but which in fact were no such thing. Starusch makes amends for his past by teaching and interacting with the young. At the end of *Local Anaesthetic*, Scherbaum has thought better of making his sacrifice and has decided to edit the school magazine and study to become a doctor. Violence is thus averted as the new values of participatory democracy win out. In the Germany outside the novel, it took a decade or more for Scherbaum's real-life counterparts to accept his teacher's arguments.

Grass knew both Meinhof and Ensslin in the latter half of the 1960s. He argued in public with the students at the "Vietnam Congress" in February 1968. After May 1970, however, he rarely referred to either the RAF or the state and media response to them. At the heart of *From the Diary of a Snail* (1972), which includes an account of the 1969 federal election, are reflections on the twin political impulses of melancholy, which induces fatalistic resignation, and utopia, which inspires revolutionary extremism. He does not mention the RAF, but the argument certainly applies to them. Grass's epic *The Flounder* (1977) does feature a trial, however, which resembles one that was taking place in Stammheim as Grass was writing the novel.

The Flounder was published at the end of August 1977 and is mentioned as a feature in the cultural landscape of the year in both *Checked* (Goetz, 1988) and *Ascent to Heaven of an Enemy of the State* (Delius, 1992). Grass uses masculinity and femininity as his two opposing principles animating world history, but opposing the Nazis with the RAF would be another way of approaching the contemporary sequences in the novel. The talking fish from the Grimms' fairy tale *The Fisherman and His Wife*, who has advised men through history, is put in the dock by a tribunal of radical women. Because the public grow ever angrier with him, ever greater security measures are required, but in Grass's novel, again as at Stammheim, it is the generations responsible for Auschwitz who are really on trial. Their accusers, the RAF at Stammheim or the radical lesbians in Grass's notorious Father's Day chapter, risk copying the behavior of their parents and grandparents in their response to Nazism. In Grass's fiction of the 1970s, the RAF is an unacknowledged presence. After *Too Far Afield*, there is one story in *My Century* (1999) on a Baader-Meinhof theme. It is narrated by the left-wing teacher from Hanover who tipped off the police that two suspicious individuals, one of whom turned out to be Meinhof, were staying in an apartment above his. Grass dramatizes the erstwhile fellow traveler's interior as he overcomes his split loyalties by betraying the terrorists to the police. Grass is unique among the writers under discussion for introducing terrorists into his work before the protestors turned to violence in the late 1960s. Like Hochhuth, his interest in politically inspired violent actions spans his writing career.

After 1968, Grass opposed the proponents of violence, which is signaled in his literary writing and political interventions; with regard to the Rohwedder assassination in 1991, the evidence from *Too Far Afield* is less clear-cut.

By depicting the Rohwedder murder as the work of a Berlin cleaning lady embittered by her husband's unemployment, Grass left himself open to accusations of justifying assassination. His boss is a likeable character, however, conforming to what has since become the stock figure in Baader-Meinhof fiction of the leading capitalist qua sympathetic liberal. In *Wessis in Weimar*, the president dismisses the danger he is courting before he is shot by an unseen hand, but the boss in *Too Far Afield* is aware that he may pay dearly for his role. As another of the novel's Fontane fans, the boss is especially deserving of readers' favor. The first Fontane novel he mentions is *Frau Jenny Treibel*, which is a satire on Berlin's nouveau riche after the first unification of Germany in 1871. It could be construed to speak in numerous ways to the new Germany post-1990, which was bent on rapid reconstruction and was inspired by business values. But the novel by Fontane that, the boss confesses, "interests me urgently," is *Quitt*, and the question which it poses: "why the poacher has to shoot the gamekeeper."[32] The anonymous narrator reflects at this point on the two main characters in *Quitt*: "A perpetrator who was likeable despite his compulsion to challenge authority; an unpleasant self-opinionated victim with abusive authoritarian tendencies" (614). His choice of the Fontane analogy for his own situation is at first sight not very astute. Lehnert Menz, the poacher, has personal reasons for his animosity towards the gamekeeper Opitz, as Opitz denied him a medal for bravery in the Franco-Prussian War. Opitz also pursues him by less-than-open means when he shoots a rabbit as it dashes from his land, where he was entitled to shoot it, into the forest, where the shooting of rabbits was reserved for others. One has to stretch the import of this poacher–gamekeeper antagonism before it fits the relationship between the boss and an ex-GDR worker in April 1991. Fonty recognizes as much, because once the boss is dead, there is no more mention of *Quitt*. Fonty's own literary detective nose now puts him on a different trail.

Grass invites his readers to turn their own sights around and to consider *Quitt* through the lens of his own novel. *Quitt* can be read as a novel about revolutionary violence, the merits of assassination, and the dangers for those in authority of behaving as if they were above the law. *Quitt* is not a great novel, as Grass's narrator all but admits. The second half, which is set mainly among American Mennonites, lacks narrative tension, although it does establish the primacy of the assassin's political motivation. The poacher Menz finds another European fugitive in the community, the splendidly named Camille L'Hermite. He was marked by the Franco-Prussian War in ways which contrast with Menz's resentment at not receiving the medal that was his by rights. In 1870, L'Hermite was a communard responsible for the execution of the archbishop of Paris. Among the Mennonites, the accent is on Christian love and forgiveness, atonement and understanding, and the first indication that Menz is on the road to expiation is his friendship with a man from the "nation's enemy" (159) from the past war. The old French revolutionary, washed up on the shores of the new world, is also a scientist and inventor, interested in chemistry and geology. Had his new German friend not known of the community's respect for L'Hermite, in view of what he has found out about his past, "he might well have assumed at the sight of all those test tubes that he had happened upon a collection of Nihilists' bombs destined for Europe" (160). Sure enough, L'Hermite used to make bombs. There is of course a line in the tradition of European terrorism that leads from these late nineteenth-century Nihilists to the RAF itself, which makes the prominence of *Quitt* in *Too Far Afield* all too appropriate.

L'Hermite is less a foil for Menz and more an indication of a potential self in a parallel existence. Had Menz been born in France, a similar career as a revolutionary militant could have beckoned. Born in the year of the July Revolution (1830), L'Hermite took to the streets at the age of 19 during the turmoil that preceded the creation of the Second Empire. As a mid-century German, Menz's opportunities were more limited. Had he been born 100 years later (as Fonty is in comparison with Fontane), however, he would have been around 19 years of age in the revolutionary year of 1968.

After the murder of the boss, Fonty begins to question the boss's reading of *Quitt*. He now recalls assassination attempts on the old Kaiser in Fontane's own lifetime before he turns to Charlotte Corday, who at the height of the Terror murdered the French revolutionary leader Marat in his bath. Fonty compares revolutionary state terror in 1793 with what is happening to the inhabitants of the "new Federal states" in 1991:

> Millions of workers and employees are being subjected to a process of beheading, the result of which may not be that the individual is made a head shorter, but the guillotine cuts of his livelihood, his job, which was said to be secure until the day before and without which, at least in these parts, he is as good as without a head (626).

The train of thought which leads Fonty to Corday leads him to announce, on nothing more than a hunch, that "only women are so consistent in their focus on a target" (627) and then to review the dozen or so "females with a strong will" in Fontane's fiction. There is no doubt in his mind when it comes to the identity of his prime suspect: Mathilde Möhring.

Mathilde's main characteristics in Fontane's eponymous novella are persistence and intelligence, but she can only get what she wants through a man. The modern-day Mathilde will have a partner or husband who has lost his job and she will now be working to feed both of them. Mathilde's greatest asset is her judgment of human character. Thus she predicts her future husband's every move when he first arrives to rent a room in her mother's house. After marriage, Mathilde pushes her husband through exams, propelling him to take up the mayoralty in a small West Prussian town. She helps him win over local dignitaries and is ready to resort to underhand tactics to reach her goals, which no one suspects her of, on account of her sex. When her husband suddenly dies, the young and clever Mathilde is left no longer a mayor's wife. But she now favors independence over a second marriage and trains to become a teacher. The controversial nature of Mathilde's story is signaled by the novella's publishing history. Fontane abandoned the manuscript of *Mathilde Möhring*, which was published posthumously, but in an altered format. In updating the material through an indirect adaptation, Grass is radicalizing a hitherto marginalized work.

Do Mathilde's qualities make her into a potential murderer, let alone a terrorist in the mold of Charlotte Corday, as Fonty believes? The new Germany supplied alternative routes for modern-day Mathildes, who no longer needed to operate through their husbands and did not have to work very long in cleaning jobs, even in the aftermath of the GDR's collapse. When Fonty identifies his suspect as Helma Frühauf, a married woman in her late thirties who works in the Treuhand building, he is convinced that she fits his profile. He correctly guesses that her husband has become unemployed. When she lets on that over the weekend in question she was visiting her sister in the western city of Duisburg, thirty minutes by train from the scene of the crime, Fonty is convinced that he has his woman.

Fonty is not likely to go to the police, and he cuts off his investigations out of fear of becoming implicated himself. Not for the first time, he ducks an issue by failing to take responsibility. What started as an intellectual challenge led to the uncovering of an unrecognized sense in *Quitt;* then a radical reading of *Mathilde Möhring* ends with what amounts to an endorsement of political assassination. Grass himself ducks out too. In the novel as a whole, the "wide field" of German ideological history, which has been characterized by so much violence for the 180 years since Fontane's birth, is finally contained by the end. Fonty finds freedom by escaping to France. Justice is not done, however, to the boss's memory. Given Grass's own spirited critique of the way unification was pushed through, it may be that he could not condemn Helma Frühauf's presumed deed in the same way as he exposed extremists in *The Flounder*. In response to the terrorism that grew out of the protest movements of the late 1960s, Grass was sure in his condemnation. However much he understood the appeal of extremism, he preached the virtues of democratic gradualism, and that spirit infused his fiction. The Rohwedder assassination was different.

So far, this chapter has concentrated on canonical figures, mostly female, that cast the RAF terrorists in an essentially positive light. Antigone, Judith, and Mathilde are brave heroines, whose only fault may be their overzealous pursuit of moral virtue. Only the Jewish outsider and Holocaust survivor Grete Weil questioned the value of such commitment. In contrast, in the 2000s, only the former East German Christoph Hein in *In His Early Childhood, a Garden* (2005) presents a modern-day Michael Kohlhaas as a potential role model. *The Last Performance* (Woelk, 2002) is rather different. The critically celebrated Ulrich Woelk uses elements of the plot of *The Magic Flute* both as the source for the central clue in a murder mystery and for his narrative of Enlightenment self-fulfillment, which sets out to harmonize differences and reconcile oppositions, albeit from the point of view of a triumphant West. Once more, acts of terrorism are barely subjected to criticism in the novel.[33] Mozart and Schikaneder's "folk opera" has a firm place in Baader-Meinhof history. It was during a performance at the Deutsche Oper on June 2, 1967 that Ohnesorg was shot and scores of other student protestors were hospitalized by Berlin police and Iranian security forces at the demonstration against the visit of the Shah of Iran. Woelk's assassinated business leader Christian Curland is entirely fictitious. In *The Last Performance,* his murder took place in the foyer of the Deutsche Oper eleven years later, after another performance of Mozart and Schickeneder's opera. The case was never cleared up. While the RAF claimed responsibility, there were reasons to believe that other forces were involved (by now a common conspiracy premise in popular Baader-Meinhof fiction): Curland was engaged in semi-clandestine financial transactions with the GDR government. Even given his link with the world of Cold War finance, he was an unlikely terrorist target.

Woelk is the first writer to explore possible connections between the plot of *The Magic Flute,* a German Enlightenment classic that Goethe considered writing a sequel to, and what was happening on the Berlin streets on that fateful summer evening when Ohnesorg was shot. After Woelk's two detectives, Paula Reinhardt and Anton Glauberg, attend a performance at the same venue in 2001, they debate whether they could relate the opera's story to the political situation in the divided Germany during the period of terrorism. The West German Glauberg believes that there are connections. In *The Magic Flute* there are two realms, one governed by the mysterious Sarasto, the other by the Queen of the Night. It is not immediately clear that one is better than the other, though by the end one realm is identified with light (and thus reason and progress) and the other with darkness (and thus superstition and ignorance). Two lovers, Pamino (Sarasto's son) and Pamina (the daughter of the Queen of the Night) are caught in the conflict between these two different ways of viewing and ordering the world. For Glauberg, the story is told from the point of view of a child who experiences his or her parents battling with each other for the child's good opinion. Glauberg is more imaginative in his reading than the East German Paula, who finds the opera's plot simply confusing. While Paula believes good and evil to be clearly distinguished from each other, which is why she became a policewoman, Glauberg counters that the two can often be close together. His reason for joining the police was to find truth.

The two cops find themselves investigating an unusual murder committed in a remote cottage on the barren coastline of Schleswig Holstein.[34] The time is November 2001, two months after the al-Qaeda attacks in New York gave Germans renewed cause to reflect on their own prior terrorist conflicts. Woelk begins the action in classic fashion with the discovery of the body by the local pastor. The body has been tied to a chair in the victim's own house, while a CD-player endlessly repeats the Queen of the Night's aria which begins: *"Der Hölle Rache kocht in meinem Herzen"* (The vengeance of Hell boils in my heart). The detectives agree that the murderer is telling them that the crime has something to do with Mozart and is an act of revenge. They both know what the pastor and the neighbors do not know: that the victim is a former RAF member. Hans Jacobi, aka Wolgast, disappeared in the late 1970s, to be found living under an assumed identity in the GDR in 1990. Since his release from prison three years later, he has lived in a house he inherited from his parents in this windswept North German hamlet. Glauberg knows his background because he is Jacobi's younger half-brother. At the end of the novel, it turns out that Paula Reinhardt is the daughter of the businessman that Jacobi (probably) murdered. As critic Sylvia Henze points out, the novel leaves the identity of Curland's killer open, as no evidence for Jacobi's involvement is produced (in contrast to the film adaptation) and he never confesses. Yet he has no other motivation for seeking refuge in the GDR, and Woelk presents his readers with no other possible culprit. The novel's open verdict on the westerner Jacobi contrasts to its depiction of the easterner Paula, who turns out to have murdered him.[35] Paula's antipathy to the old GDR is grounded in her not being permitted to visit the West after her father's murder. There are other mild anti-GDR elements in the novel, such as the Stasi obliging Jacobi's East German wife to inform on him. Restriction of movement and surveillance were two of the most pervasive everyday forms of repression in the GDR. They are also the two of the main elements of the West's critique of the East, and as such they reinforce the novel's western bias. The film adaptation, directed by the East German Matti Geschonneck under the title *Murder by the Sea* (2004), introduces a new BKA character, who is employing Paula to tail Glauberg and bug his telephone. The team listening to his conversations looks no different from one employed by the Stasi. The point here is that Stasi methods were common to both states and are still in use in contemporary Germany. In the symbolism of the (East German) film as opposed to the (West German) novel, the westerner had as much reason to dispose of the former terrorist as the easterner.

To make his novel work as a political whodunit, Woelk includes personal links that are hardly typical. Paula was seven years old when she accompanied her father to the opera and she was standing next to him when he was shot. She waited 23 years to wreak her revenge. Then she ensured that she was assigned to investigate the case in order to be sure that her guilt never came to light. Woelk makes Glauberg, rather than Paula, his narrative focalizer. She is the novel's villain, whose inability to overcome her hatred turns her into a modern-day Queen of the Night, a malign force from an alien realm that disturbs the surface harmony of a West German idyll. Paula falls away in significance once her guilt is revealed. The novel cannot accommodate her status as child victim and avenging perpetrator and cannot align her deed symbolically with her East German origin. To that extent, The Last Performance is emphatically a West German novel, showing how a West German works through the past, apparently for the benefit of the new Germany as a whole.

The Last Performance is not quite an adaptation of The Magic Flute. There are no Papageno and Papagena figures and the two main characters are not in love. But Glauberg undergoes an ordeal comparable to Pamino's by carrying out the murder investigation to its conclusion. At the end, he is reconciled with his wife and their seven-year-old son, having (shades of Pamino resisting female temptation) declined Paula's offer of a night in her bed. He has also overcome his reticence to talk to his wife about his needs and feelings, which was the cause of their estrangement. This emotional blockage was a problem he shared with other male members of his family, such as his father and his dead half-brother, and with other older male Germans in general, such as Paula's murdered father. Again there is a parallel in The Magic Flute, as Sarasto places Pamino under a speaking ban as part of his ordeal. When he is rewarded with Pamina's hand, he starts to talk once more.

As Woelk's plot incorporates characters from both former German states, a former Stasi officer, a radical pastor, student movement veterans, the wealthy widow of the assassinated business leader, and police informers, Glauberg's trial by ordeal results in a personal catharsis that is representative of the national situation. Woelk thus works through the national past by working through a national classic. The way Glauberg solves the murder, by revealing the truth about connections between past and present, should be emblematic of the newly unified Germany working through the more problematic aspects of its antagonistic history. Yet because the novel punishes the East for the sins of the West, the ending offers a false harmonization.

The next figure from the German classical repertoire unites the West and the East only insofar as he has attracted both a novelist from the former West Germany (F. C. Delius) and the former East Germany (Christoph Hein). The differences in their approaches once more reveal the fissures that still divide opinion about the contemporary German state. Michael Kohlhaas in Heinrich von Kleist's novella of the same name from 1811 has been called the "first terrorist in German literature."[36] My Year as a Murderer (Delius, 2004) contrasts Kohlhaas's spree of vengeful destruction with the patience shown by the widow of an anti-Nazi resister in her dealings with the West German state at the height of the Cold War. My Year as a Murderer, Delius's fourth novel on a terrorist theme, features two other battlers for justice: a resistance hero executed in 1943 and a young student in 1968 who plots to assassinate the judge who passed his death sentence. In *In His Early Childhood, a Garden* (Hein, 2005), a retired headmaster gives up on the legitimate institutions of the democratic state after finding that they serve only money and power. He confides to an old friend: "It is not just the press. They are all liars. The state prosecutor's office, the police, the expert witnesses, the whole state. It is like a gigantic conspiracy. Like a carbuncle full of pus."[37] In Hein's story, Richard Zurek wants to establish how his son died in a bungled arrest attempt that closely resembles the arrest of Wolfgang Grams at Bad Kleinen in 1993. The resemblance to Kohlhaas, whom Hein does not cite, was noted by reviewers.[38] Zurek's quest for justice on behalf of his dead son, Oliver, and his fading faith in legitimate means of redress take on Kohlhaasian dimensions. If he were not 72, Richard would consider taking up arms himself. His friend, who as a young man volunteered for the *Wehrmacht* and whose only regret about the war is that Hitler turned out to be a criminal, warms to the suggestion:

> We just need a little bit of skill, Richard, but with practice we can pull it off. And what I lack in youth and strength I make up for nowadays with money. After all, we are not intending to do anything wrong. We want to force the state to pronounce justice, which it is supposed to do anyway. (187)

Whereas Kleist portrayed the terrible actions of a man bent on the pursuit of a chimeric ideal of justice, Hein's novel shows little or no narrative distance to its Kohlhaas figure, although he is one who does not ultimately resort to violence himself.[39] This indictment of contemporary Germany is found otherwise only in popular fiction or some of the "revivalist" novels, which I discuss in Chapter Six. There is a nationalist element in some depictions of late left-wing terrorism. Oliver's girlfriend writes to her parents-in-law that she and Oliver were patriots: "What happened did not happen out of contempt for our country and its people, it was love and a feeling of responsibility for this society and for his homeland [*Heimat*] which led us on to this path" (192). Hein's critique of contemporary German politics closely follows that in *The Blue List. Dengler's First Case* (Schorlau, 2003), which also portrays a character based on Grams as an all but innocent fall-guy. Both draw on the work of filmmaker and author Andres Veiel, who made Grams's life and death the subject of one-half of an award-winning documentary, *Black Box BRD* in 2001. In Veiel's account, Grams senior (who is also the model for Hein's central character), is a loyal but unsophisticated man with few Kohlhaasian qualities.[40] Not believing the official version of events at Bad Kleinen, according to which their son shot himself as he fell backwards onto the railway track, Grams's parents wanted to find out why and how he died. They took their case to the Federal Supreme Court in Karlsruhe and from there to the European Court for Human Rights in Strasburg. They lost each time, but their legal progress attracted much attention and some support. Their legal failure was hardly a vindication for the police, whose version of events lacked credibility.

In Hein's novel, retired headmaster Richard Zurek is a *Beamte* (state official). When he revokes his oath of office at the end of the novel, he signals that there has been a breach of trust between him and the state. Hein's critique elsewhere goes even further. Truth is what those in power say it is. Evidence disappears. Witnesses are intimidated. State officials, whether in the law or in education, show loyalty to the state from fear that their careers will be damaged if they speak out. The people of the press are hyenas; to underline this, Hein calls Oliver Zurek's girlfriend (based on Birgit Hogefeld, who at the time of writing remains in prison) Katharina Blumenschläger in homage (one assumes) to Böll's Katharina Blum.

There is a legal basis to Richard Zurek's quarrel with the state, as there was to Michael Kohlhaas's dispute. At the start of Kleist's novella, Kohlhaas has an enviable existence: he is married, a father of two young sons, and runs a thriving business buying and selling horses. At the end of his first paragraph, Kleist calls him, in a famous phrase "one of the most upright and at the same time horrific people of his era."[41] Kleist's tale is based on a historical figure, whose travails lasted from 1532–1540, the era of robber barons, lawlessness, and the Lutheran Reformation, when the Peasants' Wars of the 1520s were fresh in the memories of rulers and ruled. Luther's famous response to the peasants' demands for justice was that they should obey their princes, since his own rebellion against the Catholic Church was not a model for political dissent. Luther plays a constructive role in Kleist's telling of the Kohlhaas saga, as he convinces Kohlhaas to give up violence and ensures that his case finally receives a fair hearing.

Kohlhaas's crisis begins when an aristocratic landowner (or Junker) refuses to let him pass from Brandenburg to Saxony, claiming that he needs to pay for a permit. Kohlhaas leaves two horses and an employee to tend to them as surety, while he rides to Dresden, where he will obtain the permission. Once there, he discovers what he suspected all along—that no permission is required—and he returns to find his horses in a parlous condition and his employee vanished. Determined to see justice done, his property restored, and the Junker punished, he quickly exhausts the legal means at his disposal because the Junker bribes the officials.

After his wife is accidentally killed while attempting to submit a petition on his behalf, Kohlhaas abandons his settled existence to raise a private army to pursue the Junker. He burns down his castle, killing all its inhabitants, and proceeds to lay waste to the cities of Wittenberg and Leipzig, believing his enemy to be hiding in them. He gives up his campaign only when he is promised a fair trial by Luther. By the end, he has succeeded in getting justice, as the Junker is sentenced to two years in prison and ordered to feed up the horses and pay damages. Kohlhaas, however, is condemned to death, yet he goes to the gallows a contented man because his quest has been successful. Kleist leaves it to his readers to decide whether his hero or the social order that prompted his behavior is more at fault. Kohlhaas is either a tragic hero or a fool.

The other Kohlhaas adaptation, *My Year as a Murderer* (Delius, 2004), includes all the ingredients for a classic terrorist drama: there are Nazis and resisters, 1960s protestors and their parents; West Germany is posited as a continuation of the Nazi state (in the shape of judges who persecute a resister's widow through a series of hostile court decisions); and hatred of West Germany is compensated by idealization of a foreign country, in this case England. The novel has three intertwining narratives. The most straightforward narrative accounts for the life and death of Georg Groscurth, the father of the narrator's close childhood friend, the personal doctor of Hitler's deputy Rudolf Hess, and an anti-Nazi conspirator who saved hundreds of lives through a mixture of bravery, daring, and low cunning. For the narrator Rolf in 1968–1969, Groscurth is a hero. But for most West Germans in the immediate postwar period, all anti-Nazi resisters were *de facto* Communists, which made their persecution by the Nazis justified and made any political activism they performed after 1945 highly suspicious. Groscurth's widow, Annaliese, comes to realize that the FRG is only interested in commemorating the officers around Claus von Stauffenberg in the plot to assassinate Hitler that was attempted on July 20, 1944. The GDR is only interested if the resisters really were communists at the time and are conformists in the present. Both postwar German states have preconceived and ideologically self-serving ideas of what anti-Nazi resistance should be.

The second strand of the story concerns Rolf's moral education. He is a student in his mid-twenties who really should be concentrating on finishing his degree by writing seminar papers on topics such as Rousseau's *Social Contract*. His life takes a different turn on the first day of Advent 1968 when he hears that a Nazi judge, Hans-Joachim Rehse, an assistant to the notorious Roland Freisler, has been acquitted on seven charges of murder. Rolf realizes that Rehse must have condemned Groscurth to death in 1943. He is outraged by the acquittal, as is most of the press, even newspapers owned by Axel Springer. His parents' dismissive comments about Groscurth are lodged in his memory. As the revolutionary year draws to a close, he resolves that he will murder Rehse to make amends for his parents and for the justice system. But Rolf is an intellectual and does not want to carry out his murder until he has fully understood the background to the case. His project is two-pronged: he will kill Rehse and write a book, which will function as a kind of manifesto for his deed.[42] The research part of the project comes to absorb his attention completely, to the extent that he neglects not only his studies but his faithful girlfriend Catherine, who at the end of the novel travels without him on a long planned holiday to Mexico, where she is senselessly killed in a random mugging.

The more scandalous third strand of *My Year as a Murderer* relates Annaliese Groscurth's entanglements with a series of Nazi judges in the Berlin courts in the first decade of the Federal Republic. After she suffers the latest in a never-ending line of unfair legal rulings, which threaten her ability to feed herself and her children, she asks:

> How would Michael Kohlhaas have reacted, if he, two days after the ver-dict of the Labor Court, which referred to a loyalty clause from the Nazi era, had been confronted with a letter like that? It can easily be imagined, a wrong, a scream for justice, more wrong, a sequence of revenge, theft, war, the story is well-known. We are stuck in the unknown twentieth century (182).

Annaliese's response is different from that of Kohlhaas. She engages another lawyer, makes another complaint: "What else can she do," Rolf wonders to himself, "if she does not want to sink into Kohlhaasian mad-ness, but submit another petition to the Administration Court?" (203). Kohlhaas is a negative model.

In 1968, young Germans no longer needed Kohlhaas either. They were inspired by "the angel from London," a Californian record-seller named Hugo who did business with the likes of the Beatles and the Rolling Stones, who tells them that every nation has its own "bullshit," the Americans cur-rently in Vietnam, the Germans in the Third Reich. He thereby admits Germany back into the community of nations by comparing and thereby relativizing the crimes of the Nazi era. In London, Rolf admires the émigré Jewish writers Erich Fried, Jakov Lind, and Elias Canetti. When Catherine visits Hugo in London, Rolf is jealous, even though Hugo is gay and thus hardly a love rival. She returns with a secondhand book written in 1947, based on the Groscurth case. Catherine and Rolf are henceforth reconciled on the subject: she has traveled to the land of the former enemy and found a book that must have belonged to one of the émigrés whom he reveres and that that he did not know existed. He in turn accepts her plans to travel to Mexico, which, although the scene of a student massacre in October 1968, represents adventure and openness to the world, which Catherine intends to explore with her camera. She is branching out in time to an epoch in

German history before the Nazis by reading Wilhelm Humboldt's account of his travels to the Americas. Rolf, meanwhile, risks allowing himself to be pulled down into the "Nazi quagmire" (135), but by the end of the novel comes to realize that he loves Berlin.

My Year as a Murderer is an account of 1968–1969, written from the perspective of the early 2000s. As Rehse dies before Rolf can shoot him, it is the book that Rolf did not write at the time, to explain the deed that he did not need to commit. Like all confessions, it is motivated by guilt, for his murderous intentions, for his recollection of his belief in his moral superiority over his parents, and, more painfully, for his neglect of Catherine. His obsession with Rehse was in turn driven by guilt for his family's lack of understanding for the plight of their neighbors. Rolf is now not only much older and wiser himself, he is aware that the national political situation has been transformed, which makes him all the more critical of his younger self. He made the wrong judgment, he was looking backwards, judging his parents, taking on another's battle without asking that person. He idealized both Georg and Annaliese Groscurth, neither of whom appears to him capable of making a mistake. They are more than heroes, they are saints. As Catherine points out, Annaliese's behavior was at times intransigent if not antagonistic after 1945. Rolf cannot accept that Annaliese's opponents had any grounds to pursue her, even in the febrile atmosphere of divided Berlin two years after the Soviet blockade and the Allied airlift. He did not notice that national politics in 1968–1969 were moving forward of their own accord. Gustav Heinemann, who in the 1950s shared Annaliese's views on rearmament, is elected federal president ("the first decent man to hold this office," in her view). This development depended ultimately on membership in the western alliance (NATO) and in the European Economic Community and was anticipated by Georg Groscurth, whose resistance group was called the "European Union." The Kohlhaas route to justice is well and truly rejected in Delius's fourth Baader-Meinhof novel.

The same is not true of Hein's *In His Early Childhood, a Garden*. Hein has always been an author who crossed boundaries. His first novel, *Der fremde Freund* (1982, *The Strange Friend*, also published as *Dragon's Blood* in the West) is a minor classic of modernist alienation, which spoke to West German readers as much as to East German readers. This was a rare feat in the 40-year history of German–German literary relations, but Hein repeated it with his next novel, *Horn's End* (1985). The end of communism prevented him from repeating it for a second time with *The Tango Player* (1989), which anticipates *In His Early Childhood, a Garden* in its portrayal of the relationship between an individual citizen and the law. In *The Tango Player*, the central character is arrested for a crime he is not aware of committing and finds his experiences of punishment and rehabilitation meaningless as a consequence. At the end, government policy changes in the wake of the Soviet invasion of Czechoslovakia in August 1968, and he gets his old job back. By the time he is released, his crime is no longer a crime. *In His Early Childhood, a Garden*, in turn, is a version of *The Tango Player* for the reunified nation, which adopted the laws and legal practices of the former West German state.[43]

Richard Zurek in *In His Early Childhood, a Garden* finds the modern world and the younger generation at fault in many things. Consumerism, foreign holidays, putting social status before moral principles, the shallowness of family relations across the generations, and drug-taking in schools are all elements of the same contemporary malaise. Some of this critique could have been written about the GDR itself during its existence, but none of it would have been out of place in a GDR denunciation of the FRG. What is new is that Hein connects the critical discourse to a fictional treatment of a well-known terrorist case and that he lets off the two terrorists, the deceased Oliver Zurek (who is reminiscent of Wolfgang Grams) and the imprisoned Katharina Blumenschläger, lightly. Oliver's sister Christine and her businessman husband offer the only countervailing viewpoints, but they are far from sympathetic characters. In the novel's indictment of the state's laws and practices, as they relate to Richard Zurek's attempts to clear his son's name, it is anti-West German, which was recognized by reviewers. Those reviews published in formerly West German newspapers dwelt defensively on Hein's stylistic weaknesses. In contrast, the lengthy review in *Freitag* saw that his critique of the relationship between the state and its citizens was not wholly unjustified.[44] Hein has no fictional counterparts for Grams's likely victims, who may have included Rohwedder and Herrhausen. Oliver's parents take the view that as long as his participation in murder cannot be proved, he is innocent. The real-life Grams may have been shot by the police, who may then lied about what happened, but even his supporters would hardly claim that he was innocent. Hein's central character is angry with contemporary Germany and reverts to an antimodern diatribe.

These two updated versions of the Kohlhaas narrative by two near-contemporary novelists could hardly be more different in their import. That by the ex-East German dissident ends by backing the Kohlhaas solution, although this remains an impulse that he does not act on. The novel by the ex-West German 68er shows that such behavior may have been warranted in the immediate postwar era of fervent anti-communism, but it is out of place by the late 1960s, let alone the mid-2000s. Yet *My Year as a Murderer* does this through a nationalist, even revisionist argument. As the "angel from London" assures Delius's fictional alter ego that all countries have their own "bullshit," not just the Germans, Delius's novel shares this nationalism with Hein's otherwise rather different adaptation of the Kohlhaas story. The two novelists have written competing ideological narratives of the evolving new German nation. By the mid-2000s, Baader-Meinhof had become if not quite a classical theme, then one which could be incorporated into reworkings of the classics. Three decades after his one-sided epistolary novel...*Already You Are an Enemy of the State* (1975), Peter Schneider adapts a Homeric myth in *Scylla* (2005). In *Autumn Messenger* (2009), Thomas Hoeth casts his terrorist femme fatale as a modern-day Circe, who bewitches her former tormentors in the police force. While Schneider's Leo Brenner is confronting the demons of his past as a student agitator in *Scylla*, his young archeologist wife is excavating a Roman mosaic that depicts the Homeric monster. The ex-terrorist Paul Stirlitz's theft of the mosaic triggers the breakup of the Brenners' marriage.[45] The allusion to *The Odyssey* underscores how the mature novelist distances his leading character from his adventurous past. There is no longer a contest for meaning: Baader-Meinhof can be approached through ancient myth, as expressed in the founding work of western literature. In *Dreamers of the Absolute* (2008), Michael Wildenhain's terrorist Tariq Fatoun quotes Adorno and Horkheimer (*The Dialectics of the Enlightenment*) on Odysseus, comparing the anonymous urban guerilla with Homer's hero, who called himself "Nobody" to escape the clutches of the Cyclops.[46] This goes to the heart of the critique of applied reason and its effect on subject identity in *The Dialectics of the Enlightenment*. By the end of the novel, when Tariq has taken up with al-Qaeda under a new identity, his old headmaster refers again to Adorno: "I cannot say what it is, but you lose something when you give up your own name" (324).

Reinvention of classical tradition becomes more playfully elaborate in the final novel to be discussed in this chapter, which is neither an intervention nor based on a historical case. Helmut Krausser began writing *Eros* (2006) in 1997, when the German Autumn was commemorated for the first time in full. By the time of publication, the novel had become a fictional retrospective of German history stretching from 1945 to 1989, written from the point of view of the beginning of the new century. *Eros* is significant for the way that it reimagines recent German history and reflects on how historical narratives, myths, and archetypes are constructed. The novel is set in the early 2000s, as the billionaire Alexander von Brücken is facing death from a painful disease. He narrates his life story to a professional writer, in particular his life-long obsession with the working-class Sofie Kurtz, who kissed him at the age of fourteen in return for 50 marks, and later on becomes a terrorist. Alexander commissions the writer to transform this peculiar love story into a novel. The "eros" of Krausser's title does not denote physical passion. Alexander is possibly impotent in the presence of the opposite sex, and his preferred sexual activity appears to be imagining Sofie during masturbation. He sublimates his erotic energies in his pursuit of money and the power that money gives him to direct the fates of others.

The unnamed writer, who is paid an enormous sum, is responsible for the allegorical meanings that the story acquires. He is the latest in a line of fictional writers who engage with the terrorist theme, but the first not to be directly engaged with it himself and instead to be entrusted with its literary historiography. If we trace his lineage to the unconfident Fritz Buchonia in *The Gentlemen of the Dawn* (Chotjewitz, 1978) through to the uninterested Roland Diehl in *A Hero of Internal Security* (Delius, 1981), to the evasive Fonty in *Too Far Afield* (1995), and to the complicit Jakob Amon and Marco Sentenza in *The Assassin's Library* (Sonner, 2001) we see increasing readiness to interpret events and to employ imagery. Krausser's direct allusion to the classic tale of "Cupid (Eros) and Psyche," which itself was embedded in a novel, alerts us to his own technique of narrative embedding. The reader is warned that Alexander von Brücken may not be a reliable source. The last, perhaps most implausible episode concerning ex-terrorist Sofie's escape from the GDR, is relayed while he is under the influence of morphine. After his death, the novelist hears from his employer's sister, who Alexander had claimed was dead; she corrects or clarifies several other significant details in those parts of her brother's life that she knew about.

In the adaptation of "Cupid and Psyche," Alexander takes the male role of Eros (or Cupid), who, against the wishes of his mother the goddess Aphrodite (Venus), falls in love with Psyche (meaning "soul" in Greek), the beautiful daughter of a poor king. The only way that Cupid can sleep with Psyche is to have her transported to a castle, in which he visits her every night without revealing his identity or even showing her his physical form. In the castle, Psyche can have everything that she could wish for, but she is lonely (this episode is the source for *Beauty and the Beast*). In another episode, Psyche travels to the Underworld and successfully returns from it. At the conclusion to the tale, she marries Eros and they have a daughter they name Voluptas (Hedone), the goddess of sensual pleasure. Krausser's *Eros*, in contrast, is a novel about lack and nonfulfillment. Alexander's love is never reciprocated by Sofie. He is out of his time, because he can no longer charm his princess with his wealth and a promise that she can share it at his side. Sofie flees from him when he has her in his grasp during her first time in his castle; and the second time, 30 years later, when he rescues her from the GDR, the contemporary equivalent of the Underworld. Understood allegorically, Sofie is postwar Germany's soul, which remains separate from the immense material wealth that Alexander amasses during the 40-year economic miracle.

Alexander and Sofie represent a series of opposites. He stands for aestheticism, irony, wealth, the upper class, power, the continuity between the prewar and postwar elites, and a disinclination to straight talking about the past. When he meets Sofie in person, he cannot cope. From a distance, his concern is well meant and even well directed. Once up close, he gets it wrong. He is in fact no good at relationships of any sort. His occasional use of Yiddish words is the only oblique acknowledgment in his narrative of the Holocaust. He ends his engagement to his secretary Silvia by removing their engagement rings from their fingers with his mouth and swallowing the rings. He cannot articulate his feelings. Sofie is on the side of honesty, working-class integrity, the vulnerability of ordinary folk, and melancholy. She takes to drink and violence as a consequence of disappointments, which are personal and political in nature. She looks for salvation in the GDR, but is more isolated there than anywhere else in her life. She is brave and resolute but unknown forces, in the shape of Alexander and his surveillance team, pull strings in her life. There are similarities and parallels that offset the differences between them: both are lonely and fail to find happiness in relationships; she is addicted to red wine, he to pills; neither has anyone to trust. Others get distracted, but they both carry on along the path they have set out on.

Krausser exploits the connections between West German terrorists and the Stasi to explore the two greatest upheavals in postwar German history: the protest of 1968 and national division. He draws on the bestselling memoirs by Inge Viett, in particular her transfer to the GDR at the beginning of the 1980s, among numerous other historical and literary sources. Ulrike Meinhof is the only other RAF figure to be mentioned, and there are elements of her biography (or at least contested perceptions of it) that go into shaping that of Sofie Kurtz. Sofie is significantly older than her comrades (she is born in 1931, Meinhof in 1934); she lets her flat be used by activists, who take advantage of her attempts to mother them, just as Meinhof accommodated Ensslin and Baader in 1970. Insofar as Sofie is an intellectual who begins a PhD (on Albert Camus) and becomes romantically involved with a virile petty criminal called Henry, who is clearly based on Baader, she also resembles Ensslin. Her alcohol dependency, which the rest of the group believes endangers them, recalls Peter-Jürgen Boock's addiction to heroin. Meinhof's suicide is a turning point for Sofie, as she observes in the novel: "How could such a strong, clever woman despair of the world, when there were still endless possibilities [...] With Meinhof, more than just an idol died, a large part of Sophie's courage and strength to resist died too."[47] The RAF's notorious sentence in their announcement of their murder of Schleyer (that they had "ended his corrupt existence") is the reason that Sofie finally quits the RAF. Already under a new identity in the GDR, she comments in her diary: "It is this sentence which forces me to say goodbye for ever to the armed struggle [...] A sentence like that takes away the legitimacy from a cause once and for all." (269)

Sofie's life and experiences are a collage put together from well-known scraps of Baader-Meinhof historiography, but the spirit of playfulness in which the novel is assembled disguises a representation of history which can be disassembled to reveal a more serious intent. *Eros* rewrites recent history as well as echoing classic narratives such as *Citizen Kane* (dir. Welles, 1941). The novel has echoes of Thomas Mann's *Doktor Faustus* (1947, an apparently less significant man telling the life story of another and interweaving it with the history of Germany) and Mann's *The Magic Mountain* (1924; the discussion between Sofie and Alexander on the night of June 2, 1967 on violence is a parody of Naphta and Settembrini). The "tower society," which secretly steers the destiny of Goethe's Wilhelm Meister, is brought to mind by Alexander's protection of Sofie. The action is referred to as a "game" on numerous occasions. Life and art overlap: Alexander's power over Sofie has resembled that of a novelist over a character. He has been like a god and an artist in her life. Without Sofie, there would be no art and no success in his life. She was his muse. The history is presented as finished by the end, but neither Alexander nor Sofie has children. The von Brücken dynasty must come to an end.

Sofie's unhappiness in love and inability to find a suitable mate are the reasons that she goes "underground." She is a variation on the by now very well-worn trope of "terrorist as woman." Sofie is not responsible for murder; in fact, she never fires a shot. She is pressed by circumstances into joining in the first place, and, once underground, she is bullied by her comrades. She is the reluctant, remorseful female terrorist. Krausser is thoroughly revisionist in his portrayal of the Left: both left-wing terrorism and the GDR represented false hopes.

Alexander claims that when he traveled to the GDR to bring Sofie back, he was, without realizing it, infected by the Left's hegemonic view that the communism in East Germany was benign. This is a thoroughly anachronistic proposition. Krausser delights in rearranging history. When Alexander intervenes directly to stop Sofie from being beaten up by the unfaithful Henry, the result is that Henry is run over by a bus. Even without Henry (Baader), terrorist groups are formed not long afterwards. Sofie stumbles into joining one after an affair with Alexander's assistant Lukian ends when she discovers that he had been stalking her, but she has taken a keen interest in politics since early adulthood. As Alexander is no longer sure where she is, he is all the more delighted when she telephones, but she does so because her comrades have suggested him as a suitable target for a kidnapping. This casts him in the role of Hanns-Martin Schleyer. Alexander is prepared to meet her and hand over whatever funds they need without going through the trouble of being kidnapped. In terms of meta-history narrated after the event, he is offering to enact the national trauma of the German Autumn as play. Once Sofie transfers to the GDR in 1976–1977, he loses sight of her once more. While the Stasi replicate his methods, indicating a basic similarity between East and West, he cannot take them on at their own game on their own turf. He sees Sofie one more time when he drives her back to the West, a couple of years before the collapse of the GDR regime, with the connivance of the Stasi.

Krausser is postmodern in his use of pastiche, indirect quotation, allusion to history and literary tradition. Several tropes and features from other novels discussed thus far in our present book play a role in *Eros* for that reason. The "chronicle novel" linking individual destinies to historical events was the central genre for postwar German novelists such as Günter Grass, Heinrich Böll, Uwe Johnson, and Siegfried Lenz. The historical narrative in *Eros* is hardly original: it is the story that the republic post-1990 likes to tell about itself, especially as there is a "happy ending," when Sofie gains her freedom in 1989.[48] Krausser includes the bombing at end of the war, postwar reconstruction, marginalized political activism in the 1950s, the watershed demonstration of June 2, 1967, armed resistance to the state by a handful of isolated individuals, and the Stasi's control of the GDR. The unspoken question in *Eros* is how much of his Nazi father's ways of thinking and doing things Alexander has inherited and has carried through the postwar period. His surname (derived from Brücke meaning "bridge") suggests that there are connections. He is buried inside a mausoleum designed after his father's egg-shaped bomb shelter. There is continuity in economics, as Alexander inherits the family fortune and business empire and amasses wealth after 1945 with apparent effortlessness.

By the end of this series of novels, the Baader-Meinhof terrorist has become a tragic figure in the national imaginary. Only in the two novels by German-Jewish authors, *My Sister, My Antigone* (Weil, 1980), which reevaluated the German tradition of Antigone adaptation, and *The Happy Ones* (Zahl, 1979), were the terrorist characters rejected as fundamentally wrong-headed. The novels that were published after reunification are fictions of national history that rewrite a classical source, either to legitimize or to challenge the new order. Each either encompasses a number of decades: 1819–1991 in *Too Far Afield* (Grass, 1995); 1945–1989 in *Eros* (Krausser, 2006); 1943–1968 in *My Year as a Murderer* (Delius, 2004); and 1967–2001 in *The Last Performance* (Woelk, 2002), or goes from the1940s to the present as in, *In his Early Childhood, a Garden* (Hein, 2005). What they have in common is that the terrorist or would-be terrorist, now re-presented as a character from the classics, is vindicated, portrayed as a victim, or reintegrated into society. By the mid-2000s, controversy has all but ceased. The topic can be presented as postmodern play or entertainment. The pattern that emerges in the popular genres is similar, as I will now try to show in the next chapter.

CHAPTER FOUR

TERRORISM AND THE GERMAN POPULAR IMAGINARY: CONSPIRACIES AND COUNTERFACTUALS

The focus in this chapter is popular fiction, principally detective novels and thrillers, or in German: *krimis*. Popular fiction is read for pleasure, but German *krimis* featuring Baader-Meinhof terrorists did not begin to get written with that principal aim until recently. More than 40 percent of Baader-Meinhof novels published between 2000 and 2010 were in the popular genres, however. There also have been a number of similarly styled popular genre films, all of which were made after 2000.[1] At last we have outrageous plot scenarios that are not rooted in historical fact or based directly on real individuals. At the beginning of the new century, cinema and popular literature quickly created a grammar of Baader-Meinhof terrorism, readily recycling tropes, motifs, and plot lines in a series of thrillers and detective novels by some of the country's leading practitioners. The uncovering of past terrorist connections among established figures in politics, the professions, and even the law and the police force, is especially common. What these *krimis* also tend to share is a left-leaning detective who believes that political change for the better is both achievable and a good thing. This makes him the terrorists' counterpart rather than their opposite number. Terrorists themselves generally get a remarkably good press in mass-market fiction. Yet as such novels enjoy less prestige than their supposedly more literary counterparts throughout Europe, not just in Germany, the critical writing on terrorist literature has so far all but ignored them.[2] "Popular" and "serious" can still be mutually exclusive categories; *trivialroman*, a term applied to novels of apparently ephemeral value, is never one of praise. As a result, there is not the same modern tradition of serious popular writing in German as there is perhaps in English. But formulas can cross genre boundaries. Literary novelists interested in Baader-Meinhof have adapted crime tropes and motifs for what are essentially novels of ideas. This started with *Katharina Blum* (Böll, 1974) and has continued with *The Assassin's Library* (Sonner, 2001), *The Last Performance* (Woelk, 2002), and *Part of the Solution* (Peltzer, 2007). In the 1970s, popular Baader-Meinhof fiction took the form of interventions. The authors, none of whom was a professional crime writer, had a point to get across. The account of a murder in *Katharina Blum* has the accent on "the why" rather than "the who" (which is never in doubt), but features police interrogations, an escape, and a violent climax.[3] Böll collaborated on the film version which deployed more overt thriller techniques and was commercially one of the most successful German films of the New German Cinema Movement.[4] *The Comrade* (Röhl, 1975) is a Cold War thriller that anticipates some of the climactic events of the German Autumn. Röhl utilizes a farfetched conspiracy theory, which resurfaces in barely altered form in some more recent thrillers. *Scenes of Fire* (Degenhardt, 1975) is an entertaining didactic novel, one of the points of which is to show that there are other more effective ways to campaign for a better life than planting bombs. Franz Josef Degenhardt explained in an interview that he had borrowed "stylistic devices from [...] various trivial genres, television soap operas, melodramas, but also comics and cabaret."[5] While Klaus Rainer Röhl's semi-amateur *The Comrade* has never been reprinted, both *Katharina Blum* and *Scenes of Fire* became bestsellers, were reprinted in the GDR, and were adapted for the screen. In 1975 "Baader-Meinhof and the novel" added up to not much more than this trio.

The Comrade is not treated seriously as a novel for a number of reasons. In the writing on the RAF, there is no more controversial figure than Röhl, Meinhof's former husband, the founding editor of *konkret* and a former Danzig schoolmate of Günter Grass (who is portrayed in *The Comrade* as the card-playing ladies' man Heiner Heck). Always ready to be interviewed, to air his views on Meinhof's reasons for joining the armed struggle, Röhl's purpose in the novel is to cast Meinhof, the mother of their twins, in a better light than Baader and Ensslin, whom he has accused of direct responsibility for her death.[6] Indirectly, he blames himself or the breakup of their marriage, which was precipitated by his philandering, for Meinhof's turn to terrorism—thus depoliticizing her actions in the eyes of his critics. In *The Comrade*, the fictional Katharina Holt needs personal, emotional security after losing both her parents in childhood. *The Comrade* whitewashes Holt (which means "innocent" or "holy"), who does not take part in the robberies or shootings (far more numerous than in reality) and is not party to the RAF's attacks in May 1972 (their so-called "May Offensive").[7] She knows nothing of the others' plans to remove her twins to a camp in Jordan for Palestinian orphans. She has had her doubts about the others all along. She is afraid of Matthias Rahner (Andreas Baader), and she thinks several times of getting out. At the end,

Holt denounces her comrades and refuses to be released from prison in exchange for the kidnapped wife of the federal chancellor. *The Comrade* is one of those *romans à clef,* in which the *clef* takes precedence over the *roman.* Röhl may not be a fluent novelist, but he is the first to exploit a number of tropes, such as that of the unwilling female terrorist as victim. *The Comrade* is also rather better than its reputation suggests. The passage describing how to lose a tail in East Berlin is richly comic. Röhl makes the crucial point that Holt / Meinhof was accustomed to illegal political activity from her days of working with him on *konkret,* which was subsidized by the GDR. He makes competent use of the flashback and also half-anticipates the climax to the German Autumn. In October 1977, it was the Palestinians who played a vital supporting role in the hijacking of a Lufthansa plane; in *The Comrade,* there are "three Arabs and a Japanese woman."[8] The actual hijacked plane landed in Rome, Lanarca, Dubai, and Yemen before it was stormed in Mogadishu; Röhl chooses Zagreb. The chief hostage is the chancellor's wife, not the president of the Employers' Association. Röhl also anticipates the role that the Stasi would play in providing new identities to West German terrorists who wanted to give up. Days after the liberation of Rahner, Holt is made an offer by a well-placed contact in East-Berlin: "Do you want to stay with us? Emigrate to the German Democratic Republic? I have not yet spoken to the leading comrades, but I think we would take you. *You!*" (260). It is a personal offer, not extended to the rest of her group, whom he describes as "bandits" and "middle-class mummies' boys," but it anticipates the arrangements made for RAF defectors in the 1980s. The GDR was ignored in other Baader-Meinhof fiction until the 2000s, when its role came to be exaggerated for the sake of including the other German state in retrospective narratives of national unity.

Röhl is also the first writer to exploit an outrageous conspiracy theory for literary effect. His idea is that Rahner / Baader is working for an international right-wing organization whose goal is to discredit the legitimate Left in Western Europe. The reason Rahner persuaded such figures as Holt to take up arms was to justify a military takeover. This is not a wholly crazy proposition. In Italy, the security services were engaged in just such a "strategy of tension." Röhl knew this all too well. A character based on the publisher Giangiacomo Feltrinelli, who accidentally blew himself up in 1972, makes an appearance in *The Comrade.* This may signal an awareness, which is lacking among some of the *krimi* writers who come after him, that he is transferring recent Italian historiography to the German context.

From this point, however, while international thriller writers continued to make German terrorism the subject of their work for a further decade, the Germans stopped. The gap in Baader-Meinhof fiction production is more obvious in the genres than elsewhere, as there follows exactly a quarter of a century during which German Baader-Meinhof novels, which come out somewhat fitfully, are exclusively serious literary fiction. My bibliography counts 18 between 1976 and 1999, compared with 28 between 2000 and 2010. No longer a suitable topic for *krimis*, Baader-Meinhof became associated with left-wing novelists published by Rotbuch (Schneider, Chotjewitz, Zahl, Geissler), whose books were read by a relatively small coterie of like-minded readers. These novels had a tendency to difficulty, even unreadability in the case of *Kamalatta* (Geissler, 1988), and basic partisanship. Literary novelists only occasionally used genre tropes and techniques in this period, such as mystery in *Dead Alive* (Demski, 1984), which was rewarded with commercial success, or suspense in *Window Seat at Mogadishu* (Delius, 1987), which did not reach a mass readerhship.

The factors that made domestic left-wing terrorism a suitable subject once more for film and literature, either popular or serious, are threefold. They are the epochal broadcast on national television of the docudrama *Death Game* (dir. Breloer, 1997), which intercuts thriller techniques with interviews with witnesses and participants; the dissolution of the RAF the following April, which has been attributed to Heinrich Breloer's influence,[9] and the election of the Red–Green Coalition in September 1998. The RAF was no longer a real or existing threat, and the former radical Left was at the helm of the capitalist economy. There was no longer anything much at stake in the fiction and films that came afterwards, which may be how the terrorists eluded censure. *Death Game*'s influence can be felt directly in *The Execution* (Brenner, 2000) and *The Assassin's Library* (Sonner, 2001), and thus it can be credited with initiating this wave of *krimis*.

After *The Execution*, the first German Baader-Meinhof *krimi* in 25 years, others by leading genre writers quickly followed. In 2002, the television series *Tatort* (*Crime Scene*) showed that formats that live by formulas can sometimes challenge clichés as powerfully as they can reinforce them. In the episode "Shadows" (dir. Näter, 2002), past association with violent protest is a guilty secret that causes a morally upright character to lead a life of failure and disappointment. As no one witnessed the unpremeditated murder he committed (shades of Joschka Fischer) on the day that Meinhof's death was announced, his guilt remains a secret that eats away at his soul for 25 years. By taking his own life after his arrest, when the truth finally comes to light, he redeems himself as he thereby saves his son, who has repeated his father's crime by killing one of his father's former comrades. The next generation still risks repeating the cycle of secret guilt. The police meanwhile know the truth about the murder that the son committed, but decide to keep it hidden. As in much popular fiction, the plot in "Shadows" revolves around individuals confronting past demons and the authorities knowing more than the public does. Like his three predecessors from the mid-1970s, Wolfgang Brenner was a politically motivated author. He aims to secure the ideological terrain for the recently elected Red–Green Coalition by exorcising its leaders' connections with the first RAF generation. Three years later, Wolfgang Schorlau used a *krimi* to enter the debate about the ill effects of reunification. *The Blue List: Dengler's First Case* (2003) is a page-turner that established Schorlau's reputation as a foremost contemporary crime writer (and campaigner). What is unusual is that he appends a mini-bibliography and essay on his research into the Rohwedder and Bad Kleinen killings, assuring readers of the underlying veracity of his conspiracy-packed narrative. *The Flight of the Seraphim* (Mock, 2003) also ends with an Afterword about the standoff between international terrorism and the European Union on the remote Cape Verde Islands, which informs this tale of counterterrorist skullduggery and capitalist exploitation of the Third World. Mock shows his sympathy for the plight of the Cape Verde islanders through three centuries of history and cites with understanding, if not approval, the welcome given in some Basque quarters to the 9/11 attacks. All three authors—Brenner, Schorlau, and Mock—use crime fiction as counter-history.

The more conservative political journalist Cora Stephen, writing under the pen name Anne Chaplet, takes a slightly different line in *The Photographer* (2002) but is similarly interested in coverups and in the past Baader-Meinhof connections of establishment figures. Ulrich Ritzel in *The Black Edges of the Fire* (2001) bases his plot on the accidental police shooting of the young Scotsman Ian Mcleod in June 1972. The police officer responsible for a similar shooting in Ritzel's novel takes his own life 29 years later. Chaplet borrows freely from Baader-Meinhof history, jumbling well-known incidents and biographies, but concentrates on two children of victims (both lightly adapted from well-known cases): the son of a chauffeur shot when his boss is kidnapped; and the daughter of a pilot executed by hijackers. Chaplet's multiple murder mystery ultimately rejects conspiracy theories, which, as a character says, only belong "in socially critical *krimis*." The novel finds the BKA's cooperation with ex-terrorists, whom it protects in return for information, to be distasteful, but ends with a homily against vigilante justice. Yet once again a conspiracy ultimately wins out: the avenging son is not brought to justice because of the embarrassment his prosecution would bring to the BKA. Thus neither his murders nor the past entanglement of a leading businesswoman become public knowledge.

By the mid-2000s, political imperatives have all but disappeared. Across the board, the trend is for commercialization. This does not diminish the status enjoyed by the terrorists in the popular imaginary; on the contrary, the unreflected nature of their representation can cast their profile into higher relief. *Wilsberg and the Third Generation* (Kehrer, 2006) and *Autumn Messenger* (Hoeth, 2009) could not be about the Russian mafia or a Chinese snake gang. In both novels, the only villains are employed by the state. In a film adaptation of a 1957 romance by the prolific Johannes Mario Simmel, *God Protects Lovers* (dir. Rola, 2008) the original heroine's guilty secret, her betrayal of her anti-Nazi Italian lover to the Gestapo, is turned into past membership in a RAF cell.[10] There are three interesting things about this unacclaimed film adaptation of a popular postwar novel: nothing is what it seems to be because conspiracies abound; RAF terrorists are a source of entertainment; and they are, on the whole, sympathetic figures. Sylvia Loredo (as so often in this type of fiction) is a dupe of the security forces, whose aim was to ambush her lover, the cell's male leader. She still has powerful enemies in the present because she knows the whereabouts of tapes of the original RAF leaders' last night in Stammheim, which demonstrate that the authorities knew all along of their suicide plans (another well-worn conspiracy theory). The film also features an avenging daughter of an RAF victim who leads Loredo's current lover, the film's tragic hero, to deliver Loredo into a trap. God and history fail this pair of lovers: Loredo shoots him, though not fatally, before turning her gun on herself.

Two more clumsily written "victim novels" from the late 2000s are constructed from the opposite perspective. Both explore the psychological damage done to children whose fathers were murdered by female RAF terrorists in the 1980s, an American soldier in *You Too Will Weep, Tupamara* (Mathiessen, 2007) and a policeman in *The End of Sleeplessness* (Marrat, 2008). These two revenge *krimis* are strongly anti-RAF, like Chaplet's *The Photographer,* but by depicting particular cases, they fail to make general connections. Both young men would have suffered similar emotional dysfunction had their fathers died in less dramatic circumstances. Several *krimis* feature terrorists who are mothers, which rehumanizes or "deterrorizes" the women in each case. In these two "victim novels" the unnaturalness of the unfeminine deed, which destroyed family life for a male teenager, is at the center of attention. Neither plot is based on a historical shooting; and both murders are recollected as aberrations from the national past that the majority now wants to forget. The central character in *You Too Will Weep, Tupamara* teaches his father's murderer about the sanctity of family life by kidnapping her baby, which was born during the last year of her prison sentence. While she has at last become feminine by giving birth, the narrator stresses that she has lost her good looks. The revenge fantasy becomes misogynist: sexual attractiveness was a prerequisite of violence, but prison transforms the murderer into a drab-looking middle-aged mother. The constellation of the sexes is inverted in the film, *Long Shadows* (dir. Walter, 2008), which revolves around the plans for revenge on a male terrorist made by his unintended victim's now grown-up daughter. She plots her revenge over more than 20 years, but in the final frame of the film, she throws away her revolver and drives away from him. The urge is to close the book on the past and to move on.

One of the RAF's real victims was the 20-year-old American GI Edward Pimental, who was lured out of a discotheque in the city of Wiesbaden on the evening of August 8, 1985 by a female RAF member (thought likely to have been Birgit Hogefeld) with the promise of sex. Instead, he was taken to some woods and murdered with a single shot to the back of the head. The motive? The RAF needed his US Army ID so that one of them could drive into the Rhein-Main Air Base the following day to deposit a bomb, which duly exploded, causing the death of two more American military personnel. Pimental and his would-be seducer are two figures who do not get written about in novels. Their symbolism is too complex.

Moral issues associated with taking lives in the name of a cause are taken lightly in most of these thrillers, if not quite swept aside. The real RAF's politics are all but ignored, their communiqués are never quoted. Of course, in a *krimi*, terrorists are not alone in their readiness to kill. The discussion in *Wilsberg and the Third Generation* (Kehrer, 2006) between the detective Wilsberg and the unrepentant female terrorist is typical of the way the question of killing is handled. Regina Fuchs shows no regrets for her past. She was the victim of the *Verfassungsschutz*, who recruited her lover and the father of her daughter to infiltrate her cell. This bolsters her self-justification, as her readiness to dedicate her life to bringing about a better world was manipulated by an unscrupulous state. Wilsberg lets her get away with her justification that the other side had more deaths on its conscience. Fuchs was the daughter of a judge, but was not interested in following in his footsteps, as the best that lawyers can do is to alleviate the present system's worst excesses. In his previous career as a lawyer, Wilsberg defended protestors who had fallen afoul of the law by throwing stones at demonstrations. He refers to this period as the best time of his life. The ending shows a good cop, the freelance Wilsberg, the ex-terrorist, and her grown-up daughter banding together to defeat evil forces, which are still identified with the state.

If a certain nostalgic romanticism for the lost era of terrorism denotes a Leftist bias in these *krimis*, in other respects they are decidedly conservative. The investigator is nearly always male and in his thirties or forties. He is unattached, though often divorced or separated, probably with a child living with his ex-partner. And of course he is white, heterosexual, and West German. The novelists are also mainly male and of roughly the same age as their detectives, born a decade or more after the original 68ers, around the mid-1950s to 1960.[11] This is the generation old enough to remember the German Autumn but too young to be marked personally by the shootings of Ohnesorg and Dutschke. Although the novels are all set in the new century, the 1980s are the favored decades of terrorist activity. The detective/investigator is sexually available and often sleeps with clients, would-be witnesses, or random women he encounters in the course of his work. This already was the case in the 1970s, and it is hardly unique to Germany. In *Scenes of Fire* (Degenhardt, 1975), Kappel's relationship to his environment is wholly libidinized: the terrorist is his and the state prosecutor's ex-girlfriend. In the American *A Disturbance in Paris* (Fick, 1981) the hero even beds a terrorist herself, who is cured of her political deviancy as a result of sleeping with him. In *You Have to Kill Birgit Haas* (Teisseire, 1978), the French police set an unlikely honey trap for the female terrorist, who falls in love with the officer employed to seduce her. *Krimi* readers expect sex scenes. Ulrich Woelk shows that he is writing a different sort of novel when Glauberg turns down Paula's offer of a night in her bed in *The Last Performance*. After allowing himself to be seduced in a chance encounter, Wolfgang Brenner's René Dörffler in *The Execution*, in contrast, reflects that he had slept with his wife only twelve hours earlier. The point is not his promiscuity, but that identifying and tracking down terrorists, restoring order, or battling to establish it in the first place is an incipiently erotic undertaking. If order *is* restored at the end, this includes the reestablishment of structured sexual arrangements.

Conspiracy theories are key to the generic plots of the post-2000 thrillers, which proceed from the premise that the truth has been hidden from the public. In *The Blue List,* the German state wants the dangerously liberal Karsten Detlev Rohwedder killed because he threatens to derail big business and the government's plans for the ex-GDR's economy. (This is, quite bizarrely, the opposite of the role that Grass and Hochhuth assign their Rohwedder characters.) In *Wilsberg and the Third Generation,* it turns out that a cabal of ruthless elderly officers was motivated to keep the RAF alive in order to justify their own budgets and surveillance practices, which is an idea as old as the RAF itself. By the mid-2000s, their motivation is to cover up their past misdeeds. The popular work of conspiracy history first published in 1992, *The RAF-Fantom: Why Politicians and Business Need Terrorists,* is acknowledged as the "inspiration" for the film *Das Phantom* (dir. Gansel, 2000),[12] but it is a key source—the blueprint even—for the thrillers by Kehrer, Mock, Schorlau, and Sonner.

Parts of this grand conspiracy are adapted from versions that were fictionalized by Röhl and in circulation in the 1970s, none of which was shown to have any truth content. When applied to the following two decades, however, it is harder to prove them wrong. Popular fiction thrives on this uncertainity. The main reasons for arguing that the RAF itself became a fiction are that no one has been arrested for the assassinations and bomb attacks of the 1980s and early 1990s, several of which, in particular the killing of Herrhausen and Rohwedder, required high levels of professional training and precision equipment.[13] The central character in Dennis Gansel's *The Fantom* is a happy-go-lucky young cop (Leo Kramer) whose colleague is shot in a "hit" that also disposes of an RAF member turned informant (Andreas Ganz) and a lawyer (Thomas Benz) who has uncovered the state's collusion in the assassination of a liberal interior minister in October 1989, the details of which recall the killing of Herrhausen. Bad Kleinen is mentioned a number of times in the film; Ganz's parents and pre-RAF life resemble those of Wolfgang Grams. In *The Fantom,* the assassinations blamed on the nonexistent RAF discredit legitimate protest and warrant crackdowns on dissent. The assassinated interior minister was moreover campaigning against Third World debt repayments and had directed attention at the real villains, who are identified as American financial institutions. The film collapses the opposition between terrorist criminal (Ganz) and detective (Kramer), as both are shot at the point they are set to reveal the conspiracy. They are also of a similar age and resemble each other physically. Kramer adopts Ganz's father as a substitute parent and is pursued by the police for most of the film, once he is wrongly suspected of shooting his own boss. In the film's refrain, Kramer and his unsuspecting colleague are singing their own version of Rio Rieser's signature protest song "If I were the King of Germany" into the tape recorder they are using to monitor the conversation between Ganz and Benz before they are both killed. By using this well-known song and associating the detective Kramer with it, the film pits the little guys in both the RAF and the police force against big business and the sinister "state behind the state." The film also makes the conspiracy into a problem that is identified with Germany and German politics. Any hope that the truth will be revealed lies with Ganz senior, to whom Kramer has succeeded in sending the tape of his son's conversation with Benz moments before they are shot. There thus remains a hope that the truth will eventually out.

The Execution (Brenner, 2000) is based on the double premise that the crisis committee chaired by Chancellor Schmidt ordered the murder of Baader and Ensslin in Stammheim. Not knowing of the RAF's collective suicide plan, the politicians agreed to put this into effect only after the storming of the *Landshut.* The Bavarian conservative politician Franz-Josef Strauss, who appears in the novel as "the candidate for the chancellorship," is said to have suggested that the RAF prisoners be shot, though it is not believed he meant his recommendation to be taken seriously (in some versions he is suspected of being drunk).[14] However, on account both of moral objections and an attachment to the Federal Republic's Basic Law, Horst Herold (aka Hans Hunold in this novel) had the terrorists' deaths faked and established them in a new life under new identities in suburban Canada. Brenner thus overlays the conspiracy theory concerning the deaths of Baader and Ensslin (that they were murdered, as their supporters outside prison asserted) with another conspiracy of his own invention. One of his points is that the murderous plan attributed to a notorious right-wing politician is thwarted by a defender of the democratic values of the republic (Herold/Hunold). Horst Herold is from this point on in the literary historiography of the RAF a positive but thwarted hero.

Herold's casting out from the BKA in 1984 and his lonely retirement in a heavily guarded bungalow on the grounds of an army base also captured the imagination of Fritz Maria Sonner in *The Assassin's Library* (2001).[15] Since *Death Game* (dir. Breloer, 1997) captivated television audiences on the 20th anniversary of the German Autumn and changed perceptions of RAF history, Herold has also appeared as a character in at least three films: *Baader* (dir. Roth, 2002); *The Baader-Meinhof Complex* (dir. Edel, 2008), in which he is played by Bruno Ganz; and *Mogadishu* (dir. Richter, 2008). He also inspired the detectives in the comedy film *What to Do in Case of Fire* (dir. Schnitzler, 2002) and *The Blue List* (Schorlau, 2003), as well as *The Ascent to Heaven of an Enemy of the State* (Delius, 1992), the first novel to portray him. Each time, his understanding of his terrorist adversary grows from empathy to something approaching outright sympathy. The Herold character is humane, self-sacrificing, committed to a good cause, and (after retirement) badly treated and unappreciated by his former employers. The RAF's number-one adversary is thus recuperated into fiction as a victim. Given how the Left demonized Herold while he still headed the BKA, this change in his reputational fortunes is, to say the least, unexpected. Nostalgia for the old Federal Republic may be one part of the explanation. In *The Assassin's Library*, Konrad Bärloch's lonely retired existence stands emblematically for the abandonment of the recent West German past. The wish for national reconciliation may be another reason. Alternatively, one could argue that Germans want to have it both ways by identifying with both the state and its adversaries. In other words, that through some apparently bizarre dialectal process the terrorists now represent the state.

Hunold / Herold comes out of retirement to track down Stürmer / Baader in *The Execution* and is the real hero and moral soul of the novel. Hunold combated the RAF in the name of progressive reform and because he believed in the democratic institutions of the new German republic. He also has a utopian plan to use information technology, which Herold pioneered for use in catching criminals, to solve all social ills. In the novel's overcomplicated finale, Stürmer is killed as his ingenious attempt to assassinate the federal chancellor is foiled. The 68er government of the SPD and the Greens survives, however, its structures solid enough to withstand an assault from a political *revenant* and his newfound allies. The democratic republican left is thus triumphant, as the new-old RAF is defeated by an alliance of Hunold and his former anti-state adversaries, who are now in power.

As this not always deft but often cerebral thriller begins, Ralf Stürmer is caught on video killing his son-in-law in a by-now uncharacteristic outburst of anger. He is frustrated at having to accept the younger man as his new employer. Stürmer promptly flees to Germany, where he has not set foot for more than 20 years. His wife Margot (Gudrun Ensslin), now debilitated by alcoholism, takes a later plane to join him, not suspecting that the friendly fellow passenger who is ever helpful with a credit card once they arrive in Germany is a Canadian detective. The Ensslin portrait is one of the novel's weaknesses and indicative of a general macho attitude in an overwhelmingly male adventure caper. Stürmer's interaction with contemporary German politics is effected through the sexually opportunistic, up-and-coming Engelhardt Seelenbinder, formerly a terrorist gunrunner. As the novel reaches its crisis, he is appointed *staatsekretär* (junior minister) in the Red–Green coalition. Seelenbinder's careerism and personal morals are not edifying, but his turning away from political violence was based on genuine insight. He saw through the self-serving bravado of his comrades. After standing up for his point of view during a drunken argument some time in 1981 or 1982, he bade farewell to his "grass-roots group" and set out on a new course.

> On this evening he got so drunk in Mehringhof that he collapsed on his way home. Two Turks took him to the Urbankrankenhaus where he had his stomach pumped. He was released again the following morning after being required to pay 187.60 DM.
> This is when the new life of Engelhardt Seelenbinder began. He avoided the bars frequented by the squatters, the autonomen, and the veteran Sixty-Eighters. He joined the Green Alternative List and set off on the campaign trail.[16]

The drunkenness that lubricates his transformation should alert us to the possible instability of his personal position, but his democratic politics are those of the novel. *The Execution* distances itself from violence, but shows that it has not been disavowed by protestors in contemporary Berlin. Stürmer falls in with two modern-day activists and makes common cause with them. The ostensible object of their protest is unemployment, which exceeded the symbolic four million mark in the year the novel was published, which it had last reached on the eve of Hitler's takeover. For Brenner, unemployment is an excuse for radical protest rather than a cause. Although the original RAF had given up on the German workers in favor of the subject peoples of Vietnam and Palestine, in the 2000s the causes of violent protest are more likely to be domestic and economic.

As it never made it to paperback and has not managed the transfer to film or television, *The Execution* must count as something of a flop. Brenner is rather careless with generic expectations. The political implausibility in the plot is less significant than the bizarre psychological characterization: neither Stürmer nor Margot is remotely convincing. Given that the historical models of the novel's characters are so well known, this must count as a failing. Yet *The Execution* heralded the beginning of the new RAF trend, which continued through the new decade. Fiction anticipated history once again: Seelenbinder's real-life prototypes were Jürgen Trittin and Joschka Fischer. Both leading Green politicians were soon caught up in very public disputes about their links with left-wing extremism in the 1970s. Both survived in office. The "revivalist fiction," which I discuss in the last chapter, posits a connection between anticapitalist activism in the 2000s and the RAF epoch.

Herold, appearing now as Konrad Bärloch, is the main character in *The Assassin's Library* (Sonner, 2001). Franz Maria Sonner sets the terrorist part of the action in the 1980s and uses the politics of that decade as the motivating factor.[17] He gives these as: NATO rearmament and the SPD-led coalition's agreement to the stationing of new atomic missiles in the FRG; the Flick corruption scandal, which involved illegal donations by the Flick conglomerate to individual politicians and political parties; the CIA campaign against the Sandinista government in Nicaragua; Ronald Reagan; and the building of another runway at Frankfurt Airport, the famous *startbahn west*. The novel is in two parts, "Damals" (Back then) and "Heute" (Today); the second part is three times as long as the first. "Damals" is set in 1984, which Günter Grass dubbed "Orwell's Year;" it recounts how the central character (Jakob Amon) comes to shoot a leading industrialist (Karmann) dead as he slept. Jakob's intention was to wound only, as he aimed his fire at what he thought were his victim's legs. Sonner makes it impossible for the reader to feel sympathy for Karmann. As an SS officer towards the end of World War II, Karmann ordered the killing of 60 civilian hostages in Czechoslovakia. In the intervening 40 years, he has become a leading figure in the business world and is now president of the "Industry Conference." He supports nuclear power and the extension of the city's airport. Sonner has borrowed some biographical details from Hanns-Martin Schleyer, but neither Schleyer nor any of the RAF's other victims could be accused of a war crime. In recent fiction and historiography, the trend has been for a more differentiated understanding of Schleyer. The idea that such a figure as Karmann could be officially protected in the Federal Republic in 1984 represents the point where this clever, highly literary novel begins to falsify rather than adapt the history that is its subject.

Sonner employs a number of tropes from detective fiction. There are two murders committed some 14 years apart (in 1984 and 1998), criminal investigations, suspicion of conspiracies, the detective knowing the criminal's mind, and the freelance maverick detective working against a corrupt system. One of the conspiracies is that Bärloch and his assistant, Horst Brill, were released from the BKA for reasons of national politics: the public did not want their repressive measures anymore. Dismissing them proves shortsighted. When Karmann is found dead in his bed, Bärloch works out immediately that Jakob was the murderer. The material for an article published by the Jewish concentration camp survivor Gabor Demeter had come via Jakob's commissioning editor at the broadcasting station Hessischer Rundfunk. The retired Bärloch does not tell anyone that he has worked out that Jakob was the murderer because he is not asked.

Not all parts of the novel add up, and the denouement is not as powerful as the first section. Jakob is finally murdered unintentionally by Bärloch's former assistant, Brill. While Jakob's original murder of Karmann is not revealed, the murder of Jakob himself is solved by a character announcing how it happened. The discovery by Jakob's friend, the writer Marco Sentenza, that Bärloch and Jakob both borrowed the same library books alerts Bärloch to the danger that Sentenza himself faces from Brill, but the plot has become overcomplicated by this stage. Its peculiar negotiation of the Jewish material notwithstanding, in its account of the reckoning for a past murder, the novel has a moral depth that distinguishes it from other *krimis*. Sonner's ideological agenda in this respect is not dissimilar to Brenner and Breloer's.

Sales figures are not the right measurement for a work like *The Assassin's Library*, which counts as a *succès d'estime* though it is yet to be reprinted.[18] It is a serious piece of literary crime fiction, inspired partly by Dostoyevsky, but more by *Crime and Punishment* than *The Possessed*. Sonner's unreadiness to take on the most sensitive issue (the legacy of the Holocaust), however, shows up the limitations of his ambition. While there is no historical model for Karmann, the Revolutionary Cells (RZ) did claim the murder of the FDP politician Heinz-Herbert Karry, economics minister for the state of Hesse, on May 11, 1981. He too was shot in his bed, in Frankfurt, and killed accidentally, his attackers claiming in a communiqué that they aimed for his legs with the intent to wound.[19] Karry supported the building of an extra runway at Frankfurt Airport, and was an advocate of nuclear power. As the national treasurer of the FDP, he was also implicated in the Flick Affair. Karry's murderers have never been identified. As the RZ did not carry out other such shootings the authenticity of the communiqué published in their name some four weeks after the murder has been questioned. It transpired, however, that the murder weapon, which was stolen from an American army base in 1970, had been found in a car belonging to Joschka Fischer three years later. In 1998, the right-wing press used Fischer's connection in their campaign to discredit him in the run-up to the elections; the story was raked over in the media once more in early 2001, when Fischer was called as a witness in the trial of former RZ member Hans-Joachim Klein. The case was ripe to be turned into a thriller.[20]

The problem for Sonner is that Karry was not in the SS. His past, in fact, could not have been more different, as he was half-Jewish. His father was sent to a concentration camp and he himself worked as a forced laborer under the Nazis. Sonner thus does more than simplify or adapt his source, as novelists are obliged to do, he turns it inside out. With such a high-profile and recent incident so rich in conflicted symbolic meanings, it is worth wondering why. The novelist's changes shed light on the fraught area of the Left's incorporation of German-Jewish history into its own narratives about itself. One explanation is retrospective wishful thinking. From the point of view of 2001, a target of the Revolutionary Cells must have had links with the Nazis rather than with their victims. Yet picking a Jewish victim would not have been completely out of step with RZ policy. Some of their members operated out of bases in the Middle East that were run by anti-Israel Arab militants, who did not always recognize the distinction between "Jewish" and "Zionist." A number worked with "Carlos the Jackal," whose own first mission was to shoot the Jewish president of the British retailer Marks and Spencer because of his support for Israel.[21] The two Germans who notoriously selected the Jewish passengers from hijacked Air France plane at Entebbe were in the RZ.

Sonner is not interested in taking on this subject, however. The political questions in his novel have to be black and white. His German-Jewish politics appear in other respects impeccable, but the suspicion lingers that he is compensating for altering his source material so radically. *The Assassin's Library* does feature, however, a Jewish character with a Holocaust past. The three other novels from the 2000s with such characters are *The Photographer* (Chaplet, 2002), which is sensationalist, and *The Pale Heart of the Revolution* (Dannenberg, 2004) and *Dreamers of the Absolute* (Wildenhain, 2008), which are both revisionist in intent. In *The Assassin's Library*, a former concentration camp inmate, Gabor Demeter, who attempts to expose leading industrialist Karmann's war record, has published a memoir of his experiences that plays a key role in the plot. Demeter himself refuses to reveal his Jewishness to newspaper editors, whom he tries to interest in the Karmann story. Were he to do so, he explains to his wife, they would take his story for that reason, and he wants them to publish it on its merits and because they are interested in exposing a war criminal. The idea here is that a Jewish journalist can get anything about the Nazi past published *because he is Jewish*. This is at best a slur and it goes unchallenged in the novel.

The Holocaust references do not end here. Sonner uses the title of Demeter's memoir, *My Life*, as the title of the last chapter of *The Assassin's Library*. This was also the title chosen by revered literary critic and Holocaust survivor Marcel Reich-Ranicki for his autobiography, published in 1999 [22] Sonner refers three times to the title of another recent representation of the Holocaust, Roberto Benigni's acclaimed but controversial film, *Life Is Beautiful* (1998).

Marco Sentenza, the writer who saves Jakob's manuscript entitled *Assassination* (*Attentat*) from destruction and also helps the retired detective Bärloch identify his erstwhile assistant Brill as Jakob's accidental murderer, resolves at the end to make the best of his future, having narrowly escaped Brill's vengeance with his life. Sentenza is approaching his threshold fortieth birthday and wants to view his problems from a sunnier perspective. After all: "Life is beautiful." The passage containing this sentence both ends *The Assassin's Library* and serves as its epigraph. But the full paragraph is only produced at the end of the novel, when it turns out that its first three lines were omitted in the epigraph. They run as follows: "I come home early in the morning. I sleep until the afternoon of the following day. First of all I will phone Helga, in the evening I will watch some films again: Roberto Benigni, *Life Is Beautiful*" (215). The life of Benigni's central character, an Italian Jew, appears to be beautiful until he and his young son are deported to a concentration camp by the Nazis. His non-Jewish wife insists on accompanying them. He attempts to hide the horrific reality of what has befallen them from their son by turning what is happening into a game. The film is about Holocaust denial by a victim in the midst of the Holocaust. Thus, as a fictitious writer character engaging with the subject of terrorism, Sentenza appropriates Jewish experience through his use of the two titles (*My Life* and *Life Is Beautiful*). This signals what Sonner himself has done more surreptitiously in his novel by obliterating his Jewish sources. As the identities of both murderers (Karmann's and Jakob's) are kept secret, the history is not worked through, but remains repressed. Without wanting to do so, *The Assassin's Library* enacts the historical forgetting that its central character, Jakob Amon, ostensibly sought to counter through his shooting. It is as if Sonner transfers Karry's Jewish identity to Demeter as a compensatory gesture for taking it away from the victim of the RZ assassination. Heinz-Herbert Karry is the novel's repressed guilty secret, which expresses itself in a series of unwanted ways.

The eponymous figure in *The Photographer* (2002, Chaplet) is the novel's first murder victim and never appears in person, despite giving the *krimi* its title. It seems that she was killed because she identified a RAF fugitive living under an assumed identity in French exile. Like the fugitive, the Jewish Ada Silbermann is a refugee from German history. *The Photographer* includes recollections of political murder, collaboration, and reprisals during the Nazi occupation of France, but he details serve little more than to provide atmospheric color to the Baader-Meinhof inspired intrigue, which is played out at the beginning of the new century. The Jewish motif is redundant. The same cannot be said of *The Pale Heart of the Revolution* (Dannenberg, 2004), which belongs in a discussion of popular fiction only insofar as it uses grotesque satire, parody, and comedy names (the real-life RAF-lawyer Klaus Croissant, for example, who identified so closely with his clients that he joined forces with them, is portrayed as Borsalino von Baguette). One plot strand is based in a fictional version of the Institute for Social Research, founded by the critical theorists Theodor Adorno and Max Horkheimer, who both fled the Nazis on account of their Jewish heritage. Dannenberg draws on the view that concerted harassment by student protestors in lectures hastened Adorno's death from a heart attack in 1969. The students were angry with him because, despite his avowed Marxist-inspired critique of capitalism, he refused to play a leading role in their struggle. Residual anti-Semitism is not usually given as a cause of their grievance. In the novel, Aaron Wizent is called a "Pentagon Jew" during one disturbance;[23] in the next protest, which kills him, a Molotov cocktail is hurled in is direction. Killing a Jew is the 68er generation's original crime in the symbolic scheme of this revisionist novel. It binds together its perpetrators who, after reenacting their fathers' Oedipal revolt, control intellectual debate and academic research in the FRG over the next three decades. In popular German Baader-Meinhof fiction, the Jewish or Holocaust theme is thus either guiltily ignored (Sonner), employed to evoke a mood (Chaplet), or orchestrated into a fierce polemic (Dannenberg).

Wolfgang Mock in *The Flight of the Seraphim* (2003) is not as fluent as some of the *krimi* writers, but he has doses of sex, fighting, and nocturnal ambushes in a lavishly exotic setting. Mock's *krimi* is also a closure narrative. His James Bond style villain is working for the European Union to build a rocket-launching site on the mid-Atlantic Cape Verde Islands. Mock is telling a story that he wants his readers to believe has been suppressed. It involves the Basque terrorist separatists in ETA collaborating with the RAF to hole up on the Verdes with the government's tacit consent.

There are in fact two villains in *The Flight of the Seraphim*. One is the European Union itself, with its neocolonialist plans to develop the islands. The other is Sarrazin, an egomaniacal secret-service chief, who gets his comeuppance at the hands of Max Danco, the younger brother of a RAF terrorist who was killed while collaborating with ETA. In the summer of 1989, Alex Danco was lured by Sarrazin into a shootout in Spain. For the next 12 years, his younger brother feels the responsibility for his death, because he believed Sarrazin shared his aim of persuading Alex to leave the RAF/ETA and Max had been collaborating with him on that basis. When Max learns the truth, he can begin to take his life in a new direction. Once more the past relinquishes its grip on an individual, after the truth about his own past is discovered, but the wider injustice lives on.

The Blue List: Dengler's First Case, which also was published in 2003, shows Wolfgang Schorlau to be a sure-footed genre writer. *Dengler* quickly became a domestic hit. By 2009, the first book in the series had been through 11 reprints and had inspired four sequels. Here at last is the successful Baader-Meinhof thriller. Schorlau uses a number of formulas. The narrative is fast-paced. The sex, violence, humor, intrigues, and subplots are all cleverly woven together. Dengler is an ex-BKA man who left the force because he could not stomach its compromises with the truth. While he is likeable, quirky, highly competent, and honest, his own integrity is compromised by occasional personal weakness as he battles against an intrinsically corrupt world. These are often twin premises of detective novels.

What is striking in Schorlau's debut is the extremism of its antistate and anticapitalist politics, which are qualified by nostalgia for the economic and social conditions of "real existing socialism" in the German Democratic Republic. As in Wolfgang Becker's hit film *Goodbye Lenin!* which appeared in 2003, nostalgia for East German communism has a West German stamp here. Regret that an alternative to western capitalism had ceased to exist on the other side of the Wall produces a rosy retrospective representation of it. Whereas one interpretation of *Goodbye Lenin!* is that it works through this nostalgia to expose the fantasy on which it is based, no such self-reflexive mechanism is present in *The Blue List*. For Schorlau, the economic and social history of the past 15 years in the "new federal states" is a story of what would not have happened if Karsten Detlev Rohwedder, head of the Treuhand agency charged with finding buyers for GDR state enterprises, had not been assassinated on April 1, 1991. The plan for a select number of these state-owned comapnies, the names of which are on the "blue list" of the novel's title, to become, in effect, self-managing workers' cooperatives could have changed the course of history. Devised by an economics professor from the University of Innsbruck, it was modeled on the experiences of an Austrian firm taken over by its employees at the end of World War II that eventually enjoyed great success. In 1990–1991, West German business saw its own interests threatened by Rohwedder's enthusiasm for this socialist policy. West German firms wanted to buy up their rivals in the East in order to close them down and take over their markets. Less than two months after Rohwedder's assassination, an Austrian Lauda passenger jet crashed into the jungle, shortly after taking off from Bangkok en route to Vienna. On board was the academic economist who had been advising the Treuhand boss. Schorlau imagines what could have happened had the professor, whom he calls Paul Stein, missed the plane, which, in *The Blue List*, was brought down in order to kill him. As Brenner did in *The Execution*, Schorlau thus explores the realm of the counterfactual, but with the opposite ideological intention.

Another strand in the novel is a fictionalized account of the attempted arrest and shooting of Wolfgang Grams. The Grams case has been more discussed than any other terrorist death, including the Stammheim suicides, and Grams has been the subject of more fictional and filmic treatments than any other RAF member since the original leadership trio. This is remarkable, given that little is known about him in between his "going underground" around 1984 and his death at Bad Kleinen some nine years later. In his afterword, Schorlau describes Grams as a care-free young hippie who could not have also been an assassin and maker of state-of-the-art bombs. Schorlau appears not to accept that in the seven years Grams spent in the RAF before the Herrhausen killing, during which time he is believed to have lived in the Middle East, where he could have received all manner of training, he could have learnt the skills of a professional marksman.

In Schorlau's story, Grams is called Uwe Krems and is gulled by an undercover police agent into taking part in the Rohwedder assassination. Krems is naïve and wants to please and to compensate for his past failings. Once again we have terrorist as victim of the state. His bungled arrest and killing at Bad Kleinen are a result of another conspiracy, but this time it is not one that Dengler can sort out. Dengler does succeed in unraveling what befell Professor Paul Stein, and he reunites him with his beautiful young daughter, who has begun a passionate affair with Dengler. Before there can be a happy ending, the three of them overcome a trio of hired killers at Stein's Tuscan hideaway. At the end, the price that must be paid for the happy reunion of Stein with his daughter is silence on the Rohwedder scandal. Big finance is still pulling all the strings. The novel thus has its cake and eats it by uncovering the scandal and explaining in the next breath why it must stay a secret.

The Blue List established the conventions for a terrorist thriller. *Wilsberg and the Third Generation* (Kehrer, 2006), the work of a consummate specialist, rearranges a number of them excitingly, but they are by now familiar. Two Baader-Meinhof *krimis* from 2009 are even more formulaic. The good and bad cops in *Autumn Messenger* (Hoeth, 2009) are named just that: Good and Bad, as if to underline their generic function. *Murderer's Child* (Mayer, 2009) follows a teenage girl's investigation into her parents' dark pasts, which is prompted by her discovery of a corpse on the beach near her mother's home. *Murderer's Child* is written for education, *Autumn Messenger* for entertainment. Hoeth's portrayal indicates a turning away from political controversy, which is evident in other Baader-Meinhof fiction from the end of the 2000s. The trend mirrors national consensus on economic and foreign policy in the wake of the financial crisis of 2008 and the military stalemate in Afghanistan.

In Thomas Hoeth's *Autumn Messenger,* a thirty-year-old woman believes that her mother, a notorious terrorist who played a key role in the events of the German Autumn, was killed shortly after her own birth. Her life changes when she sees a woman who looks like her mother on a news report of the Stuttgart Easter March, next to a banner protesting against the presence of German soldiers in Afghanistan. A small group of characters who played key roles in the events of 1977 now decide to settle old scores, once the daughter has hired a detective to find her mother. The terrorist defense lawyer, the former terrorist who is now a senior academic, the former inmate of a *Fürsorgeheim* who made the RAF into a substitute family, as well as the police are all trapped in some sort of time warp.

Monika Gürtle is an unwilling woman terrorist whose loyalties were tested when she became pregnant. She really only joined the RAF because she was required to repeat a year's schooling. There is plenty of action in *Autumn Messenger;* the settings range from a monastery to a high-class S&M brothel frequented by local dignitaries, which Monika Gürtle now runs. The novel exploits its material along with its readers. In a discussion of the "libidinal bonds" between the RAF and its supporters, which depended on the masochism of the radical Left, Kraushaar writes that "Ulrike Meinhof and Gudrun Ensslin would have played the role of dominatrix equally effectively."[24]

On the whole, the female terrorist is rarely sexualized in German novels, in contrast to international fiction. Hoeth is the first novelist to do so overtly in *Autumn Messenger,* albeit with respect to the female terrorists' effect on the police and general public. The young Monika, beautiful and pregnant, was set up by the malign terrorist mastermind Christian Mohr to be arrested. He wanted her to be punished because she wished to give up. Apart from Mohr, who is now coming to the end of a long jail sentence, all the characters associated with terrorism in the late 1970s wanted to get out (*aussteigen*). All live in fear of exposure in the present. Monika was carrying photographs that Mohr wanted to fall into police hands. They showed the Baader-Meinhof trial judge having sex with an underage male prostitute, who was acting on Mohr's own instructions. The plot is foiled because one of the arresting officers is Monika's childhood sweetheart. This married father of three is also the father of Monika's child to be. In an even less expected twist, he is shot by his own friend and colleague in moral outrage at his sexual duplicity. Monika, who adopts the role of the Homeric Circe in the novel's denouement, 30 years later, represents a sexual rather than a violent danger. Social identity depends on the exclusion of a sexual threat embodied by a traditional femme fatale. But Monika's pregnancy and her desire to leave her terrorist cell indicate that she has been falsely labeled. All she wanted to do was to settle down with her baby. In the intervening 30 years, after giving birth in secret and giving up her baby for adoption, she has been a plaything of the security services, first in the Middle East, then the GDR. At the end of *Autumn Messenger,* mother and daughter are reunited, while the father's murderer is punished when he succumbs to the same sexual temptation as his late colleague and photographs are published on the Internet. The murderer's lover is not a terrorist but a Polish prostitute employed by Monika herself. Society no longer projects its fears of its own desires on to terrorist women and it applauds the exposure of hypocrisy. Once more the villains work for the state and most of the terrorists are reluctant resisters to it.

Murderer's Child, although a very different kind of book, is similar in its use of formulas. The middle-aged characters remain trapped by their past, because they have covered it up, rather than address it. They are scarred by their experiences, living in fear that their past deed will one day catch up with them. It finally does so in the shape of Viktoria, the long-lost daughter of a now leading Green Party politician. At age three, Viktoria was sent by her terrorist mother to an orphans' camp in Jordan, and she did not return to Germany until her grandparents tracked her down eight years later. (This is the fate that Meinhof planned for her twin daughters in 1970.) Now in her early thirties, Viktoria is getting her revenge on her mother's ex-comrades, who she is convinced were responsible for her mother's aberrant behavior. For her to retain her image of her mother intact, however, she targets the men before turning the gun on herself. The novel features two daughters who are in different ways dealing with their mothers' terrorist legacies. Viktoria is convinced that her mother was an unwilling terrorist, led astray by her contemporaries. She could not have been both a mother and a murderer. The bad mother is punished as her career is ruined when her past comes to light, thanks to her daughter's revenge murders. Levke's mother, in contrast, is redeemed through her daughter's actions, because she finally faces up to her past when the pair discuss it together.

Gina Mayer is an excellent teacher, because she presents her school-age readers with the conclusion that the past is a project that needs to be worked on. There cannot be closure, only a working solution. The romantic subplot between Levke and a Polish builder ends when Tom returns to Poland to be with his fiancée. A romantic happy ending is postponed. Yet the final scene takes place in Berlin with the surviving characters reflecting on all the changes the country has gone through. The past is the past, they agree.

Even if cover-ups and conspiracies are the *krimi*'s lifeblood, the shape that they take is revealing of their readers' and authors' anxieties, repressed wishes and fears. One explanation of conspiracy theories is that history's losers latch onto them to rationalize their own failures.[25] In the Baader-Meinhof context, they also imply a denial of agency on the part of the key figures who are revealed not to be responsible for their own actions. Cultural representations generally play a subsidiary role in the elaboration of conspiracy theories, whereas in the 2000s in Germany with respect to Baader-Meinhof, the conspiracies and the theories that underpin them are largely delegated to fiction and cinema.[26] Does this show that nobody really believes in them but that novelists wonder what the world would look like if they were true? In other words, is the whole point that it is not for real? In German popular fiction, we have untold histories that *they don't want you to know*; suppressed family ties to the terrorists or to their adversaries; extreme suspicion of all forms of state authority; and collusion between police and terrorists. We also have the past haunting the present as uncompleted business and a refusal to incorporate Jewish source material, except for instrumental ends. The recent *krimis* also reflect political developments since 1998: first, a legitimization of the Red–Green Coalition; then a pro-RAF critique of contemporary society. Dissatisfaction with market economics, criticism of the European Union, and a conviction that what passes for Anglo-Saxon neoliberalism may be inherently un-German results in the RAF's becoming equated in the national symbolic memory with "upright revolt." This leads to a nonconfrontational, default identification with a domesticated form of historical terrorism that casts the state as villain and allows the reader to identify with the former terrorist, quite often as the victim.

CHAPTER FIVE

BAADER-MEINHOF TRANSLATED:
FROM *DIE HARD* TO AL-QAEDA

Until recently, German history thrillers were more likely to get written abroad than in Germany itself. Cold War spy fiction, although often set in a divided Germany, overwhelmingly was produced by British or American authors. Such novels often confront a compromised individual with a final set of deep moral choices in the midst of a crumbling order. The questions that they address are universal rather than specifically German. Today there is a thriving subgenre of crime fiction set against the background of German twentieth-century history, mainly in the Nazi era but also including the Weimar Republic and the aftermath of World War I. For German novelists, the division of the country was too immediate or painful a subject for it to be turned into entertainment, however thought-provoking and morally engaged much of the English-language fiction might be. In comparison with *The Spy Who Came in from the Cold* (John le Carré, 1963) and *The Innocent* (Ian McEwan, 1989), German novels which feature the Berlin Wall are ponderous and worthy, when they are not driven by ideology.[1] East German writers faced censure for so much as alluding to "the anti-Fascist protection barrier," while their West German counterparts were more likely to pretend that it did not exist. *The Happy Ones* (Zahl, 1979) is typical. Although the book is set in a corner of West Berlin hemmed in by the Wall the characters appear barely to notice it.

The situation is rather different with Baader-Meinhof novels as most of them are written in German by Germans. International novelists do fill gaps, however, by incorporating source material that the Germans ignore. They also continued to write on the subject when the Germans stopped. In the 1990s the most popular Baader-Meinhof novel in Germany was a translation from the Swedish by Jan Guillou, *The Democratic Terrorist* (1987, tr. into German 1990). There are, however, two phases of interest, which do correspond to those in Germany itself. In the first of these, Baader-Meinhof terrorism is a key component of the novelists' understanding of contemporary Germany, which they interpret through the prism of Nazism and the Holocaust; in the second, they are more likely to explore the Arab-Israeli conflict or Islamic extremism in the wake of 9/11. International authors exploit the Baader-Meinhof theme to address political questions in their own countries and seem unaware of the German fiction, most of which was written for a national readership and was not usually translated out of German.[2] None of the novels by Zahl, Delius, Goetz, or Geissler, for instance, which Sandra Beck dubs "canonical," nor those by Scholz and Woelk, published more recently, have come out in English.[3] In contrast, classic German fiction set in Nazi Germany (by authors such as Grass, Böll, Wolf, and Schlink) made an instant international impact. Whether writing literary or popular fiction, international novelists cannot be said to write in a contemporary "terrorist tradition" any more than German novelists harked back to Dostoyevsky and Conrad. But their knowledge of contemporary German history is usually faultless. Stefan Aust is often a key source.

Foreign writers rarely engage directly with German politics, but they are ready to show sympathy with idealist German revolutionaries. In his book about the RAF, British anarchist Tom Vague quotes from *Hamlet* in his epigraph (which is superimposed onto an image of a hand grenade), asking:

Whether 'tis nobler in the mind to suffer
the slings and arrows of outrageous fortune,
or to take arms against a sea of troubles,
and by opposing end them?[4]

He then punctures his own dramatic pathos by adding at the base of the page: "Well, it's better than bottling it up!" Vague paraphrases Aust and Bommi Baumann for a mildly alternative readership, but he anglicizes RAF history so that the group becomes a German version of the Sex Pistols, whose heyday was also 1976–77. The Baader-Meinhof cult is sustained today by websites such as that run by Richard Huffman (www.baader -meinhof.com) and is expressed in such self-publications as the print-on-demand novel, *Love, Gudrun Ensslin* (Corbin, 2010), which seems to have been inspired in part by the film of Aust's book. When international novelists make claims on behalf of German terrorists, they exceed anything expressed by German writers and reflect their own national context. In the dramatic monologue *I'm Ulrike—Screaming* (1975) Franca Rame, an activist playwright and wife of Dario Fo, takes every detail of RAF propaganda on prison mistreatment as fact. In *It Happened Tomorrow* (Rame, 1977), she even dramatizes the murder of Baader, Ensslin, and Raspe in

Stammheim.[5] In the novel *A Disturbance in Paris* (Fick, 1981), the central character, who is an American film director named Alexander Marin, is asked by the terrorists to make a documentary on Meinhof's life from footage and photographs that are provided for him. The purpose is to reassert core values after her death and other recent defeats. Fick invents not only individual quotations from Meinhof but a whole revolutionary ideology. She is to be depicted as a reincarnation of the republican heroine from the Spanish Civil War, *La Pasionaria,* whom Marin has always revered.

In international work, extremist politics is also taken more readily to be an extension of avant-garde art. *Journeys from Berlin/1971* (dir. Rainer, 1980) is the prime example in film. It is matched by Alban Lefranc's trilogy of novelettes in literature. In *The Invisible Circus* (Egan, 1995), a relatively brief association with the RAF is part of the heroine's pattern of self-destructive behavior, which ends in suicide. In Jennifer Egan's novel, which was made into a film starring Cameron Diaz, the 1960s were about hedonism and escape from convention: teaming up with the RAF was part of a program of pushing life to the limits, otherwise expressed through experiments with drugs and sexuality. Lefranc published the first two of his brief novels in French; the third has so far only appeared in German.[6] Each is centered on a German radical, from the world of film (Rainer Werner Fassbinder, 1945–1982); literature (Bernward Vesper, 1937–1971); and popular music (Christa Päffgen, known as Nico, 1938–1988). The hallmark of each life is self-destruction, brought on by an inability to break free emotionally from the ties to the Nazi past or to heal the wounds caused by early experiences of war and ideological indoctrination. Lefranc's narrative style is fragmentary and associative. He juxtaposes imagined conversations or interior monologues with chunks of quotation from outside sources (which are acknowledged at the end of the book). Each life was lived on the edge, and moments of joy were snatched from periods of mental suffering. Lefranc sees the experiences and achievements of both Fassbinder and Vesper through the prism of the RAF and their own entanglement with it (Fassbinder through making films about them; Vesper through his relationship with Ensslin). This perspective becomes forced for Fassbinder while for Nico it is quite perverse, but in Lefranc's vision, modern Germany is a land of extremes.

For all the differences in approach in what is a disparate body of work, the pattern of publication dates for international fiction is in line with that for the German novels. The dip in interest between the mid-1980s and the beginning of the 2000s is somewhat briefer. *You Have to Kill Birgit Haas* (Teisseire, 1978), *Nothing Lasts Forever* (Thorp, 1979), *How German Is It. Wie Deutsch ist es* (Abish, 1979), and *A Disturbance in Paris* (Fick, 1981) were written in the wake of 1977, when international interest in German terrorism was most intense. All are more adventurous and politically more imaginative than the contemporaneous German novels. By the end of the Cold War, this interest dried up, reviving in the 2000s in the wake of al-Qaeda, rather than because of developments in Germany. For the two characters in Don Delillo's short story "Looking at Meinhof," which begins at the exhibition of Gerhard Richter's *18 Oktober 1977* in New York's Museum of Modern Art, discussing the RAF is a form of therapy.[7]

The first foreign state to produce a writer—or at least a filmmaker—who showed an interest in Baader-Meinhof terrorism was the German Democratic Republic. The film was an adaptation of the West German left-wing detective thriller, *Scenes of Fire* (Degenhardt, 1975). Thus, if there is a GDR take on Baader-Meinhof terrorism, it is to be found in this East German cinematic adaptation of a West German novel. This situation was unusual. German–German literary crossovers usually entailed republishing works that were successful in one German state by a publisher in the other. Although the two states existed next to each other, there was no tradition of western writers setting their fiction in the east, or vice versa. This is what makes the postunification *Too Far Afield* (Grass, 1995) a pioneering feat of the imagination. For one thing, novelists lacked the basic knowledge of everyday life in the other Germany. Also, an East German novel on West German terrorism would also have been obliged to toe the party line and would have risked being very dull. Official GDR quarters showed an interest in Baader-Meinhof as a theme. *The German Sisters* (dir. von Trotta) won the GDR Critics' Prize in 1984. Heinrich Böll's writings were distributed widely throughout the eastern bloc, including *Katharina Blum* and *Safety Net*. *My Sister, My Antigone* (Weil, 1980) was reprinted by the GDR publishers Volk & Welt immediately after it appeared in the West. In his most famous play, *The Hamletmachine* (1977) the GDR's most celebrated dramatist, Heiner Müller (who was for long periods also among the most persecuted), conflates Ulrike Meinhof ("the woman at the end of the rope") with Shakespeare's Ophelia. When he was awarded the Büchner Prize in 1985, he hushed his western hosts when he referred to Meinhof as if she were a literary character:

> daughter of Prussia and latter-day mistress of one of German literature's other foundlings, who dug his own grave on the Wannsee [Heinrich von Kleist], protagonist in the last drama of the bourgeois world, the armed RETURN OF THE YOUNG COMRADE FROM THE LIMEPIT [from Brecht's *The Measures Taken*], [...] a sister with Marie's bloody necklace [from Büchner's *Woyzeck*].[8]

Meinhof was the only actor from the postwar West in Müller's tortured drama of German twentieth-century history.

The novel *Scenes of Fire* was first published in Bertelsmann's *Autorenedition* in 1975 and was issued in the GDR by Aufbau in 1976 and 1977. In 1978, it was made into a film by the DEFA studios under the direction of the veteran Horst E. Brandt. It is the novel about West German protest politics in the mid-1970s that a GDR author could have written, had one tried to do so and had he or she possessed the requisite knowledge of left-wing politics in the FRG. Degenhardt was a member of the Deutsche Kommunistische Partei (DKP), which was formed in 1968 after the banning of the original Kommunistische Partei Deutschlands (KPD) as unconstitutional in 1956. The new party officially supported the GDR, which in turn supported it with funds. Degenhardt's central character is a 34-year-old radical lawyer named Bruno Kappel who up to seven years earlier (the novel is set in 1974) had shared a girlfriend called Karin Kunze, an underground member of an unnamed far-Left terrorist group, with his friend Baller, now a state prosecutor. Kappel is caught between the two. The novel follows his search for Kunze to pass on a tip-off from Baller that her group has been infiltrated by the *Verfassungsschutz*. Kappel wants her to give up. During his search, Kappel comes across a campaign to save an expanse of countryside from being turned into a military reservation for NATO exercises, which is called "Klein-Schweden" because of battles fought there during the Thirty Years' War. Kunze and her friends are likely to want to subvert this campaign, which is run by grassroots activists who have mobilized local opposition.

At the heart of the novel is the question of the appropriate and most effective means of political action, which are debated by the characters within a broad frame of theoretical and historical reference. Klein-Schweden is the focus of a much wider struggle, which is waged on the ground but also in the press. The terrorists are parasites on the popular cause, unintentionally acting against the interests of the working classes. Uncertain of his direction, signaled by his series of erotic encounters, Kappel learns to value solidarity and community. The novel posits a direct connection between NATO and capitalist economics and shows up the ruthlessness of the West German state, which relishes the excuse that the terrorists have given them to use violence on the protestors. At the end, Kappel, having failed to influence Kunze, appears to want to stay in his working-class hometown, which recalls the ending of Peter Schneider's *Lenz* (1973).

The film of the novel is the first Baader-Meinhof thriller. In the film *Scenes of Fire*, Karin Kunze plays a bigger role, thus breaking the taboo of representing terrorists as terrorists that was in effect in West German novels and films of the 1970s and beyond. In other respects, the adaptation is remarkably faithful, but in a GDR context, the role played by the *Verfassungsschutz* inevitably brings to mind the Stasi. Critique of the West thus merges with veiled critique of the East. The GDR argument against terrorism is no different than that of the orthodox Marxist Left in the FRG. West Germany comes across as full of critical protocommunists with no political home, part of a protest movement going nowhere. In comparison, forms of protest and dissent in the East were considerably restricted. Set in one German state and made in the other, the film *Scenes of Fire* can now be viewed as a prereunification national-unity narrative.

Sometimes international authors took on themes that their German counterparts avoided. *The Democratic Terrorist* (Giullou, 1987; tr. from Swedish, 1990) was readily received in the FRG for this reason, and it was immediately made into an action film, becoming the second popular Baader-Meinhof film to be made in Germany.[9] The Swiss-German detective thriller *Snow Trap* (Blatter, 1981) also quickly went through a number of reprints. The German version of Doris Lessing's *The Good Terrorist* (1985; tr. 1986), which is not concerned directly with Baader-Meinhof, went through ten editions in German in the same time that it was reprinted only three times in the original English. Lessing's young heroine wants nothing so much as to tidy up the London house that she squats with some mysterious housemates. Unwittingly, she becomes embroiled in a criminal plot involving both the IRA and the KGB and ends up responsible for a fatal explosion. She fits easily into the trope "terrorist as woman" from Chapter One, but the German translation of the title shows up the limits of what could be said in public on the subject. As the good "terrorist" is female, Lessing's title has to be gendered in German (*Terroristin*), but for the first 17 years and 9 editions of the translation's publishing history, the qualifying adjective was omitted. Only in 2003 was the same translation published as *Die gute Terroristin*.[10]

Roderick Thorp's action thriller *Nothing Lasts Forever* (1979) is an ephemeral best-seller, but it earned itself a place in Hollywood history as the basis for the first in the *Die Hard* series of movies (dir. McTiernan, 1988). In contrast to the more famous film, the book's political tendency is liberal but its conclusions about terrorist attacks on international business could be construed as more than a little troubling. *Die Hard*, which made Bruce Willis into a star, spreads the image of "terrorists" being long-haired young German men. Led by Hans Gruber (Alan Rickman), they tote machine guns to hold innocent Americans to ransom. While none of them shout *Raus, raus!* or *Schnell, schnell!*, they quite easily could be Hollywood Nazis. Unlike its source, *Die Hard* is concerned with the reassertion of traditional gender roles. In *Nothing Lasts Forever* there are women terrorists, whom Joe Leland, an ex-World War II fighter pilot, has to get used to killing along with the men. Bruce Willis, in contrast, is fighting for the macho values of Reagan's resurgent America and could not be seen shooting the fairer sex.

Willis is on the premises of a tower block that is taken over by a group from the fictitious *volksfrei* movement, because he is tracking down his estranged wife, who is portrayed as a typically modern woman who has put career before marriage and even reclaimed her maiden name. The terrorists represent a wholly alien intrusion into the peaceful setting of corporate America. Willis's character realizes "these guys are mostly European," "well financed and very slick," making them "bad-arsed perpetrators." Their ruthlessness appears irrational but turns out to be motivated by material greed. Gruber pretends to have mounted the attack in order to gain the release of various comrades held in prisons around the world, who belong to such organizations as the New Provo Front (Northern Ireland), Liberté de Quebec (Canada), and Asian Dawn (Sri Lanka). But what he really wants is millions of dollars. His plan includes faking his own death, so that the FBI will leave him in peace. The revolutionary aims thus turn out to be a cover for a massive bank heist; political terrorism is a front for good old-fashioned crime. The difference between *Die Hard* and the German films is that the terrorists in *Die Hard* are just greedy bad men whose politics have no meaning other than as a means to make their fortune. Baader-Meinhof never has this function in the German imagination.

If *Die Hard*'s politics are those of an assertive American right wing, on the point of triumph in the Cold War, *Nothing Lasts Forever*, published in 1979, bears the stamp of the less self-confident era of President Jimmy Carter. Joe Leland is a more complicated character than Willis's Roy Rogers. He flies to Los Angeles to visit his successful daughter and two grandchildren. His uncertainty over her brash male colleagues, expensive new habits, and his suspicion that she has become a cocaine user are not antifeminist; they indicate a lack of enthusiasm for the new face of the American business world. Leland has worked in antiterrorism and recognizes his adversary, Tony the Red, who is the leader of a mixed group of twelve third-generation RAF terrorists. Leland knows some German. The reason he takes on Tony the Red and his gang barefoot (just as Rogers fights Gruber) is that a German businessman once told him that washing your feet was the best way to refresh yourself at the end of a tiring day and he was doing just that when Tony the Red struck. The German businessman also recalled meeting Hitler, said to have been a peasant who could never change his opinion about anything. Such details place the novel firmly in a post-Nazi context. Thorp caricatures left-wing European nihilist extremists, recalling "Ursula Schmidt, the German poetess who celebrated death, the Italian kids who specialized in killing politicians slowly, or Little Tony the Red, from Germany again, who loved the drama of death."[11]

Tony may be politically motivated, but his methods of killing are those of a gangster. His trademark dispatch of his victims entails straightening their lapels before shooting them. Tony comes from a wealthy family, his father was an SS man, and he hung out on the arty fringe of Baader-Meinhof before joining them. Yet his motivation is political. His group attacks the Klaxon Oil building where Leland's daughter works because the company has just concluded a multimillion dollar arms deal with the military junta in Chile. Joe Leland understands their politics. He reflects towards the end: "University kids in Germany had been cheering for these bums for more than a decade. Not that they were completely wrong" (133). Leland does nothing to stop Tony from shooting his daughter's two unscrupulous male bosses. Tony may be a cold-blooded killer, but there is something of a modern-day Robin Hood to him when he promises to throw six million dollars out of the window for passersby. At the end of the novel *Nothing Lasts Forever*, Tony kills Leland's daughter, before being shot himself by Leland. This ending is unlike the triumphal conclusion to the first *Die Hard* film. Leland is an uncertain hero who is caught between the two sides.

Walter Abish was born in Vienna in 1931 into a Jewish family. After fleeing the Nazis, his family lived in several countries, including Israel. He moved to the United States in 1957 and became a citizen. When he published *How German Is It*, his fourth prose work, he had never visited Germany. German-speaking critics have reacted to him as a transnational rather than a foreign author.[12] *How German Is It. Wie deutsch ist es* (Abish, 1979; tr. 1984) seems to have been given a German translation from a sense of obligation, owing to the author's Austrian Jewish background. The central character, Ulrich Hargenau, who has recently been on trial for terrorism, believes himself to be the son of an anti-Nazi resistance fighter who was executed in 1944 after the failed von Stauffenberg plot to kill Hitler. It is revealed by the end, however, that his supposed father was killed more than nine months before he was born, and he is unlikely to find out who his real father is. Abish posits a line from the anti-Nazi resistance to the present-day *Einzieh* (literally "move-in") group, his fictional equivalent for the RAF. The real questions Abish addresses are: How German was Nazism and how Nazi is Germany 34 years after the end of the war? The Federal Republic is superficially peaceful and prosperous, but is disturbed by regular explosions in public places and the discovery of mass graves dating from the Third Reich. *How German Is It?* is kind of state-of-the-nation social panorama, which works from the premise that the Federal Republic can only be understood and is only interesting at all through reference to Hitler's Germany.

The novel is rich in literary, cultural, and historical, and philosophical allusions. Ulrich Hargenau, who is named after the central characters in major novels by Robert Musil (*The Man without Qualities*) and Hermann Broch (*The Sleepwalkers*), is a successful writer whose girlfriend

Paula got him involved with *Einzieh*. This sexualizes the male intellectual's connection to terrorist violence while keeping him at one remove from it. Unwanted reminders of the Nazi past appear at socially embarrassing moments—in speech, for instance, through chance remarks by marginalized characters. The ugly truth about the past is not confronted, except by an outsider such as Franz, a waiter who is building a scale-model out of matchsticks of the Durst concentration camp, on the site of which the new city of Brumholdstein has been built. In contemporary Germany, violence is latent; the terrorists both react against this state of affairs and are an expression of it, making them a symptom of a much bigger problem. While the surface is calm and social class and rank are no longer supposed to count, the working classes all live in the town of Damling and the bourgeoisie, who employ servants, live in Brumholdstein, named after the recently deceased philosopher who is modeled on Martin Heidegger (1889–1976). None of the bourgeois characters appears capable of sustaining a relationship, let alone a marriage. Ulrich's brother Helmut is the most promiscuous, and as an architect he is identified with postwar reconstruction, which is why the *Einzieh* group blows up a police station and a post office that he has designed. There are also attempts on his life. In the final section of the novel, an apparently contented working-class character is persuaded after a brief meeting with two women terrorists to help them. He promptly shoots two policemen and blows up the sluice gate that he has faithfully operated for years. The scenarios are fictitious in the manner of a film by Jean-Luc Godard, who supplies the novel's epigraph. German writers could not or would not emulate this style and approach to domestic left-wing terrorism. Their novels stick closely to plots taken from recent history or social reality and they bracket out the Nazi past.

A Disturbance in Paris (Fick, 1981), a conventional thriller written for the mass market, is a very different sort of novel, but it too does something that to this day German authors are wary of doing: it mentions the Palestinians. The novel concerns a kidnapping of an Israeli intelligence chief named Efraim Litvak by an international commando that includes an Arab and a Japanese and is led by the urbane middle-aged Professor Manfred Uvald Prinz. The kidnapping in the story is carried out in the 1978, the year after Schleyer's kidnapping. The aim of the new kidnapping is to secure the release from Stammheim of two other German prisoners. After pressure on the Germans from the Israeli government, this pair is flown to Algiers, from which they quickly make their way back to Europe (as actually happened after the release of the Yemeni Five in February 1975 following the kidnapping of Peter Lorenz). The elderly Holocaust survivor Efraim Litvak, on the other hand, is returned dead, seemingly from a heart attack, his body missing a finger, which was cut off by his kidnappers.

Prinz is an intellectual mastermind and ruthless operator with no historical counterpart, as the narrator tells us:

> Taught at Hamburg, University of Exeter and Munich. Multilingual. Father figure to the others. About forty-five. Erudite. Gives impression of omniscience [...] Favorite phrases: "The sword also means cleanness and death," and "There are no innocents." Early friend of Ulrike Meinhof. Not keen on Andreas Baader. [...] Well-versed in terrorist literature from sixteenth century on.[13]

Carl Fick is not exploring contemporary relations between Germans, Arabs, and Israelis, nor making an explicit point about Baader-Meinhof's anti-Zionism. He exploits the themes as plot ingredients to fashion an exciting and at times sensationalist story. The central character is an American film director named Alexander Marin, who unwittingly finds himself wanted for murder and suspected of defecting to the terrorists when he inadvertently lands in their clutches. Yet were it not for their practice of what Marin regards as "random killing," he admits that he could have thrown in his lot with Prinz's group, as he is inspired by other aspects of their idealistic commitment.

Fick employs two other tropes identified in the German fiction. The German terrorist who features most prominently is a sexy young woman. An Israeli agent describes Janna Macklenburg-Konrad as "a blond woman, young, reputed to be constructed in the fashion of Catherine Deneuve, but who dresses like a beggar and wears her hair like a witch" (191). Marin takes the role of the libidinous middle-aged male investigator. Macklenburg-Konrad is as unreflective as she is attractive, having committed murder without thinking through her motivation or the consequences of her actions. Of course, she can be redeemed through her love for Marin and his good example. Unfortunately for both of them, *A Disturbance in Paris* ends with a shootout in which all the terrorists, their latest hostage, the German justice minister, and Marin get killed.

In this unevenly written American thriller, the unscrupulous German state is represented by Dr. Kurt Karl Gebhardt, "the prosecutor general of the West German Office to Protect the Constitution" (241). As we have seen, German novels often depict BKA investigators but rarely employees of the *Verfassungsschutz*, whereas foreign novelists are more likely to pit the terrorists against an undercover agent (the so-called *V-Mann*). The *Verfassungsschutz* may formally be the successor organization to the Gestapo, and up to 1990 the West German counterpart of the Stasi, but its designation (the protection of the constitution) indicates the difference between the democratic postwar order and the totalitarian German regimes. For a German writer, it is difficult to portray the *Verfassungsschutz* as villainous, perhaps because the constitution itself was essentially written against the state in the name of the citizenry. Yet, as I argued in the last chapter, through focusing on a figure based on Horst Herold, the German novelists also make the BKA into would-be good guys. The Germans thus have an ultimately collapsible dualist opposition.

Gebhardt is being duped by his nubile mistress and junior employee, who feeds Prinz all his plans, but the chief defender of the constitution is ready to sacrifice the Minister of Justice and renege on his deal with Marin. This leads to an exchange which reveals, in an aside, American attitudes to the Third Reich. When Marin offers to lead Gebhardt to Prinz and the kidnapped minister, in return for an amnesty for himself and Janna, Gebhardt shows more interest in pursuing Janna than in liberating the kidnap victim:

> *Gebhardt*: The Macklenburg-Konrad woman is a killer bitch.
> *Marin*: She called you a killer dog. She hasn't made any lampshades lately. Who the hell do you want, Gebhardt: Macklenburg-Konrad or Mohler? (252)

The reference to lampshades is to the practice at Auschwitz of making them from human skin. In American narratives, the connections between Nazism and Baader-Meinhof are explicit. Fick's Baader-Meinhof narrative differs from the standard German version through his reference to the massacre of the Israeli athletes at the Munich Olympics in 1972 and to the events at Entebbe in June 1976. At Entebbe, as someone points out in the novel, the Israelis showed the GSG-9 what to do in a hostage crisis. Earlier in the discussion, Marin has told Gebhardt that he has killed the Lebanese member of Prinz's gang after the Lebanese shot an Israeli agent. The Israeli was the innocent party, since he was on Prinz's tail for the kidnapping and killing of Litvak. Telling the Israelis the whereabouts of the agent's body "might help to make amends for Munich" (249), according to Marin's daughter's British boyfriend. Gebhardt, however, cares nothing "about the Israeli or the Lebanese" (248). The reason that Fick is not interested in dwelling on the possible anti-Semitism of the younger generation of German terrorist killers is that he pins the charge on the older Gebhardt.

A Disturbance in Paris underlines an uncomfortable fact that all too often gets written out of the German accounts of the period, whether fictional or historical: revolutionary young Germans ganging up with Palestinians against Israelis is part of the complex called "Baader-Meinhof." In non-German literary and cinematic representation, German–Palestinian collaboration is central. Within two years of the Entebbe raid, it had become the subject of two Hollywood action films as well as one made in Israel.[14] The Black September attack on the Israeli athletes was first brought to the screen in an American made-for-television film, starring William Holden and Franco Nero, *21 Hours at Munich* (dir. William Graham, 1976), and more recently and to greater acclaim in *One Day in September* (dir. Kevin Macdonald, 1999), which won an Oscar for best documentary, and *Munich* (dir. Steven Spielberg, 2005). The historiography of Munich is firmly in non-German hands too.[15] For Israeli storytellers and Hollywood directors sympathetic to Israel, Entebbe was a propaganda gift: here were Israel's Arab foes working with Germans, who once again selected Jews for death or punishment. In the Entebbe films, German hijackers persecute Jews/Israelis, which contrasts sharply with the trio of German Mogadishu thrillers discussed in Chapter Two.

The novelist Gerhard Seyfried is a partial exception. As as a cartoonist, Seyfried supplied the Student Movement with some of its most famous images and catch phrases, which were mass produced on radical posters that were displayed on bedroom walls the length and breadth of the republic. In its disavowal of lethal violence, Seyfried's *The Black Star of the Tupamaros* (2004) is disingenuous, however. In a "News" section midway through the novel, Seyfried says that the Entebbe hijackers released 147 hostages, but does not specify that they were the non-Israelis or non-Jews. His readers do learn, however, that it was an Israeli unit that raided Entebbe on July 4, 1976 and that they killed 20 Ugandans, all 4 hijackers, and destroyed the fighter planes in the Ugandan Air Force. In the mid-2000s, the old 68er Left, as represented by Seyfried is still in denial about Entebbe. Henryk M. Broder, a German 68er of Polish-Jewish heritage, recalled that after the raid his left-wing friends were united in their condemnation of Israel. Entebbe made Broder aware of what the German Left insisted could not exist because it was a contradiction in terms: left-wing anti-Semitism.[16]

Entebbe plays a central role for foreign historians.[17] British writer Hans Kundnani sees it as constitutive of Joschka Fischer's change of heart, which saw him forsake provocative street violence in favor of democratic politics through the vehicle of the Green Party. Although Gillian Becker begins *Hitler's Children* (1978) with Entebbe, the standard histories written in German by Stefan Aust (1985/97) and Butz Peters (2004) omit it entirely. Klaus Pflieger (2004) includes Entebbe but leaves out Munich. It is only in 2007 that Willi Winkler gives full accounts of both.[18] It is justifiable *up to a point* for historians of the RAF to ignore Entebbe and Munich, as the RAF is itself was not directly involved on either occasion.[19] Yet, given that the first generation of RAF began their training at the Fatah camp and that their history ended at Mogadishu in a plane hijacked by Palestinians, the link with the Arab–Israeli conflict can hardly be ignored. After releasing all the non-Jewish passengers, the Entebbe hijackers demanded the release of more than 50 "political prisoners," mostly Palestinians held in Israeli jails but also six Germans, three of whom were RAF members.[20] From jail, Meinhof welcomed the Munich killings; among Black September's demands was her release and Baader's release.[21] The RAF knew very well that the events were connected: the day of Schleyer's kidnap (September 5, 1977) was the fifth anniversary of Munich. Apart from retelling the famous episode at the training at the Fatah camp in July 1970, German writers have barely attempted to reimagine the role played by the Middle East in Baader-Meinhof history.[22] They prefer either the narratives that are already well known (the Baader-Ensslin love story, the drama of the German Autumn) or semi-fictionalized events from the 1980s, which can be assimilated into a less complicated and more positive national myth. The situation is beginning to change. *Carlos* (dir. Assayas, 2010) in a Franco-German coproduction, only reports on Entebbe because the hero of the film was not selected to lead the mission. But in the film Hans-Joachim Klein explains that he wants to leave the RZ because Germans of his generation have no place separating Jews from non-Jews as if they were on the ramp at Auschwitz. Oliver Assayas's multi-part television film *Carlos* does show more comprehensively than any German account up to 2010 how closely the Revolutionary Cells worked with Palestinian organizations with links across the Middle East. The dramatic center of the film is the raid on the OPEC conference on December 21, 1975, in which Germans played central roles. Carlos was also closely allied with Johannes Weinrich and married Magdalena Kopp, both from the RZ.

The only Swiss-German take on Baader-Meinhof also highlights a number of things that the West German writers were not doing. Silvio Blatter's perfectly serious use of a popular form is signaled in his dedication of *The Snow Trap* (1981) to Heinrich Böll. This short detective novel reflects contemporary concerns about the security response to terrorist attacks, in this case a bank robbery in Zurich that left a terrorist and a passerby dead. The surviving robbers get away, as most of them did in real life on November 19, 1979 when Rolf Klemens Wagner and three accomplices raided a branch of the Swiss Volksbank in Zurich. They accidentally shot dead a passerby and injured another, as well as two policemen, as they fled. In Blatter's *krimi*, the Swiss police work with the BKA to follow a false lead through the winter snow to a remote Alpine refuge. Blatter turns the detective genre on its head. The Swiss and German detective duo does not get their woman. They do not even follow up clues that they have identified for themselves, as they rely on a tip-off from a member of the public who is influenced by the general mood of suspicion and prejudice. In contrast to private detectives, they are not thinking for themselves but acting as part of a machine. As the narrative reaches its climax, the readers know what the detectives do not: the young couple in the refuge is innocent. Elsewhere in the novel, the police are hunting chimera. A real terrorist fails to make an appearance. Instead, an innocent group of young Germans are arrested at gunpoint in a restaurant and a young man who has borrowed his father's car without permission crashes through a police roadblock. Blatter shows up the limits of Herold's technique of *rasterfahndung* and also how the techniques of crime detection, as reproduced as tropes in crime fiction, were not appropriate in the pursuit of terrorist adversaries.

Sweden was part of the Baader-Meinhof story following the hostage-taking in the West German Embassy in Stockholm in April 1975.[23] Jan Guillou makes much of Swedish connections in *The Democratic Terrorist* (1987). He also sets key episodes in the Middle East and is explicit about his own pro-Palestinian sympathies, as is his central character, Count Hamilton alias "Le Coq Rouge," an action hero in the James Bond mold. Terrorists and counterterrorist agents thus have anti-Zionism in common; as Hamilton is Swedish, his hostility to Israel comes guilt-free to German readers, who devoured the novel in translation. At the beginning of *The Democratic Terrorist*, the BKA intercepts a conversation between two RAF men a few days after an attack on a German army barracks. The BKA concludes that they are now looking for a Swedish comrade to assist with an operation in Sweden. The RAF is internationalizing, with homegrown offshoots in Belgium and France. The *Verfassungsschutz* responds by recruiting Hamilton and tasking him with infiltration of the RAF cell. He wins the terrorists' trust and succeeds in directing operations to such an extent that the two cells are smashed and an operation to blow up the fourth floor of the American Embassy in Stockholm, which houses the CIA, is foiled. *The Democratic Terrorist* is the only Baader-Meinhof novel with a *V-Mann* as its central character. Guillou also does what no German novelist up to this point had attempted: he imagines everyday life among RAF terorrists.

Hamilton is good looking, well educated, and has a taste for fine wine and Beethoven. Above all, he is well versed in the art of killing. As only a Swedish secret agent in the Social Democrat era of Olof Palme could do, he boasts a revolutionary past. In his student days, he was a Marxist-Leninist member of an organization called Clarté. He has not lost all his youthful idealism, but his political interests are now limited to the Arab–Israeli conflict. Although he has always rejected acts of individual terrorism, his past allegiance enables him to understand what motivates the RAF and removes the need of a cover identity. The space in which he works between the *Verfassungsschutz*, who turn out not to be interested in taking any terrorists alive, and the RAF is morally murky. From a political point of view, he appears to have nothing against the plan, which he proposes to the cell, to blow up the CIA's Swedish HQ. The killing will be targeted, not random. He is personally motivated to prevent it happening only when the PLO turn out to be against it. Their reason is that violence on such a scale, which could be traced to the Middle East, where Hamilton sources the rocket launchers and missiles, may derail diplomatic efforts to secure a peace deal with Israel. Thus Hamilton can have his German comrades liquidated without betraying his own pro-Palestinian allegiance.

The Democratic Terrorist is not the Le Carré-esque masterpiece that it could have been because at crucial points in the plot, Giullou puts genre conventions ahead of politics or psychology. Hamilton gets to know some of the terrorists, even falling in love and having an affair with one. They are introduced to readers as kindly, fair-minded warriors for a better world. While they are ruthless when they need to be, their relative lack of military training makes them vulnerable. In the crisis in Syria, however, when he and two Germans are taken prisoner, Hamilton does not hesitate in eviscerating his German comrades at the command of the Palestinian leader. He never shows remorse for his deed. He later leads the others, including Ursula, his girlfriend, into an ambush that leaves them all dead. He even shoots Ursula himself. In order for these deeds to be motivated, Guillou suddenly "others" the terrorists. From being reliable comrades in a noble cause, they mutate into fanatics, as a blankness opens up behind their eyes. After her death, Ursula is worth the merest mention to Hamilton's controlling officer: an emotional entanglement is an occupational hazard on such a mission. Guillou thus ultimately has it both ways: he replays the terrorist dream of fighting for a better world before brutally killing them off.

The German-Swedish film of the novel directed by Pelle Bergland in 1992, which co-stars Ulrich Tukur, who played Baader in Stammheim (dir. Hauff, 1985) as a Verfassungsschutz controller, went into production the year after the German translation was published. As it was sponsored by the state television channel ZDF, who could not broadcast the film for eight years because of the controversial subject matter, it counts as a German adaptation of a foreign source, despite a Swedish director and principal actor. The film is the first postunification treatment of a Baader-Meinhof theme and includes for the first time a RAF–Stasi connection: part of Hamilton's cover story is that he has been kicked out of the Swedish military because of his work with the East German secret service. A more significant difference is that his political motivation for helping the RAF to assist the PLO is downplayed. In place of politics is his affair with the RAF comrade, now called Monika. She is feminized more than Ursula in the novel and even is given a child, whom, as she confides tearfully to Hamilton, she has not seen for four years. This makes her another reluctant female terrorist who regrets her abandonment of conventional family life. In the film, rather than shooting Monika at the point of crisis, as happened to Ursula in the novel, Hamilton tries to save her. In the final scene, she does not understand why he is not armed, as they are surrounded by police, and she dies in a hail of bullets when she reaches into her pocket for own gun. She is thus shown her to be irredeemable at the last. She is also the second female terrorist to be shot on screen. When their cell was raided and its members eliminated one by one, we see a masked commando hesitate before pulling the trigger on the blonde Fredericke Kunkel. He shoots her only after she shouts to him to do so, sensing the sexist reason for his chivalrous reluctance. After doing so, he removes his balaclava and is sick.

After *The Democratic Terrorist,* the only international Baader-Meinhof novels to be published until the new century are the experimental *Lisbon Last Margin* (Volodine, 1990) and *The Invisible Circus* (Egan, 1995). The second phase of international Baader-Meinhof fiction coincides with the much larger number of German novels published in the 2000s. Given that Baader-Meinhof has lately been an overwhelmingly male topic, it is striking that the only two comic novels in any language are by women. Before the satire in *The Pale Heart of the Revolution* (Dannenberg, 2004), the American Erin Cosgrove published a spoof romantic novel set on a campus of a wealthy East Coast university. Cosgrove mocks contemporary fascination with Baader-Meinhof terrorism of the 1970s; her novel also enjoyed some success in German translation. For Cosgrove, any rebellion worth the name could only be in aid of furthering the spread of true romance so that the world becomes a replica of romantic fiction. *The Baader-Meinhof Affair* (Cosgrove, 2003) is so entitled because the fabulously rich and devastatingly handsome male lead, named Holden after the narrator of J. D. Salinger's *The Catcher in the Rye,* is the head of a clandestine student society that reenacts the story of the RAF. Cosgrove's knowledge of the material and her feel for its meanings cannot be faulted. Playing Andreas Baader, Holden exudes sexual charisma. Baader and his comrades are presented as at-heart spoilt rich kids who rebel against their own privileges. The student members of the "B-M Gang" identify with the historical Baader-Meinhof Group in a parody of the adulation of their German counterparts a generation previously. For some of the novel's comic purposes, any other sect from history could have served just as well. Cosgrove does make a number of contemporary connections and she is, like all the Americans, interested in the Jewish, Nazi, and Israeli–Palestinian connections. The heroine Mara, whose own intellectual passion is the study of serial killers, is drawn to the group because she is in love with Holden/Baader. As she tries to make sense of its activities, she draws some conclusions that historians took rather longer to reach (her thoughts are given in italics in the novel):

Maybe, the RAF traded their fascist German ancestry for victim status. That would explain why they trained with the Palestinians. Somewhere in their twisted minds it wasn't enough to assert themselves as victims of World War II instead of the Jews; they also had to side with the self-proclaimed victims of Israel: the Palestinians.

It's probably the same reason why Holden and the rest are so drawn to the B-M gang. They know their junk-bond and old-money nepotistic class is the reason America is in such a shambles. It's their parents' class feasting on the middle and lower class's desiccated body. [...] Although Holden and the others happily reap the benefits of their class, they envy its victims. [...] So they recast themselves as casualties of the state through identification with the Baader-Meinhof Group. Oh my. All this German/Jew stuff gives me a headache. And it's time for me to go.[24]

As *The Baader-Meinhof Affair* is a romance, Mara's purpose is to get her man. This she finally does after her rival for his affections is foiled from turning a make-believe reenactment into a real-life bloodbath. Mara falls into Holden's arms, the B-M Gang is wound up, and the villain, the aptly named Regan, who played Gudrun to Mara's Ulrike in the "B-M Games," is led away by the police. The novel sets out reasons to rebel against the America of George W. Bush's neo-Cons, but then takes them all back. The would-be terrorist outlaws see the error of their ways as both the state and the media had been monitoring their activities from the start.

Cosgrove is not a professional romantic novelist, but a multitalented installation artist who also writes. She came to find about the RAF after seeing Gerhard Richter's cycle of paintings and spending a year in Berlin in 1995.[25] The general butt of her parodic satire is the trend in the genre to romanticize the outlaw. Her avant-garde combination of political humor, sex, and terrorism anticipates *The Raspberry Reich* (2004) by the Canadian director Bruce LaBruce, who appropriates RAF themes for similar and even more outré purposes. It is the only "gay porn" film to engage with the Baader-Meinhof legacy, indeed the only porn film of any sort that is recorded as doing so. The film begins, however, with a shot of a young male Asian, reciting verses from the *Koran*: contemporary terrorism is religiously rather than politically motivated, as it was in the recent past. Gudrun is the domineering leader of a revolutionary cell that venerates the heroes of the 1960s and 1970s, Angela Davis and Che Guevara, and the RAF leaders. Revolutionary slogans appear at regular intervals on the screen: "Private property cannot be stolen, only liberated," "Corporate hip hop is counterrevolutionary," but also the more contemporary "Meat is murder." Gudrun's guru, the "Reich" of the title, is the sexologist and theorist of the orgasm, Wilhelm Reich. After making vigorous love in public to one of her male followers, which encourages a respectable middle-aged couple who see them in the elevator to follow their lead, she announces that men have to overcome their repressed homosexuality by seducing each other to "join the homosexual intifada." Sexual obsession with Gudrun Ensslin is the reason the central character in the self-published British novel *Love, Gudrun Ensslin* (Corbin, 2010) becomes associated with the RAF.

The main interest in two other British Baader-Meinhof novels is Palestine and/or Islamic extremism in the wake of 9/11. *Absolute Friends* (le Carré, 2004) traces a line from 68er militants to al-Qaeda and the post-9/11 "war on terror." *Unity* (Arditti, 2005) explores an individual's motivation to commit "an act of evil," in this case planting a bomb in an enclosed space with the intention of killing as many people as possible. The bomber is an aristocratic British actress, playing the title role in a German film about Unity Mitford's involvement with Hitler in the 1930s. The time is November 1977 and the occasion is a memorial event for the Israeli athletes killed at the Munich Olympics. Felicity Bentall succeeds in killing herself, the British ambassador, who happens to be her own uncle, "his deputy, two secret servicemen and the Polish chargé d'affaires."[26] As a piece of ideology, the novel is an attack on British anti-Zionism.

John le Carré's *Absolute Friends* takes a rather different ideological line. It tells the story of the British Ted Mundy and the German Sasha who share a room in a Kreuzberg commune in West Berlin in 1969. Their life-long friendship is forged after Ted risks his life to save Sasha's life during a demonstration, as a result of which Ted is deported and comes to the attention of the British secret services. One or two other communards end up with the RAF, getting blown up in Lebanon. For a mixture of rather confused moral and emotional reasons, which include a cussed dash of idealism, Ted and Sasha later find themselves working together as a duo of double agents on opposite sides of the Iron Curtain. The novel reaches its climax a dozen years after the fall of the Berlin Wall, when both are gulled into signing up to an educational organization that purports to be promoting world peace through teaching an alternative syllabus of radical economics and sociology. In fact, it is an elaborate cover for an American neo-Con plot. The two friends are shot on the Heidelberg premises of the proposed alternative university and are posthumously framed as western al-Qaeda operatives, the point being the CIA's need to demonstrate to the German and French people and their governments, who had both opposed the Iraq War in 2003, that the threat of radical Islamic extremism is as real on the European continent as it is in New York. The symbolism is bitter: the rekindled fire of youthful radicalism in two middle-aged men, whose personal lives were ruined by their cross-border clandestine activities, results in their being shot to pieces by the adversaries of their youth, the CIA.

Michael Arditti does not allude directly to 9/11 in *Unity. Reflections on the personalities and politics behind Wolfgang Meier's legendary lost film.* But the novel's editor and narrator, who is a fictional version of Arditti himself,[27] assembles the documents to explain the terrorist deed over the years 2001 and 2002. The novel's center of gravity is the Nazi past, but the real present is not 1977, when most of the action is set, but the contemporary conflict between the West and militant Islam. In the novel, the memorial service to the Israeli athletes was to be held on September 11, 1977, but, in the words of the pro-Palestinian leftist British actress Geraldine Mortimer, "Germans, in thrall to history and desperate to appease Zionists, are determined that everything should go 100% according to plan. So service postponed until Schleyer crisis resolved" (228). Felicity Bentall did not apparently mean to blow herself up at Munich's Olympic Stadium, but doing so accidentally makes her into a suicide bomber. She has recently graduated from Cambridge where the original script for the film was devised by three friends, one of whom now pieces together the narrative of the novel 24 years after Felicity's fatal mission. As the filming of "*Unity*" coincides almost exactly with the Schleyer kidnapping and the director, Wolfgang Meier, a fictional amalgam of Brecht and Fassbinder, is a more or less open Baader-Meinhof sympathizer, Felicity is exposed on set to far-left West German politics. She leaves her Cambridge boyfriend Luke Dent, the author of the screenplay, and starts an affair with a mysterious Palestinian. The Arab terrorist Ahmet, who arrives on set as a friend of the German actors, has a policy of "My enemy's enemy is my friend," which gives Geraldine Mortimer (who must be based partly on the actress and activist Vanessa Redgrave) some pause for thought, as she confides to her journal:

> Felt squalid. Not only buying from rabid neo-fascist but using authentic Nazi guns. A. displayed no such qualms. Guns highly efficient, readily available and hard to trace. Besides, in late capitalist society, there can be no untarnished transactions. Last year, PFLP delegates guests at both communist and fascist rallies in Italy during same week. (272)

Arditti thus works back and forward in time from 1977 and extends geographically to Britain and the Middle East. The contexts are different each time, but the basic questions that he poses are the same. He extends the collaboration between Palestinians and Germans in order to internationalize the fictional atrocity into a British-German-Arab operation directed against Israel.

Unity was well received and short-listed for the Wingate *Jewish Quarterly Prize* in 2006. Arditti is more interested in the Third Reich and in the connections that he can make between the Nazis and his other contexts, which are Britain in the 1930s, the 1970s, and the present, as a possible site of extremism, either radical or reactionary; the Middle East; and West Germany in 1977. The German Autumn enabled all the novel's characters to discover how they could have behaved had they lived through the 1930s and 1940s in Germany. This is made more poignant by the presence of Third Reich survivors, victims and perpetrators, and the knowledge of roles played by older family members. The character of Wolfgang Meier is dictatorial on set and obsessed with psychosexual explanations of Hitler's behavior. He even takes over the role of Hitler in the film. Some of the Germans assert that the British have no cause for moral smugness: Unity Mitford's flirtation with an extremist cause she did not fully comprehend is repeated by Felicity's infatuation with German and Arab extremism. Felicity's killing of her own uncle in the explosion at the Munich Stadium suggests that she was rebelling against her privileged background. Her father was an English anti-Semite, which prompts the narrator to remark that "it can be no coincidence that, for all their ideological polarity, the Far Right in the 1930s and the Far Left in the 1970s both chose to target the Jews" (185). In this second phase of Anglo-American Baader-Meinhof fiction, the German conflict is either a cover for the battle with al-Qaeda or is connected closely with it.

The last international novel is from Austria, which, being German-speaking, was the most obvious bolt hole for German terrorist fugitives, though it was not a source of recruits. *Schäfer's Torments* (Haderer, 2009) adapts elements of the German Baader-Meinhof *krimi*, but treats the RAF as an alien intrusion. Austria is connected dramatically with Baader-Meinhof history through the raid on the OPEC conference at Christmastime in 1975 and a copycat hostage-taking in 1977, organized by activists from the June 2nd Movement and carried out by Austrian students. This was also the subject of an Austrian documentary film made in 2007, *No Island. The Palmers Kidnapping of 1977* (dirs. Binder and Gartner). In contemporary interviews and news footage, the kidnappers come across as naïve, amateur, and foolish, as well as political romantics, who were motivated, among other things, to rescue their small country's reputation for conservatism by taking part themselves in the revolutionary events unfolding on the other side of the border. One Austrian take on the kidnapping is that the Viennese students were taken for a ride by their German comrades, who pocketed the ransom money and let them face the consequences of their actions. The critique is iterated in Georg Haderer's political crime novel, *Schäfer's Torments* (2009). As the detective is beginning to piece together the clues to a series of murders in the wealthy ski resort of Kitzbühel, he recalls what he knows of the Palmers case:

> The time of the RAF. In 1977 the head of a clothing company had been kidnapped in Austria. Schäfer remembered a lecture at the university by one of those involved after his release at the beginning of the 1990s. And the shame that he had felt at the relatively long sentences and the inhumane prison conditions which had driven one of the three kidnappers to suicide.[28]

Perhaps the most striking moment in the film *No Island* comes with learning that the directors' main source of information, Thomas Gratt, who was the force behind the kidnapping, committed suicide shortly after filming was finished.

In the elegantly written and often witty *Schäfer's Torments*, the murder victims, all successful local businessmen in their fifties, had secretly taken part in a similar kidnapping 30 years before. The novel is not narrated from the perspective of aging former participants; the detective's sympathy is with the young ex-RAF member Andreas Radner, who disappeared after the successful copycat kidnapping, which, in contrast to Palmers kidnapping, never became public knowledge (like so much Baader-Meinhof history in German popular fiction). Now working in Vienna, Schäfer grew up in Kitzbühel, which is why he was assigned the case, but his feelings about his hometown are highly ambivalent. Speculators, second-home owners from outside, have destroyed it in his eyes; whoever is now killing off the local bigwigs is a kind of alter ego, acting out his wishes in liquidating the local business elite. His former girlfriend even reveals her suspicion that he is responsible for the murders: "You used to have extreme views about a few people...that they should be done away with and so on" (142). He is also called Johannes, like his informant, who served a ten-year prison sentence for his part in bombing an American army base and killing three soldiers. Although Johannes was caught by the police, it turns out that Andreas Radner was done away with by his Austrian accomplices, who are now getting bumped off in quick succession, usually in bizarre circumstances.

The murderer turns out to be a young police inspector who has been investigating the case with Schäfer and is Radner's secret love child. *Schäfer's Torments* is another RAF revenge thriller, but with the difference that it is the terrorist's son who avenges his father's murder on the common criminals, now pillars of local Austrian society, who took his father's life to ensure their own enrichment. The young German with political ideals at the heyday of Baader-Meinhof was the patsy of his cynical money-grabbing Austrian neighbors. By revisiting Kitzbühel, Schäfer relives his own past and reviews the emotions that drove him from there as a young man. He recognizes that he externalized the reasons for his anger by messing up his own love life. Still, his sympathy is with the murderer rather than with his victims, with Radner and his son rather than with the Kitzbühel elite. Haderer imports a RAF story to articulate a critique of contemporary mores in small-town Austria and projects his own political analysis of the late 2000s to the RAF in the late 1970s.

What has emerged in this chapter is that Baader-Meinhof terrorism, as I have defined it in this book, has been a thematic export to a variety of other contemporary literatures. Baader-Meinhof is at once very German in its specificity and universal, in that American, British, Austrian, French, and Swedish characters recognize part of themselves in the terrorists. International novelists stick to the popular genres, with occasional recourse to the avant-garde and to parodies of Germanic high seriousness. For Swiss-German, Swedish, and Austrian novelists, this entailed using their national connection with an episode in Baader-Meinhof history. For the American and British novelists of Jewish origin (Abish and Arditti), it meant expanding the scope of Baader-Meinhof history to include the Holocaust and the contemporary conflict between the state of Israel and the Palestinians. Thematically, international novelists make the conflict more international, linking Baader-Meinhof with Palestine or Chile in the 1970s or al-Qaeda in the 2000s. Conversely, comparison with the German novels shows conspiracy theories about secret-service collusion and police coverups to be the result of German insecurities. Even in the popular genres, international novelists tend to be serious rather than exploitative, interested in politics rather than in serving up stereotypes to create an effect. They had a greater distance from the history, which led to greater imaginative freedom and an ability to break taboos that inhibited their German counterparts, who only half caught up in the 2000s. The nuances of German Baader-Meinhof history are largely lost on them, but they plug gaps in the German-language fiction, while by and large ignoring the episodes, the German Autumn, the assassinations of Herrhausen and Rohwedder, and many of the personalities (Herold, Schleyer, Baader) that fascinated the Germans. While "Baader-Meinhof" is a fundamentally different phenomenon outside Germany, it was not turned against contemporary Germans. On the contrary, its literary representation (though not always its depiction in cinema—witness *Die Hard*) has served an integrative purpose, bringing postwar Germany and Germans closer to international readers. Not only did 1970s German terrorists act against a backdrop of recent Nazi history, in fiction they competed with the more numerous and inevitably less sympathetic depictions of Nazis. German terrorists have potential to be the good guys, even the "good Germans" that international writers are more likely to seek in recent history than the Germans are themselves.

CHAPTER SIX

RAF REVIVALISM IN THE 2000S

Younger German writers in the 2000s are angrier with contemporary politics than are the aging 68ers, whose late terrorist fiction is predicated on characters' remorse for their association with violence. German political fiction as a whole enjoyed a renaissance in the decade of the 2000s. Urban guerillas battling the system come in a number of guises. They may be embittered former Stasi operatives, as in the surreal social panorama *The Good and the Bad* by André Kubiczek, (2003) or an inscrutable group of underground bomb makers, as in Michael Kumpfmüller's *Message to Everybody* (2008), which is set in the near future in an unnamed European country.[1] The most talked about novel of 2008 was Uwe Tellkamp's epic of GDR life *The Tower*, but three years earlier in *The Kingfisher* (2005) he portrays a right-wing terrorist movement that calls itself "The Rebirth," and is inspired by RAF methods, if not their ideology.[2] *Where Will You Be* (Hammerstein, 2010) is set in the near future after a complete meltdown of the world financial system.[3] A group calling themselves the Victims takes Germany's most infamous stock market speculator, Lisa Locust, hostage in an imitation of the RAF's ambush of Hanns-Martin Schleyer, except that nobody is killed. While "Lisa Locust" is a villain *de nos jours,* representing international finance capital, the Victims are postmodern protestors, who are convinced that nothing they can do will have any effect, in contrast with the heroic era of protest in the recent past. The idea of setting the RAF on corporate financiers who had brought the western world to the brink of economic ruin was not limited to Germany. In *Love, Gudrun Ensslin* (Corbin, 2010), a British Baader-Meinhof enthusiast persuades a former German RAF member to come out of retirement to assassinate city financiers, such as hedge fund managers and bond dealers responsible for the financial crisis.

After the financial crisis of 2007–08, a second factor that influenced how Baader-Meinhof is depicted and understood, was the al-Qaeda attack on the United States on September 11, 2001. In cinema, this resulted in a pause in the production of Baader-Meinhof feature films. In German fiction, the opposite is the case, but only two novels, both published in 2008, allude to 9/11 directly. In *The Weekend* (Schlink, 2008), which takes place in 2007, it is suggested that Jan, originally the seventh member of the group of friends, who are gathering to welcome the convicted terrorist Jörg out of prison, did not really commit suicide in the mid-1970s. In the novel that Ilse starts writing at the beginning of the weekend, she imagines that Jan faked his death in order to join the RAF. In her story, he even pulls the trigger on Schleyer. Ilse further imagines that Jan found himself at the top of one of the Twin Towers on September 11, 2001, there to deposit a suitcase for a Lebanese contact, and that he jumped to his death once the floor began to melt. It seems likely that, unbeknownst to Jan, the suitcase contained a transmitter that guided one of the hijacked planes to the tower. Thus for Ilse, al-Qaeda finally killed off the dream of the Red Army Faction. Indeed, she lays 9/11 at the door of the RAF.

Like the trio of novelists who are the main subject of this chapter, Bernhard Schlink recognized that Baader-Meinhof veterans could inspire a new generation. Schlink's Jörg, whose case is based on that of Christian Klar, shows no explicit regrets, but on release from prison has no intention of picking up where he left off or of recommending that anyone else do so, despite being encouraged by a young hanger-on. For Jörg, the past is past, the "war" that he was fighting is over. Jörg's reason has not got much to do with politics. His big surprise for his friends is that he has inoperable prostate cancer and has been given just months to live. This explains why he panicked when the 18-year-old Dorle, daughter of his friend Ulrich, presented herself naked to him on the first night. This rather implausible episode is designed to show that an aging terrorist can still appear glamorous to a teenager in 2007. Dorle, however, is attracted by his charisma as mediated in the press and television, but nothing else. After failing to seduce Jörg on Friday, which the whole house discovers because of his loud protests, Dorle beds his son on Saturday, which represents a more wholesome romantic outcome.

In *Dreamers of the Absolute* (Wildenhain, 2008) the same trope of terrorist as alter ego or onetime close friend is employed, and its general tenor is similarly critical. Michael Wildenhain (b. 1958) retells some of the history of the Kreuzberg squatters' movement from the 1980s, which was the subject of some of his earlier fiction. In a plot line that occurs for the first time in a German novel, however, he fictionalizes the career of a clandestine Revolutionary Cells activist with connections, not least through his Lebanese father, with the Middle East. *Dreamers of the Absolute* is infused with the narrator's disaffection with all forms of militant activism and as such is an antidote to even the most melancholic Baader-Meinhof novels that have been the subject of this book; it narrates an emotionally compelling story. Wildenhain's Tariq Fatoun (based on Tarek Mousli) does not lay down his arms with his comrades in the early 1990s. After cooperating with the state prosecutor during his trial in 1999 for possession of explosives, he is released with a new identity and resumes what has become a battle with the West in the ranks of al-Qaeda.

A resurgence of left-wing terrorism seemed a possibility as the anti-capitalist movement gained supporters at the turn of the new century. In Germany, the American firm of management consultants McKinsey & Company was one of the new bogeymen. The writer and *Spiegel* journalist Dirk Kurbjuweit revealed in 2003 that he had been approached to write a screenplay in which "a [female] opponent of globalization drifts into terrorism." For some, it seemed that this could quite easily happen for:

> Social conflicts are becoming harder. The world created by McKinsey provokes resistance because it splits society. In America and Europe it is less the losers who are defending themselves but, as usually happens, people whose sense of justice has been offended. That means above all sections of the youth. You can see it in the protests against neo-Liberal globalization, which have become more radical over the years, street battles, or the young man who was shot by the police in Genoa.[4]

Kurbjuweit's original title for his book on the "dictatorship of the economy" was *The McKinsey Society*; it was published in 2003, the same year that Rolf Hochhuth's *McKinsey Is Coming* created waves because of the advocacy of assassination expressed in it. It was, however, once again a film that made more plausible connections. Hans Weingartner's *The Edukators* (released in Germany as *Die fetten Jahre sind vorbei*, 2004) was the international anticapitalist film of the decade. It features a trio of young activists, played by three rising stars, Daniel Brühl, Julia Jentsch, and Stipe Erceg (who would play Holger Meins in *The Baader-Meinhof Complex*), who repeat the original generation's slide from playful violence against property (rearranging expensive furniture in rich people's houses while they are on holiday) to endangering human life by taking a hostage. Weingartner also replays the Schleyer kidnapping. The hostage, played by Burghart Klaußner, who bears some physical resemblance to Joschka Fischer, is the human connection to the "years of lead." Thirty-five years before the time of the story, this millionaire owner of a luxury villa was a street-fighting revolutionary, even claiming to have been a close friend of Rudi Dutschke. Once he has befriended his captors, as Schleyer attempted to do, he takes charge of the situation, rolling spliffs and giving advice. The political conclusion to the film is disillusioning, as on his release he wastes no time in betraying the youngsters to the police. He is their negative role model, the man they do not want to end up like, whose personal evolution is part of a generational cycle that they have to break. But the activist trio regroups after this betrayal, which they predicted, and embark on another intrepid mission, this time to commit criminal damage to satellite TV transmitters. *The Edukators,* in fact has a double ending. First it appears that they will be caught, as the film shows a heavily armed police unit storming their apartment. Then, it turns out the apartment is empty as the camera focuses on a message to their onetime prisoner pinned to the wall: "Some people never change." The activists meanwhile are in the Mediterranean and free to plan another, more worthwhile action.[5] In cinematic terms, we are back to Louis Malle's *Viva Maria!* (1965), despite their reexperiencing most of the arc of Baader-Meinhof terror from 1968 to 1977. In Weingartner's follow-up, *Free Rainer or Your Television Is Lying* (2008), which may be wittier and more poetic despite its lack of box-office success, the emphasis is no longer on symbolic gestures but on direct action that has an effect. This time, the German Autumn is referenced through the films that the German television-viewing public wants to see once they are liberated from media corporations and advertisers.

One factor in the renaissance of domestic political fiction was the return of political dissent at the end of the Kohl era in 1998, which was also the year that the remnants of the RAF announced their disbandment. Politics were contested once more. The merits and defects of globalization with its mantras of deregulation, efficiency, and a shrunken state dominated discussion. In the domestic arena, Gerhard Schröder's Agenda 2010 welfare reforms, which he pushed through at the start of his second term in office beginning in 2002, polarized debate for the first time in three decades. The Iraq War, which began in March 2003, revived the anti-Americanism of the 1960s and the 1980s. Schröder's opposition to the plans for an invasion insured his reelection in 2002, which gave the historic Red–Green Coalition a second term in office. Agenda 2010 was designed to reduce unemployment by cutting pay to the long-term jobless, thus encouraging them to take lower-paid and usually lower-skilled jobs. It was hardly a set of measures for the Left to celebrate, and it caused the SPD to lose every electoral contest after 2002. In domestic and economic policy, it is Red–Green's enduring legacy. As in 1918–1919, when Gustav Noske and Friedrich Ebert deployed the *Freikorps* to quell the Spartacists, though with far less bloody consequences, the reformist Left appeared to be working against the interests of its own supporters. Agenda 2010 ultimately split the SPD once again, when former party chairman and finance minister Oskar Lafontaine broke away to join the East German reform communists in what ultimately became *Die Linke.*

When the SPD stronghold of North Rhine Westphalia fell to the Christian Democrats in regional elections in May 2005, Schröder announced that he wanted new national elections, one whole year before they were due. This was a highly unusual move, which reflected the instability of the times. He petitioned the president to dissolve the Bundestag after proposing a vote of "no confidence" in his own government. Yet the CDU under Angela Merkel campaigned for even more radical free-market reforms, which enabled Schröder to position himself to her left. In the words of Sebastian Singer from *The Loaded Shooter of Andreas Baader* (Bock, 2009): "He forgot that he was the Chancellor and started campaigning against his own policies."[6] On September 18, Schröder very nearly avoided a defeat that had seemed a certainty when he called the election. The end result was a Grand Coalition of CDU and SPD (minus Schröder) led by Merkel, which pursued basically Social Democratic economic policies. Stability and consensus returned. The most influential of the three smaller parties not in government, however, was the newly formed *Die Linke*, which shifted the balance of power leftwards. The world financial crisis of 2007–08 was seen as proof by many Germans that the Anglo-Saxon neoliberal model of capitalism had failed. The 2009 elections, which resulted in a right-of-center government of Merkel's CDU with the liberal FDP, were once more about personnel and personalities rather than policy differences.

This chapter is dedicated to three novels published after 2000 and set in or near the new German capital of Berlin in the first decade of the new century. Each makes explicit links between the violent activism in the present, which is fictitious, and the historical violence of the 1970s.[7] The three novels are by authors born over three decades: Ulrich Peltzer, b. 1956, *Part of the Solution*, (2007); Thomas Weiss, b. 1964, *The Death of a Truffle Pig* (2007); and Thilo Bock, b. 1973, *The Loaded Shooter of Andreas Baader* (2009). They take the political realities of the 2000s as their starting point, as they are set in 2003 (*Part of the Solution*), at the time of the election summer of 2005 (*The Loaded Shooter of Andreas Baader*), and over a period of several months in 2006–2007 (*Death of a Truffle Pig*). Peltzer and Bock have Berlin settings; Peltzer even locates much of his action in the legendary Kreuzberg district. Weiss's novel, which is based on a real case, is set in Berlin's immediate historic hinterland of Brandenburg. The cause of the political action each time is globalized capitalism and its effects on German society. The novels feature activists or protesters who believe themselves to be disenfranchised from decision making and take direct steps, ultimately including violence, even murder, to make a difference, show defiance, live the right life, or perhaps for other, less upright motives. Their exploration of violence is surely nourished also by the continuation of acts of sabotage ("violence against things") still carried out by low-profile anarchist groupings, operating mainly in Berlin, and by sporadic outbursts of street violence, such as seen most years on May 1st.[8]

The novels also react to the worldwide anticapitalist and antiglobalization movements that have been a focus for protest since the late 1990s. Peltzer's *Part of the Solution* is a significant work on a number of counts. Peltzer attempts to devise a narrative form that accomplishes two things: it is an aesthetic counterbalance to the new electronic media with which the novel is directly concerned (closed circuit television, mobile telephones and text messages, e-mail, Internet searches, and video clips); and it encapsulates his theme of surveillance. The RAF novel it most resembles, although *Part of the Solution* is more readily readable, morally complex, and uses irony, is *Kamalatta* (Geissler, 1988), which may account for Peltzer's calling his central character Christian (after Christian Geissler). Peltzer starts from the proposition that most experience in the contemporary world is mediated. What we say and what we do has been said and done in advance by others who have produced images or written descriptions of it that we know. Originality and authenticity with respect to either action or expression are in decline, but there is still space for them which has to be negotiated.

The journalist Christian and German literature student named Nele conduct a courtship by e-mail, leaving each other messages on answering machines that are verbal traces. They go to the cinema, rather than seeing a live theatre performance. They have their first conversation at a party, in front of a dresser covered with family photographs of their host's wife's family. Christian plays back the recording of Nele's voice when she has disappeared and he misses her. As the novel reaches its anticlimactic finale, Nele obsessively photographs everything that she sees, making an image before she has an impression. Christian, a freelance journalist and aspiring novelist, and Nele, an advanced student researching a dissertation on the Romantic novelist Jean Paul, spend their working hours in front of computer screens. Christian reviews films, is helping a friend with a restaurant guide, and hawks around what he writes to editors of newspapers and magazines. For his day-to-day writing, words are interchangeable. There are only so many adjectives or phrases that are acceptable in any given context. Individuality of expression is limited. He is paid on commission, a typical representative of what came to be known as the *prekariat*, a brain worker who makes a modest living from short-term or part-time contracts, one of an army of freelancers dependent on Berlin's cheap rents. As a journalist, he is part of this same world, turning reality into verbal patterns that Nele protests against. Once more, terrorism and its symbolic significance in contemporary culture are addressed through the intermediary of a professional writer. Diehl in *A Hero of Internal Security* (Delius, 1981) failed to engage with the history that was unfolding around him; the unnamed novelist in *Eros* (Krausser, 2006) gave exaggerated symbolic meanings to the tale dictated to him; but Peltzer's Christian withholds his judgment. Three generations are present in *Part of the Solution*. The 89ers, born in the mid-1960s, are represented by Christian and his two friends, Jakob and Martin. The twenty-somethings are represented by Nele. The original 68ers are represented by another all-male trio, Eberhard Seidenhut, the BKA inspector; Klaus Witzke, his opposite number from the *Verfassungsschutz*; and Carl Brenner, Jakob's university boss, who is a professor of Italian Studies. As a Baader-Meinhof novelist, Peltzer is highly conservative in one respect: The revolutionary is an attractive young woman who is sexually involved with his central character. She is, however, elusive, and her character refuses to be allegorized, pitied, or redeemed. The cop whose understanding of his adversary runs over into sneaking respect is, of course, another well-worn trope. His analysis shows more than a hint of sympathy for the protestors:

> If you were young, dissatisfied with how the world is, angry about poverty and hunger, escalating unemployment, and you realize that you do not really have any legal means of changing anything. No mass movement, no party that you can join. Instead weasel words from politicians in alliance with bankers who you hold responsible for everything and who earn as much in a month as a million Africans [earn] in a year. That radicalizes you all by itself.[9]

Seidenhut and Witzke have collaborated since the late 1960s, when Witzke supplied the BKA with a report on the West Berlin "Wandering Hash Rebels." Given their experience, it is little wonder that they make such short work of Nele's cell. Witzke has infiltrated it through a *V-Mann*, who he estimates will take two years to produce results. Seidenhut has moved with the times and has two cyber hackers working on their e-mails. The actions of Nele's cell are escalating. A burlesque performance in a shopping mall off Friedrichstrasse results in a violent assault on a protester by a security guard and the eight protestors being bundled by force onto the street. The protestors then spray graffiti on a Lufthansa office, participate in a demonstration against a World Bank meeting in Zurich, at which a demonstrator next to Nele was crushed to death by a police vehicle, and set fire to municipal offices in the outlying Berlin district of Treptow, which results in four new VW cars at a next-door garage being burnt to cinders. The stakes are getting higher for both sides. The death of a demonstrator calls for a response from the protestors. On their arrest, members of the cell are found to have rudimentary bomb-making equipment in the cellar of their house.

Nele's interest in novelist Jean Paul signals her intellectual eccentricity, as Jean Paul was an anti-classical, comic, ironic novelist. Her clandestine protest activities are more direct gestures of defiance. As such they have to be brought under control by force. Christian's novel stands apart from the media-saturated world that he inhabits; writing it is one form of rebellion. His research into the extradition from France to Italy of former Red Brigade militants is the other. Between 250 and 300 Red Brigaders had fled to France by the beginning of the presidency of the socialist François Mitterand in 1981, who agreed that they could remain on condition that they had not been involved in killings. Twenty years later, it suited Italian Prime Minister Silvio Berlusconi to blame this Paris-based Left for a resurgence in political violence. Mitterand's Gaullist successor, Jacques Chirac, agrees to the Red Brigaders' repatriation. Christian sees the commercial potential that writing about such a topic could have: he could sell feature articles and interviews to newspapers and magazines. Both his research and his novel are eminently susceptible to co-option into the mediated world that provides him with his bread and butter. This is the contradiction in which Christian lives.

Christian's experience of adolescent revolt three years after Moro's kidnapping by the Red Brigades is entirely mediated. A concert given by the Clash in Düsseldorf when he was fifteen is his key memory, as it marks a turning point in his life. It resulted in parental punishment for both him and for his friend Jakob, because they missed the last train home and spent the night wandering through the city. Christian gives Jakob the original concert ticket that he has found secreted in his unread copy of Elias Canetti's *Crowds and Power* as a birthday present at the party where he meets Nele. They recall the songs and the album titles, *White Riot, Combat Rock, Spanish Bombs, Sandinista*. The Clash themselves knew about the Spanish Civil War and the Nicaraguan Sandinistas only indirectly; Jakob and Christian's experience of the two very real revolutionary conflicts from the 1930s and 1980s is thus mediated one step further. For all their charisma, there is a suspicion that the Clash could have been fake: "Did the kids in Brixton listen to The Clash? Or are they just middle-class simulacra of political resistance?" (172–73). Yet because 1981 counts as the media Stone Age, Christian and Jakob had to attend a concert in person in order to see the group, whose images were otherwise available only on record covers.

The duo of Christian and Jakob was once a trio. Martin, its third member, was a theatre director who suffered a nervous breakdown and took to drink. He is the novel's deranged conscience. Towards the end, news of his suicide makes both friends reflect that they could have done more to help him. Martin does not appear in person and he does not even succeed in having a conversation with either friend when he phones. The narrative has been punctuated by mad messages to Christian and Jakob from Martin, about being followed or getting to the bottom of a conspiracy against him. His awareness of reality is heightened either by alcohol or by a medical condition. Other characters really are being followed. The Red Brigade veterans have every reason to be wary of conspiracies. Nele and her comrades have their e-mails intercepted. The voices that Martin hears are echoes through a microphone, recordings of what has been said a second previously.

Although the novel ends with an authentic encounter in Paris with a Red Brigade contact, it begins with research on the Internet when, with his best friend from school and university, Jakob Schussler, an academic Italianist, Christian looks at a videotaped documentary of the kidnapping of Italian Prime Minister Aldo Moro in March 1978, in circumstances that resembled the kidnapping of Schleyer six months earlier. Their dialogue proceeds as follows:

"When did that take place?"
"At the beginning of seventy-eight."
"Can you remember anything?"
"We were eleven."
"Twelve," said Jakob and drank a gulp of beer. "Play a bit more." (21)

For many of their contemporaries, the kidnapping and murder of Aldo Moro was a rerun of the Schleyer kidnapping and murder the previous autumn. Christian's interpretation of why the Italian government in 2003 is seeking the extradition of long-forgotten Red Brigade activists, which the French government for its part also welcomes, is that the system cannot allow even the memory of its contestation. It requires victory over the past as well as the present, and this applies to Germany as well as its two neighbors.

For Peltzer, referring to the parallel struggle in Italy in the 1970s, instead of the better-known *bleierne Zeit* in Germany, has the advantage of defamiliarizing recent history. There were numerous links between the two countries, which are also reflected in fiction. No other Western countries witnessed ideologically motivated antistate violence on the same scale, despite the existence of groups with similar aims in France, the UK, and the United States. West Germany and Italy shared a background of Nazism or Fascism and were both on NATO's front line against communism, West Germany because of the GDR, Italy because of its strong domestic Communist Party. RAF fugitives traveled to Italy, Dutschke recuperated there, and Lenz, the eponymous hero of Peter Schneider's seminal novella from 1973, rediscovered himself and his politics on an Italian journey. *Scylla* (Schneider, 2005) is set exclusively in Italy. Italian characters appear in a number of German novels as writers, journalists, and intellectuals who are interested in documenting the German terror scene. In *The Happy Ones* (Zahl, 1979), an Italian journalist named Rossi is ready to pay thousands of marks for an interview with one of the "Unnameables," as RAF members are known in that novel. Maurizio Serrata in *Ascent to Heaven of an Enemy of the State* (Delius, 1992) is a professor of German from Ferrara; the two murders in *The Assassin's Library* (Sonner, 2001) are cleared up by a German with the Italian-sounding name of Marco Sentenza.

What distinguishes the Italian from the German experience are its murkier battle lines, the involvement of the state in orchestrating or colluding with the left-wing "terrorists" and the presence of a militant Right that reverted to violence, aiming to prepare the ground for a coup, as happened in Chile in 1973. The ground is more fertile for conspiracy theories, which appear to have more substance than north of the Alps.

Through the character Professor Karl Brenner (the same name as that chosen by Schneider for the central character in *Scylla*), Peltzer links the postwar protests in both countries, as the Brenner Pass over the Alps connects the countries themselves. Brenner's biography has a certain binational typicality, and he divulges its bare essentials when he takes Christian and Jakob to view a broken-down property on the German–Polish border that he is planning to buy. Past the age of 60, Brenner is taking two steps that more usually taken at thirty: investing in property and getting married. His delayed personal development is accounted for by the politics he encountered in his younger days.

Like his two main characters, Peltzer abhors cliché. Essential details about birth and background, which a nineteenth-century realist like Fontane delivers in a first paragraph, emerge as incidentals in subordinate clauses. He proceeds in this way with respect to the connections among the present of Nele's cell of activists, Christian's precarious professional existence, and the RAF of the 1970s. German readers are likely to recognize the novel's title from a prison communication written by Holger Meins just before his death in November 1974. Meins is replying to a fellow prisoner who is considering giving up his hunger strike. His words, which have been much quoted, are strangely poetic in the brutality of their crude binary logic:

either person or pig
either survival at any price or
struggle to the death
either problem or solution
there is nothing in between.[10]

No one refers to the phrase "problem or solution" in the novel or even mentions Meins or any of the other RAF by name. One of Nele's activist comrades is named Holger, however, like Rolf Tolm's two sons, whom he calls Holger I and Holger II, in *Safety Net* (Böll, 1979).[11] Gudrun Ensslin not only played the cello, she studied German literature, like Nele. In an argument between Holger and an unnamed female comrade over ways and means, the purpose of carrying out actions, and the way forward, Holger quotes another famous line. His comrade's point has been that revolutionary action has to have an effect. He argues: "Signs are emptied of meaning if they do not have consequences" (390). For Holger, it is more a question of personal probity, of showing where you stand:

> Because some time or other you have to draw a line of separation. Perhaps that is the only reason.
> And perhaps that is not enough.
> You have to decide that for yourself. (391)

The Maoist notion of "drawing a line of separation" (*einen Trennungstrich ziehen*) between the activist and the oppressive pig system was an essential tenet of RAF doctrine.[12]

The consensus view on the left in Germany is that Meins and the rest of the RAF, while undoubtedly brave, did not point the way forward. To give a novel a title that brings to mind one of their best-known phrases must suggest that the novelist has found an answer to the question of what being "part of the solution" in real life is. As the narrative focus throughout the novel is on Christian and Nele, it must lie with them. The most significant piece of missing information relates to the ending, after Nele has accompanied Christian to Paris to carry out the Red Brigade interview. After she has discovered by text message that two of her comrades back in Germany have been arrested, she accuses Christian of using the Red Brigade survivors for his newspaper story—in other words, of being part of the manipulative media system that serves the interests of big business that she is combating. If Christian is to be "part of the solution," then he must have another purpose for the information. After separating from him, we last see her at the end of the novel go back to him in the café where he is sitting. What will happen to her as a result of her cell being broken up is left open. We do not know either whether he will get his interview. He was met as arranged and then apparently was dropped before the interview could take place (perhaps because his concern for Nele led him to disregard an instruction, which the Red Brigaders in turn could have noticed if they were watching him). It is also possible that he has dropped the idea of an interview because of what Nele has said to him.

Part of the Solution is a Berlin novel, in which locations and place names resonate. Berlin is a united city: Christian, a Westerner from the Rhineland, lives in the old East Berlin district of Prenzlauer Berg, Nele is from the Mecklenburg Lakes in still radical Kreuzberg in the former West. Any big novel about Berlin gets compared with Alfred Döblin's *Berlin Alexanderplatz* (1929), and there are some overlaps in their shared multi-stranded construction. It is not *Berlin Alexanderplatz* that is Pelzer's most significant intertext, however, but the twentieth-century novel of surveillance par excellence, George Orwell's *1984* (1949). Orwell's Winston Smith is an everyman (like that other Christian from *Pilgrim's Progress*). He also represents the last possibility for a novel hero under totalitarianism. Winston Smith has pieces of memory, which are the basis of his integrity, an individual conscience, and a will to act, to make a difference. But by the end he is not only crushed by O'Brien's Thought Police, he is worked over to the point that he believes that two plus two equals five. He not only has no will of his own any more, but no memory of his own will. After *1984* there could be no individuals, only automata. It is the bleakest novel, written at the century's ebb, when one form or another of totalitarianism was destined to triumph.

Peltzer, in contrast, shows greater faith in individuals doing the right thing, or in other words being part of a solution. Winston betrays Julia (and she betrays him) under interrogation; their bond of love was not strong enough and could never have been strong enough. In contrast, Christian and Nele are together at the end of *Part of the Solution*. There are superficial similarities in the plot of the two novels, such as the age of the central male characters (both of whom have a failed marriage or relationship in their recent pasts); their professions; and their affairs with younger, braver women, which are each time a locus for defiance. Christian and Nele make love out of view of the CCTV cameras, as Julia leads Winston to the unsurveyed countryside for their tryst. Each time, the security services know all along everything that is happening.

Contemporary electoral politics are not addressed in *Part of the Solution,* but they lurk in the background. The next two novels are more obviously topical. *The Loaded Shooter of Andreas Baader* (Bock, 2009) is set against the backdrop of the election of 2005, which was one of the most bizarre contests in the history of the Federal Republic. It centered on the fundamental question of which economic model was right for the country: neoliberal capitalism, identified increasingly with George W. Bush's America and Tony Blair's Britain, or a reinvention of Ludwig Erhard's social-market economics. Schröder was a reluctant neoliberal who partially recovered his position during the campaign because he could argue against the more extreme economic measures recommended by his opponent. The students' plan in *The Loaded Shooter of Andreas Baader*—to gun down Schröder in order to win sympathy votes for the SPD and keep the left in office—is no more illogical than Schröder's own behavior.

The controversy that erupted in the run-up to the 2005 election is the inspiration for Thomas Weiss's political murder investigation, *Death of a Truffle Pig*, published in December 2007 at the tail end of the thirtieth anniversary commemoration of the German Autumn. Weiss's novel encompasses most of the economic topics that had been in the news. In March 2005, SPD chairman Franz Münterfering referred to hedge funds and private equity firms as "locusts." He was looking for votes: the Red–Green Coalition was on the brink of collapse. He was prompted to make his intervention after Grohe, a profitable German manufacturer of bathware equipment, was bought up by a private equity firm and swiftly closed down. After being sold by a British consortium to the (American) Texas Pacific Group for an estimated 1.5 billion euros in 2005, the new owners shut its factory in Herzberg in the former East Germany, resulting in the loss of 300 jobs. The fate of Grohe and the further controversy over Müntefering's populist intervention generated headlines, books, and an award-winning television documentary.[13] Outside Germany, however, Münterfering was accused of using anti-Semitic rhetoric on the grounds that he was comparing individual businessmen to pests or vermin, as the Nazis compared the Jews to undesirable creatures.[14] This was unfair, since he was criticizing the institutions rather than individuals and there was no evidence that he was aware that any individual or institution had Jewish origins. In his novel, Weiss makes up for this on both counts: his eponymous "truffle pig" is an individual who may well be Jewish.

Death of a Truffle Pig consists of 63 sections, varying in length from a paragraph to four to five pages. Each purports to be an authentic document of one sort or another: a newspaper article, a transcript of an interview, a court judgment. Frank Finlay has called it a "polyphonic novel" because of the range of voices that an invisible authorial hand has assembled, apparently to illuminate the case from a variety of angles.[15] It seems to me that for polyphony to be an appropriate term, some of the voices need to contradict each other, and the sources need to be questioned, or at least submitted to irony. This does not happen.[16] Nobody defends the murder victim, who is the chief executive of a private equity firm; nobody explains what such firms are and what else they do, or questions the motivation of the murderer, who happens to be a retired member of the same GSG-9 unit that stormed the hijacked *Landshut* plane in Mogadishu. The nearest the book has to a controlling narrative presence is a journalist on the local newspaper whose name is Wolfgang Marx. This results in what perhaps amounts to the novel's nicest conceit: contemporary economic history is being reported back to Marx.

Weiss gives the facts a further twist, however, by reproducing a distinctly nationalist account of postwar German economic history in his thumbnail sketch of his fictional Grothe Company's fortunes. Founded in 1922, the firm's breakthrough came in the 1930s, with the production of a new handheld shower device. "Then the war, the ups and downs in which they get through; there is war damage but it can repaired."[17] The Nazis are not mentioned and the firm's war record appears not worth reporting on. There are questions that surely need to be posed. Was the company's production switched to military purposes? Did Grothe supply concentration camps? Were trade unionists or other "agitators" in the work force deported? Did the company employ forced labor from the countries conquered by Germany? The narrative picks up again in 1954, when Hermann Grothe's son Heinrich takes over. He brings some changes, introduces an advertising department, and shows himself in tune with the new age. Although the name of Hitler's Minister for War Production, Albert Speer, is conspicuous by its absence, the architect of the postwar "economic miracle," Ludwig Erhard, is associated closely with the Grothe Company and its owner.

> Black-and-white photos from the Berlin *Tagesspiegel* show Heinrich Grothe with Ludwig Erhard in 1963 at the opening of a new factory. Both in dark suits, with cigars and glasses of bubbly. Then Ludwig Erhard behind the lectern, in the background the new factory, decorated for the occasion, the flowers etc. by the lectern. Workers from the factory floor and the offices listening attentively. Heinrich Grothe, looking confident with his hands in his pockets. Germany and Grothe are on the move. (30)

The "oil crisis" in the mid-1970s is overcome with no great difficulty. Reunification in 1990 presents new opportunities, and the firm moves from Spandau in West Berlin to Nierenberg, where Heinrich Grothe has acquired premises from a state-run GDR enterprise for the symbolic price of 1 German mark. Grothe is still moving with the tide of history. The real problems start eleven years, later with Heinrich's retirement and his sale of the family firm to an "English investment group, British Commerce Partners" (30). They reduce the work force, extract profit that is not reinvested in the company, and just five years later sell the company to the Texas Atlantic Group. Passing from the British to the Americans is like being tossed from the frying pan into the fire. Antiglobalization has distinctly nationalist overtones in this novel. The date that the Texas Atlantic Group take over is May 8, 2006, the 61st anniversary of the unconditional surrender and the end of World War II in Europe. May 8th was known as the "Day of Liberation" in East Germany and the "Day of Capitulation" in the West. In this novel the resonance is clear: once again, Germany has been defeated by American forces—military in 1945; financial in 2006. The characters, newspaper reports, and interviews in *Death of a Truffle Pig* are all invented, as is the case at its center: the murder of the American Marc Schworz, the leading representative of Texas Atlantic Group, by a Grothe employee of 30 years' standing, Klaus Heuser, who is the company chauffeur and an ex GSG-9 commando. Weiss gives both Schworz and Heuser significant back stories, this time not based on real individuals. Heuser's personal link with the German Autumn is underscored by reports of the impending release from prison of RAF members Christian Klar and Brigitte Mohnhaupt. For his critics, Klar's anticapitalist statements were a sign that he was not fit for a pardon. They show that he has no remorse and cannot distance himself from his past. For the citizens of Nierenberg in Weiss's fictional account, Klar's arguments are correct, however. Weiss quotes the theater director Claus Peymann on Klar's comments from prison on resistance to global capitalism: "He articulates what by far the greater part of the world population outside Western Europe and America thinks" (106). According to Peymann:

> These terrorists killed because they believed that with their murders they were able to do something against the murder of hundreds of thousands of children and women in Vietnam, because they believed they had to do something against poverty in the Third World. As Brecht has his Saint Joan of the Stockyards say: "Only violence will do where violence rules..." For me, Christian Klar is for this reason a tragic figure. (95)

The real-life Christian Klar congratulated the author of *Death of a Truffle Pig* after reading it in prison.[18]

The fake documentary style of *Katharina Blum* is one literary model. A fellow Nobel Laureate had more recently explored the multiple meanings of a controversial historical event and revised public perceptions of it. In *Crab Walk* (2002) Günter Grass addressed the difficult question of commemorating German suffering in World War Two by rehearsing multiple accounts of how a German ship transporting thousands of refugees was sunk by a Soviet submarine in January 1945.[19] The difference between Grass and Weiss, however, is that through an elaborate narrative setting Grass weighs up the import of the different meanings that were always attached to this catastrophe.

Martin Walser's controversial *Death of a Critic* (2002) is recalled in Weiss's title.[20] As in Walser's novel, there is uncertainty surrounding the question of the Jewish identity of the murder victim (or presumed murder victim in the case of *Death of a Critic*). Like Walser, Weiss does not mention Jewishness, but, again like Walser, he drops hints. As they are not picked up by any of the characters in the book, they must be aimed directly at his readers. New Yorkers of Austrian descent, as Schworz is said to be, tend overwhelmingly to be Jewish refugees from Nazi Germany or the descendants of refugees. They were born at least 30 years before May 1, 1968, which is given as Schworz's birthday. The symbolic date indicates that the hopes of the Left for international revolutionary solidarity have come to nothing; the children of '68 went to business school. Schworz's date of birth does not match up with his Austrian origins. Schworz is not an obviously Jewish name. Weiss gives an account of Schworz's funeral which, halfway through, is revealed to have been presided over by a "Reverend Williams" and thus must take place under the auspices of a church. Schworz's children are called Paul and Jonathan. His wife's name is not given, but we learn that she has a friend called Ruth Morgenthaler, who can only be Jewish.

Weiss juxtaposes three historical time sequences: the present of 2006–07; the Third Reich of 1933–45; and the "years of lead," which stretch from 1972, the massacre at the Munich Olympics, to 1977. Heuser's killing of Schworz in a wooded area, and his choice of words in his communiqué recall the killing of Schleyer. Heuser entitles his text "MAKE A SIGNAL AGAINST NEOLIBERAL GLOBALIZATION! ANOTHER WORLD IS POSSIBLE!"[21] It ends: "We have therefore ended the disgusting grubbing through the Brandenburg soil by Schworz's greedy snout in the search for profit" (19). Weiss also reproduces the RAF's communiqué dated October 19, 1977, after his account of Mogadishu. It begins with a notorious sentence which Heuser evidently echoes: "we have after 43 days ended hanns-martin schleyer's miserable and corrupt existence" (74), even reproducing the RAF's avoidance of the upper case in their publications.

Heuser's cold-blooded murder of Schworz is compared directly to the famous attempt by Georg Elser on Hitler's life in November 1939. Heuser names his one-man "commando," in true RAF tradition, after Elser, whose bravery and singlemindedness, the novel tells us, have never been granted their due. Another echo of the past, which Weiss this time did not invent, is that the code name for the operation in Mogadishu, *Feuerzauber* (fire magic), was the same as that used by the Legion Condor in Spain, which carried out the bombing of the Basque town of Guernica on April 26, 1937. The continuity that Weiss thereby establishes is between Hitler's Germany and Helmut Schmidt's, which revives the RAF's original critique of the FRG. But Schmidt is mentioned in the novel as the author of articles in *Die Zeit* criticizing "predatory capitalism." Thus he, like Heuser, has switched sides.

Heuser joined GSG-9 from conviction, having been revolted by the massacre of the Israeli athletes in Munich, which resulted from a bungled

German attempt to release them and which in turn was the reason for the creation of the GSG-9 crack force. In the years following 1977, however, Heuser found out about the Palestinian hijackers of the *Landshut*. Weiss also explains what motivated Black September in Munich. Heuser's change of sides thus has two origins: his experience in working for a private equity firm and his increased knowledge of the Arab–Israeli conflict, which leads him to sympathize with the Palestinians. Weiss's political instincts are in each respect thoroughly revisionist. This strain in contemporary German political thought is usually given voice by Rolf Hochhuth, whose *McKinsey Is Coming* (2003) has a similar nationalist message to that of *Death of a Truffle Pig*.

There arguably had been a nationalist dimension to the RAF and the protest movements in the late 1960s, and this was given greater emphasis in some of the fiction of the 2000s. In *The Loaded Shooter of Andreas Baader* (Thilo Bock, 2009), the plan to assassinate a politician is part of a patriotic mission to save German town centers from the uniformity that the multinationals, with their identical chain stores and fast food outlets, would impose. The "deed" has a religious function too:

> "We are doing in the end for our country," said Leander, his voice full of pathos.
> "For our country?"
> "Yes, what else," said Leander. "Our deed is supposed to help Germany!" (277)

By the end of the novel, before he is taken to a psychiatric hospital, Leander has mutated into a neo-Nazi thug. *The Loaded Shooter of Andreas Baader* opens at the beginning of July 2005 and follows the fortunes of a small group of Berlin students through the summer of the election. Other news events included a G8 summit in Scotland; the London bombings on July 7th, in which 56 people were killed by Islamist extremists; and Hurricane Katrina in the United States, which exposed George W. Bush's uncaring attitude to the African American inhabitants of New Orleans. Not only Germany, but the Western world seemed to be in crisis. Bock's novel is told in the first person by Sebastian Singer and is half *Bildungsroman*, half *Desillusionierungsroman* (half novel of education, half novel of disillusionment). It is also one hundred percent "pop." Bock chronicles Sebastian's belated self-discovery and his process of social, sexual, and political maturation, at the end of which he has rid of himself of what he took to be his ideals. Born in 1978, thus not even alive at the same time as Baader, whose gun his friend Leander claims to possess, Sebastian is approaching his twenty-seventh birthday. His age is perhaps the least convincing part of the novel and is included for symbolic reasons: it means that he voted for the first time in the 1998 election. He admits towards the beginning that he does not understand much about politics, the welfare state, and Schröder's reforms, but knows that

> the federal election of nineteen hundred and ninety-eight, the first that I was allowed to participate in [...] brought about a decisive change for my generation: Helmut Kohl could be voted out; politicians could make a likeable impression, perhaps not exactly nice but somehow you could imagine having a conversation with them at a party. (44)

Politics is confusing for these 98ers. They deplore the fact that 85 percent of Germans shop at the discounter Aldi, but Sebastian boycotts its rival Lidl because Lidl exploits its workers. They complain that all main streets are the same because the same multinational chains have shops on all of them, but are outraged too that it is no longer possible to buy single postage stamps, that there is a ban on barbecues in public parks and restrictions on drinking in public spaces. As Sebastian's friend Luzie says, "We are furious but do not know what with" (377). Most of the time, most seem well-adjusted to their environment. They fantasize about violence: exploding a bomb or shooting a politician. Kai, who is stopped by police as he wanders through a rally addressed by the CDU-rightwinger Roland Koch in Charlottenburg, wants to massacre the crowd. When it comes to politicians, according to Kai: "In the final analysis it really does not matter whom we shoot [...] They are all corrupt" (112).

The Loaded Shooter of Andreas Baader is arch in a postmodern sort of way. Sebastian knows at one point that he is a character in a cheap novel. There is sex, suspense, and semi-slapstick comedy in between the politics. When his girlfriend Rieke turns up in Sebastian's bedroom with a gun, which falls out of her handbag as they begin to make love, the explanation is that Leander has got it from his father, who was a RAF lawyer in the 1970s. This turns out to be untrue. Leander's father specializes in traffic accidents and speeding offenses. He never met Baader. The students' knowledge of the RAF comes from a mixture of books and hearsay, pop music, and consumer culture. Stefan Aust's *The Baader-Meinhof Complex* is passed around.

But even if Rieke is a femme fatale for the 2000s and Sebastian is excited by the gun in the bed with her, it is less a thriller than a remake of the 68er student novel. This subgenre was perfected by writers such as Peter Schneider in *Lenz* (1973), Uwe Timm in *Hot Summer* (1974), and F. C. Delius in *America House and the Dance around the Women* (1997).[22] Bock obliquely refers to Timm's *Red* (*Rot*, 2001) when the discussion turns to blowing up Berlin's Victory Column. The central character in these novels tends to be a male student or ex-student, who is usually fretting over an essay or seminar presentation on German literature. Timm's Ulrich Krause is trying to read Hölderlin; Delius's Martin is trying to give an account of the titles of classic German poetry anthologies. Their topics illustrate the fusty, unimaginative way of academic life in pre-68 West Germany. In 2005, students have a wider range of areas of study. Rieke appears genuinely absorbed by her assignment on Expressionist apocalyptic poetry, to the horror of her boyfriend Sebastian:

> "Going to the library on a Saturday!"
> "On account of a seminar presentation on Apocalyptic Imagery in Expressionist Poetry."
> "They almost caused the First World War to happen by imagining it in their poems," Rieke said (21–22).

Given that she shoots Sebastian on the last page of the novel, her enthusiasm for her literary studies could be taken as evidence of incipient mental instability.

We never see Sebastian actually studying, but he does come face to face at a social occasion with a tutor who has started a relationship with a student friend of Sebastian's. Sebastian tries to be relaxed about this, but his social skills abandon him during an argument on the topical subject of political assassinations. He hurriedly leaves the beer garden in embarrassment. This is not the only time that he finds himself unequal to a social occasion, which is a sign of his immaturity. His studies should be helping him make sense of the political world, but on sitting down opposite his tutor, he thinks to himself: "I cannot even get my head round the topic, something to do with constitutions and political crises" (354).

In the 68er student novel, the academics were out of step with contemporary life and politics, which contributed to the alienation experienced by the central character. Here, the alienation cannot name its cause or find a referent. When first Sebastian's and then Leander's father appears towards the end of the novel, Bock comes close to denouncing the students. Leander and Sebastian are from prosperous middle-class backgrounds. Neither appears to need a part-time job because they receive financial support from their parents. The sole function of Sebastian's dad, Herr Singer, is to supply his son with money. He turns up to get his signature for a life insurance policy that should give him security. Inadvertently, he also saves Sebastian from the crazed Leander, who is threatening to shoot him.

Bock sets his novel in what appears to be the same milieu as Weingartner's "Edukators" and puts some of their slogans into the people's mouths, but the political tendency of *The Loaded Shooter of Andreas Baader* could not be more different. Like Weingartner's film, the novel has two endings. The first is harmonious and sees Sebastian and the sensible Luzie, who thought of voting for Merkel and who slowly but surely has won Sebastian's heart through persistent attention, watching the election results on television. Rieke then returns, after an absence of several days. Contradicting his assertion that they have split up, she produces the "shooter" of the novel's title and aims it straight at her errant former boyfriend. The last line of Sebastian's narrative, which is also the last line of the novel, leaves little doubt that she shoots him dead: "And then Rieke pulled the trigger" (471).

Rieke's loss of control was anticipated by Leander's losing his mind, but Sebastian has himself to blame for becoming involved in their assassination fantasy. His relationship with Luzie was beginning to teach him about himself. After fleeing from the conversation in the beer garden, they spend an enchanting and chaste night walking through a Berlin park. The conversation eventually turns to her current topic of study. She hesitates before telling him.

"I am learning," she said, "about masturbation."
"About what?" I turn my head to Luzie but she is still staring at the stars, but the corner of her mouth which is turned in my direction is pointing upwards. She must be grinning.
"Masturbation is one of the most frequent forms of sexual activity, for which furthermore you do not need a partner."
"I am aware of that."
"I find that reassuring," Luzie says, and looks at me grinning in a way that could be called suggestive.
"And you are preparing that for an exam? "
"Well, why not, even thwarted reproduction is part of biology and the examiners will find it a bit different, but I know men don't like talking about it."
"Really, is that true?"
"When did you last have a wank?" Luzie asks and I feel that she has caught me out. (382)

Sebastian's problem with Luzie is that he can never tell her what he has been doing with Rieke and Leander, their weekend in Rieke's grandparents' old cottage in the Lausitz, when they practice shooting, the "conspiratorial" apartment for Leander, and the theft from H&M, all of which are preparation for their assassination of a politician. Luzie misreads his embarrassment over her question. Not long ago, Rieke ordered him at gunpoint to masturbate in front of her. He is embarrassed about his secret life with Rieke, which centers on the gun and their shared dark fantasies. Luzie's seminar topic also highlights the real purpose of their project, which is entirely self-centred, satisfying their wants, quelling their anger, or distracting them from their boredom. Bock's novel is a comic caper, but it has a serious point to make in the context of fiction about the RAF and its would-be imitators. The novels engaging with the RAF that appeared in the 2000s by older writers, such as Timm, Schneider, Delius, and Schlink distanced themselves from violent protest, which seemed an attractive option to some of their colleagues in the 1970s and to some younger characters in their novels now. Michael Wildenhain even draws a direct line of connection between the Revolutionary Cells and Al Qaeda. The young generation, which is exploring a political landscape that does not appear to have changed fundamentally since then, needs to learn the same lessons over again. The findings of this chapter are that there are still fissures in the understanding of terrorism as it is represented in contemporary fiction. A resurgent economic nationalism that instrumentalizes the memory of Baader-Meinhof for its own ideological purposes is set against a romantic anticapitalism, which is still hopeful of finding a route to "the right life." The past is either an inspiration or a warning.

CONCLUSIONS

In this book I have treated a large corpus of narrative fiction as one enormous, multifaceted literary text, which I have taken to be a kind of unacknowledged political unconscious for the 40-year period 1970–2010. While the novelists are not always in step with one another, they were working on a common, indeed national project, which developed over those 40 years in response to violence committed by left-wing extremists and developments in German history in general. The narratives from Baader-Meinhof history that have been fictionalized reveal the stories that the fractured German nation wanted and needed to tell itself. They are national, sometimes nationalist, but ultimately reassuring, featuring the renegade terrorists alongside their adversaries or principal victims, who for them represented the state or the imperialist capitalist system. The love affair between Baader and Ensslin, the drama of the German Autumn, the killing of Herrhausen and Rohwedder during the tumult of reunification, and the role of the police chief Horst Herold tell us as much about Germany's self-image as the figures and episodes that are usually excluded from the novels: Horst Mahler, Ulrich Schmücker, and Hans-Joachim Klein, as well as Munich and Entebbe or the murder of the American soldier Edward Pimental in 1985. I have made a number of other findings. The first is that the impulse for reconciliation, expressed in fiction as efforts to reintegrate the errant terrorist, was dominant, if not quite from the mid-1970s then certainly from the end of the German Autumn in 1977. It carried on most powerfully into the 2000s. Characters based on Herold are portrayed in the main as heroes too; even (ex-Nazi) capitalist villains turn out to be dignified human beings with their own ideas for liberal reform. While the RAF existed, fictional treatments were decidedly guarded; only once the threat that they posed had receded was the subject freely explored in the imagination. In retrospective fiction, "Baader-Meinhof" is a far bigger entity, involving far more individuals than ever it did in reality. Only because armed revolt was a heroic failure, however, do ex-terrorists get basically good press in these novels. There is a deep-reaching sense that terrorist violence on behalf of a righteous case was only justified as long as nobody got hurt. Killing people did not correspond with the terrorists' own self-understanding and certainly did not fit the image that writers wanted to have of them. The problem was that as they used guns and bombs, people were inevitably going to end up hurt. Most of the literature got written out of this self-evidently contradictory position. The terrorist in literature is for this reason not a wholly serious figure. She belongs in the realm of the imagination as a symbolic possibility only, often compensating for the past failure to resist Hitler. The experience of Nazism bred a suspicion of authority, which expressed itself in popular fiction through conspiracy theories that cast the state in the role of villain. The terrorist was not supposed to get real; once she did so, novelists were likely to be in denial. The greatest Baader-Meinhof crime is the killing of the 62-year-old industrial leader and ex-SS officer Hanns-Martin Schleyer, which was effected from a moral logic that was implicit in their undertaking from the start. Yet Schleyer never appears as a character in a novel, despite novelists' fascination with his case. His kidnapping is subject to a taboo, which like most such taboos is all the more powerful for being unacknowledged. Among other things, the RAF was a martyr cult whose supporters found mourning for their fallen comrades to be cathartic for less easily recognized losses. In fiction, guilt is generated by the immediate terrorist events, such as responsibility for a death, but it was attached as well to the events of 1933–1945, which is one reason that Baader-Meinhof accrues so many religious and mythological meanings when transferred to literature. Its literary treatment is thus placed at the heart of contemporary German self-understanding, its politics and its culture.

NOTES

A Brief History

1. F. C. Delius, *Himmelfahrt eines Staatsfeindes*, in *Deutscher Herbst Trilogie* (Reinbek bei Hamburg: Rowohlt, 1997), 440.
2. Erin Cosgrove, *The Baader-Meinhof Affair* (New York: Printed Matter, 2003), 68.

Introduction: The Baader-Meinhof Myth Machine

1. The figures vary according to who is counted. Pflieger counts 34 victims and 27 from their own side (making 61 in total), Augustin counts 41 and 35 (76 in total). Klaus Pflieger, *Die Rote Armee Fraktion—RAF—14.5.1970 bis 20.4.1998* (Baden-Baden: Nomos, 2004), 66-67; Ron Augustin, Labourhistory.net/raf/other (accessed 16 June 2010).
2. Alan O'Leary, Ruth Glyn, and Giancarlo Lombardi give the figure of 374 fatalities, in the introduction to O'Leary, Glyn, and Lombardi (eds.), *Terrorism, Italian Style: The Representation of Terrorism and Political Violence in Contemporary Italian Cinema* (London: IGRS, 2011), 1–15, p. 2.
3. Wolfgang Kraushaar, *1968 als Mythos, Chiffre und Zäsur* (Hamburg: Hamburger Edition, 2000), 166.
4. Klaus Theweleit, "Bermerkungen zum RAF-Gespenst. Abstrakter Realismus und Kunst," in *Ghosts. Drei leicht inkorrekte Vorträge* (Frankfurt: Stroemfeld, 1998), 59.
5. One reason that she finds this gap so striking is because she leaves out a number of novels, for instance: *The Happy Ones* (Zahl, 1979); *Safety Net* (Böll, 1979); *My Sister, My Antigone* (Weil, 1980), and *Dead Alive* (Demski, 1984). See Luise Tremel, "Literrorisierung. Die RAF in der deutschen Belletristik zwischen 1970 und 2004," in Wolfgang Kraushaar (ed.), *Die RAF und der linke Terrorismus*, 2 vols. (Hamburg: Hamburger Edition, 2006), vol. 2, 1117–54, 1130.
6. Wolfgang Kraushaar, *Fischer in Frankfurt: Karriere eines Außenseiters* (Hamburg: Hamburger Edition, 2001).
7. See *The Attorneys: A German Story* (dir. Schulz, 2009), a documentary on the lives and careers of Mahler, Schily, and the RAF defense attorney turned Green politician, Hans Christian Ströbele.
8. Gillian Becker, *Hitler's Children. The Story of the Baader-Meinhof Gang* (New York: Lippincott, 2nd ed. 1978). On her semi "fictionalization," see Gerrit-Jan

Berendse, *Schreiben im Terrordrom. Gewaltcodierung, kulturelle Erinnerung und das Bedingungsverhältnis zwischen Literatur und RAF-Terrorismus* (Munich: edition text & kritik, 2005), 174–84.

9. For a classic account, see Michael Schneider, "Väter und Söhne, posthum. Das beschädigte Verhältnis zweier Generationen," in *Der Kopf verkehrt aufgesetzt oder Die melancholische Linke* (Neuwied: Luchterhand, 1981), 8–64.

10. Aust may have borrowed the idea of a "complex" from Christopher Dobson and Ronald Payne's, *The Carlos Complex: A Pattern of Violence* (London: Book Club Associates, 1977).

11. Dorothea Hauser, *Baader und Herold – Beschreibung eines Kampfes* (Berlin: Fest, 1997/2007), 230 and 231.

12. Gerd Koenen, *Vesper, Ensslin, Baader: Urszenen des deutschen Terrorismus* (Cologne: Kiepenheuer & Witsch, 2003).

13. Dea Loher, *Leviathan*, in *Olgas Raum. Tätowierung, Leviathan. Drei Stücke* (Frankfurt: Verlag der Autoren, 1994), 145–229.

14. Jeremy Varon, *Bringing the War Home. The Weather Underground, the Red Army Faction, and Revolutionary Violence in the Sixties and Seventies* (Berkeley CA: University of California Press, 2004), 20.

15. Colvin points out that "she forgot her handbag, and the police report describes a revolver found inside it, a detail that casts doubt on the version of events that says her decision to leave with the group was unplanned and taken at the very last moment." Sarah Colvin, *Ulrike Meinhof and West German Terrorism: Language, Violence and Identity* (Rochester NY: Camden House, 2009), 80.

16. Peter Schneider calls it "the language of the Wannsee Conference," in Peter-Jürgen Boock and Peter Schneider's, *Ratte tot... Ein Briefwechsel* (Neuwied: Luchterhand, 1985), 108.

17. Quoted by Stefan Aust in *Der Baader-Meinhof Komplex*, 2nd ed. (Munich: Goldmann, 1998), 646.

18. Gerd Koenen, *Das rote Jahrzehnt. Unsere kleine deutsche Kulturrevolution 1967–1977* (Frankfurt: Fischer, 2001), 364.

19. Thomas Elsaesser, "Antigone Agonistes: Urban Guerillas or Guerilla Urbanism? The Red Army Faction, Germany in Autumn and Death Game," in *Giving Ground. The Politics of Propinquity*, eds. Jean Copjec and Michael Sorkin (London / New York: Verso, 1999), 267–302, p. 268–69.

20. Norbert Elias, *Studien über die Deutschen. Machtkämpfe und Habitusentwicklung im 19. und 20. Jahrhundert*, ed. Michael Schröter (Frankfurt: Suhrkamp, 1992), 343.

21. The poem is Celan's "Death Fugue" ("Todesfuge"), written in 1944–1945 and first published in 1948. Koenen writes: "We have everything that we need here for modern myth making–with traces of an antique tragedy or Teutonic *Götterdämmerung*. Even the names sound like theatrical inventions: "Stammheim," for instance, could be from a national drama by Richard Wagner. A haunted castle at any event, on the seventh floor of which, freely adapted from Theweleit, the "killer flesh" of the parents cried out to be redeemed through a sacrifice on the part of the children. But Oedipus Rex and Antigone are close by too—and the topic of collective patricide, which we can understand the murder of Schleyer as having been." Koenen, *Das rote Jahrzehnt* (2001), 363–64.

22. The phrases "German Autumn" and "years of lead" are taken or adapted from Heinrich Heine and Friedrich Hölderlin, respectively. The films are *Deutschland im Herbst* [Germany in Autumn] (dir. Kluge et al, 1978) and *Die bleierne Zeit* [The Leaden Time] (dir. von Trotta, 1981), known in English as *The German Sisters* or *Marianne and Juliane*. Kraushaar calls the German Autumn a "Pseudopoem." See Wolfgang Kraushaar, "Der nicht erklärte Ausnahmezustand. Staatliches Handeln während des sogenannten Deutschen Herbstes," in Kraushaar (ed.), *Die RAF und der linke Terrorismus* (2006), vol. 2, 1011–25, p. 1012.

23. Helmuth Krausser, *Eros* (Munich: btb, 2008), 184.

24. Whether the "selection" was undertaken by nationality (Israeli and non-Israeli) or ethnic origin (Jewish and non-Jewish) was always disputed by the Revolutionary Cells. See Oliver Tolmein, *Vom deutschen Herbst zum 11. September. Die RAF, der Terrorismus und der Staat* (Hamburg: Konkret, 2002), 254.

25. Hans-Joachim Klein, *Rückkehr in die Menschlichkeit. Appell eines ausgestiegenen Terroristen* (Reinbek: rororo, 1979). Foreword by Daniel Cohn-Bendit. Memoirs by former terrorists are generally marred by the authors' priority of self-justification. Inge Viett was commercially the most successful, Margrit Schiller (after Klein) the most astute. Inge Viett, *Nie war ich furchtloser. Autobiographie* (Nautilus: Hamburg, 1996); Margrit Schiller, *Es war ein harter Kampf um meine Erinnerung. Ein Lebensbericht aus der RAF* (Hamburg: Konkret, 1999).

26. *Hans-Joachim Klein: My life as a terrorist* (dir. Oey, 2005).

27. The affair generated 900 newspaper articles between July and November 2003. See Heinz-Peter Preusser, "Warum *Mythos* Terrorismus? Versuch einer Begriffserklärung," in Matteo Galli and Preusser (eds.), *Mythos Terrorismus. Vom Deutschen Herbst zum 11. September—Fakten, Fakes und Fiktionen* (Heidelberg: Universitätsverlag, 2006), 69–83, esp. 70–73.

28. Anne Siemens, *Für die RAF war er das System, für mich der Vater: Die andere Geschichte des deutschen Terrorismus* (Munich: Piper, 2007).

29. Ulrich Woelk, *Die letzte Vorstellung* (Hamburg: Hoffmann & Campe, 2002), 49.

30. Inge Stephan and Alexandra Tacke (eds.), *NachBilder der RAF* (Vienna: Böhlau, 2008).

31. *Der Baader Meinhof Report. Aus Akten des Bundeskriminalamtes, der "Sonderkommission" und des Bundesamtes für Verfassungsschutz* (Mainz: Hase and Kochler, 1972).

32. Ibid., 20 and 35.

33. Wolfgang Schorlau, *Die blaue Liste. Denglers erster Fall* (Kiepenheuer & Witsch, 2003), 77 and 78.

34. Peter-Paul Zahl, *Die Glücklichen. Schelmenroman* (Munich: dtv, 2001), 462–63. First published in 1979 and frequently reprinted.

35. *The Baader-Meinhof Report* (1972), 43.

36. For an amusing demolition of this section, see Colvin, *Ulrike Meinhof and West German Terrorism* (2009), 191–92.

37. Hans Kundnani, *Utopia or Auschwitz. German's 1968 Generation and the Holocaust* (London: Hurst, 2009), 161.

38. Aust, *Der Baader-Meinhof Komplex* (1998), 396.
39. See Bianca Dombrowa et al, *GeRAFtes. Analysen zur Darstellung der RAF und des Linksterrorismus in der deutschen Literatur* (Bamberg: Lehrstuhl für Neuere deutsche Literatur, 1994), 13.
40. Thomas Hoeps, *Arbeit am Widerspruch. Terrorismus in deutschen Romanen und Erzählungen (1837–1992)* (Dresden: Thelem, 2001).
41. Vesper is portrayed most notably in *The German Sisters* (dir. von Trotta, 1981), Dea Loher's play *Leviathan* (1993), the novelette by Alban Lefranc, *Attaques sur le chemin, le soir, dans la neige* [Attacks on the road, in the evening, in the snow] (2005), and *Who If Not Us* (dir. Veiel, 2011), as well as in the film version of his "novel-essay," *The Trip* (dir. Imhof, 1985).
42. Elsaesser makes *The Trip* sound more exciting and relevant to Baader-Meinhof history than it is, referring to a visit to Sicily with Gudrun and Andreas, guerilla training by Libyans, and the kidnap of baby Felix. The explanation must be that he is thinking of Imhof's 1985 film, which does indeed contain these episodes.
43. See Michael Kappeln, *Doppelt Leben: Bernward Vesper und Gudrun Ensslin. Die Tübinger Jahre* (Tübingen: Klöpfer & Meyer, 2005).
44. Gillian Becker, *Hitler's Children*, 3rd ed. (London: Pickwick, 1989), 94.
45. Quoted by Gerd Conradt in *Starbuck Holger Meins. Ein Porträt als Zeitbild* (Berlin: Espresso, 2001), 155.
46. Christoph Hein, *In seiner frühen Kindheit ein Garten* (Frankfurt: Suhrkamp, 2005), 41–42.
47. See Margaret Scanlan, *Plotting Terror: Novelists and Terrorists in Contemporary Fiction* (Charlottesville and London: University of Virginia Press, 2001). Her Baader-Meinhof novel is the French *Lisbonne dernière marge* [Lisbon Last Margin] (Volodine, 1990) and her only German-language novel is Friedrich Dürrenmatt's *The Assignment* (1985).
48. Steven Crashaw, *Easier Fatherland* (London: Continuum, 2004); Tony Judt, *Postwar. A History of Europe since 1945* (London: Vintage, 2010), 470–72.
49. Quoted by Stephen Schindler, "Bombige Bücher: Literatur und Terrorismus," in *Wendezeiten Zeitenwenden. Positionsbestimmungen zur deutschsprachigen Literatur 1945–1995*, eds. Robert Weninger and Brigitte Rossbacher (Tübingen: Stauffenberg, 1997), 55–78, p. 55.
50. *Der demokratische Terrorist* (dir. Bergland, 1992), an adaptation of the Swedish thriller of the same title by Jan Guillou, and *Die Terroristen!* (dir. Gröning, 1992).
51. See Rachel Palfreymen, "The Fourth Generation: Legacies of Violence as Quest for Identity in Post-unification Terrorism Films," in David Clarke (ed.), *German Cinema since Unification* (London / New York: Continuum, 2006), 11–42.
52. Gretchen Dutschke, *Wir hatten ein barbarisches, schönes Leben. Rudi Dutschke: Eine Biographie* (Cologne: Kiepenheuer & Witsch, 1996), 78.
53. Klaus Rainer Röhl, *Fünf Finger sind keine Faust. Eine Abrechnung* (Munich: Universitas, 1998), 3rd ed., 186. Becker's *Hitler's Children* begins with a reference to the film.
54. Klaus Stern and Jörg Hermann, *Andreas Baader. Das Leben eines Staatsfeindes* (Munich: dtv, 2007), 90, 106, and 111.

55. See Koenen, *Das rote Jahrzehnt* (2001), 15.
56. Aust, *Der Baader-Meinhof Komplex* (1998), 223–24.
57. Günter Grass, "Politisches Tagebuch." *Wiederholter Versuch," Essays und Reden II 1970–1979, Werkausgabe* (Göttingen: Steidl, 1997), edited by Volker Neuhaus and Daniela Hermes, vol. 15, 210–213, p. 211.
58. Stern and Hermann, *Andreas Baader* (2007), 35–42.
59. Ibid., 104–06.
60. Marianne Herzog, *Von der Hand in den Mund. Frauen im Akkord* (Berlin: Rotbuch, 1976); *From Hand to Mouth. Women and Piecework*, tr. Stanley Mitchell (Harmondsworth: Penguin, 1980); *Nicht den Hunger verlieren* (Berlin: Rotbuch, 1980); and *Suche* (Darmstadt: Luchterhand, 1988).
61. See the reconstruction of Katharina de Fries's story in the ghost-written memoirs by Ulrike Edschmid, *Frau mit Waffe. Zwei Geschichten aus terroristischen Zeiten* (Frankfurt: Suhrkamp, 2001), 69.
62. Kurt Held (pseudonym of Kurt Kläber), *Die rote Zora und ihre Bande* (Aarau: Sauerländer, 1941).
63. Kawaters is quoted in "Als wenn es mich nicht gäbe," *Der Spiegel*, 2 June 2001. See also www.freilassung.de
64. Kawaters's novel *Zora Zobel findet die Leiche* (1984) was followed by *Zora Zobel zieht um* (1986). Both Frankfurt: Zweitausendeins. After her return to Germany and legality, she published *Zora Zobel auf Umwegen* (Berlin: Espresso, 2001).
65. Bernhard Schlink, *Das Wochenende* (Zurich: Diogenes, 2008), 103.

1 Avoiding the Subject: Six Tropes in 68er Fiction

1. This is the subject of Uwe Timm's *Der Fremde und der Freund* (Frankfurt: Suhrkamp, 2005).
2. The driving license is said to have been issued to "Peter. C, born on 14.6.34 in Berlin," Aust, *Der Baader-Meinhof Komplex* (1998), 93.
3. For a review of recent literature, see Patricia Melzer, "Maternal Ethics and Political Violence: The 'Betrayal' of Motherhood among the Women of the RAF and June 2 Movement," *Seminar* 47:1 (2011), 81–102.
4. Three recent films have had female directors: *Schattenwelt* [released as *Long Shadows*], (dir. Walter, 2008); *The Day Will Come* (dir. Schneider, 2009); and *The Attorneys: A German Story* (dir. Schulz, 2009).
5. Christine Brückner, "Kein Denkmal für Gudrun Ensslin. Rede gegen die Wände der Stammheimer Zelle," in *Wenn Du geredet hättest Desdemona. Ungehaltene Reden ungehaltener Frauen* (Hamburg: Hoffmann & Campe, 1983), 109–122.
6. Baader is the model in: *The Comrade* (Röhl, 1975); *Gentlemen of the Dawn* (Chotjewitz, 1978); *Ascent to Heaven of an Enemy of the State* (Delius, 1992); *The Execution* (Brenner, 2000); and *Rose Party* (Scholz, 2001). *The Blue List* (Schorlau, 2003) and *In His Early Childhood, a Garden*, (Hein, 2005) feature characters based on Grams. Klar is the model in *The Weekend* (Schlink, 2008) and *Autumn Messenger* (Hoeth, 2009).
7. For Claire Bielby, this has its origins "in the print media of the 1970s where the woman terrorist became a print media phenomenon and was set up as 'other' to the German mother and, arguably too, to the German nation."

Bielby, "Remembering the Red Army Faction," *Memory Studies* 3:2 (2010), 137–50, p. 139.

8. See Varon, *Bringing the War Home* (2004), "Democratic Intolerance," 254–64.

9. Revolutionary Cells activist Gerd Albartus, for example, who would be "executed" by Palestinians in 1987, was sentenced to four years, nine months for arson attacks on cinemas showing the Entebbe films. See Tolmein, *Vom deutschen Herbst zum 11. September* (2002), 254. See also *Dreamers of the Absolute* (Wildenhain, 2008), 156.

10. Peter-Paul Zahl, *Die Glücklichen. Schelmenroman* (Munich: dtv, 2001), 461.

11. On the RAF as "death cult," see Matteo Galli, "'Mit dem Einkaufswagen durch den Geschichts-Supermarkt'? Zu einigen Bestandteilen des sogenannten Mythos RAF in den Künsten: Entstehung, Entwicklung und Neukontextualisierung," in Galli and Preusser (eds.), *Mythos Terrorismus* (2006), 101–16, esp. 110–14.

12. Judith Kuckart, *Wahl der Waffen* (Frankfurt: Fischer, 1990), 9.

13. Eva Demski, *Scheintod* (Munich: Hanser, 1984), 217.

14. Renate Klöppel, *Der Pass* (Hamburg: Rotbuch, 2002), 98.

15. Wolfgang Brenner, *Die Exekution* (Frankfurt: Eichborn, 2000), 281.

16. This at least was the how the original film released to cinemas ended. The DVD version ends with their escaping German repression by going to Italy, which is another time-honored practice, both in German literature (Goethe) and Baader-Meinhof history.

17. Meinhof was still idealizing the "Baader action" from prison in 1974. Colvin remarks, "It is difficult not to feel that the group never got beyond its one significant success," *Ulrike Meinhof and West German Terrorism* (2009), 174.

18. Kochstraße, which ran parallel to the Berlin Wall, has now been re-named: one half after Axel Springer, the other half after Rudi Dutschke.

19. Günter Herburger, "Lenau" (1972), in *Die Eroberung der Zitadelle. Zwei Erzählungen* (Neuwied: Luchterhand, 1991), 111–70, p. 121–22.

20. Dated May 24, 1967. Dieter Kunzelmann, *Leisten Sie keinen Widerstand! Bilder aus meinem Leben* (Berlin: Transit, 1998), 79.

21. The films are *The Legends of Rita* (dir. Schlöndorff, 2000) and the documentary featuring Viett herself, *Big Freedom, Little Freedom* (dir. Konrad, 2000); the play is Andreas Dresen, *Zeugenstand. Stadtguerilla-Monologe* (*In the Witness Box. Urban Guerilla Monologues*), which premiered in 2002 at the Deutsches Theater, Berlin. Arguably all post-2000 novels with a GDR dimension owe a debt to Viett.

22. For Viett's own account, see *Nie war ich furchtloser. Autobiographie* (Reinbek bei Hamburg: Rowohlt, 2000), 135-49. See also Till Meyer, another participant in the kidnapping, *Staatsfeind. Erinnerungen* (Hamburg: Spiegel Buchverlag, 1996), 323–32.

23. The terrorists were Verena Becker, Rolf Heissler, Gabriele Kröcher-Tiedemann, Rolf Pohle, and Ina Siepmann. Horst Mahler refused to be exchanged as he had left the RAF and preferred to serve out his prison sentence.

24. See Koenen, *Das rote Jahrzehnt* (2001), 374–75, who points out that they were lucky that nothing went wrong and did not have to put the contingency plan, which involved taking another hostage, or, in the case of their

hideaway being found, leading out Lorenz with the barrel of a shotgun secured against his head by masking tape. Chancellor Helmut Schmidt was furious at the outcome, which he claimed he would never have allowed had he not been laid low with a heavy cold, which strengthened his resolve to stand firm in 1977.

25. Viett, *Nie war ich furchtloser* (1996), 94.
26. Gerhard Seyfried, *Der schwarze Stern der Tupamaros* (Berlin: Aufbau, 2006), 315.
27. Theweleit, "Bemerkungen zum RAF-Gespenst" (1998), 46–47.
28. Kraushaar, *1968* (2000), 165.
29. Elsaesser, "Antigone Agonistes" (1999), 284.
30. Herburger, "Lenau" (1972), 124.
31. Peter O. Chotjewitz, *Die Herren des Morgengrauens. Romanfragment* (Berlin: Rotbuch, 1978), 93.
32. See Hoeps, *Arbeit am Widerspruch* (2001), 164.
33. Uwe Timm, *Rot* (Cologne: Kiepenheuer & Witsch, 2001), 111.
34. Auster recalls his sudden realization that he had known a number of America's most wanted men from his days as an activist at Columbia University. "In the summer of 1969, I walked into a post office in western Massachusetts with a friend who had to mail a letter. As she waited in line, I studied the posters of the FBI's ten most wanted men pinned to the wall. It turned out that I knew seven of them." Paul Auster, *Hand to Mouth. A Chronicle of Early Failure* (Faber and Faber: London/Boston, 1997), 34–35.
35. Scanlan, *Plotting Terror* (2002), 1–2.
36. F. C. Delius, *Mein Jahr als Mörder* (Berlin: Rowohlt, 2004), 9.
37. Delius has denied that this was ever the case. See Sven Kramer, "Demarcations and Exclusions: Terrorism, State Violence, and the Left in German Novels of the 1970s and 1980s," in Robert Weninger (ed.), *Gewalt und kulturelles Gedächtnis. Repräsentationsformen von Gewalt in Literatur und Film seit 1945* (Tübingen: Stauffenberg, 2005), 255–65, p. 262. See also Keith Bullivant, "F. C. Delius's 'Deutscher Herbst' Trilogy," ibid., 267–77, esp. 274, note 6.
38. Peter Schneider, *Messer im Kopf. Drehbuch* (Berlin: Rotbuch, 1979).
39. Boock / Schneider, *Ratte tot* (1985), 8–9.
40. Ibid., 67.
41. Peter Schneider, *Rebellion und Wahn. Mein '68. Eine autobiographische Erzählung* (Cologne: Kiepenheuer & Witsch, 2008).
42. Schneider said in 1985 that the idea of using violence to bring about a revolution was at the heart of discussions among students in 1968: "The idea of the urban guerrilla and of armed struggle in the big cities was by no means restricted to a handful of isolated individual warriors. Right from the beginning it played a central role in the thoughts and feelings of the 68er generation and was discussed quite openly at teach-ins attended by thousands in a way which is unimaginable today." Boock / Schneider, *Ratte tot* (1985), 9.
43. Colvin, *Ulrike Meinhof and West German Terrorism* (2009), 38. She identifies the other authors as Enzensberger, Gaston Salvatore, and Bahman Nirumand, 36.
44. See Gudrun Ensslin, Bernward Vesper, *"Notstandsgesetze von Deiner Hand." Briefe 1968/1969* (Frankfurt: Suhrkamp, 2009), 48.

45. See Inge Stephan, "'Raspe-Irrweg' und 'Baader-Schwachsinn.' Dekonstruktion des Deutschen Herbstes in Rainald Goetz' Roman *Kontrolliert* (1988)," in Stephan and Tacke (eds.), *NachBilder der RAF* (2008), 39–62. See also Uwe Schütte, *Die Poetik des Extremen. Ausschreitungen einer Sprache des Radikalen* (Göttingen: Vandenhoeck & Ruprecht, 2006), esp. 83–96 ("Sympathy for the Devil—Zwischen Nähe und Abgrenzung zum Terrorismus").

2 From Stechlin to Stammheim: F. C. Delius as Pioneer

1. The *German Autumn* novels by F. C. Delius are: *Ein Held der inneren Sicherheit* (1981), *Mogadischu Fensterplatz* (1987), and *Himmelfahrt eines Staatsfeindes* (1992). All published Reinbek bei Hamburg: Rowohlt. References are to the *Deutscher Herbst Trilogie* (Reinbek bei Hamburg: Rowohlt, 1997).

2. As Bullivant points out "the festivities envisioned by Nagel [Baader] are unimaginable without all the public celebrations that came after the fall of the Berlin Wall," which surely underlines the fact that the first two novels were products of their time of publication too. Keith Bullivant, "F. C. Delius's 'Deutscher Herbst' Trilogy," in Weninger (ed.), *Gewalt und kulturelles Gedächtnis* (2005) 267–77, p. 273.

3. Theodor Fontane, *Der Stechlin* [1898], in *Sämtliche Werke, Romane, Erzählungen, Gedichte*, vol. 5, ed. Walter Keitel (Munich: Hanser, 1966), 7–388, pp. 8–9.

4. Futterknecht argues that Diehl "walls himself up behind the thick and attractive façade of an ultramodern building" and speaks of "the dead souls in their palatial splendour," whose lives continue as if nothing has happened—-for the time being anyway. Franz Futterknecht, "Die Inszenierung des Politischen. Delius' Romane zum Deutschen Herbst," in *F. C. Delius: Studien über sein literarisches Werk*, eds. Manfred Durzak and Hartmut Steinecke (Tübingen: Stauffenberg, 1997), 69–88, p. 77.

5. According to Theweleit, this reaction was typical of what actually happened: "The non-sympathy for Schleyer was mercilessly explicit: when you have a system of abstract identification, anything that does not belong is split off unceremoniously. Schleyer, 'representative in chief of German capital,' hoped in vain that a tear be shed for him." Theweleit, "Bemerkungen zum RAF-Gespenst" (1998), 75.

6. Quoted by Futterknecht, "Die Inszenierung des Politischen," (1997), 75, note 7.

7. Delius moves the German Autumn to 1979; if Diehl were eleven in 1953, he would have been 35 in 1977. Büttinger would have been 63. There are a number of other deliberate divergences from the facts, which mark out the novel as fiction: that is a work of symbolic rather than historical truth.

8. See Dominick LaCapra, *Writing History, Writing Trauma* (Baltimore/London: The Johns Hopkins University Press, 2001), esp. 21.

9. Lutz Hachmeister, *Schleyer. Eine deutsche Geschichte* (Munich: C. H. Beck, 2004).

10. See Schütte, *Die Poetik des Extremen* (2006), 399.

11. Christian Hißnauer, "'Mogadischu.' Opferdiskurs doku/dramatisch. Narrative des Erinnerns an die RAF im bundesdeutschen Fernsehen 1978–2008," in Ächtler and Gansel (eds.), *Ikonographie des Terrors?* (2010), 99–125.

12. Scribner places Delius in this company: "Through his hostage Andrea, he engenders Germany as a victim and enters the events of 1977 into a skewed account of history." Charity Scribner, "Engendering the Subject of Terror: Friedrich Christian Delius and Friedrich Dürrenmatt in the Mid-1980s," in Berendse and Cornils (eds.), *Baader Meinhof Returns* (2008), 125–36, p. 134.

13. Robert Coover, *The Public Burning* (New York: Viking, 1977), or *Die öffentliche Verbrennung* (Neuwied: Luchterhand, 1983). See also Klaus Modick, "Die öffentliche Verbrennung. Friedrich Christian Delius' Romangroteske *Himmelfahrt eines Staatsfeindes*," *Frankfurter Rundschau* 30.09.1992.

14. Schütte writes of *Ascent to Heaven of an Enemy of the State* that "Delius shows himself to be one of the few authors who have recognized the messianic dimension of the RAF." Uwe Schütte, "'Heilige, die im Dunkel leuchten.' Der Mythos der RAF im Spiegel der Literatur nachgeborener Autoren," in *Counter Cultures in Germany and Central Europe: From Sturm und Drang to Baader-Meinhof,* eds. Steve Giles and Maike Oergel (Berne: Lang, 2003), 353–72, p. 362.

15. *La mort d'Ulrike Meinhof: rapport de la Commission international d'enquête* (Paris: Maspero, 1979). [The death of Ulrike Meinhof: Report of the International Commission of Enquiry]. One reviewer identifies Serrata with Delius himself, calling him "eine Nebenfigur, hinter der nach Hitchcock-Manier die intellektuelle Physiognomie des Autors aufscheint." See Hannes Krauss, "Politisches Begräbnis, Medienspektakel. Plädoyer für F. C. Delius' umstrittenen Terroristen-Roman," *die tageszeitung* 06.01.1993.

16. See Jutta Ditfurth, *Ulrike Meinhof. Die Biographie* (Hamburg: Ullstein, 2007), 444–46 and Pflieger, *Die Rote Armee Fraktion* (2004), 66.

17. Peter Schneider, "Der Sand an Baaders Schuhen," *Kursbuch* 51 (1978), 1–15.

18. Erich Fried, "Vorbeugemord" (1974), in *Anfragen und Nachreden. Politische Texte* (Berlin: Wagenbach, 1994), ed. Volker Kaukoreit, 11850. Even lists are highly contentious in this context. Fried names the police responsible for the deaths and their victims as follows: "Kurras, Salzwedel, Schulz [...] Ohnesorg, Rauch, Schelm, Weissbecker, Epple, Macloed, and the Fedayin [from Black September] and the Munich athletes" (129–30). He thus leaves out the victims from among the German police but includes both the Palestinians responsible for the massacre of the Israeli athletes at the Munich Olympics and leaves out the athletes themselves.

19. See Karin König, "Zwei Ikonen des bewaffneten Kampfes. Leben und Tod Georg von Rauchs und Thomas Weissbeckers," in Kraushaar (ed.), *Die RAF und der linke Terrorismus* (2006), 430–71.

20. Elsaesser, "Antigone Agonistes" (1999), 285.

21. One chapter of the novel is a montage of truncated quotations from *The Baader-Meinhof Complex*, where Nagel reflects "Wie ich mir diese Sprache stehle, in der ich euch vormache, wie ihr mit mir umgeht" (473). Aust, "Andreas Baader" and "Andreas Baader geht nach Berlin," in *Der Baader-Meinhof Komplex* (Munich: Knaur, 1989), 16–19 and 38–40.

22. Heinrich Heine, *Deutschland. Ein Wintermärchen*, Caput 26, in Heine, *Sämtliche Schriften*, ed. Klaus Briegleb (Frankfurt: Ullstein, 1981), 571–644, p. 639.
23. See Kirsten Prinz, "Umkämpft und abgeschlossen? Narrative über die RAF im Spiegel ihrer Rezeption. Überlegungen zu Bernhard Schlinks Roman *Das Wochenende* und Bernd Eichingers Film *Der Baader Meinhof Komplex*," in Ächtler and Gansel (eds.), *Ikonographie des Terrors?* (2010), 311–32, esp. 324–25.
24. See Gabriele Mueller's excellent exegesis, "Imagining the RAF from an East German Perspective: Carow's *Vater, Mutter, Mörderkind* and Dresen's *Raus aus der Haut*," in Berendse and Cornils (eds.), *Baader Meinhof Returns* (2008), 269–84.

3 Retelling the Classics: Baader-Meinhof and the German Literary Canon

1. Böll admitted only "an unconscious association" with Schiller. J. H. Reid points out that "the dual title is also archaic [and] takes the reader back to the eighteenth century [...] This post-modernist quotation of earlier forms implies a didactic stance (*How* violence arises) and simultaneously parodies the didactic stance." Reid, *Heinrich Böll* (1988), 185.
2. Hans Egon Holthusen, *Sartre in Stammheim. Zwei Themen aus den Jahren der großen Turbulenz* (Stuttgart: Klett-Cotta, 1982).
3. Also known in English as *The Possessed* and *The Devils*.
4. Von Trotta originally meant the phrase to refer to her central characters' formative childhood decade of the 1950s. See back cover of *Die bleierne Zeit. Ein Film von Margarethe von Trotta*, edited by Hans Jürgen Weber with Ingeborg Weber (Frankfurt: Fischer, 1981).
5. According to *The Black Star of the Tupamaros* (Seyfried, 2004) 93–98.
6. See, for example, Herbert Kraft, *Mondheimat: Kafka* (Pfullingen: Neske, 1983).
7. Peter O. Chotjewitz, *Die Herren des Morgengrauens. Romanfragment* (Berlin: Rotbuch, 1978), 22.
8. Kafka: "Jemand musste Josef K verleumdet haben, denn ohne daß er etwas Böses getan hätte, wurde er eines Morgens verhaftet." Chotjewitz: "Jemand musste in Fritz Buchonia ein schlechtes Gewissen erzeugt haben, denn ohne daß er sich einer Schuld bewußt gewesen wäre, hatte er eines Morgens einen Traum." Franz Kafka, *Der Proceß. Roman in der Fassung der Handschrift* [The Trial, written 1914–15, first published 1925], in *Gesammelte Werke in zwölf Bänden*, vol. 3, ed. Malcolm Pasley (Frankfurt: Fischer, 1994), 9.
9. *The Gentlemen of the Dawn*'s place in the literary mythology of the RAF is assured after the scandal of its publication history. Bertelsmann refused to publish the novel after the series, edited by authors themselves (the *Autorenedition*), had chosen it, which caused the innovative series to fold. The novel found a home instead with Rotbuch, which has reissued it on the 20th and 30th anniversaries of the German Autumn in 1997 and 2007. See Hoeps, *Arbeit am Widerspruch* (2001), 217.

10. Pierre Bertaux, *Hölderlin und die französische Revolution* (Frankfurt: Suhrkamp, 1969). Peter Weiss's play *Hölderlin* premiered in 1971.

11. Theodor W. Adorno, "Parataxis." Zur späten Lyrik Hölderlins" (1964), in *Noten zur Literatur* (Frankfurt: Suhrkamp, 1974), 447–91.

12. Oliver Tolmein comments that Geissler's novel was "a kind of cult book of the anti-imperialist scene, but in fact much more multi-layered." "*RAF—Das war für uns Befreiung.*" *Ein Gespräch mit Irmgard Müller über bewaffneten Kampf, Knast und die Linke* (Hamburg: Konkret, 1997), 269.

13. See Peter Langemeyer, "Moralische oder politische Anstalt? Zur Standortsbestimmung des politischen Dramas und Theaters bei Rolf Hochhuth," in *Rolf Hochhuth: Theater als politische Anstalt*, eds. Ilse Nagelschmidt, Sven Neufert, and Gert Ueding (Weimar: Denkena, 2010), 73–98.

14. Moray McGowan, "Ulrike Meinhof im Deutschen Drama der Neunziger Jahre: Drei Beispiele," in Giles and Oergel (eds.), *Counter Cultures in Germany and Central Europe* (2004), 373–93.

15. "As the story of a girlfight it has a certain popular appeal, but its basis in fact has never been properly demonstrated, neither by Aust nor anyone else," comments Colvin in *Ulrike Meinhof and West German Terrorism* (2009), 172–73; see also 209–15.

16. Werner Hecht (ed.), *Brechts Antigone des Sophocles* (Frankfurt: Suhrkamp, 1988).

17. Blum's choice between "loyalty to lover over loyalty to the state" is not unlike Antigone's. See Sven Kramer, "Demarcations and Exclusions: Terrorism, State Violence, and the Left in German Novels of the 1970s and 1980s," in Weninger (ed.), *Gewalt und kulturelles Gedächtnis* (2005), 255–65, p. 258.

18. At the time, productions of Camus's *Les Justes* were taken off theater programs and there were rumors that the same fate had befallen Mozart's *Die Entführung aus dem Serail*, because of the word "kidnapping" in the title. Reid, *Heinrich Böll* (1988), 193.

19. Theweleit, "Bemerkungen zum RAF-Gespenst" (1998), 71.

20. George Steiner, *Antigones* (Oxford: Clarendon Press, 1984), 151.

21. Elsaesser, "Antigone Agonistes" (1999).

22. Within the narrower confines of German Studies, it has been the subject of sustained scrutiny, however. See Moray McGowan, for instance, "Myth, Memory, Testimony, Jewishness in Grete Weil's *Meine Schwester Antigone*," in Helmut Peitsch, Charles Burdett and Claire Gorrara (eds.), *European Memories of the Second World War* (New York / Oxford: Berghahn, 1999), 149–58.

23. Grete Weil, *Meine Schwester Antigone* (Zurich: Benziger, 1980), 6.

24. Pascale R. Bos, *German-Jewish Literature in the Wake of the Holocaust: Grete Weil, Ruth Kluger and the Politics of Address* (New York/Basingstoke: Palgrave, 2005), 53. Bos argues that the younger generation, like the narrator, is caught up in its own "Antigone Complex," "overcompensating in such a way that their protest deteriorates in extremism and more violence," 54.

25. The action in Boock (*Descent*, 1988), Geissler (*Kamalatta*, 1988), and Giullou (*The Democratic Terrorist*, 1987) is based each time on plots against NATO targets.

26. The story is perhaps better known outside Germany as a source of motifs for painters, such as Donatello, Mantegna, Caravaggio, and Artemisia Gentileschi, among a great many others.

27. Rolf Hochhuth, *Judith*, in *Alle Dramen*, 2 vols, vol. 2 (Reinbek bei Hamburg: Rowohlt, 1991), 2127–2330, p. 2300.

28. For a full list, see Nagelschmidt, Neufert and Ueding (eds.), *Rolf Hochhuth* (2010), 414–18.

29. See Oskar Negt (ed.), *Der Fall Fonty. "Ein weites Feld" von Günter Grass im Spiegel der Kritik* (Göttingen: Steidl, 1996).

30. Theodor Fontane, *Quitt* [1890], in *Sämtliche Werke, Romane, Erzählungen Gedichte*, ed. Keitel (1966), vol. 1, 213–452; *Mathilde Möhring* [1907], ibid., vol. 4, 577–674.

31. Gerhard Wisnewski, Wolfgang Landgraeber, Ekkehard Sieker, *Das RAF-Phantom. Wozu Politik und Wirtschaft Terroristen brauchen* (Munich: Knaur, 1997), 230–79. First published 1992.

32. Günter Grass, *Ein weites Feld*, Werkausgabe (Göttingen: Steidl, 1997), eds. Volker Neuhaus and Daniela Hermes, vol. 13, ed. Hermes, 613.

33. Tremel points out that just about all the characters are RAF sympathizers, at least after the event. See Tremel, "Literrorisierung" (2006), esp. 1148–51. Alongside *Rose Party* (Scholz, 2001) among the Baader-Meinhof novels published in the 2000s, *The Last Performance* has been the object of the most critical scrutiny from Germanists, making it "canonical" in the sense suggested by Beck, *Reden an die Lebenden und an die Toten* (2008), 16. No one has noticed the connection with the plot of *The Magic Flute*.

34. The novel was adapted for television under the title *Murder by the Sea* (*Mord am Meer*, 2004, dir. Geschonneck), which makes it the first film adaptation of a German Baader-Meinhof novel since *Scenes of Fire* (Degenhardt, 1975; dir. Brandt, 1978).

35. See Sylvia Henze, "Die RAF und die DDR—Zur künstlerischen Darstellung eines 'blinden Fleckes' in Ulrich Woelks *Die letzte Vorstellung*, Ulrich Plenzdorfs *Vater, Mutter, Mörderkind* und Volker Schlöndorffs *Die Stille nach dem Schuss*," in Ächtler and Gansel (eds.), *Ikonographie des Terrors?* (2008), 179–98, esp. 185, note 19.

36. See Schütte, *Die Poetik des Extremen* (2006) who treats the novella as "a handbook for the revolution," 84. Also Troy A. Pugmire, "Ein Vergleich: Heinrich von Kleists Michael Kohlhaas und die 'Rote Armee Fraktion,'" *Utah Foreign Language Review* (1993–94), 124–37. [No vol. no.]

37. Christoph Hein, *In seiner frühen Kindheit ein Garten* (Frankfurt: Suhrkamp, 2005), 183.

38. E.g. Hubert Spiegel, "Bleierner Tanz," *Frankfurter Allgemeine Zeitung*, February 5, 2005. It must be one of the reasons that there is already a book of study notes for use in German schools on the novel: Rüdiger Bernhardt, *Interpretationen zu Christoph Hein. In seiner Kindheit ein Garten: Lektüre- und Interpretationshilfe*. Königs Erläuterungen und Materialien (Hollfeld: Bange, 2010).

39. The opposite interpretation was adopted in a dramatization by a Berlin theatre in 2007, according to Anne-Kathrin Griese. "A stage version adapted by Jens Groß presents the hero of the novel as deluded. The whole plot is performed

for the father who needs the idea of proximity to his son and righteous commitment in order to come to terms with his loss." Griese, "Der familäre Blick: Andres Veiel *Black Box BRD* (2001) und Christoph Hein *In seiner frühen Kindheit ein Garten* (2005)," in Stephan and Tacke (eds.), *NachBilder der RAF* (2008), 165–80, p. 177.

40. Veiel reports that both Werner Grams and Wolfgang's brother Rainer lost their trust in the workings of the law in the democratic state (the "Rechtsstaat"). See Andres Veiel, *Black Box BRD. Alfred Herrhausen, die Deutsche Bank, die RAF und Wolfgang Grams* (Stuttgart/Munich: Deutsche Verlags-Anstalt, 2002), 26–27.
41. Heinrich von Kleist, *Michael Kohlhaas (Aus einer alten Chronik)*, in *Werke in einem Band*, ed. Helmut Sembdner (Munich: Hanser, 1966), 587657, p. 587.
42. See Stuart Taberner, "The Art of Delay: Protest and Prose in F. C. Delius's *Mein Jahr als Mörder*," in Brigid Haines, Stephen Parker, and Colin Riordan (eds.), *Aesthetics and Politics in Modern German Culture. Festschrift in Honour of Rhys Williams* (Oxford: Lang, 2010), 91–102.
43. David Clarke, "Requiem für Michael Kohlhaas: Der Dialog mit den Toten in Christoph Heins *Horns Ende* und *In seiner frühen Kindheit ein Garten*," in Arne de Winde and Anke Gilleir (eds.), *Literatur im Krebsgang. Totenbeschwörung und memoria in der deutschsprachigen Literatur nach 1989, Amsterdamer Beiträge zur neueren Germanistik* 64 (2008), 159–79.
44. Mario Scalla, "Republik ohne Bürger," *Freitag*, 28.01.2005.
45. For Cornils, the novel *Scylla* "can be interpreted as a further aesthetic and creative allegory of the [student] movement: once a beautiful maiden, corrupted through no fault of her own, she kills those who come too near. Innocence and violence are the two halves of her being, and Odysseus thought she was the lesser of two evils." See Ingo Cornils, "Joined at the Hip? The Representation of the German Student Movement and Left-Wing Terrorism in Recent Literature," in Berendse and Cornils (eds.), *Baader Meinhof Returns* (2008), 137–55, p. 148.
46. Theodor W. Adorno and Max Horkheimer, *The Dialectics of the Enlightenment* (1947). Michael Wildenhain, *Träumer des Absoluten* (Stuttgart: Klett-Cotta, 2008), 75–76.
47. Helmut Krausser, *Eros* (Munich: btb, 2008), 246.
48. According to Krausser, quoted by Steffen Markus, "Am Ende. Zu Helmut Kraussers Eros," *Text und Kritik* (187), 2010, 94–107, p. 105.

4 Terrorism and the German Popular Imaginary: Conspiracies and Counterfactuals

1. The German films are: *Das Phantom* (dir. Gansel, 2000); the literary adaptation *Murder by the Sea* (dir. Geschonneck, 2004); and *God Protects Lovers* (dir. Rola, 2008,). There is also an episode of the long-running television crime series *Tatort* entitled *Shadows* (dir. Näter, 2002). The first German terrorist detective film was the GDR adaptation of Degenhardt's *Scenes of Fire* (dir. Brandt, 1978), which was followed by the German-French co-production of *We Have to Kill Birgit Haas* (dir. Heynemann, 1981), adapted from the 1978

novel by Guy Teisseire, and the German-Swedish co-production of another literary adaptation, *The Democratic Terrorist* (dir. Bergland, 1992) after the Swedish novel by Jan Guillou. *Mogadishu* (dir. Richter, 2008) adheres to thriller conventions, as does, up to a point, *The Baader-Meinhof Complex* (dir. Edel, 2008) and, last but not least, *Death Game* (dir. Breloer, 1997) in its nondocumentary sections.

2. A number of essays in Tacke and Stephan (eds.), *NachBilder der RAF* (2008), concern "pop literature" but none is about popular fiction. Sandra Beck lists a number of *krimis* too, but devotes her attention to the already much-discussed *The Last Performance* (Woelk, 2002). Beck, *Reden an die Lebenden und an die Toten* (2008), 160–87, esp. 167, note 198, and bibliography.

3. Böll also called *Safety Net* a *krimi*, quoted in Reid *Heinrich Böll* (1988), 20405.

4. See Hans-Bernhard Moeller and George Lellis, *Volker Schlöndorff's Cinema: Adaptation, Politics, and the "Movie-Appropriate"* (Carbondale and Edwardsville: Southern Illinois University Press, 2002), 128–43.

5. Quoted by Hoeps, *Arbeit am Widerspruch* (2001), 212. Thomas Hoeps has a section on Degenhardt in *Arbeit am Widerspruch* (2001), 209–13. Like Dombrowa et al. and Berendse, he lists *The Comrade* (Röhl, 1975) in his bibliography, but offers no comment on it.

6. Röhl did this most recently in *Mein langer Marsch durch die Illusionen. Leben mit HITLER, der DKP, den 68ern, der RAF und ULRIKE MEINHOF* (Vienna: Universitas, 2009), 224.

7. Katharina Holt may be named Katharina, which means "the pure one," after Katharina Blum.

8. Klaus Rainer Röhl, *Die Genossin* (Vienna: Molden, 1975), 12.

9. Elsaesser, "Antigone Agonistes" (1999), 298.

10. Johannes Mario Simmel, *Gott schützt die Liebenden* (Hamburg: Zsolnay, 1957) was filmed first by Alfred Vohrer in 1973.

11. The rule is broken if we count Zora Zobel in Corinna Kawaters's popular alternative 1980s series, but she operates on the periphery of Baader-Meinhof territory. *The Photographer* (Chaplet, 2002) has a male-female duo, as does *Shadows* (dir. Näter, 2002).

12. This book was first published in 1992 and was reissued in updated form for the 1997 anniversary. Outside popular fiction, the book's exciting thesis has gained little credence. Gerhard Wisnewski, Wolfgang Landgraeber, Ekkehard Sieker, *Das RAF-Phantom. Wozu Politik und Wirtschaft Terroristen brauchen* (Munich: Knaur, 1997).

13. Butz Peters entitles one of his concluding chapters "Thirteen Riddles," counting nine unsolved murders. Peters, *Tödlicher Irrtum. Die Geschichte der RAF* (Berlin: Argon, 2004), 738–54, esp. 738–39. See also Wolfgang Kraushaar, *Verena Becker und der Verfassungsschutz* (Hamburg: Hamburger Edition, 2010), in which the experienced RAF researcher weighs the evidence in favor of one of the possible assassins of Siegfried Buback in April 1977 having worked as an informer for the secret services.

14. Strauss's biographer dismisses the rumor as a slur. Stefan Finger, *Franz Josef Strauß. Ein politisches Leben* (Munich: Olzug, 2005), 411–12. According to Kraushaar, the proposal to reintroduce the death penalty for imprisoned

terrorists was made by the General State Prosecutor, Kurt Rebmann, but was discussed by a number of politicians in all parties. Wolfgang Kraushaar, "Der nicht erklärte Ausnahmezustand" in *Die RAF und der linke Terrorismus* (2006), 1015.

15. Some of the interest in Herold could have been inspired by Dirk Kurbjuweit's commemorative article, "Gefangen für alle Zeiten," *Die Zeit*, 08.08.1997. Wisnewski, Landgraeber, and Sieker cite Herold in support of their thesis that the post-77 RAF was controlled by the state. *Das RAF-Phantom* (1997), 19.

16. Wolfgang Brenner, *Die Exekution* (Frankfurt: Eichborn, 2000), 211.

17. Some historians see the 1980s as more violent than the preceding decade. Jeremy Varon, for instance, writes that "Armed struggle, by the mid-1980s, appeared to be a permanent feature of West German political life, carried out by a host of clandestine cells and supported by a loose network of radical bookstores, legal collectives, independent militants, and semi-legal groups like the Autonomen, who used violence as a street tactic." Varon, *Bringing the War Home* (2004), 302. While it did not always feel like that at the time, he does have a point.

18. *The Assassin's Library* was adapted for radio in 2004, however. Reviewers in the quality press on the whole liked it. See Volker Breidecker in the *Süddeutsche Zeitung* (10.10.2001), Jens Hohensee in *Die Zeit* (17.01.2002), and Sascha Verna in the *Neue Zürcher Zeitung* (27.04.2002).

19. See "Heiße Spur im Mordfall Karry," *Der Spiegel*, 22.06.1981 and "Perle im Dreck," *Der Spiegel*, 22.08.1983.

20. See Kundnani, *Utopia or Auschwitz* (2009), 176 and 214. See also the chapter "Shots to the Stomach" ("Schüsse in den Unterleib") in Wisnewski, Landgraeber and Sieker, *Das RAF-Phantom* (1997), 84–90. *Unterleib* can also mean "groin," which could give the murder a ritualistic dimension.

21. See Dobson and Payne, *The Carlos Complex* (1977), 41–42.

22. Marcel Reich-Ranicki, *Mein Leben* (Berlin: Deutsche Verlags-Anstalt, 1999).

23. Sophie Dannenberg, *Das bleiche Herz der Revolution* (Berlin: Deutsche Verlags-Anstalt, 2004), 66.

24. Kraushaar, *1968* (2000), 169.

25. See David Aaronovitch, *Voodoo Histories. How Conspiracy Theory has Shaped Modern History* (London: Vintage, 2010), 328.

26. See Mark Fenster, *Conspiracy Theories: Secrecy and Power in American Culture* (London / Minneapolis: University of Minnesota Press, 2008), 2nd ed.; and see Gordon B. Arnold, *Conspiracy Theory in Film, Television, and Politics* (London/Westport: Praeger, 2008).

5   Baader-Meinhof Translated: From *Die Hard* to al-Qaeda

1. Uwe Johnson, *Zwei Ansichten* (*Two Views*, 1965) and Peter Schneider's *Der Mauerspringer* (*The Wall-Jumper*, 1982) fall into the first category; Christa Wolf's *Der geteilte Himmel* (*The Divided Sky*, 1963) falls into the second. See Peter Hutchinson, *Literary Presentations of Divided Germany: The Development*

of a Central Theme in East German Fiction (Cambridge: Cambridge University Press, 1977). Martin Walser courted opprobrium for criticizing the fact of division in Cold War spy novel, *Dorle und Wolf* (1987, tr. Leila Vennewitz as *No Man's Land*).

2. *Katharina Blum* did inspire an American made-for-television remake, however: *The Lost Honor of Kathryn Beck* (dir. Langton, 1984). See Moeller and Lellis, *Volker Schlöndorff's Cinema* (2002), 142.

3. Beck, *Reden an die Lebenden und an die Toten* (2008), 16.

4. Tom Vague, *The Red Army Faction Story 1963–1993: Televisionaries* (Edinburgh/San Francisco: AK Press, 1994).

5. In Franca Rame and Dario Fo, *A Woman Alone and Other Plays*, tr. Gillian Hanna, eds. Emery and Christopher Cairn (London: Methuen, 1991), 181–92.

6. Alban Lefranc, *Angriffe. Drei Romane* (Munich: Blumenbar, 2008), tr. Katja Roloff. *Attaques sur le chemin, le soir, dans la neige* (*Attacks On The Path, in the Evening, in the Snow*), which is about Fassbinder, was originally published in Montreal by Le Quartanier in 2005. *Des foules, des bouches, des armes* (*Crowds, Mouths, Arms*), about Vesper, was published in Paris by Melville/Leo Scheer in 2006. *Sie waren nicht dabei* (*They Were Not There*) about Nico, has only appeared in German translation.

7. Delillo's story was published in *The Guardian*, August 17, 2002.

8. Quoted by Galli in "'Mit dem Einkaufswagen durch den Geschichts-Supermarkt'" (2006), 108.

9. The film was *Der demokratische Terrorist* (dir. Bergland, 1992).

10. *The Good Terrorist* (London: Cape, 1985) and *Die Terroristin*, trs. Manfred Ohl and Hans Sartorius (Frankfurt: Fischer-Goverts, 1986) and finally, *Die gute Terroristin* (Munich: Goldmann, 2003). On account of her German name, which she acquired by marrying the German-Jewish émigré communist Gottfried Lessing, Doris Lessing is treated as something of an honorary German. When she was awarded the Nobel Prize for Literature in 2007, it emerged that she was related by marriage to Gregor Gysi, one of the leaders of the reform communists, by then renamed *Die Linke*.

11. Roderick Thorp, *Nothing Lasts Forever* (London: Corgi, 1981), 44.

12. Robert Leucht, *Experiment und Erinnerung: Der Schriftsteller Walter Abish* (Vienna: Böhlau, 2006).

13. Carl Fick, *A Disturbance in Paris* (London: Gollancz, 1983), 246.

14. See Annette Vowinckel, "Skyjacking: Cultural Memory and the Movies," in Berendse and Cornils (eds.), *Baader Meinhof Returns* (2008), 251–68. See also Giles Foden, *The Last King of Scotland* (London: Faber & Faber, 1998), 234 and the film adaptation, directed by Kevin Macdonald in 2006).

15. This started with Serge Groussard's *The Blood of Israel: The Massacre of the Israeli Athletes. The Olympics 1972* (New York: Morrow, 1975), tr. from French by Harold J. Salemson, and Simon Reeve's, *One Day in September. The Full Story of the 1972 Munich Olympics Massacre and the Israelis' Revenge Operation 'Wrath of God'* (London: Faber & Faber, 2000). There is now a German novel by Ulrike Draesner, *Spiele* (Munich: Luchterhand, 2005), which uses the Olympics as a backdrop for a story about adolescent love and cites Reeve and Macdonald as historical sources.

16. Henryk M. Broder, *Der ewige Antisemit. Über Sinn und Funktion eines beständigen Gefühls* (Frankfurt: Fischer, 1986), 61–66.
17. The first "instant" account was by William Stevenson with material by Uri Dan, *90 Minutes at Entebbe* (Toronto / London: Bantam, 1976), which was translated into German the following year.
18. Willi Winkler, *Geschichte der RAF* (Berlin: Rowohlt, 2007), 216–20 (on Munich) and 271–74 (on Entebbe).
19. Contrary to what is often asserted, "there is no evidence of cooperation over the attack" between the Palestinians of Black September and German supporters on the ground in Munich, according to Kay Schiller and Christopher Young, *The 1972 Olympics and the Making of Modern Germany* (Berkeley: University of California Press, 2010), 204.
20. The Germans they wanted released were Werner Hoppe, Jan-Carl Raspe, Ralf Reinders, Ingrid Schubert, Fritz Teufel, and Inge Viett, but not Baader or Ensslin. See Pflieger, *Die Rote Armee Fraktion* (2004), 67. Hoppe, Raspe, and Schubert were from the RAF, which makes Entebbe part of RAF history.
21. See Aust, *Der Baader-Meinhof Komplex* (1998), 272–73.
22. The exception among works of history is Wolfgang Kraushaar's excellent *Die Bombe im jüdischen Gemeindehaus* (Hamburg: Hamburger Edition, 2005), and among the novels *Dreamers of the Absolute* (Wildenhain, 2008).
23. This has been the subject of a Swedish documentary film, *Stockholm–75* (dir. Aronowitsch, 2003), based mainly on the role played by Karl-Heinz Dellwo, who is interviewed in the film.
24. Cosgrove, *The Baader-Meinhof Affair* (2003), 106–07.
25. See Annabel Wahba's review of the German translation, "Der Blick durch die Sonnenbrille," *Der Tagesspiegel*, March 22, 2005.
26. Michael Arditti, *Unity. Reflections on the Personalities and Politics Behind Wolfgang Meier's Legendary Lost Film* (London: Maia, 2005), 15.
27. The reviewer in *The Times* of London refers to him in quotation marks as "Michael Arditti" to underline the postmodern play in the novel, which extends to a fictional bibliography. Jane Shilling, "Twisted Sister's Radical Turn," *The Times*, June 4, 2005.
28. Georg Haderer, *Schäfers Qualen* (Innsbruck/Vienna: Haymon), 130–31.

6 RAF Revivalism in the 2000s

1. André Kubiczek, *Die Guten und die Bösen* (Berlin: Rowohlt, 2003). Michael Kumpfmüller, *Nachricht an alle* (Cologne: Kiepenheuer & Witsch, 2008).
2. Uwe Tellkamp, *Der Eisvogel* (Frankfurt: Suhrkamp, 2005) and *Der Turm* (Frankfurt: Suhrkamp, 2008).
3. Lukas Hammerstein, *Wo wirst du sein* (Frankfurt: Fischer, 2010).
4. Dirk Kurbjuweit, *Unser effizientes Leben. Die Diktatur der Ökonomie und ihre Folgen* (Berlin: Rowohlt, 2003), 183–84. He does not pause to wonder why the protester who becomes a terrorist has to be female.
5. This, at least, is how the version released for screening in German cinemas in 2004 ended. The version released on DVD cut the final scene showing them setting off on their final mission.

6. Thilo Bock, *Die geladene Knarre von Andreas Baader* (Cologne: Kiepenheuer & Witsch, 2009), 315.
7. See Roman Halfmann, "Neo-Terrorismus im Zeichen der RAF: Die Aufarbeitung des Deutschen Herbstes in der deutschen Gegenwartsliteratur zwischen Klischee und Absetzung," in Ächtler and Gansel (eds.), *Ikonographie des Terrors?* (2010), 333–47.
8. Violence such as burning expensive cars in areas of the capital that are on the point of being gentrified. See for instance brennendeautos.de
9. Ulrich Peltzer, *Teil der Lösung* (Zurich: Amman, 2007), 349–50.
10. Quoted by Gerd Conradt in *Starbuck Holger Meins. Ein Porträt als Zeitbild* (Berlin: Espresso, 2001), 155.
11. In Böll's novel, Holger I was taken by his mother Veronika Zelger when she eloped with the terrorist Heinrich Bewerloh. Rolf named his second son with his new partner "Holger" in defiance of critics, who said the name was now tainted by association with Holger Meins.
12. And it was quoted as an epigraph to the RAF's first manifesto, "Das Konzept Stadtguerilla" (1971); quoted by Koenen, *Das rote Jahrzehnt* (2001), 359.
13. See, for instance, Katrin Bischoff, "Verspekuliert," *Berliner Zeitung*, 06.06.2005, and Nils Klawitter, "Schmeißen Sie die raus," *Der Spiegel*, 28.11.2005; see *Und du bist raus—Wie Investoren die Traditionsfirma Grohe auspressen* (dir. Hubert Seipel, West Deutscher Rundfunk, 2006).
14. See Wolfgang Munchau in the British conservative weekly, *The Spectator*, "Anti-Americanism, anti-Semitism, anti-capitalism," 21 May 2005.
15. Frank Finlay, "Thomas Weiss's 'Polyphonic' novel *Tod eines Trüffelschweins*," in Haines, Parker, and Riordan (eds.), *Aesthetics and Politics in Modern German Literature* (2010), 117–29.
16. Walter Delabar notes its onesidedness, "Für das System oder dagegen? Thomas Weiss über den Tod eines Trüffelschweins," *literaturkritik.de*, 3 March 2008.
17. Thomas Weiss, *Tod eines Trüffelschweines* (Göttingen: Steidl, 2007), 29
18. As reported by Dieter Stolz, introducing Thomas Weiss at a reading at the University of Leeds, September 18, 2009. Peter O. Chotjewitz, writing in Meinhof's old magazine, which made Weiss's novel its book of the month, took a conventional Marxist line that killing individuals never changes anything. He praised *Death of a Truffle Pig* for its acumen in other respects and for the way that Weiss dispatches his villain. See Chotjewitz, "Thomas Weiss *Tod eines Trüffelschweins*," *konkret*, January 2008, 45.
19. Günter Grass, *Im Krebsgang* (Göttingen: Steidl, 2002).
20. Martin Walser, *Tod eines Kritikers* (Frankfurt: Suhrkamp, 2002).
21. "Another world is possible" was the motto of the Direct Action Network, which was set up to protest against the World Trade Organization in Seattle in 1999.
22. Uwe Timm, *Heisser Sommer* (Munich: Bertelsmann, 1974), F. C. Delius, *Amerikahaus und der Tanz um die Frauen* (Reinbek bei Hamburg: Rowohlt, 1997). See Ingo Cornils, "Writing the Revolution: the Literary Representation of the German Student Movement as Counter Culture," in Giles and Oergel (eds.), *Counter Cultures in Germany and Central Europe* (Berne: Lang, 2003), 295–314.

BIBLIOGRAPHY

In order to show the chronological clustering of interest in Baader-Meinhof terrorism, the first sections of the bibliography are arranged by ascending year of publication rather than alphabetically by author. My criterion for selection is that a figure who may be broadly identified as a Baader-Meinhof terrorist appears in the novel (or film or play for the films and plays sections). I give here the original date of publication and publisher, which sometimes are different from the editions I have quoted from in the chapter Notes (details of which are given there). If there is no English translation of the work, I give a literal translation of the title.

German Fiction

1974
Heinrich Böll, *Die verlorene Ehre der Katharina Blum* (Cologne: Kiepenheuer & Witsch). English: *The Lost Honour of Katharina Blum*, tr. Leila Vennewitz (London: Secker and Warburg, 1975).

1975
Franz Josef Degenhardt, *Brandstellen* (Munich: Bertelsmann). [Scenes of Fire].
Klaus Rainer Röhl, *Die Genossin* (Vienna: Fritz Molden). [The Comrade].
Peter Schneider,... *schon bist du ein Verfassungsfeind* (Berlin: Rotbuch) [...Already You Are an Enemy of the Constitution].

1978
Peter O. Chotjewitz, *Die Herren des Morgengrauens. Romanfragment* (Berlin: Rotbuch). [The Gentlemen of the Dawn. Novel fragment].

1979
Heinrich Böll, *Fürsorgliche Belagerung* (Cologne: Kiepenheuer & Witsch). *Safety Net*, tr. Leiela Vennewitz (London: Secker and Warburg, 1981).
Peter-Paul Zahl, *Die Glücklichen* (Berlin: Rotbuch). [The Happy Ones].

1980
Grete Weil, *Meine Schwester Antigone* (Zurich: Benziger). *My Sister, My Antigone*, tr. Krishna Winston (New York: Avon, 1984).

1981
F. C. Delius, *Ein Held der inneren Sicherheit* (Reinbek bei Hamburg: Rowohlt). [A Hero of Internal Security].

1984

Inge Buhmann, *Mazedonischer Grenzfall* (Pendragon: Bielefeld). [Macedonian Border Case].

Eva Demski, *Scheintod* (Hanser: Munich/Vienna). *Dead Alive*, tr. Jan van Heurck (New York: Harper and Row, 1986).

1987

F. C. Delius, *Mogadischu Fensterplatz* (Reinbek bei Hamburg: Rowohlt). [Window Seat at Mogadishu].

1988

Peter-Jürgen Boock, *Abgang* (Göttingen: Lamuv). [Descent].

Christian Geissler, *Kamalatta* (Rotbuch: Berlin). [Kamalatta].

Rainald Goetz, *Kontrolliert* (Suhrkamp: Frankfurt). [Checked].

Eva Zeller, *Heidelberger Novelle* (Deutsche Verlags-Anstalt: Stuttgart). [Heidelberg Novella].

1990

Judith Kuckart, *Wahl der Waffen* (Frankfurt: Fischer). [Choice of Weapons].

1992

F. C. Delius, *Himmelfahrt eines Staatsfeindes* (Reinbek bei Hamburg: Rowohlt). [Ascent to Heaven of an Enemy of the State].

1994

Ulrich Plenzdorf, *Vater, Mutter, Mörderkind* (Rostock: Hinstorff). [Father, Mother, Murderer's Child].

1995

Günter Grass, *Ein weites Feld* (Steidl: Göttingen). *Too Far Afield*, tr. Krishna Winston (London: Faber & Faber, 2000).

1996

Ulrike Edschmid, *Frau mit Waffe. Zwei Geschichten aus terroristischen Zeiten* (Reinbek bei Hamburg: Rowohlt). [Woman with Gun. Two Stories from Terrorist Times].

1999

Günter Grass, *Mein Jahrhundert* (Göttingen: Steidl, 1999). *My Century*, tr. Michael Henry Heim (London: Faber & Faber, 1999).

2000

Wolfgang Brenner, *Die Exekution* (Frankfurt: Eichborn). [The Execution].

2001

Leander Scholz, *Rosenfest* (Hanser: Munich/Vienna). [Rose Party].

Franz-Maria Sonner, *Die Bibliothek des Attentäters* (Munich: Kunstmann). [The Assassin's Library].

Ulrich Ritzel, *Die schwarzen Ränder der Glut* (Lengwil: Libelle 2001). [The Black Edges of the Fire].

Uwe Timm, *Rot* (Cologne: Kiepenheuer and Witsch). [Red].

2002

Peter-Jürgen Boock, *Die Entführung und Ermordung Hanns-Martin Schleyers. Eine dokumentarische Fiktion* (Frankfurt: Eichborn) [The Kidnapping and Murder of Hanns-Martin Schleyer. A Documentary Fiction]

Anne Chaplet [Cora Stephen], *Die Fotografin* (Munich: Kunstmann) [The Photographer].

Renate Klöppel, *Der Pass* (Berlin: Rotbuch). [The Mountain Pass]

Ulrich Woelk, *Die Letzte Vorstellung* (Hamburg: Hoffmann & Campe). [The Last Performance].

2003

Wolfgang Mock, *Der Flug der Seraphim* (Leipzig: Militzke). [The Flight of the Seraphim].

Wolfgang Schorlau, *Die blaue Liste. Denglers Erster Fall* (Kiepenheuer & Witsch: Cologne). [The Blue List. Dengler's First Case].

2004

Sophie Dannenberg, *Das bleiche Herz der Revolution* (Berlin: Deutsche Verlags-Anstalt). [The Pale Heart of the Revolution].

F. C. Delius, *Mein Jahr als Mörder* (Berlin: Rowohlt). [My Year as a Murderer].

Gerhard Seyfried, *Der schwarze Stern der Tupamaros* (Frankfurt: Eichborn). [The Black Star of the Tupamaros].

2005

Christoph Hein, *In seiner frühen Kindheit ein Garten* (Frankfurt: Suhrkamp). [In His Early Childhood, a Garden].

Peter Schneider, *Skylla* (Hamburg: Rowohlt). [Scylla].

2006

Jürgen Kehrer, *Wilsberg und die dritte Generation* (Dortmund: Grafit). [Wilsberg and the Third Generation]

Helmut Krausser, *Eros* (Munich: btb). *Eros*, tr. Mike Mitchell (New York: Europa Editions, 2008).

2007

Hinrich Matthiesen, *Auch du wirst weinen, Tupamara* (Hamburg: Quermarken). [You Too Will Weep, Tupamara].

Ulrich Peltzer, *Teil der Lösung* (Zurich: Ammann). *Part of the Solution,* tr. Martin Chalmers (Chicago: University of Chicago Press, 2011)

Thomas Weiss, *Tod eines Trüffelschweins* (Göttingen: Steidl). [Death of a Truffle Pig].

2008

Helmut Marrat, *Das Ende der Schlaflosigkeit. Eine Geschichte in zwei Teilen* (Frankfurt: Verlag Neue Kritik). [The End of Sleeplessness. A Story in Two Parts].

Bernhard Schlink, *Das Wochenende* (Zurich: Diogenes). *The Weekend,* tr. Shaun Whiteside (London: Weidenfeld, 2010).

Michael Wildenhain, *Träumer des Absoluten* (Stuttgar: Klett Cotta). [Dreamers of the Absolute].

2009

Thilo Bock, *Die geladene Knarre von Andreas Baader* (Cologne: Kiepenheuer & Witsch). [The Loaded Shooter of Andreas Baader].

Thomas Hoeth, *Herbst-Botin. Ein Stuttgart-Krimi* (Tübingen: Silberburg). [Autumn Messenger: A Stuttgart Crime Novel].

Gina Mayer, *Mörderkind* (Ravensburger: Ravensburg). [Murderer's Child].

2010

Lukas Hammerstein, *Wo wirst du sein* (Frankfurt: Fischer). [Where Will You Be].

International Fiction

1978
(France) Guy Teisseire, *Il faut tuer Birgit Haas* (Paris: Livre de poche). [You Have to Kill Birgit Haas].

1979
(US) Walter Abish, *How German Is It. Wie Deutsch ist es* (New York: Norton).
(US) Roderick Thorp, *Nothing Lasts Forever* (New York: Norton).

1981
(Switzerland) Silvio Blatter, *Die Schneefalle* (Benziger: Zurich). [The Snow Trap].
(US) Carl Fick, *A Disturbance in Paris* (Boston: Little Brown).

1987
(Sweden) Jan Guillou, *Den demokratishe terroristen* (cited: *Der demokratische Terrorist. Ein Coq-Rouge-Thriller*, tr. from Swedish to German by Hans-Joachim Maass. Munich: Piper, 1990). [The Democratic Terrorist].

1990
(France) Antoine Volodine, *Lisbonne dernière marge*. (Paris: Minuit). [Lisbon Last Margin.]

1995
(US) Jennifer Egan, *The Invisible Circus* (New York: Doubleday).

2003
(US) Erin Cosgrove, *The Baader-Meinhof-Affair* (New York: Printed Matter, Inc.).

2004
(UK) John le Carré, *Absolute Friends* (London: Hodder and Stoughton).

2005
(UK) Michael Arditti, *Unity. Reflections on the personalities and politics behind Wolfgang Meier's legendary lost film* (London: Maia).
(France) Alban Lefranc, *Attaques sur le chemin, le soir, dans la neige* (Montreal: Le Quartanier, 2005). [Attacks along the Path, in the Evening, in the Snow].

2006
(France) Alban Lefranc, *Des foules, des bouches, des armes* (Paris: Melville/Leo Scheer, 2006). [The Crowds, the Mouths, the Weapons].

2007
(Austria) Michael Scheuermann, *RAF Gier. Hans Sachs Zweiter Fall* (Marchtrenk: Federfrei). [RAF Greed. Hans Sachs' Second Case].

2009
(Austria) Georg Haderer, *Schäfers Qualen* (Innsbruck/Vienna: Haymon). [Schäfer's Torments].

2010
(UK) Simon Corbin, *Love, Gudrun Ensslin* (No Place of Publication: New Generation)

German Films and Plays

Note: Where I know them, I give the published English titles, otherwise I give a literal translation.

Mutter Kösters Fahrt zum Himmel (dir. Rainer Werner Fassbinder, 1975). [Mother Köster's Trip to Heaven].

Die verlorene Ehre der Katharina Blum (dir. Volker Schlöndorff with Margarethe von Trotta, 1975). [The Lost Honor of Katharina Blum].

Das Zweite Erwachen der Christa Klages (dir. Margarethe von Trotta, 1976). [The Second Awakening of Christa Klages].

Deutschland im Herbst (dir. Alexander Kluge et al, 1978). [Germany in Autumn].

Messer im Kopf (dir. Reinhard Hauff, 1978). [Knife in the Head].

Dritte Generation (dir. Rainer Werner Fassbinder, 1978). [Third Generation].

Die bleierne Zeit (dir. Margarethe von Trotta, 1981). [*The German Sisters* (UK) / *Marianne and Juliane* (US)].

Judith [1984] by Rolf Hochhuth, in *Alle Dramen*, 2 vols, vol. 2 (Reinbek bei Hamburg: Rowohlt, 1991), 2127–2330.

Stammheim (dir. Reinhard Hauff, 1985). [Stammheim].

Die Reise (dir. Markus Imhof, 1985). [The Trip].

Die Erpresser. Eine böse Komödie by Peter-Paul Zahl (Berlin: Kramer, 1990). [The Blackmailers. A Nasty Comedy].

Die Terroristen! (dir. Philip Gröning, 1992). [The Terrorists!].

Vater, Mutter, Mörderkind (dir. Heiner Carow, 1993). [Father, Mother, Murderer's Child].

Wessis in Weimar. Szenen aus einem besetzten Land by Rolf Hochhuth (Munich: dtv, 1994), [1993], [Wessis in Weimar. Scenes from an Occupied Country].

Leviathan, by Dea Loher, in *Olgas Raum. Tätowierung, Leviathan. Drei Stücke* (Frankfurt: Verlag der Autoren, 1994), 145–229.

Todesspiel (dir. Heinrich Breloer, 1997). [Death Game].

Raus aus der Haut (dir. Andreas Dresen, 1997). [Out of Your Skin].

Die innere Sicherheit (2000, dir. Christian Petzold). [The State I'm in].

Die Stille nach dem Schuß (dir. Volker Schlöndorff, 2000). *The Legends of Rita.*

Große Freiheit, kleine Freiheit (dir. Kristin Konrad, 2000). [Big Freedom, Little Fredom].

Das Phantom (dir. Dennis Gansel, 2000). [The Phantom].

Black Box BRD (dir. Andres Veiel, 2001).

Andreas Dresen, *Zeugenstand. Stadtguerilla-Monologe* (premiered at the Deutsches Theater, June 2002, unpublished script). [Witness Box. Urban Guerilla Monologues].

Was tun, wenn's brennt? (dir. Gregor Schnitzler, 2002). [What to Do in Case of Fire].

Baader (dir. Christoph Roth, 2002). [Baader].

Tatort: Schatten (dir. Thorsten Näter, 2002). [Crime Scene: "Shadows"].

Mord am Meer (dir. Matti Geschonneck, 2004). [Murder by the Sea].

Die fetten Jahre sind vorbei (dir. Hans Weingartner, 2004). [*The Edukators*].

Das Wunder von Mogadischu (dirs. Stefan Brauburger, Oliver Halmburger, Stephan Vogel, 2007). [The Miracle of Mogadishu].

Der Weiße mit dem Schwarzbrot. Christof Wackernagel in Mali (dir. Jonas Grosch, 2007). [White Man with Black Bread. Christof Wackernagel in Mali].

Mogadischu (dir. Roland Suso Richter, 2008) [Mogadishu].

Schattenwelt (dir. Connie Walter, 2008) [Long Shadows].

Gott schützt die Liebenden (dir, Carlo Rola, 2008). [God Protects Lovers].

Der Baader-Meinhof Komplex (dir. Uli Edel, 2008). [The Baader-Meinhof Complex].

Free Rainer oder Dein Fernseher lügt (dir. Hans Weingartner, 2008). [Free Rainer or Your Television Is Lying].

Es kommt der Tag (dir. Susanne Schneider, 2009). [The Day Will Come].

Die Anwälte. Eine deutsche Geschichte (dir. Birgit Schulz, 2009). [The Attorneys. A German Story].

Wer wenn nicht wir (dir. Andres Veiel, 2011). [Who if not Us].

International Films and Plays

(Italy) *I'm Ulrike—Screaming* (1975) and *It Happened Tomorrow* (1977), in Franca Rame and Dario Fo, *A Woman Alone and Other Plays*, tr. Gillian Hanna (London: Methuen, 1991).

(US) *Raid on Entebbe* (dir. Irwin Kershner, 1977).

(US) *Victory at Entebbe* (dir. Martin J. Chomsky, 1977).

(GDR) Heiner Müller, *Die Hamletmaschine*, in Theo Girshausen (ed.), *Die Hamletmaschine: Heiner Müllers Endspiel* (Cologne: Prometh, 1978) [1977, The Hamletmachine]

(Israel) *Operation Thunderbolt* (dir. Menahem Golan, 1978).

(GDR) *Brandstellen* (dir. Horst E. Brand, 1978). [Scenes of Fire].

(US) *Journeys from Berlin/1971* (dir. Yvonne Rainer, 1980).

(France) *Il faut tuer Birgit Haas* (dir. Laurent Heunemann, 1981). [We Have to Kill Birgit Haas].

US) *The Lost Honor of Kathryn Beck* (dir. Simon Langton, 1984).

(US) *Die Hard* (dir. John McTiernan, 1988).

(Sweden/Germany), *Der demokratische Terrorist* (dir. Pelle Bergland, 1992). [The Democratic Terrorist].

(UK) *Baader-Meinhof: In Love with Terror* (dir. Ben Lewis, 2002).

(Sweden) *Stockholm-75* (dir. David Aronowitsch, 2003).

(Canada/Germany) *The Raspberry Reich* (dir. Bruce LaBruce, 2004).

(Netherlands) *De Terrorist Hans-Joachim Klein* (dir. Alexander Oey, 2005). [Hans-Joachim Klein: My Life as a Terrorist].

(Austria) *Keine Insel. Die Palmers Entführung 1977* (dirs. Alexander Binder and Michael Gartner, 2007). [No Island. The Palmers Kidnapping].

(Austria) *Ulrike Maria Stuart von Elfriede Jelinek: Uraufführung am Thalia-Theater* (Würzburg: Königshausen & Neumann, 2007).

(France/Germany) *Carlos* (dir. Oliver Assayas, 2010).

Other Primary Material

Lucius Apuleius, "Cupid and Psyche," in *The Transformations of Lucius Otherwise Known as The Golden Ass*, tr. Robert Graves (Harmondsworth: Penguin, 1950), pp. 97–133.

Paul Auster, *Leviathan* (Faber and Faber: London, 1992).

Paul Auster, *Hand to Mouth. A Chronicle of Early Failure* (Faber and Faber: London/Boston, 1997).

Wolfgang Becker (dir.), *Goodbye Lenin!* (Germany, 2003).

Bertholt Brecht, *Brechts Antigone des Sophocles* (Frankfurt: Suhrkamp, 1988), ed. Werner Hecht. [Brecht's Antigone by Sophocles]

Bertolt Brecht, *Die Maßnahme. Lehrstück* [1930, *The Measures Taken* or *The Decision*], in *Die Stücke von Bertolt Brecht in einem Band* (Frankfurt: Suhrkamp, 1978), 255–68.

Hermann Broch, *Die Schlafwandler. Eine Romantrilogie. Kommentierte Werkausgabe*, ed. Michael Lützeler (Frankfurt: Suhrkamp, 1994) [The Sleepwalkers].

Christine Brückner, "Kein Denkmal für Gudrun Ensslin. Rede gegen die Wände der Stammheimer Zelle," in *Wenn Du geredet hättest Desdemona. Ungehaltene Reden ungehaltener Frauen* (Hamburg: Hoffmann & Campe, 1983), 109–122. [No Monument for Gudrun Ensslin. Speech to the Walls of the Stammheim Cell].

Albert Camus, *Les Justes* (Paris: Gallimard, 1950). [*The Just Assassins*].

John le Carré, *The Spy Who Came in from the Cold* (London: Pan Books, 1965) [1963].

G. K. Chesterton, *The Man Who Was Thursday. A Nightmare* (London: Arrowsmith, 1908).

Joseph Conrad, *The Secret Agent: A Simple Tale* (London: Harper & Brothers, 1907).

Joseph Conrad, *Under Western Eyes* (London: Methuen, 1911).

Robert Coover, *The Public Burning* (New York: Viking, 1977).

Costa-Gavras (dir.), *State of Siege* (France, 1972).

Don Delillo, "Looking at Meinhof," *The Guardian*, 17 August 2002, published as "Baader-Meinhof," in *The Angel Esmeralda: Nine Stories* (London: Picador, 2011).

F. C. Delius, *Ein Bankier auf der Flucht: Gedichte und Reisebilder* (Berlin: Rotbuch, 1975) [A Banker on the Run: Poems and Travel Pictures].

F. C. Delius, *Amerikahaus und der Tanz um die Frauen* (Reinbek bei Hamburg: Rowohlt, 1997). [House of America and the Dance around the Women].

F. C. Delius, *Die Birnen von Ribbeck* (Reinbek bei Hamburg: Rowohlt, 1991) [The Pears of Ribbeck].

Fyodor Dostoyevsky, *Demons: A Novel in Three Parts*, translated and annotated by Richard Pevear and Larissa Volokhonsky (London: Vintage, 1994), [first published in Russian in 1872, also known as *The Possessed* and *The Devils*].

Ulrike Draesner, *Spiele* (Munich: Luchterhand, 2005) [Games].

Friedrich Dürrenmatt, *Der Auftrag, oder, Vom Beobachten des Beobachters der Beobachter: Novelle in vierundzwanzig Sätzen* (Zurich: Diogenes, 1985) [The Assignment, or, On the Observing of the Observer of the Observers].

Joseph von Eichendorff, "Mondnacht," in *Historisch-Kritische Ausgabe*, eds. Hermann Kunisch and Helmut Koopmann, *Gedichte*, vol. 1, eds. Harry Fröhlich and Ursula Regener (Stuttgart: Kohlhammer, 1993), 327–28 [1837, Moonlit Night, set to music by Robert Schumann, 1840].

Hans Magnus Enzensberger, *Durruti oder der kurze Sommer der Anarchie* (Frankfurt: Suhrkamp, 1972) [Durruti or the Brief Summer of Anarchy].

Giles Foden, *The Last King of Scotland* (London: Faber & Faber, 1998).

Theodor Fontane, *Der Stechlin* [1898], in *Sämtliche Werke, Romane, Erzählungen, Gedichte*, vol. 5, ed. Walter Keitel (Munich: Hanser, 1966).

Theodor Fontane, *Quitt* [1890], in *Sämtliche Werke, Romane, Erzählungen, Gedichte*, vol. 1, ed. Walter Keitel (Munich: Hanser, 1966), 213–452.

Theodor Fontane, *Mathilde Möhring* [1907], in *Sämtliche Werke, Romane, Erzählungen, Gedichte*, vol. 4, ed. Walter Keitel (Munich: Hanser, 1966), 577–674.

Theodor Fontane, *Frau Jenny Treibel* [1893], in *Sämtliche Werke, Romane, Erzählungen, Gedichte*, vol. 4, ed. Walter Keitel (Munich: Hanser, 1966), 297–478.

Johann Wolfgang von Goethe, *Die Leiden des jungen Werther*, in *Gedenkausgabe der Werke, Briefe und Gespräche*, ed. Ernst Beutler, vol. 4, *Der junge Goethe* (Zurich / Stuttgart, 1949), 268–511 [1774, The Sorrows of Young Werther].

Jean Genet, *Les Bonnes* [1947], *The Maids. A Play with an introduction by Jean-Paul Sartre*, translated by Bernard Frechtman (New York: Grove, 1956).

William A. Graham (dir.) *21 Hours at Munich* (1976).

Günter Grass, *Die Blechtrommel* (Neuwied: Luchterhand, 1959). [*The Tin Drum*].

Günter Grass, *Hundejahre* (Neuwied: Luchterhand, 1963). [*Dog Years*].

Günter Grass, *Örtlich betäubt* (Neuwied: Luchterhand, 1969). [*Local Anaesthetic*].

Günter Grass, *Aus dem Tagebuch einer Schnecke* (Neuwied: Luchterhand, 1972) [*From the Diary of a Snail*].

Günter Grass, *Der Butt* (Neuwied: Luchterhand, 1977). [*The Flounder*].

Günter Grass, *Das Treffen in Telgte* (Neuwied: Luchterhand, 1979) [*The Meeting in Telgte*].

Günter Grass, *Im Krebsgang* (Göttingen: Steidl, 2002). [*Crabwalk*].

Jakob and Wilhelm Grimm, "Von dem Fischer un zyner Frau" [The Fisherman and His Wife] and "Von dem Machandelboom" [The Juniper Tree], in *Kinder- und Hausmärchen* [1812] (Frankfurt: Insel, 1984), 3 vols., vol.1, 134–43 and 266–77.

Hans Jakob Christoffel von Grimmelshausen, *Der abenteuerliche Simplicissimus Teutsch* [1688] (Berlin and Weimar: Aufbau, 1984). [Simplicissimus Teutsch].

Friedrich Hebbel, *Judith* [1840], in *Werke*, vol. 1, *Dramen 1*, eds. Gerhard Fricke, Werner Keller, and Karl Pörnbacher (Munich: Hanser, 1963), 7–76.

Christoph Hein, *Der fremde Freund* (Berlin and Weimar: Aufbau, 1982) [The Distant Lover].

Christoph Hein, *Horns Ende* (Berlin and Weimar: Aufbau, 1985) [Horn's End, 1985].

Christoph Hein, *Der Tangospieler* (Berlin and Weimar: Aufbau, 1985) [The Tango Player].

Heinrich Heine, *Deutschland. Ein Wintermärchen* [1844], *Sämtliche Schriften*, ed. Klaus Briegleb (Frankfurt: Ullstein, 1981), 571–644. [Germany: A Winter's Tale]

Kurt Held, *Die rote Zora und ihre Bande* (Aarau: Sauerländer, 1941). [Red Zora and Her Gang].

Gunter Herburger, "Lenau," in *Die Eroberung der Zitadelle. Zwei Erzählungen* (Neuwied: Luchterhand, 1972), 113–70. [The Conquest of the Citadel. Two Stories].

Marianne Herzog, *Von der Hand in den Mund. Frauen im Akkord* (Berlin: Rotbuch, 1976). [From Hand to Mouth. Women and Piecework].

Marianne Herzog, *Nicht den Hunger verlieren* (Berlin: Rotbuch, 1980). [Don't Lose the Hunger].

Marianne Herzog, *Suche* (Darmstadt: Luchterhand, 1988). [Search]

Werner Herzog (dir.), *Alle für sich und Gott gegen alle* [*The Enigma of Kaspar Hauser*] (1976).

Hermann Hesse, *Der Steppenwolf* (Frankfurt: Suhrkamp, 1974) [1927, *Steppenwolf*].

Rolf Hochhuth, *Der Stellvertreter. Ein christliches Trauerspiel*, in *Alle Dramen* (Reinbek bei Hamburg: Rowohlt, 1991), vol.1, 9–448 [1963], [*The Representative. A Christian Tragedy*].

Rolf Hochhuth, *McKinsey kommt. Molières Tartuffe. Zwei Theaterstücke*. Mit einem Essay von Gert Ueding (Munich: dtv, 2003). [McKinsey Is Coming; Moliere's Tartuffe. Two Plays].

Friedrich Hölderlin, "Der Gang aufs Land" [1801, The Step into the Countryside], in *Sämtliche Werke, Grosse Stuttgarter Ausgabe*, ed. Friedrich Beissner, vol. 2 (Stuttgart: Kohlhammer, 1951), 84–85.

Homer, *The Odyssey*, tr. and intro by Richard Lattimore (New York: Harper and Row, 1975).

Henry James, *The Princess Casamassima* (Edinburgh: Macmillan, 1886).

Elfriede Jelinek, see *Ulrike Maria Stuart*.

Uwe Johnson, *Zwei Ansichten* (Frankfurt: Suhrkamp, 1965). [Two Views].

Franz Kafka, *Der Proceß. Roman in der Fassung der Handschrift* [The Trial, written 1914–15, first published 1925], in *Gesammelte Werke in zwölf Bänden*, vol. 3, ed. Malcolm Pasley (Frankfurt: Fischer, 1994).

Corinna Kawaters, *Zora Zobel findet die Leiche* (Frankfurt: Zweitausendeins, 1984). [Zora Zobel Finds the Corpse].

Corinna Kawaters, *Zora Zobel zieht um* (Frankfurt: Zweitausendeins, 1986). [Zora Zobel Moves House].

Corinna Kawaters, *Zora Zobel auf Umwegen* (Berlin: Espresso, 2001). [Zora Zobel on a Detour].

Heinrich von Kleist, *Michael Kohlhaas (Aus einer alten Chronik)*, in *Werke in einem Band*, ed. Helmut Sembdner (Munich: Hanser, 1966), 587–657. [Michael Kohlhaas. From an Old Chronicle].

Doris Lessing, *The Good Terrorist* (Cape: London, 1985).

Louis Malle (dir.), *Viva Maria!* (France, 1965).

Kevin Macdonald, (dir.) *One Day in September* (Switzerland / Germany / UK, 1999).

Kevin Macdonald, (dir.), *The Last King of Scotland* (Germany / US / UK, 2006).

Thomas Mann, *Der Zauberberg* (Frankfurt: Fischer, 1924) [The Magic Mountain]

194 / BIBLIOGRAPHY

Thomas Mann, *Doktor Faustus. Das Leben des deutschen Tonsetzers Adrian Leverkühn erzählt von einem Freunde* (Stockholm: Bermann Fischer, 1947). [Doctor Faustus. The Life of the German Composer Adrian Leverkühn, as Told by a Friend]

Ian McEwan, *The Innocent* (London: Cape, 1990).

Ulrike Meinhof, *Bambule. Fürsorge—Sorge für wen?* (Berlin: Wagenbach, 1971) [Riot. Welfare—Caring for Whom?]

Herman Melville, *Moby Dick* (New York: Harper and Brothers, 1851).

Eduard Mörike, *Mozart auf der Reise nach Prag* (Stuttgart/Augsburg: Cotta, 1856) [Mozart on the Journey to Prague].

Wolfgang Amadeus Mozart (composer*), Die Zauberflöte* [1791, *The Magic Flute*] from a libretto by Emanuel Schikaneder.

Robert Musil, *Der Mann ohne Eigenschaften*, 2 vols (Frankfurt: rororo, 1994), ed. Adold Frisé [The Man without Qualities].

George Orwell, *1984* (London: Secker & Warburg, 1949).

Arthur Penn (dir.), *Bonny and Clyde* (1967).

Gilles Pontecorvo (dir.), *The Battle of Algiers* (France / Italy, 1965).

Rio Rieser, "If I were the King of Germany" (first recorded 1976 by *Ton Steine Scherben*).

J. D. Salinger, *The Catcher in the Rye* (New York: Little Brown & Co, 1951).

Jean-Paul Sartre, *Les mains sales. Pièce en sept tableaux* (Paris: Gallimard, 1948) [Dirty Hands or *Crime Passionel*].

Friedrich Schiller, "Der Verbrecher aus verlorener Ehre. Eine wahre Geschichte" [The Criminal of Lost Honor. A True Story, 1786], in *Schillers Werke. Nationalausgabe*, eds. Julius Petersen and Hermann Schneider, vol. 16, *Erzählungen*, ed. Hans Heinrich Borcherdt (Weimar: Böhlaus Nachfolger, 1954), 7–29.

Friedrich Schiller, *Maria Stuart* [1800], in *Schillers Werke. Nationalausgabe*, eds. Julius Petersen and Hermann Schneider, vol. 9, *Maria Stuart, Die Jungfrau von Orleans*, eds. Benno von Wiese and Lieselotte Blumenthal (Weimar: Böhlaus Nachfolger, 1948).

Friedrich Schiller, *Wilhelm Tell* [1804] in *Schillers Werke. Nationalausgabe*, eds. Julius Petersen and Hermann Schneider, vol. 10, *Die Braut von Messina, Wilhelm Tell, Die Huldigung der Künste*, ed. Siegfried Seidel (1980).

Bernard Schlink, *Der Vorleser* (Zurich: Diogenes, 1995) [*The Reader*].

Peter Schneider, *Lenz* (Berlin: Rotbuch, 1973) [Lenz].

Peter Schneider, *Messer im Kopf. Drehbuch* (Berlin: Rotbuch, 1979). [Knife in the Head]

Peter Schneider, *Der Mauerspringer* (Darmstadt: Luchterhand, 1982) [The Wall Jumper].

Friedrich Schubert (composer), *Die Winterreise* [*The Winter's Journey*, 1827, Op. 89], poem cycle by Wilhelm Müller (1823).

Johannes Mario Simmel, *Gott schützt die Liebenden* (Hamburg: Zsolnay, 1957). [God Protects Lovers].

Sophocles, *Antigone* [442 BC], in *The Theban Plays* (Harmonsworth: Penguin, 2011), tr. and intro. E. Watling.

Uwe Tellkamp, *Der Eisvogel* (Frankfurt: Suhrkamp, 2005) [The Kingfisher].

Uwe Tellkamp, *Der Turm* (Frankfurt: Suhrkamp, 2008) [The Tower].

Uwe Timm, *Heisser Sommer* (Munich / Vienna: Autorenedition, 1974). [Hot Summer].

Uwe Timm, *Kerbels Flucht* (Munich / Vienna: Autorenedition, 1980). [Kerbel's Flight].

Uwe Timm, *Der Fremde und der Freund* (Frankfurt: Suhrkamp, 2005). [The Stranger and the Friend].

Margarethe von Trotta (dir.), *Rosa Luxemburg* (West Germany, 1986).

Bernward Vesper, *Die Reise* (Berlin: März, 1977). [The Trip].

Martin Walser, *Dorle und Wolf* (Frankfurt: Suhrkamp, 1987) [1987, *No Man's Land*].

Martin Walser, *Tod eines Kritikers* (Frankfurt: Suhrkamp, 2002) [Death of a Critic].

Peter Weiss, *Hölderlin. Stück in zwei Akten* (Frankfurt: Suhrkamp, 1971).

Peter Weiss, *Die Ästhetik des Widerstands* (Frankfurt: Suhrkamp, 1975-81), 3 vols. [The Aesthetics of Resistance].

Christa Wolf, *Der geteilte Himmel* (Berlin: Aufbau, 1975), [1963, *The Divided Sky*].

Thomas Wolfe, *You Can't Go Home Again* (New York: Harper and Row, 1940).

Sönke Wortmann (dir.), *Das Wunder von Berne* (Germany, 2003). [The Miracle of Bern].

Sönke Wortmann (dir.), *Deutschland. Ein Sommermärchen* (Germany, 2006) [Germany. A Summer's Tale].

Secondary Literature

David Aaronovitch, *Voodoo Histories. How Conspiracy Theory Has Shaped Modern History* (London: Vintage, 2010).

Norman Ächtler and Carsten Gansel (eds.), *Ikonographie des Terrors? Formen ästhetischer Erinnerung an den Terrorismus in der Bundesrepublik 1978–2008* (Heidelberg: Winter, 2010).

Theodor W. Adorno, "Parataxis. Zur späten Lyrik Hölderlins" (1964), in *Noten zur Literatur* (Frankfurt: Suhrkamp, 1974), 447–91.

Theodor Adorno and Max Horkheimer, *Dialektik der Aufklärung. Philosophische Fragmente* (Amsterdam: Querido, 1947).

Gordon B. Arnold, *Conspiracy Theory in Film, Television, and Politics* (London/Westport: Praeger, 2008).

Ron Augustin, *Labourhistory.net/raf/other* (accessed 16 June 2010). www.labourhistory.net

Stefan Aust, *Der Baader Meinhof Komplex* [1985] (Munich: Goldmann, 1998), 2nd ed.

Der Baader Meinhof Report. Aus Akten des Bundeskriminalamtes, der Sonderkommission und des Bundesamtes für Verfassungsschutz (Hase and Kochler: Mainz, 1972).

Sandra Beck, *Reden an die Lebenden und an die Toten. Erinnerungen an die Rote Armee Fraktion in der deutschsprachigen Gegenwartsliteratur* (St. Ingbert: Röhrig, 2008).

Gillian Becker, *Hitler's Children. The Story of the Baader-Meinhof Gang* (New York: Lippincott, 1977). 3rd ed. (London: Pickwick, 1989).

Gerrit-Jan Berendse, *Schreiben im Terrordrom. Gewaltcodierung, kulturelle Erinnerung und das Bedingungsverhältnis zwischen Literatur und RAF-Terrorismus* (Munich: edition text & kritik, 2005).

Gerrit-Jan Berendse and Ingo Cornils (eds.), *Baader-Meinhof Returns. History and Cultural Memory of German Left-wing Terrorism* (Amsterdam: Rodopi, 2008), *German Monitor* 70.

Rüdiger Bernhardt, *Interpretationen zu Christoph Hein. In seiner frühen Jugend ein Garten: Lektüre- und Interpretationshilfe. Königs Erläuterungen und Materialien* (Hollfeld: Bange, 2010).

Pierre Bertaux, *Hölderlin und die französische Revolution* (Frankfurt: Suhrkamp, 1969).

Claire Bielby, "Remembering the Red Army Faction," *Memory Studies* 3:2 (2010), 137–50.

Peter-Jürgen Boock/Peter Schneider, *Ratte-tot…Briefwechsel* (Neuwied: Luchterhand, 1985).

Pascale R. Bos, *German-Jewish Literature in the Wake of the Holocaust: Grete Weil, Ruth Kluger and the Politics of Address* (New York/Basingstoke: Palgrave, 2005).

brennendeautos.de (accessed 17 October 2010).

Henryk M. Broder, *Der ewige Antisemit. Über Sinn und Funktion eines beständigen Gefühls* (Frankfurt: Fischer, 1986).

Keith Bullivant, "F. C. Delius's 'Deutscher Herbst' Trilogy," in Weninger (ed.), *Gewalt und kulturelles Gedächtnis* (2005), 267–77.

Peter O. Chotjewitz, "Thomas Weiss *Tod eines Trüffelschweins*," *konkret*, January 2008, 45.

David Clarke, "Requiem für Michael Kohlhaas: Der Dialog mit den Toten in Christoph Heins *Horns Ende* und *In seiner frühen Kindheit ein Garten*," in Arne de Winde and Anke Gilleir (eds.), *Literatur im Krebsgang. Totenbeschwörung und memoria in der deutschsprachigen Literatur nach 1989, Amsterdamer Beiträge zur neueren Germanistik* 64 (2008), 159–79.

Sarah Colvin, *Ulrike Meinhof and West German Terrorism: Language, Violence and Identity* (Rochester NY: Camden House, 2009).

Commission international d'enquête. *La mort d'Ulrike Meinhof: rapport de la Commission international d'enquête* (Paris: Maspero, 1979).

Gerd Conradt, *Starbuck Holger Meins. Ein Porträt als Zeitbild* (Berlin: Espresso, 2001).

Ingo Cornils, "Writing the Revolution: the Literary Representation of the German Student Movement as Counter Culture," in Giles and Oergel (eds.), *Counter Cultures in Germany and Central Europe* (2003), 295–314.

Ingo Cornils, "Joined at the Hip? The Representation of the German Student Movement and Left-Wing Terrorism in Recent Literature," in Berendse and Cornils (eds), *Baader Meinhof Returns* (2008), 137–55.

Steven Crashaw, *Easier Fatherland* (London: Continuum, 2004).

Helena Darwin, "Terror als Ausweg aus der Tristesse? (Pop-)Kulturelle Erinnerungen an die RAF," in Stephan and Tacke (eds.), *NachBilder der RAF* (2008), 313–23.

Walter Delabar, "'entweder mensch oder schwein.' Die RAF in der Prosa der siebziger und achtziger Jahre," in Walter Delabar/Eberhard Schmitz (eds.), *Deutschsprachige Literatur der 70er und 80er Jahre* (Darmstadt: Wissenschaftliche Buchgesellschaft, 1997), 154–87.

Walter Delabar, "Für das System oder dagegen? Thomas Weiss über den Tod eines Trüffelschweins," *literaturkritik.de*, 3 March 2008.

F. C. Delius, "Die Dialektik des deutschen Herbstes. Drei Thesen über das Terrorjahr 1977 und dessen Folgen," *Die Zeit*, 25 June 1997.

Jutta Ditfurth, *Ulrike Meinhof. Die Biographie* (Hamburg: Ullstein, 2007).

Christopher Dobson and Ronald Payne, *The Carlos Complex: A Pattern of Violence* (London: Book Club Associates, 1977).

Bianca Dombrowa (et al.), *GeRAFtes. Analysen zur Darstellung der RAF und des Linksterrorismus in der deutschen Literatur* (Bamberg: Lehrstuhl für neuere deutsche Literatur, 1994).

Gretchen Dutschke, *Wir hatten ein barbarisches, schönes Leben. Rudi Dutschke: Eine Biographie* (Cologne: Kiepenheuer & Witsch, 1996).

Norbert Elias, *Studien über die Deutschen. Machtkämpfe und Habitusentwicklung im 19. und 20. Jahrhundert*, ed. Michael Schröter (Frankfurt: Suhrkamp, 1992).

Thomas Elsaesser, "Antigone Agonistes: Urban Guerillas or Guerilla Urbanism? The Red Army Faction, Germany in Autumn and Death Game," in *Giving Ground. The Politics of Propinquity*, eds. Jean Copjec and Michael Sorkin (London/New York: Verso, 1999), 267–302.

Gudrun Ensslin, Bernward Vesper, *"Notstandsgesetze von Deiner Hand." Briefe 1968/1969*, eds. Caroline Harmsen, Ulrike Seyer, and Johannes Ullmaier. With an Afterword by Felix Ensslin (Frankfurt: Suhrkamp, 2009).

Mark Fenster, *Conspiracy Theories: Secrecy and Power in American Culture* (London / Minneapolis: University of Minnesota Press, 2008), 2nd Ed.

Stefan Finger, *Franz Josef Strauß. Ein politisches Leben* (Munich: Olzug, 2005).

Frank Finlay, "Thomas Weiss's 'Polyphonic' novel *Tod eines Trüffelschweins*," in Haines, Parker, and Riordan (eds.), *Aesthetics and Politics in Modern German Culture* (2010), 117–29.

Erich Fried, "Vorbeugemord" (1974), in *Anfragen und Nachreden. Politische Texte*, ed. Volker Kaukoreit (Berlin: Wagenbach, 1994), 118–50.

Franz Futterknecht, "Die Inszenierung des Politischen. Delius' Romane zum Deutschen Herbst," in *F. C. Delius: Studien über sein literarisches Werk*, eds. Manfred Durzak and Hartmut Steinecke (Tübingen: Stauffenberg, 1997), 69–88.

Matteo Galli and Heinz-Peter Preusser (eds.), *Mythos Terrorismus Vom Deutschen Herbst zum 11. September—Fakten, Fakes und Fiktionen* (Heidelberg: Universitätsverlag, 2006).

Matteo Galli, "'Mit dem Einkaufswagen durch den Geschichts-Supermarkt'? Zu einigen Bestandteilen des sogenannten Mythos RAF in den Künsten: Entstehung, Entwicklung und Neukontextualisierung," in Galli and Preusser (eds.), *Mythos Terrorismus.* (2006), 101–16.

Steve Giles and Maike Oergel (eds.), *Counter Cultures in Germany and Central Europe: From Sturm und Drang to Baader-Meinhof* (Berne: Lang, 2003).

Ruth Glyn, Giancarlo Lombardi, and Alan O'Leary, "Introduction," in Glyn, Lombardi, and O'Leary (eds.), *Terrorism, Italian Style: The Representation of Terrorism and Political Violence in Contemporary Italian Cinema* (London: IGRS, 2011), 1–15.

Günter Grass, "Politisches Tagebuch. Wiederholter Versuch" (1972), *Essays und Reden II 1970–1979, Werkausgabe* (Göttingen: Steidl, 1997), eds. Volker Neuhaus and Daniela Hermes, vol. 15, 210–213.

Anne-Kathrin Griese, "Der familäre Blick: Andres Veiel *Black Box BRD* (2001) und Christoph Hein *In seiner frühen Kindheit ein Garten* (2005)," in Stephan and Tacke (eds.), *NachBilder der RAF* (2008), 165–80.

Lutz Hachmeister, *Schleyer: Eine deutsche Geschichte* (Munich: Beck, 2004).

Roman Halfmann, "Neo-Terrorismus im Zeichen der RAF: Die Aufarbeitung des Deutschen Herbstes in der deutschen Gegenwartsliteratur zwischen Klischee und Absetzung," in Ächtler and Gansel (eds.), *Ikonographie des Terrors?* (2010), 333–47.

Brigid Haines, Stephen Parker, and Colin Riordan (eds.), *Aesthetics and Politics in Modern German Culture. Festschrift in Honour of Rhys W. Williams* (Oxford: Lang, 2010).

Dorothea Hauser, *Baader und Herold– Beschreibung eines Kampfes* (Berlin: Fest, 1997).

Sylvia Henze, "Die RAF und die DDR – Zur künstlerischen Darstellung eines 'blinden Fleckes' in Ulrich Woelks *Die letzte Vorstellung*, Ulrich Plenzdorfs *Vater, Mutter, Mörderkind* und Volker Schlöndorffs *Die Stille nach dem Schuss*," in Ächtler and Gansel (eds.), *Ikonographie des Terrors?* (2010), 179–98.

Christian Hißnauer, "'Mogadischu.' Opferdiskurs doku/dramatisch. Narrative des Erinnerns an die RAF im bundesdeutschen Fernsehen 1978–2008," in Ächtler and Gansel (eds.), *Ikonographie des Terrors?* (2010), 99–125.

Thomas Hoeps, *Arbeit am Widerspruch. Terrorismus in deutschen Romanen und Erzählungen (1837–1992)* (Dresden: Thelem, 2001).

Hans Egon Holthusen, *Sartre in Stammheim. Zwei Themen aus den Jahren der großen Turbulenz* (Klett- Cotta: Stuttgart, 1982).

Peter Hutchinson, *Literary Presentations of Divided Germany: the Development of a Central Theme in East German Fiction* (Cambridge: Cambridge University Press, 1977).

Tony Judt, *Postwar. A History of Europe since 1945* (London: Vintage, 2010), 470–72.

Michael Kapelln, *Doppelt Leben: Bernward Vesper und Gudrun Ensslin: Die Tübinger Jahre* (Tübingen: Klöpfer and Meyer, 2005).

Gerd Koenen, *Das rote Jahrzehnt. Unsere kleine deutsche Kulturrevolution 1967– 1977* (Kiepenheuer & Witsch: Cologne, 2001).

Gerd Koenen, *Vesper, Ensslin, Baader. Urszenen des deutschen Terrorismus* (Cologne: Kiepenheuer & Witsch, 2003).

Hans-Joachim Klein, *Rückkehr in die Menschlichkeit. Appell eines ausgestiegenen Terroristen* (Reinbek: rororo, 1979). Foreword by Daniel Cohn-Bendit.

Karin König, "Zwei Ikonen des bewaffneten Kampfes. Leben und Tod Georg von Rauchs und Thomas Weissbeckers," in Kraushaar (ed.), *Die RAF und der linke Terrorismus* (2006), vol. 1, 430–371.

Herbert Kraft, *Mondheimat: Kafka* (Pfüllingen, Neske, 1983).

Sven Kramer, "Demarcations and Exclusions: Terrorism, State Violence, and the Left in German Novels of the 1970s and 1980s," in R. Weninger (ed.), *Gewalt und kulturelles Gedächtnis* (2005), 255–65.

Wolfgang Kraushaar, *1968 als Mythos, Chiffre und Zäsur* (Hamburg: Hamburger Edition, 2000).

Wolfgang Kraushaar, *Fischer in Frankfurt: Karriere eines Außenseiters* (Hamburg: Hamburger Edition, 2001).

Wolfgang Kraushaar, *Die Bombe im jüdischen Gemeindehaus* (Hamburg: Hamburger Edition, 2005).

Wolfgang Kraushaar (ed.), *Die RAF und der linke Terrorismus* (Hamburg: Hamburger Edition, 2006), 2 vols.

Wolfgang Kraushaar, "Der nicht erklärte Ausnahmezustand. Staatliches Handeln während des sogenannten Deutschen Herbstes," in Kraushaar (ed.), *Die RAF und der linke Terrorismus* (2006), 2 vols, vol. 2, 1011–25.

Wolfgang Kraushaar, *Verena Becker und der Verfassungsschutz* (Hamburg: Hamburger Edition, 2010).

Hannes Krauss, "Politisches Begräbnis, Medienspektakel. Plädoyer für F.C. Delius' umstrittenen Terroristen-Roman," die *tageszeitung* 06.01.1993.

Hans Kundnani, *Utopia or Auschwitz. Germany's 1968 Generation and the Holocaust* (London: Hurst, 2009).

Dieter Kunzelmann, *Leisten Sie keinen Widerstand! Bilder aus meinem Leben* (Berlin: Transit, 1998).

Dirk Kurbjuweit, "Gefangen für alle Zeiten," *Die Zeit*, 08.08.1997.

Dirk Kurbjuweit, *Unser effizientes Leben. Die Diktatur der Ökonomie und ihre Folgen* (Berlin: Rowohlt, 2003).

Dominick LaCapra, *Writing History, Writing Trauma* (Baltimore/London: The Johns Hopkins University Press, 2001).

Peter Langemeyer, "Moralische oder politische Anstalt? Zur Standortsbestimmung des politischen Dramas und Theaters bei Rolf Hochhuth," in *Rolf Hochhuth: Theater als politische Anstalt*, eds. Ilse Nagelschmidt, Sven Neufert, and Gert Ueding (Weimar: Denkena, 2010), 73–98.

Robert Leucht, *Experiment und Erinnerung: Der Schriftseller Walter Abish* (Vienna: Böhlau, 2006).

Steffen Markus, "Am Ende. Zu Helmut Kraussers Eros," *Text und Kritik* (187) 2010, 94–107.

Moray McGowan, "Myth, Memory, Testimony, Jewishness in Grete Weil's *Meine Schwester Antigone*," in Helmut Peitsch, Charles Burdett and Claire Gorrara (eds.), *European Memories of the Second World War* (New York/Oxford: Berghahn, 1999), 149–58.

Moray McGowan, "Ulrike Meinhof im Deutschen Drama der Neunziger Jahre: Drei Beispiele," in Giles and Oergel (eds.), *Counter Cultures in Germany and Central Europe* (2003), 373–93.

Patricia Melzer, "Maternal Ethics and Political Violence: the 'Betrayal' of Motherhood among the Women of the RAF and June 2 Movement," *Seminar* 47:1 (2011), 81–102.

Till Meyer, *Staatsfeind. Erinnerungen* (Spiegel: Hamburg, 1996).

Klaus Modick, "Die öffentliche Verbrennung. Friedrich Christian Delius' Romangroteske *Himmelfahrt eines Staatsfeindes*," *Frankfurter Rundschau* 30.09.1992.

Hans-Bernhard Moeller and George Lellis, *Volker Schlöndorff's Cinema: Adaptation, Politics, and the "Movie-Appropriate"* (Carbondale and Edwardsville: Southern Illinois University Press, 2002).

Gabrielle Muller, "Imagining the RAF from an East German Perspective: Carow's *Vater, Mutter, Mörderkind* and Dresen's *Raus aus der Haut*," in Berendse and Cornils (eds.), *Baader Meinhof Returns* (2008), 269–84.

Wolfgang Munchau, "Anti-Americanism, anti-Semitism, anti-Capitalism," *The Spectator*, 21 May 2005.

Oskar Negt (ed.), *Der Fall Fonty. "Ein weites Feld" von Günter Grass im Spiegel der Kritik* (Göttingen: Steidl, 1996).

Rachel Palfreyman, "The Fourth Generation: Legacies of Violence as Quest for Identity in Post-unification Terrorism Films," in David Clarke (ed.), *German Cinema since Unification* (London/New York: Continuum, 2006), 11–42.

Butz Peters, *RAF. Terrorismus in Deutschland* (Munich: Knaur, 1993).

Butz Peters, *Tödlicher Irrtum. Die Geschichte der RAF* (Berlin: Argon, 2004).

Klaus Pflieger, *Die Rote Armee Fraktion—RAF—14.5.1970 bis 20.4.1998* (Baden-Baden: Nomos, 2004).

Benjamin Piel, *Terror-Böll. Terrorismus im Werk von Heinrich Böll* (Munich: Medienbauer, 2009).

Heinz-Peter Preusser, "Warum *Mythos* Terrorismus? Versuch einer Begriffserklärung," in Galli and Preusser (eds.), *Mythos Terrorismus* (2006), 69–83.

Kirsten Prinz, "Umkämpft und abgeschlossen? Narrative über die RAF im Spiegel ihrer Rezeption. Überlegungen zu Bernhard Schlinks Roman *Das Wochenende* und Bernd Eichingers Film *Der Baader Meinhof Komplex*," in Ächtler and Gansel (eds.), *Ikonographie des Terrors?* (2010), 311–32.

Troy A. Pugmire, "Ein Vergleich: Heinrich von Kleists Michael Kohlhaas und die 'Rote Armee Fraktion'," *Utah Foreign Language Review* (1993–94), 124–37. [No vol. no.].

J. H. Reid, *Heinrich Böll: A German of this Time* (Oxford/New York: Berg, 1988).

Klaus Rainer Röhl, *Fünf Finger sind keine Faust* (Munich: Universitas, 1998). 3rd Ed.

Klaus Rainer Röhl, *Mein langer Marsch durch die Illusionen. Leben mit HITLER, der DKP, den 68ern, der RAF und ULRIKE MEINHOF* (Vienna: Universitas, 2009).

Mario Scalla, "Republik ohne Bürger" [review of Christoph Hein, *In seiner frühen Kindheit, ein Garten*], *Freitag*, 28.01. 2005.

Margaret Scanlan, *Plotting Terror: Novelists and Terrorists in Contemporary Fiction* (Charlottesville and London: University of Virginia Press, 2001).

Kay Schiller and Christopher Young, *The 1972 Olympics and the Making of Modern Germany* (Berkeley: University of California Press, 2010).

Margrit Schiller, *Es war ein harter Kampf um meine Erinnerung. Ein Lebensbericht aus der RAF* (Konkret: Hamburg, 1999).

Stephen Schindler, "Bombige Bücher: Literatur und Terrorismus," in *Wendezeiten Zeitenwenden. Positionsbestimmungen zur deutschsprachigen Literatur 1945–1995* eds. Robert Weninger and Brigitte Rossbacher (Tübingen: Stauffenberg, 1997), 55–78.

Michael Schneider, "Väter und Söhne, posthum. Das beschädigte Verhältnis zweier Generationen," in *Der Kopf verkehrt aufgesetzt oder Die melancholische Linke* (Neuwied: Luchterhand, 1981), 8–64.

Peter Schneider, "Der Sand an Baaders Schuhen," *Kursbuch* 51 (1978), 1–15.

Peter Schneider, *Rebellion und Wahn. Mein '68. Eine autobiographische Erzählung* (Cologne: Kiepenheuer & Witsch, 2008).

Uwe Schütte, "'Heilige, die im Dunkel leuchten.' Der Mythos der RAF im Spiegel der Literatur nachgeborener Autoren," in Giles and Oergel (eds.), *Counter Cultures in Germany and Central Europe* (2003), 353–72.

Uwe Schütte, *Die Poetik des Extremen. Ausschreitungen einer Sprache des Radikalen* (Göttingen: Vandenhoeck & Ruprecht, 2006).

Charity Scribner, "Engendering the Subject of Terror: Friedrich Christian Delius and Friedrich Dürrenmatt in the Mid-1980s," in Berendse and Cornils (eds.), *Baader Meinhof Returns* (2008), 125–36.

Jane Shilling, "Twisted Sister's Radical Turn" [Review of Michael Arditti, *Unity*], *The Times*, 4 June 2005.

Anne Siemens, *Für die RAF war er das System, für mich der Vater: Die andere Geschichte des deutschen Terrorismus* (Munich: Piper, 2007).

Hubert Spiegel, "Bleierner Tanz" [Review of Christoph Hein, *In seiner frühen Kindheit, ein Garten*], *Frankfurter Allgemeine Zeitung*, 5 February 2005.

George Steiner, *Antigones* (Oxford: Clarendon Press, 1984).

Inge Stephan and Alexandra Tacke (eds.), *NachBilder der RAF* (Vienna: Böhlau, 2008), 39–62.

Inge Stephan, "'Raspe-Irrweg' und 'Baader-Schwachsinn.' Dekonstruktion des Deutschen Herbstes in Rainald Goetz' Roman *Kontrolliert* (1988)," in Stephan and Tacke (eds.) (2008), 39–62.

Klaus Stern and Jörg Hermann, *Andreas Baader: Das Leben eines Staatsfeindes* (Munich: dtv, 2007).

William Stevenson with material by Uri Dan, *90 Minutes at Entebbe* (Toronto/London: Bantam, 1976).

Robert Storr, *Gerhard Richter October 18, 1977* (New York: Museum of Modern Art, 2000).

Stuart Taberner, "The Art of Delay: Protest and Prose in F. C. Delius's *Mein Jahr als Mörder*," in Haines, Parker, and Riordan (eds.), *Aesthetics and Politics in Modern German Culture* (2010), 91–102.

Klaus Theweleit, "Bermerkungen zum RAF-Gespenst. Abstrakter Realismus und Kunst," in *Ghosts. Drei leicht inkorrekte Vorträge* (Stroemfeld: Frankfurt, 1998), 13–99.

Oliver Tolmein, *Vom deutschen Herbst zum 11. September. Die RAF, der Terrorismus und der Staat* (Hamburg: Konkret, 2002).

Oliver Tolmein, *"RAF—Das war für uns Befreiung." Ein Gespräch mit Irmgard Müller über bewaffneten Kampf, Knast und die Linke* (Hamburg: Konkret, 1997).

Luize Tremel, "Literrorisierung. Die RAF in der deutschen Belletristik zwischen 1970 und 2004," in Kraushaar (ed.), *Die RAF und der linke Terrorismus* (2006), vol. 2, 1117–54.

Tom Vague, *The Red Army Faction Story 1963–1993: Televisionaries* (Edinburgh/San Francisco: AK Press, 1994).

Jeremy Varon, *Bringing the War Home. The Weather Underground, the Red Army Faction, and Revolutionary Violence in the Sixties and Seventies* (Berkeley / London: University of California Press, 2004).

Andres Veiel, *Black Box BRD. Alfred Herrhausen, die Deutsche Bank, die RAF und Wolfgang Grams* (Stuttgart/Munich: Deutsche Verlags-Anstalt, 2002).

Inge Viett, *Nie war ich furchtloser. Autobiographie* (Nautilus: Hamburg, 1996).

Anette Vonwinckel, "Skyjacking: Cultural Memory and the Movies," in Berendse and Cornils (eds.), *Baader-Meinhof Returns* (2008), 251–68.

Annabel Wahba, "Der Blick durch die Sonnenbrille," *Der Tagesspiegel*, 22 March 2005 [review of German translation of Erin Cosgrove, *The Baader-Meinhof Affair*].

Hans Jürgen Weber with Ingeborg Weber, eds., *Die bleierne Zeit. Ein Film von Margarethe von Trotta*, (Frankfurt: Fischer, 1981).

Robert Weninger (ed.), *Gewalt und kulturelles Gedächtnis. Repräsentationsformen von Gewalt in Literatur und Film seit 1945* (Tübingen: Stauffenberg, 2005).

John Wieczorek, "From Wallerfang to Auschwitz: Aspects of the Novels of Judith Kuckart," *The Scope of German Studies in the Twenty-First Century*, eds. Holger Briel and Carol Fehringer (Berne: Lang, 2003), 291–308.

Willi Winkler, *Geschichte der RAF* (Berlin: Rowohlt, 2007).

Gerhard Wisnewski, Wolfgang Landgraeber, Ekkehard Sieker, *Das RAF-Phantom. Wozu Politik und Wirtschaft Terroristen brauchen* (Munich: Knaur, 1997). First published 1992.

Uwe Wittstock, "Der Terror und seine Dichter," *Die Neue Rundschau* 101 (1990), H.3, 65–78.

INDEX